COLIN KAY was born in Nigeria, grev[...] history at Cambridge. After teaching [...] Colin finally settled in Wiltshire whe[...] works as a self-employed consultant, and is also deeply involved in his local community. He is a passionate supporter of Bath Rugby and enjoys the theatre, cinema and walking.

After a lifetime immersed in and dominated by educational development and academic study, Colin now has the time to return to his first love of creating fiction. *Fateful Gift* is his first novel to be published. His second: *The Bank of the Holy Grail* is a racy thriller set against the background of the euro crisis. His third: *Arrowhead* is a historical fantasy that takes place in third-century Germany.

To Tracy
Thanks for all your
support and for being a
guinea pig

Colin

FATEFUL GIFT

COLIN KAY

SilverWood

Published in 2014 by SilverWood Books

SilverWood Books Ltd
30 Queen Charlotte Street, Bristol, BS1 4HJ
www.silverwoodbooks.co.uk

ISBN 978-1-78132-275-8 (paperback)
ISBN 978-1-78132-276-5 (ebook)

British Library Cataloguing in Publication Data
A CIP catalogue record for this book is available from
the British Library

Set in Sabon by SilverWood Books
Printed on responsibly sourced paper

This book is dedicated to Teresa. At an early stage of writing it she asked what the book was about. When told it was a mystery she replied, "What, you mean you don't even know what it's about?" Perhaps she was right.

Contents

1   Spain, May 2011   9

2   New Orleans, August 1994   11

3   England, September 2004 – June 2005   35

4   England, June 2006 – August 2009   111

5   England, September – October 2009   190

6   Spain, October 2009 – May 2011   271

1

Spain, May 2011

The young woman leaned on the rail of the narrow balcony. Between the hotel tower blocks in front of her, she could see the sea and beach. It was late May and the afternoon sun was already sweltering. Its dusty heat was reflected back by the roads and buildings. She sipped the gin from the plastic cup and let the cold sharpness catch the back of her throat. There had been no tonic and no glasses so she drank it neat in the plastic cup from the bathroom, taking the vodka first and saving the gin till last. She sipped it again slowly, trying to make the moment last.

The air was still. After the chaos of their journey, everything seemed suddenly to have stopped. It was a stillness without calm and it did not lessen the intensity of the emotions struggling inside her. Everything had a vividness about it: the heat, the balcony, the blue of the sea. She looked around, trying to fix each dimension of this moment forever in her memory.

On the beach there were brightly coloured sun beds, white pedalos and figures in the water. Memories of other summers and other beaches flowed into her mind. She dared not let herself dwell on them. With a slow, deliberate movement she drained the plastic cup. Taking one more look at the sea, she turned and moved quietly into the room.

Inside the air was dark and cool. Her two children lay asleep on the bed. She could hear their breathing above the hiss of the air conditioning. Pausing for a moment, she listened and watched their chests rise and fall. A violent tremor ran through her body. She clenched her fists and closed her eyes, trying to reassert control over herself. It passed like a wave on the seashore. She stood completely motionless, then taking a deep breath, walked up to the left-hand side of the bed where the youngest lay, bent over and gazed at his peaceful face. She kissed him on the forehead and whispered something to herself. Then she picked up the large white pillow from the bed.

2

New Orleans, August 1994

Mike was soaked with sweat. His tee shirt stuck to his chest and back, and his jeans stuck to his legs. The auditorium was airless and made almost unbearable by the stage lights and the mass of sweating bodies. He took off his headphones and put them next to the control panel. Despite them, his head was ringing with the rhythm of the music. It was as if it had engulfed him completely and become the pulse of his body. He knew it would pound on for a couple of hours until it finally drained away. The house lights had come on now and the crowd was disappearing fast. He stood up and stretched, stiff from bending over the controls for the last three hours. Before the auditorium was empty they had begun packing up the gear, dismantling it and then carrying it out the back to their truck. The hard work soon got rid of the stiffness in his muscles. The kit piled up: amplifiers, speakers. cables, his sound desk and all the rest. He wondered if they would get it all in. There seemed so much. He always wondered that, but they always did. The effort of carrying and lifting made him sweat even more. Outside it was hardly any cooler. His mouth and throat were dry. He was desperate for a drink. At last it was all stowed away. He stretched back against the side of the truck to his full six foot, breathing heavily.

"Want a beer, Mike?" Steve, one of the other roadies, tossed him a can. He opened it and drank, relaxing. The pounding of the music in his head was beginning to ease off.

"It was a good set." Steve, dark and wiry compared to Mike's tall blondness, joined him.

"Yeah." It had been good. The hall had been packed and the kids had really warmed to the band. Who would have thought it? A small-time British rock band getting crowds in New Orleans.

11

"Hey, you guys, how yer doing?" It was Eddie, one of the locals who'd done the lighting. "Great gig. You Brits certainly can play rock and roll."

"Thanks, man," Steve said. "You finished now?"

"Yes, sir. Hey, you want to come and hear some real music?"

They looked at him.

"Jazz, man. You're in New Orleans. You can't come to New Orleans and not hear some jazz."

They looked at each other.

"Come on," he said persuasively, "it's just a few steps away."

Steve looked at his watch. They had to be on the road in the morning, but it wasn't a long drive.

"What about this?" He banged on the truck.

"Your truck'll be okay here. I put the word out. Nobody will touch it. I got a friend who'll keep an eye on it for you."

"Why not?" Steve looked at Mike.

"Okay by me." Mike shrugged his shoulders. "I'll fetch Dougie." He started off, but then Dougie appeared round the corner with another of the lighting guys.

"We're going to go and hear some jazz. You coming?"

"Sure." He locked the back doors of the truck and turned to Eddie. "Lead on, my man."

Eddie led them off down the street. Steve walked beside him, asking questions about the city. Dougie and Isaac, the other lighting technician, followed them, Isaac adding in some answers to Steve's questions. Mike tagged behind, listening. He didn't feel much like talking. After gigs he rarely did. The pounding music made it hard to think of things to say. He was just happy to listen, to let the words flow over him.

They turned right outside the hall and then cut down a back alley between tall buildings. It was really dark here. No street lights, only the light from shaded windows picking up the white of Eddie's tee shirt. Mike was glad Eddie and Isaac were with them. On his own he wouldn't have had a clue. In foreign cities you had to be careful. In his five years travelling with bands as a sound engineer that was one thing he'd learnt. Even in his home city of Manchester there were places it was better not to go. But then he knew where was safe and where was not. In other places you needed to be alert, even in England. A group of young men on the street at night, you could easily walk into trouble, or simply attract it. Abroad was worse. Until you'd worked out the dynamics of a place it was difficult to be safe; not only knowing where to go, but the pattern of its night life. This was something he could do quickly. He seemed to have some kind of extra sense that enabled him to feel tension or aggression before they landed in the middle of it. All bands he'd worked with valued him for his ability to steer them safely to drink, food or whatever kind of entertainment they wanted, without getting them into a fight.

America, though, was a real challenge. All the cities they'd played in were different and their stays were so short. Making sense of them wasn't easy, but reading a bit about a place first helped him to build up a picture, so that he could find his way around. Then it was about picking up the vibes, sensing the atmosphere.

He glanced up at the houses they passed between, open windows; their lights shaded behind blinds, the hum of voices. He wondered what was happening behind each one. Who was there? What were they doing? He tried to picture the men and women.

There was a sudden outburst of shouting above them to his left. A woman's voice screamed. He did not need to understand the language to recognise a stream of abuse. Then came the smash of crockery breaking as it hit a wall or a floor, and an angry male voice began to shout.

Eddie stopped and listened and then laughed. "This is a place of passion," he said. "The hotter it gets, the hotter the passion."

There was the sound of more crockery breaking above them. The woman's voice began again, a torrent of anger and scorn. They heard a blow and it stopped in mid-flow. The woman screamed. There was the sound of a struggle and bodies crashing to the floor.

"C'mon," Eddie said, "our entertainment isn't far away."

They continued down the alley as the woman above them screamed again. Mike stood for a moment in the darkness, listening intently. Then, realising he had been left behind, hurried to catch up with them.

Suddenly they came out of the maze of backstreets and alleys. They were in a larger street lined with trees. Mike blinked for a moment – the streetlights seemed suddenly bright compared with the blackness they'd been walking through. The houses were taller and obviously once grand, but now had plaster peeling off the walls. Eddie turned right and they followed him along the street to a small square with a fountain in the middle. Around it there were cafes and bars. They could hear the unmistakable sound of a saxophone playing. Eddie crossed the street and led them to a doorway, above which there was a painted sign: *Jay's Place.*

They followed him down rickety wooden stairs and into a large smoke-filled room. To their right, along one side, was a brightly lit and crowded bar. Facing them on a raised platform a five-piece group with a singer was playing. In-between were round tables surrounded by chairs. Most of the tables were full of men and women drinking. Waitresses in red dresses moved to and fro carrying trays of drinks. Eddie pushed his way through and found a table. They each grabbed one of the cane chairs and sat down. Although it had only been a short walk, Mike was glad to rest his legs.

"Kitty?" Dougie said, putting some dollars in the middle of the table. Despite Eddie's protests, Mike and Steve followed suit. Eddie waved and a waitress came towards them.

"What do you guys want? The wine is good here."

"Beer," Steve said. "We're parched."

"*Cherie*," Eddie greeted the waitress, putting his arm round her waist. "A big pitcher of Bud for five thirsty men. My friends, this is Annette, the best waitress in the whole of New Orleans."

Annette smiled at them warmly, taking in the whole table. She was slim with a mischievous air, as though about to tease them. The red dress, low at the front with a short skirt, showed off her figure in a way that was definitely teasing.

"Of course, Monsieur Eddie," she said mockingly, running her fingers through his hair. Then she adroitly disengaged herself from his arm and turned away to the bar.

Mike looked round the room. He noticed that they were the only white people there. Yet oddly, he didn't feel conspicuous. Nobody seemed to care. Everyone was too focused on the music.

"This is the real thing," Eddie was saying. "None of your tourist shit. This is the best jazz in the whole of New Orleans."

Mike looked at the band. They were immersed in the sound they were producing. The pianist was old and grizzled, with grey hair and grey stubble. He was wearing a blue open-necked shirt and black braces. Old he may have been, but his fingers flashed across the keys and he bent and swayed. Centre stage was the saxophone player, tall and angular in a white shirt, black denims and red waistcoat. In his hands the saxophone moved from side to side, as though it was in control rather than being played. He too swayed and moved his instrument around. Beside him, instrument in hand, tapping his feet, stood the trumpet player, waiting for his time to come. Beyond him the bass guitarist, a red cap jauntily perched on his head, worked the chords with his fingers, swaying and moving like the others to the power of the music. At the back the drummer, a young lad with a thick, curly mass of hair, was frenzied, sweat pouring down his face, as his sticks and hands moved between his drums and cymbal.

Mike had listened to a bit of jazz, but he was really a rock and roller at heart. He had never heard anything like this before. The mellow poignancy of the saxophone contrasted with the dynamic beat of the drums and bass. There was a brashness and a rawness about the sound, especially from the trumpet player, who now added the raucous, strident voice of his instrument to the mix. Mike was fascinated as the different elements blended together, separated and then wove in and out of each other. It was as though he was seeing with his ears; seeing a tapestry of bright colours and emotions.

Then, as the saxophone and trumpet stopped, the singer moved to the centre of the stage. She was slight and plain and very black. Mike had not realised until now that black people could come in so many different shades. He wondered if this was a racist thought. If the singer's appearance was plain and nondescript, her voice was not. Deep, with a soulful huskiness, it was almost like another instrument in the band, rather than a voice. A human foil for the saxophone with the same mellow quality that pulled at the emotions. It was not the words she sang, but the sound itself that touched you. The room fell silent. Even the hubbub by the bar was stilled. As she sang, she movedd to the rhythm and moved with small, precise steps. Mike was transfixed. He let himself drift with the music. The singer paused and the trumpet player picked up the refrain, but he did not have the range to match the quality of her voice. She stepped forward and began again. Her voice, through the magic of its tone rather than the meaning of the lyrics, filled the room with feeling, like a wave breaking on the shore. It washed away the last pounding remnants of the rock and roll and left him clean and renewed. As the song ended, the room applauded. The band struck up a different piece, quicker and more urgent.

People began to talk. The waitress came over with a large pitcher of beer and glasses. Mike drank deeply. He suddenly felt so thirsty that the first cold glass hardly seemed to make any difference. Eddie refilled their glasses. He called the waitress for another pitcher. "Thirsty men here," he said, laughing and patting her playfully on the bottom.

Eddie and Steve were talking about the music, about jazz and rock and roll. Isaac and Dougie occasionally made comments. Mike was happy to let them talk. Half listening, he stretched back in his chair and sipped the cold beer. Now that the urgency of his thirst was gone, he could savour the taste and let the coldness seep through him. He looked around the room. People were dancing now. There were some couples, some pairs of girls dancing together and some dancing on their own. They moved with an ease and freedom that he envied. He had a good sense of rhythm, and safe behind his control desk he could tap and nod in time. The dance floor was a different thing. In the spotlight he became clumsy and self-conscious. He had seen good dancers in other parts of the world, but not quite like this. They seemed so natural; so much part of the music, as though it had entered their being and flowed out through them in their movements.

One girl in particular caught his attention. She was dancing on her own. Lighter skinned than most of them in the room, with fine high cheekbones, she wore a simple white dress. The cleavage of her breasts showed brown against the cotton and her skirt revealed the smoothness of her long legs. Her hair was a reddish blonde, clustered around her face in banks of curls that fell to her shoulders. A necklace of figures glowed pale ivory against her skin, and bracelets of the same kind were around her wrists.

Eyes half closed, she danced as if obeying a higher command in a world that was parallel, yet separate. Her movements were entirely for herself and yet in a way divorced from her. She moved around the floor between tables and between couples. At times she danced close to a table, as though she was searching for someone. Her face scanned each person and then moved on.

Mike watched, fascinated. There was something almost unbearably sensual about her. The way her breasts moved to the music, revealing most, but not all, of their curves. How her skirt clung to her thighs and her bottom. And yet at the same time, there was a kind of innocence about her. He had seen dancers before, who deliberately flaunted the sexuality of their bodies to arouse the males in their audience. They were offering an open invitation, a business deal. Each exaggerated movement said "You can have all this and more if you will only pay the price, credit cards gladly accepted. I am here for the taking so take me if you can afford me." This was not the message. This was a sexuality that was wild and intense, but was not for sale. The movements of the body said "This is how I am. I move my breasts because they are part of me. They show the way I feel. I do not do this because I want you to buy me. I am beyond the price of your dollars and your credit cards. If you want me, then you must meet the challenge and tame me. If you can match my wildness then I can be yours."

The woman moved around the edges of the dance floor. She danced up and between the tables closest to it. As she approached each table it would become quiet. It was as if those sitting there were afraid. When she scanned their faces with her half-closed eyes, those sitting there would avoid her gaze, look at the floor and shrink down into their chairs. Once she had moved away they would relax and start to talk again, but glancing after her in dread, as if frightened that she might return.

Mike was so absorbed in watching her that he did not realise that she had approached their table. Suddenly she was in front of him. Their conversation stopped. He sensed Eddie and the others turn away, but he was unable to take his eyes from her. Her eyes met his and opened wide. Mike was held by them, blue-green and as bottomless as the deep sea. Her stare drew him in and seemed to reach right down inside him, as though she was searching his innermost self. He could not break the contact and draw his eyes away. Her lips moved as though she was speaking and she fingered the charms around her neck. The moment seemed to last a long time then suddenly she was gone. She had moved on to another table and Mike was left staring at empty space. Eddie breathed out and mopped his face with a large handkerchief.

"This is bad news," he said, looking round at the others. He turned to Mike. "Man, be careful, she gave you the look. You want a woman, I can find you one. There are plenty of fine women here." He gestured round the room. "You just say. You choose anyone and I can get them for you. They will give you a good time and make you happy. But not that one." He spat on the floor. "That one is a bad woman; she will only bring you sorrow."

"What do you mean?" Mike struggled to make the words come. His mouth seemed suddenly dry again. "What is wrong with her?"

"She is a voodoo woman. She can see things, she knows things. There is a power inside her. It flows through her. Look how she dances."

"I was worried for you." Isaac joined in, his voice full of concern. "She looked at you and you did not look away. How did it feel?"

"Like she was looking deep inside me. Looking into the inner me. Looking into my soul, I guess."

"The voodoo woman is always searching. She is looking for someone else with the power. Someone to connect with. Or someone to whom she can pass on her power. I was afraid for you because she looked at you for so long. But she passed by, so you are okay."

Steve laughed. "Hey, what is this shit? This is the twentieth century, man, not the middle ages. What is all this mumbo jumbo? Voodoo, it's just a lot of rubbish."

Eddie and Isaac looked at him quietly.

"Listen, this is New Orleans. This is a strange city and even in the twentieth century, a strange world. Voodoo is as much a part of New Orleans as jazz."

"You are joking," Steve went on. Mike knew he loved to be pro-vocative.

"You heard the lady sing. Didn't she cast a spell over you?" Eddie asked.

"Sure, but that was different."

"It was a kind of magic," Eddie went on. "Voodoo is magic too, but it is different. Voodoo and jazz, they are part of the same thing."

"Come on, let's get some more beer," Dougie interrupted them. "All this talking about magic is making my head ache and my throat dry." They all laughed and relaxed. Eddie called the waitress and soon their glasses were full again.

The dancer had moved on and vanished into the crowded room. The singer sang again and they drank more beer. The talk turned to sound and lighting and rigs and technical things and where they were going next.

Mike sat half listening as usual. He was still thinking about that look. The deepness of those eyes, the way they had seemed to see right into his inner being. Eddie was right about the power that flowed through her. Voodoo was something he'd vaguely heard of, but only in horror movies or cheap bestsellers. He wasn't religious or even superstitious. He just got on with his life and took each thing as it came. Spirits and that sort of stuff were not things he'd ever thought about. It seemed to have so little to do with his reality. Yet Eddie had a point about the power of music, and he certainly believed in that. It did not matter whether it was the rawest rock or this jazz, music could move you in a way that words alone could not.

Mike became aware of pressure building in his bladder. The beer was beginning to make itself felt.

"Where's the john?" he asked, getting to his feet. He felt light-headed. Lots of beer and no food, he thought. Eddie gestured to the other side of the room. Mike concentrated hard and picked his way carefully between the tables and the people, trying not to appear unsteady. At the end of the room there was a passageway with the WC sign above it. He walked down it and felt a bit steadier. The air was fresher here. He paused a moment and leant against the wall. Then he continued to the far end where there were two doors. Finding the men's he went in. He unzipped and stared down at the stream of liquid hitting the bowl of the urinal and felt relief begin to seep through him. The image of the dancer came into his mind. The sensuous way she had moved her body, the brownness of her thighs, the cleavage of her breasts. Mike finished, zipped up his jeans and crossed to the basin. He washed his hands and splashed some cold water on his face, ran his fingers through his hair and left.

A little way down the corridor, two hands grabbed him from behind and pulled him into a doorway. Caught off balance, he staggered slightly down a step. He was in a small room of some kind. The only light was coming in from the corridor. Looking up into his eyes was the dancer. He opened his mouth to speak, but she put her finger against it, motioning him to be quiet. She pulled him further into the room until her back was against the far wall. Taking one of his hands, she slipped it inside the front of her dress. Her breast was soft against his hand; the skin was deliciously smooth to his fingers; her nipple hardened as he touched it. He bent to kiss her but she moved her head so that his lips only brushed her cheek. Her scent filled his nostrils: fragrant, mysterious, exciting. She reached for his other hand and guided it down beneath her skirt and between her legs. He felt the short cropped hair and then the wetness between her legs. Her hands were unzipping his fly. She reached inside and pulled out his penis. The shock of intimate contact, combined with the alcohol, inflamed his desire so that he was already erect. She moved his hands and placed them on her back and then, opening her legs, pulled him towards her. He needed no encouragement and thrust up, entering her. As he did so she leaned back against the wall. He thrust up inside her and heard her moan. Thrusting again, deeper, he tried to find a rhythm. Then her muscles tightened around his penis and she began to rock back, echoing his thrusts as though she was sucking him up inside her. He felt himself beginning to climax and heard her panting quicken. As they came together, she bent her head upwards and placed her lips on his, pushing her tongue inside his mouth and breathing into him. The shudder of their climax and of her breath seemed to go right through him like an electric shock. He blacked out.

Mike came to, sitting on the floor in what seemed to be a store cupboard of some kind. He wasn't sure at first where he was. He got to his feet unsteadily. There was a pain in the side of his head, where he had banged it. He had no idea how long he had been unconscious. His head ached. He staggered up the step and back into the passageway. Had he tripped and fallen? Mike struggled to recall what had happened. Then he remembered the girl. He looked around, but there was no sign of her. Standing in the corridor, he breathed the cool air and tried to get his bearings. Had he imagined it all? It seemed so real. Mike felt confused and disorientated. He could clearly remember going to the john – but after that? He shook his head. The others must be wondering what had happened to him. He made his way slowly along the passage and back to the room and their table.

"Where have you been?" Steve greeted him. "We were just about to send out a search party for you. Sit down and have some more beer."

Mike mumbled something about having a long pee and sank gratefully into his chair. He took a gulp of beer, but it seemed warm and flat and no longer refreshed him. His head was spinning and he felt dizzy. He was finding it hard to decide what was real and what wasn't.

Dougie leant over to him and said quietly, "Do your flies up, Mike, before you expose yourself to the world."

Mike grinned and zipped himself up. The others were passing a joint around, but he simply took it and passed it on.

"You okay, mate?" Steve asked.

"I feel a bit feverish but it's probably nothing." He was desperate to seem okay and tried to focus on the room. Looking around, he saw with a start that the dancer was back. She was on the far side of the room. He watched her intently. Her dance was different now; she no longer went out among the tables as though she was searching for someone. Instead she stayed close to the band. Her body still moved in the same sensuous way beneath her dress, but the dance was calmer, more resigned. Her eyes were fully open and yet did not really seem to see those around her. He remembered what Eddie had said about the spirit moving her and controlling her. Had the experience in the cupboard really happened? Or was it just a fantasy? He remembered thinking about her as he peed and then when he was walking down the passageway. He looked across at her, trying to catch her eye, but she did not seem to notice him.

Three large men entered the room. They were tall and very black. Each was wearing a charm necklace the same as the dancer's. They moved towards the dance floor and people parted to let them through and then looked away.

Eddie was leaning over towards him. "Hey, man. It's time we went. This is not good." The others were getting to their feet. Mike stood up, still watching what was happening on the dance floor. The three men approached the dancer. Two of them stood on either side of her. They seemed to want her to go with them and she appeared to refuse. She took a step away from them, but the men on each side of her held her back.

"Come on, man. We've got to go." Isaac was pulling him by the arm, leading him towards the door. He moved slowly, looking over his shoulder.

The men on either side of the woman had hold of her arms so she could not move. They reached behind her and, each taking a handful of her hair, pulled her head back. When they had first held her she had struggled to get free. Now she was no longer struggling, just standing calmly. The third stood in front of her. In one hand he held a small bowl. He drew his other hand back and something in it flashed in the light. He suddenly drew his hand across her neck. As he did, she let out a terrible scream and an ugly red gash ruined the perfection of her throat.

Isaac pulled Mike after him as they struggled across the room and up the staircase. Once outside they did not stop. Eddie and Isaac hurried them across the lighted street and into the darkness of the alleys.

"That was such bad news," Eddie kept saying as they moved quickly.

"I think we got out in time," said Isaac. "The cops won't be there for a while."

"Will they want witnesses?" Steve asked.

"Yeah, but nobody will have seen anything and maybe nobody will even report it," Eddie replied.

"But it was murder," Mike said, "bloody murder."

"Yeah, but do you want to spend the next six months here as a witness?" Steve said.

"We certainly would stand out like a sore thumb," said Dougie.

"Don't worry, man. Sometimes these things happen and everyone knows except the cops. Sometimes lots of people see something, but if it's voodoo then nobody sees nothing."

"Still, I think we better hit the road," Steve said. "We wouldn't be popular if the tour finished in New Orleans."

"Right," said Dougie. So they hurried through the alleys back to their lorry.

*

22

Mike was walking down a dark passageway. At the end of it, waiting for him, was the dancer. Her arms were stretched out towards him. The corridor seemed very long and his legs seemed to be made of lead. He struggled, then just as he was about to reach her, three men appeared; two stood either side of her holding her arms and pulling her head back by her hair. She looked towards him, her blue-green eyes appealing for help. He tried to run, but his legs would not move. They pulled her head back, revealing her throat. He tried to shout to them to stop; no words came out. The knife flashed; red welts spread across the brown throat. All was darkness. Then he was in the passageway again. She was there at the end waiting for him. He ran but the passageway was long. He had to get to her before they came. At last he reached her. She was in his arms. He tried to tell her that she was in danger, that they must go, but she wouldn't listen. She took his hand and put it on her breast. She unzipped his fly and reached in to touch him. Then they were there. They pulled her away from him. He couldn't move or speak. Her eyes looked at him, the blue-green of them suddenly moist and appealing. They held her. She didn't struggle. They forced her head back. Her eyes still held his. The knife flashed. She screamed and Mike woke.

He was lying in darkness. There was motion. His head ached. His mouth felt like sandpaper. It took him a moment to realise that he was in the back of the truck. They had created a place where they could sleep, whether they stopped in a lay-by or needed to take turns to drive. He lay there for a while, feeling nauseous. The events of the night before came back to him. He remembered hurrying back through the alleys to the truck. Then, nothing. The motion meant that they were on the road. He sat up; his head was spinning. What had happened since they reached the truck? Working his way forward, he opened the panel that gave access to the cab.

"The sleeping beauty wakes at last." Steve said looking back at him from the passenger's seat. Dougie was driving. "You okay?"

"What time is it?"

"A little after nine."

"What happened?"

"When we got back to the truck you passed out. We put you in the

23

back and started driving. Eddie felt it would be good if we got out of New Orleans. After a couple of hours we stopped and slept for a bit. We had a nap and then started again about six. Sure you're okay? It's not like you to pass out after a few beers."

"I don't know," Mike said. "Maybe I've got a touch of fever. Maybe I'm just dehydrated." He passed his hand over his forehead. It wasn't hot but it felt clammy with sweat.

"Have some water." Steve passed him a bottle. Mike took it and drank deeply.

"Want me to drive?" he asked.

"No, it's okay. We'll stop for some coffee in a couple of hours. You can take over then if you feel up to it. Go back and get some more sleep."

"Okay," Mike said and shut the hatch. He crawled back to his sleeping bag, drank some more water and tried to get comfortable. It was difficult to sleep. He kept thinking about last night, trying to separate what had actually happened from what he must have imagined. Rolling over he felt something hard against his thigh. There was an object in his pocket. It was smooth against his fingers. He pulled it out of his pocket and found his lighter. By its flickering light he saw a small figure. Carved in ivory was a woman with bare breasts and a long skirt. It looked just like the figures he'd seen around the dancer's neck and wrists. He stared at it and wondered how it came to be in his pocket.

The humid summer heat had stayed with them as they drove north up through the Carolinas and Virginia towards Pennsylvania. It made sleeping hard. Mike drank a shot of whisky and lay back on the bed. He looked around the motel room then closed his eyes, relaxed and waited for the dreams to come, as he knew they would. Every night on the tour, since New Orleans, he had had the same dream.

Always he was walking along a passageway towards the girl. Always in the end she was pulled away. Sometimes it was before he reached her. Sometimes he reached her, touched her, embraced her, and entered her. Sometimes he came and when he woke he found that he had actually come. It was like being a teenager again and having a wet dream. But always at the end they took her, held her and cut her throat. And always, her eyes held his with that fixed, imploring look.

So he lay back and waited for sleep and what it would bring. Mike still found it hard to work out what had actually happened that night at the jazz club. He supposed he was in some kind of shock because of what he'd seen. He didn't really know and he wasn't sure what to do about it. And the little ivory figure. How had he got it? He kept taking it out of his pocket and looking at it as though it held the answer to his questions. At first sight the carving had seemed crude. When he looked at it more closely, however, he saw that the body, and especially the breasts, had been fashioned with such care and delicacy that it showed a wild beauty. Only the face was blank and expressionless, as if waiting for life to be breathed into it. The woman had long hair and there was something old fashioned about her skirt. There was a feeling of great age about it, a smoothness of usage, as though many fingers had touched it as his did. He didn't know who it was supposed to be, or what it meant and he couldn't really talk to Steve and Dougie about it. Neither had said much about the evening. It was as though they both wanted to forget it. Mike had felt feverish for a couple of days, and, at first, he thought the dreams were part of that. Now he wasn't sure. All he could do was put up with them and hope that as time went on they would fade, or pass, or something. At last he fell asleep.

He was in a room in some sort of hotel. Although he could see around him, it was as though he was not really present. Sitting on a stool in front of the dressing table was a young woman he did not know. She must have been in her late twenties. She had a pale complexion that had no trace of a tan. Her face was striking in a forceful way, but not pretty, and her hair was black mid length and styled with a wave. She was wearing a red dress, low cut with straps that revealed her white shoulders and back. Before her on the dressing table was her make-up: lipstick, mascara and eyeliner. Also on the dressing table was a litre bottle of vodka, two-thirds full, and two bottles of pills. One of the bottles of pills was open with its top beside it. She was putting on lipstick. It was a deep blood red that stood out garishly against the paleness of her skin. As he watched, she stopped and looked at herself in the mirror. She took a handful of pills from the bottle, put them in her mouth and washed them down with the vodka. Then she refilled her glass to the top and continued with the lipstick. The television was on loud. It was on a music channel and she stopped at times to listen. She continued with her lipstick. Then she put some powder on her cheeks, did her eyebrows and eyelids. All the time she kept stopping to take more pills and refill her glass. Her head and shoulders moved in time to the beat of the music and her lips mouthed something. When the first bottle of pills was empty, she undid the top of the other one and continued. She took great care with the make-up, stopping to look at herself in the mirror and redoing bits that she wasn't satisfied with. By the time she had finished, both bottles of pills were empty and the vodka bottle only had two or three inches left in it.

She stood up a little unsteadily and looked in the mirror. Then she blew a kiss to herself and said something in a low voice. Picking up the vodka bottle, she cradled it in her arms like a dancing partner and moved slowly to the middle of the room. She turned to face the television and began to dance to the music. Her skirt fell to her mid-thigh and her long legs stood out in sheer black stockings. One black strap of her bra had escaped from under her dress and slipped down onto her arm.

As she danced she raised the vodka bottle to her lips and drank. Some of the liquid spilled and ran down her chin, dropping onto her breasts and dress. She clasped the bottle to her and closed her eyes. Her lips mouthed something he could not hear. The movements became slower and slower and more and more unsteady as the drugs and alcohol took effect. Suddenly she staggered and fell, still holding the vodka bottle. He heard a crack as her head hit the floor. One side of her dress rode up almost to her waist. He was standing over her, looking down at the crumpled pale figure in black and red, lying like a broken doll that some child had tossed away.

Mike woke in the darkness and lay staring at the ceiling. The image of the woman on the floor was vivid before him. For a moment he could not move or think. This dream was as real as the others, but so completely different. He looked at his watch; it was 2.30 in the morning, so there was a lot of the night still to come. He poured another glass of whisky and lay back, looking at the ceiling. When he closed his eyes he could still see the figure on the floor.

He woke again with the light streaming through the thin curtains. It was eight o'clock. There had been no more dreams, and for the first time for a while he felt refreshed by sleep. But the image of the woman lying on the hotel room floor and all that he had seen was still clear.

He got up, showered, shaved and pulled on his tee shirt and jeans. The only mirror in the room was on the dressing table, so he sat for a moment on the stool in front of it, looking at himself carefully. As he did so, it was as though he saw a different image – a woman in a red dress with lipstick in her hand. With a start he got up and took a couple of steps into the middle of the room. He looked around him. This was the room in his dream. The dressing table, the television, the carpet, it was all the same. He told himself he was being stupid. Every room in this motel must look like this. But he could not rid himself of the feeling. He was absolutely sure this was the room in his dream.

The others were already having breakfast and talking about the next gig. They were pleased to have had a night in a motel instead of sleeping on the road. The tour had gone well, and it was only right that they should get a bit of comfort. Soon it would be over and they would be back home. They were already looking forward to that and planning the things they would do. Mike listened to them. He still felt haunted by the image of the woman. Their normality and certainty were things he suddenly felt envious of.

"So, what are you going to do when we get back, Mike?" He realised Steve had asked him a question.

"Dunno, really. Sleep, I guess. Then look for another band."

"Ah the enthusiasm of youth," Dougie said mockingly. They were only four or five years older than Mike, but at times they liked to pretend he was the youngster on the tour. Mike felt in no mood to respond. He finished his coffee and got up, saying he was just going to put his things together and that he would see them at the truck

As he checked out at reception, Mike had a sudden urge to ask what was in his mind.

"I know this is an odd question, but has anything strange ever happened in the room I had?"

"What room did you have?" The brunette behind the desk looked up at him and checked his room number. "Oh sure, that was really sad. This woman OD'd in it about eighteen months ago. It was strange. She drove down from Philadelphia. Attractive looking, some kind of executive, I think, with an expensive car. I remember checking her in. When she didn't appear by lunchtime and didn't answer the phone, they went and opened up the room. They found her on the floor." She searched for something under the counter. "It made the local paper." She pulled out a wallet file and handed it to him. "It's the only publicity we've ever had. Not that it would make most people want to stay here."

Mike took the file and opened it. He knew what he would find before he looked, but it still made him breathe in deeply. The photograph on the front page of the paper was the woman from his dream. He scanned the newsprint. Twenty-eight-year-old Roberta McNeill had died of an overdose of sleeping tablets. There were no suspicious circumstances. It was clearly intended because a bottle of vodka and two bottles of pills had been found in her room. There was no suicide note. She was single, a high flyer who worked as a financial assistant for a big corporation. There was no obvious motive and the police were still investigating it.

"Sad," Mike said. "Did they ever find out why she did it?"

The receptionist sighed. "I think it was to do with some guy. It often is." She looked at him with curiosity. "What made you ask?"

Mike stared at her for a moment, not knowing what to say. "I don't really know." He shrugged his shoulders. "Just something about the room, I guess. Strange vibes, you know."

She looked at him with interest. "Some people say that if a terrible thing has happened in a place or a room, you can sense it. What do you think?" Her manner was open and friendly.

"I don't know. I've never really felt that way before."

"Maybe you've never stayed somewhere where a person has committed suicide before. I once went to a place in Kentucky where the Indians massacred some pioneers in the early days. You could just feel the sadness."

"Perhaps you're right." Mike shrugged his shoulders again. At least she didn't seem to think he was crazy. "Thanks for the information." He handed her back the file.

"You're welcome." She smiled at him. "So, you're moving on today?"

"Yeah, we've got a gig in Philadelphia. A couple more after that and then we're back to the UK."

"Well, I hope it all goes well." She smiled again and looked as though she was going to say something else. It was as if she wanted to prolong their conversation.

"Thanks again," he said, returning her smile and picking up his bag. Then, on an impulse, he put it down again. "Do you fancy coming to see the band? I can give you a free pass to get in." Feeling embarrassed, he added, "I'd really like to hear more about this place in Kentucky."

"I'd like to, but I'm probably working." There was a tinge of regret in her voice. "When is it?"

"Tomorrow night in Philadelphia."

"Hey," she brightened up, "that's my day off. I don't have to be back here until lunchtime the next day. So I can stay over in Philly and drive back in the morning."

"You'll come, then?" Mike suddenly felt unsure. "It's only a bit of British rock and roll."

"Of course I'll come. That's really kind of you." There was warmth in her voice.

"Okay, let me write you out a pass." He took a piece of notepaper from the desk and the pen and began to write on it. He suddenly stopped and looked at her. "I'm sorry, I don't even know your name."

She laughed and pointed to the badge on her blouse. "Sandra. Sandie, actually, Sandie Wilson. And you're...?"

"Mike," he said and held out his hand. Then realised what an English thing it was to do. She took it, laughing.

"Nice to meet you, Mike." Her hand was soft and warm. He looked at her properly for the first time. Her light brown hair was styled and part of it fell across her forehead. Below it, he met her eyes; they were brown and full of friendliness. Freckles dusted her cheeks and snub nose and her mouth turned up at the corners, like she was someone who was always smiling. Even though they had only exchanged a few words, he felt they had somehow made contact with each other. He let her hand go, realising he had probably held onto it for too long and seemed ridiculous.

He returned to writing, then folded the piece of paper in half and handed it to her. "The gig starts at eight, but get there early and I'll come down and meet you. Give this to the guy on the door and he'll let you in and get a message to me."

"That's kind of you, Mike." As she took the paper from him, her fingers brushed against his hand.

"Maybe afterwards we can have a meal or a drink or something."

"I'd like that."

They looked at each other as if neither wanted to end this moment. Mike could think of nothing else to say so he picked up his bag again.

"So, Sandie, I'll see you in Philadelphia." He used her name for the first time.

"Yes."

He turned to go and then turned back. "Oh, and thank you for telling me about the room."

"You're welcome." Her voice had reverted to standard receptionist good manners, but the smile that accompanied it was far more personal.

Mike walked out to the truck where the others were waiting. He no longer felt alone. The conversation with Sandie seemed to have lifted the burden that had been pressing down on him ever since New Orleans.

They drove to Philadelphia that day and stayed in a cheap hotel near the venue. It gave them a day to set up for the gig. They ate in a cheap diner across the road. Steve and Dougie talked about going out for some beers, but Mike said he was tired and still felt feverish. He didn't want to be hung-over for the gig, so he went back to the hotel early. It was an old thirties building and the rooms were gloomy with high ceilings.

Mike lay down on the bed and stared at the ceiling. The streetlights threw patterns on it through the gaps in the curtains. He could hear cars going by in the street outside and in the distance, a train. Somewhere there was a siren. He thought of Sandie, as he had kept thinking of her since they had left the motel. Trying to picture her – the styled brown hair, the brown eyes, the smiling lips; he realised again that he knew nothing about her. She had been sitting behind the reception desk in a white blouse. He had never seen her stand up, so he didn't know if she was tall or short. In fact, he had paid very little attention to her physical appearance. And yet that didn't matter. His dream in the room, her experience in Kentucky, seemed to have created some kind of bond

30

between them. He wondered if he could talk to her about New Orleans. He needed to share it with somebody. She had seemed so open to ideas and so curious about them. Whether he would be able to talk to her about it he wasn't sure.

Looking up, he saw the ivory figure which he had put on the bedside table. He wondered what Sandie would make of it, this small, expressionless woman hiding her secrets like a sphinx. Picking it up between his finger and thumb, he stared at it. As he did so, it seemed to him as though the blank face became Sandie's, looking at him with that open, friendly smile.

He must have fallen asleep because he woke to find the light turning a pale grey outside the window. His watch said five-thirty. Traffic was beginning to pass on the street below. Perhaps it was the noise that had woken him. He lay for a while listening to it and realised that he must have slept without dreaming. It was too early to get up, so he lay and dozed, not sure whether he was awake or asleep. He heard cars and imagined he was in the truck and they were driving down the state highway to Philadelphia. Signposts flashed by the window. Then he heard sirens. A police car accelerated past them, its lights flashing. They came to a stop. In front of them the traffic was at a standstill. He wound down the window to try to see what the problem was.

"Big pile up ahead," he heard a car driver say. Getting out of the truck he walked up between the stationary cars. He came to a place where the highway was covered with debris. Cars were on their sides. Some were burnt out. He felt suddenly gripped by anxiety. The medics were there. They were carrying bodies out on stretchers. He stood watching as they passed. A man with a badly burnt face, writhing in pain, came first. Next, a young boy who with a broken leg. As each case went by, he scanned the face anxiously, filled with a growing sense of foreboding. Then he saw her. He recognised her immediately, even though he had only seen her once. The styled brown hair that fell across her forehead had fallen back from her face; the brown eyes were open, sightless.

"What a shame, such a pretty girl," he heard one of the medics say.

"No," he shouted. "No, it can't be!"

*

31

Mike woke, suddenly filled with panic. He had to do something. Sandie was going to drive up today. He needed to stop her. But how? He had no phone number for her. The motel, he thought, he must phone the motel. They would have a number for her. He sat on the bed, trying to remember what it was called and where it was. But he hadn't really paid much attention to it at the time. It had seemed just the same as all the others they had passed along the highway. Mike looked at his watch. It was seven o'clock. She had said that she had the day off and he had no idea what time she would leave. He pulled on his jeans and tee shirt. How could he find out the name of the motel and its number? Perhaps Steve or Dougie would know. He stood up and out of habit, thrust his hands into the pocket of his jeans. One came in contact with a folded piece of paper. He pulled it out and looked at it. It was a flyer for the motel. He must have picked it up automatically and put it in his pocket. Quickly he went to the phone and dialled the number. He waited for the sound of ringing, but there was only silence. He looked again at the flyer. In his hurry, he realised he hadn't used the code. He tried again. This time the phone rang. Mike stood, listening, holding his breath. He pictured the reception area as it had been when he had spoken to her and willed for someone to pick it up. Eventually the ringing stopped and a female voice recited the number.

"I wonder if I could speak to Sandie Wilson?"

"I'm afraid not, it's her day off."

"Is it possible that you could give me her number? I need to contact her urgently."

There was silence on the other end for a moment. Then the voice said, "And who are you?"

"My name's Mike. I stayed with you the night before this."

"I'm sorry, we don't give staff numbers out over the phone."

"But I need to contact her urgently."

"I'm sorry, but that's the rule."

"Could you possibly give her a message for me? It's really important."

"Okay, let me just get some paper." There was the sound of an object being picked up. "Okay, go ahead." Mike tried to think of what to say. "Look, I gave her a pass for a gig in Philadelphia tonight but she mustn't come."

"Is the gig off?"

"No, it's not that. Look, it's hard to explain. I really need to talk to her. I'm staying at the Hotel…" He read the name off the notepad by the phone. "Can you ask her to call me here? But she must not drive to Philadelphia today. Have you got that?"

"Mustn't drive to Philadelphia today and to ring you. Okay, I'll do my best. I'm sure I've got her number here somewhere."

"You will make sure she gets the message?"

The voice sounded irritated. "Look, I said I'd do my best. Now would you get off the phone? I have a guest to attend to."

Mike started to thank her, but the receiver at the other end clicked as she put the phone down.

Mike stood looking at the phone. There was nothing more he could do. He just had to depend on her to ring Sandie. If he tried to ring again he would just annoy her more. Undressing, he showered and shaved, listening out all the time for the ringing of the phone, but it remained silent. For a while he sat down on the bed, staring at the receiver. It did not ring. When he went down to breakfast he stopped at reception and told them he was expecting a call and could they let him know if one came in. Over breakfast he tried to pull himself together. He'd just had a bad dream. It probably meant nothing at all. She would phone in a minute and he would be embarrassed about trying to explain and she would laugh at him. But she didn't phone. After breakfast there was still no message for him. He had to go to start setting up for the gig.

After a long morning's work they went to get some food from a diner near the venue. As they sat eating, the television was showing the local news. Suddenly the screen was filled with pictures of damaged cars. Mike froze. It was exactly what he had seen in his dream. As soon as they started showing pictures of the dead and injured he felt a sickness in his stomach. Sandie's face filled the screen and he knew at once that she was dead.

That night, Mike lay on his bed in the hotel, feeling completely alone. He had had to tell the others part of what had happened. How he'd given Sandie a pass to the gig and he had recognised her face on the screen. They could see that he was upset. His sense of grief had been impossible for him to hide. He did not tell them about his dream. They would not have understood. It sounded crazy that he could dream about something that then came true. That was not possible. He couldn't shake off a feeling of guilt. If he had not invited Sandie to come to the gig, she would still be alive. It wasn't just that his message had not got through, that he had failed to warn her. Part of him wondered if, in some way, by dreaming about her death he had caused it.

That night he was back in the passageway. It seemed longer this time. She stood waiting for him right at the end of it, a very long way away. As usual, his legs were unable to move him forward. There was a kind of light behind her that he had not noticed before. It made her appear almost radiant. At last he reached her. She was looking at him and holding out her hand. He came closer. Tonight her look was different. Her eyes were no longer imploring; they were calmer. She was smiling with a warmth he'd never seen before. Stretching out, she took his hand and pulled him close to her. Her scent filled his nostrils. With her other hand she pressed something into his fingers. It was one of the small carved ivory figures that hung round her neck and wrists. As she handed it to him she began to fade away. He tried to hold her, but she had gone and he stood alone in the passageway with the small figure glowing in the palm of his hand.

Mike woke and put his hand in his pocket. It was still there, hard and smooth beneath his fingers, the small carved ivory figure that was the one tangible thing, the one piece of evidence that proved something had happened that night in New Orleans. He did not know what it meant, only that somehow it was important. Perhaps it was the key to his dreams or a burden that he must carry. Whatever it was he would now have to face it on his own.

3

England, September 2004 – June 2005

The policeman stepped forward and knocked on the door for a second time. Again he shouted, demanding that those inside open it. Again there was no response. He turned to his two colleagues.

"Alright," he said, "break it down." They stepped forward with large sledgehammers and began smashing the door in around the lock. At once a dog started barking furiously from inside and children started screaming.

Laura stood back and watched. She hated forced entries. She'd done two before this one and they had really affected her. In her job as a social worker she had seen and heard many disturbing things, but these upset her more than anything else. She wasn't sure if it was the violence of the entry itself, with the sound of splintering wood, or what followed – the forced separation of children from parents. Then there was the uncertainty. You never knew what would be behind the closed door; violence almost always provoked violence. Laura had seen plenty of squalor. She had dealt with victims of abuse, been sworn at and threatened, all in the course of her job, but none of it made her feel like this.

The door splintered and hung on its hinges. The three policemen stepped through it and into the front room of the two-up two-down terraced house. Immediately a large black dog rushed forward and attacked one of them. He pushed it back with the handle of his sledgehammer and pinned it against the wall.

"Grab its collar, Jimmy," he shouted. One of his colleagues hurried over and grabbed hold of the dog. It twisted and struggled, trying to bite him while he looked round for something to tie it with. An unshaven man in a vest and jeans staggered to the doorway of the second room.

From either side of him peered the faces of two frightened girls. The house smelt of dog, urine, alcohol and tobacco.

"Get out of my fucking house, you bastards," he shouted, waving a baseball bat at them.

"Paul McIntyre," the policeman said in a calm voice, "I am arresting you on suspicion of burglary and drug dealing. Put the bat down or you'll just make things more difficult."

"Get out of my fucking house," the man repeated, gesturing with the bat. The dog struggled and snarled. The children began screaming. Their strident, high-pitched voices filled the room.

"Come on, Mr McIntyre, put the bat down." One of the constables walked across the room towards him. McIntyre lunged for him, but the constable caught him by the wrist and bent it. McIntyre cried out with pain and dropped the bat. At once the other constable was there. He pinned McIntyre's arms behind him and handcuffed him. Then, one on each side, they began to pull him out of the room. At that point, the dog escaped from the man who had been holding it and launched itself at the nearest constable, sinking its teeth into his leg. He hit it across the head with the sledgehammer he still held and stunned it. The third constable was able to grab it and put a rope around it. Then they dragged McIntyre and the dog out of the house towards the waiting van. The constable who had been bitten was swearing loudly with the pain.

"Okay, love, the kids are all yours," one constable said to Laura as they left the house.

"Come on, Rob," she said over her shoulder to her colleague and stepped across the room towards the girls. They stopped screaming and vanished into the inner room, where they stood with their backs against the wall. Kim, aged nine and Tracey, aged five, Laura remembered from the files she had read.

"Come on, Kim," she said, "we're not going to hurt you." She stepped towards them. The room was a shambles of dirty plates, mugs, empty bottles and tins.

"Fuck off," the older girl shouted back. The younger one was clinging onto her, terrified. "Leave us alone."

"Listen, Kim, we're not going to hurt you. We just want to take you where we can get you cleaned up." Laura kept her voice low and calm and stood still for a moment.

"I want my Dad," Tracey, the younger one, sobbed. Kim shielded her protectively. "Go away and leave us alone," she shouted. Suddenly she moved forward and picked up a knife out of a drawer. She waved it at Laura. "Go away or I'll fucking cut you, you bitch," she shouted.

Laura looked round. She picked up a towel from a chair and held it in front of her. "Come on, Kim." Her voice was soft. "Don't be silly. You can't stay here now your Dad's gone." She took a careful step forward, sensed that Rob was moving to her right. "You want to see your Dad, don't you?" She continued in a low voice and took another tentative step. Kim lunged towards her, slashing the air with the knife. Laura steadied herself, holding the towel in front of her. Kim slashed again. Laura thrust the towel forwards. The knife caught on the towel. Rob rushed forward and grabbed Kim, pinning her arms to her sides. The knife clattered to the floor. He lifted her off her feet and carried her, kicking and swearing, outside. Laura quickly put her arm round Tracey, who burst into tears. She led the sobbing child out of the house.

Outside, Rob was still struggling with Kim.

"Open the door for me," he said. She left Tracey for a moment and opened the back door of the car. Rob bundled Kim inside. Laura pushed Tracey in as well and locked the car with the remote. Kim was screaming and trying to get out; Tracey was crying. They both waited a few minutes for the noise to subside. Once in the back of the car, all the fight went out of Kim and she too burst into tears. Then they got in and Laura spoke to her again, gently.

"It's all going to be okay, Kim. We are going to take you somewhere where you can get cleaned up. Then we will have to find somewhere for you both to stay until you can see your Dad." Kim said nothing, just continued sobbing. Rob drove the car off, while Laura kept talking to the girls and reassuring them.

Once they got to the social services offices, they took them out of the car and into the building. There they were met by Carol from the child protection team. She helped Laura to get the girls to shower and put on clean clothes. Laura kept talking to them all the time, but Kim said nothing and Tracey kept sobbing. Then Carol started to interview them, while Laura tried to find a placement where they could stay for the next few days. Normally they would have tried to find another member of the family who would look after them. For Kim and Tracey this wasn't possible. Laura had already tried before they went to the house. They had not been able to get in touch with the mother and there were no suitable family members living locally. There was an aunt in Stoke, but they had still not been able to contact her, either. There was a short-term foster family that Laura had already spoken to. She rang them again; they agreed to come in and meet the two girls and to take them until at least Monday. They were an experienced couple who had taken difficult youngsters before. Laura was confident that they would cope with Kim and Tracey, at least for the first few days.

By five fifteen they had come and collected the two girls. The first interview had not gone well. Neither girl wanted to say anything about their father or what had been happening in their house. Carol decided to give up for the day. Laura went back to her desk to write her report, feeling completely drained. She looked at her watch. It was Thursday and she was going out at seven thirty. The report would be needed tomorrow, so she took a deep breath and then made a start. By six she was on her way out of the offices, as usual one of the last to leave.

Laura parked her car on her drive. It was only a small, modern terraced house, but it was hers. She always felt that sense of pride when she came home after work. It had taken a lot of saving and a little help from her parents, until fifteen months ago she had moved in. She unlocked her front door and looked around. Furnishing it had been hard and had taken time, looking for deals, trying to find the right things, but now it was more or less complete and she could feel that it was really hers.

Dropping her bag on the floor, Laura picked up the post. There was nothing of interest, so she put it on the coffee table in the lounge. The room had a two-seater settee and two armchairs. She had bought them at an auction and spent the whole winter recovering them. Going into the kitchen, she opened the fridge and poured herself a glass of white wine. Then she picked up the phone and dialled.

"Hi, Lottie. Are you still okay for tonight? Good. Look I've only just got in so I might be a bit late. No, it's been a pig of a day. You too, eh? I'll tell you about it later. See you in the Crown at about eight. Don't worry if I'm a bit late."

Laura took a deep drink of wine and thought about food. She wasn't really hungry. The forced entry still left her feeling churned up, but she had better eat something. "It's no good drinking on an empty stomach," she thought. She needed something quick. Back in the kitchen she looked in the fridge and found the remains of some Bolognese sauce. It took no time to boil some spaghetti and heat up the sauce. Within fifteen minutes it was ready, and she was sitting at the table in the dining room, leafing through the local paper while she ate. As soon as she had finished, Laura washed up, poured another glass of wine and took it upstairs with her. In her bedroom, she drew the curtains, undressed and undid her hair – tied up for work – letting it fall over her shoulders. Her watch said twenty to seven, so there was enough time to wash it before she had to leave. Going into the bathroom, she turned on the shower and stood under the warm water. It ran through her hair and over her face and body. She felt it wash the grime of her day away and began to think about the night ahead. Thursday nights were one of her nights out in the week. The Corn Exchange in the town centre normally had a band of some kind playing. Sometimes they were local ones she'd never heard of. Occasionally they got a more well-known one. Not someone really famous, but maybe a group that were just beginning to make their name. It was fun and it was different. After the shower, she wrapped a towel round her and went back into the bedroom to dry her hair.

Laura stood up and walked across the room to her underwear drawer. Buying nice underwear was one of her indulgences. She rummaged through for a few minutes thoughtfully and chose a matching set of bra and pants in ivory. The bra was low cut and slightly see-through. The pants were see-through at the side with a lacy pattern over the crotch. She put them on and looked at herself in the mirror. They looked good. Wearing sexy underwear made her feel sexy and slightly aroused. Frequent visits to the gym and the pool had kept her in shape. Her breasts were firm and did not sag, her hips were wide but her waist slim, and her bum was okay. She turned sideways and was satisfied. Though who it was for, she had no idea. Laura hadn't had a date since she'd moved into her house. She kept hoping that she might meet someone nice, but most of the men seemed too young, or creeps who just tried to get you drunk.

She closed the drawer and took a pair of skin-tight jeans from her cupboard. With some effort she managed to wriggle into them, making a mental note to make sure she got to the gym on Saturday. Then she put on a simple white short-sleeved top. It had a rounded neckline that revealed a bit of cleavage and clung to her body, accentuating the curve of her breasts. Laura returned to the dressing table and took another sip of wine. She dried her hair, applied a deep red lipstick and added a little make-up. Not too much, she wanted to look sophisticated, not like a slag. For a final touch, she added a simple gold chain and a pair of hooped gold earrings. She sat back and looked at the effect, brushed her hair out and then smiled at herself in the mirror, almost ready for action. She took the bottle of perfume from the dressing table and applied a little to her neck. Perfume was another passion of hers. Chanel N° 5 she loved more than any other, but the bottle was getting low and it was a long time till her birthday.

Laura looked at her watch: seven twenty-five. Where had the time gone? She threw her work clothes into the cupboard, shut the door and took the towel back to the bathroom. Finishing the wine, she took the empty glass downstairs, then rushed upstairs again for shoes and a handbag. Equipped with these, she hurried downstairs and, picking up a jacket and her keys, was out of the door.

Outside her house she turned right and walked to the end of the street, reaching the bus stop on the corner just as the green single-decker came into view. The bus wasn't full so she sat on her own halfway down on the kerb side. She took out her mirror and checked her appearance in case rushing had dishevelled her hair, but she was fine.

Lottie was her best friend. She went right back to the first day at secondary school. They had both come, as the only pupils from different, tiny village schools, to the large comprehensive. Somehow on that first day they had ended up sitting together and had become friends at once. At first they clung together for some kind of mutual support amid the chaos of new people, bigger people and sometimes rougher people. That mutual security had turned into a genuine liking for each other, and as they grew older they had developed common interests.

They had both stayed on in the sixth form, though doing slightly different subjects. When Laura went to Swansea to study Sociology, the first step to working for social services, Lottie had studied English at Cardiff. The towns were so close that it had been easy to keep in touch and share their experiences of university and men. When Lottie went to Exeter to do her PGCE they had lost touch a little. Then she had turned up in the same town as second in English at one of the local secondary schools, about a year after Laura had moved there to be one of social services' team leaders. For a while they had thought of sharing a flat or even buying a house together. In the end they decided that such close proximity might spoil their friendship. Lottie rented a flat on the other side of town. She said she was saving for a deposit on a house, following Laura's example, but she liked foreign holidays too much and was not as good at saving as Laura. They always met on a Thursday to go to the Corn Exchange to see whatever group was playing. It was their girls' night out of the week. At first they had gone hoping that they might meet someone interesting. Now it was just fun to be out having a few drinks and a bop and thinking that it was almost the end of the week. Sometimes they would go out for meals or trips to the theatre. Lottie was a good friend, and that sense of mutual support was still very strong between them.

The bus reached the market square. Laura got off and crossed the road to the Crown. She headed for the so-called Farmers' Bar. It was normally less crowded and not as noisy as the Ploughboys, one on the other side, and there was less chance of Lottie bumping into some of her sixth formers. That was one of the drawbacks of being a teacher in a small town.

Laura went in. Lottie was already there at a seat in the corner sipping a gin and tonic. As Laura came over she stood up. She was wearing a loose black top with red flowers, caught in at the waist by a belt and black jeans. Her straw blonde hair fell to her shoulders and she had a sense of style that Laura both admired and envied.

"Hi," said Laura, embracing her and giving her a kiss on the cheek. Their friendship had always had the warmth of physical contact. "Are you ready for another one?"

Lottie looked down at her almost full glass. "Not quite," she said, "but it's tempting." She thought for a moment. "No, I shall begin with restraint."

"I can't see that lasting long," Laura laughed and turned to go to the bar. She ordered a gin and tonic for herself and then came back to the table to join Lottie. She normally drank wine, but sometimes a gin and tonic had that little extra kick, especially after a trying day.

"Cheers," said Lottie as they clinked glasses. "Now unburden yourself about the hard and unappreciated lot of the country's favourite scapegoat and then I'll tell you about my horrors in Year Nine. Assuming, that is," she looked around furtively, "that none of them or their delightful parents are skulking anywhere in the shadows."

Laura leaned back in her chair and took a deep drink of the gin. Lottie was always good for her and she could already begin to feel herself relax.

"It was a forced entry," she said. "Absolute chaos. One of the police got bitten by a dog. This little girl tried to attack me with a kitchen knife."

"Well, even my Year Nines cannot compete with that scale of violence." Lottie looked at her with concern. "Are you okay?"

"Yes, really. It wasn't her fault, poor kid. She was scared stiff. God knows what her father had been doing to her. Neglect at the very least." She dropped her voice also, looking round. "I guess we will spend most of tomorrow extracting all the sordid details."

"A bit unnerving though, for you. What exactly happened?"

Laura moved closer so she could speak in a low voice and described the scene in the house.

"It was a bit scary I suppose, but there wasn't really time to think. I just knew we had to get the girls out of there. You know, some people live in a completely different world." She gestured around the bar with its well-dressed clientele. "You would never believe that such things could exist in a town like this."

"Will the girls be alright?" Lottie asked.

"I doubt it," Laura said heavily. "If he hasn't physically fucked them, he has certainly fucked up their lives. He'll probably go to prison and they will end up in foster care. As they are young it might work, but probably not. Never mind, tell me about the horrors of Year Nine. Are they really worse than we were?"

"You bet," said Lottie and began to describe the antics of her group. Laura was never sure how true it really was, but it always made her laugh and moved her thoughts away from the endless squalor and sadness that she dealt with. She sometimes wondered why she had ended up working for social services. As Lottie had said, social workers did seem to be the scapegoats of the nation. They were either villains because they took children away from their parents when they shouldn't, or villains because they did not take children away from their parents when they should. Sociology had fascinated her at school and had made her want to make things better for people, with the belief that she actually could. The reality was proving to be something different. She bought them another drink and asked Lottie, "Do you know anything about the band playing tonight?"

"Not really. Although Paul, who teaches drama, said he'd heard they were okay. He said they were real rock and may be on the verge of a record deal."

Laura smiled. Through her school Lottie was always a mine of information. Anything local, somebody, staff or pupils, knew something about. You would have thought social services would be a good network, but they weren't. Rob, who'd been on the entry, was okay, though he was newly married and didn't socialise much. Most of the others seemed to be middle-aged women, more interested in talking about their own kids that anything else. She sighed. "Well I could certainly do with something to blow my mind away tonight."

"Cheer up, old girl," Lottie said, "after all, tomorrow's Friday. I know you've got a pretty grotty day, but after that it's the weekend and freedom at least for a while. Have you got anything planned?"

"Not much, though there's an auction I might go to on Saturday. I'd love to get a desk. What about you?"

"You really are obsessive about your house, aren't you? Must be your nest-building instinct. I have been summoned home. It's my Nan's birthday, so we're all going out for a meal."

"Oh." Laura had hoped they might do something together. She tried not to look disappointed.

"Why don't you come along? I'm sure your folks would be glad to see you and you're almost part of our family. Mum and dad could squeeze another place at the meal."

Laura looked doubtful. "I'm not sure. I've got to write up my case notes on Sunday."

"We'd be back by lunchtime. I've got essays to mark too. Go on, it would be fun. We could look up some of our old friends."

"Maybe. I'll think about it."

It was tempting. She wanted to do something that weekend, a trip home though wasn't quite what she was thinking of.

"Well, I'm going straight after work, so give me a ring if you want to come. "

They were silent for a few moments, then Laura looked at her watch.

"Come on, drink up. The support group must be nearly done. Time for battle."

One of the reasons for going to the Crown first was that it was directly opposite the Corn Exchange. They could sit and have their drinks in comfort, then go across when they were ready. It saved standing outside and queuing, which Lottie didn't like because there was more chance of seeing some of her pupils. Usually they missed the supporting band; experience had taught them that they were pretty dire, with sound systems that seemed permanently distorted.

At the Corn Exchange they showed their tickets on the door and went in. The hall was about three-quarters full. Quite a good turnout, thought Laura. Maybe this band would be good. They made their way towards the front. Their timing was just right; the support group had finished. Lots of people were coming out to get drinks or go to the loo. They were able to move forward easily and ended up near the front on the right. Laura looked round. The place always looked so ordinary with the house lights on, just a room and a stage with people milling around aimlessly. She looked at the rest of the audience. There were people of all ages; some teenagers but also some older people. She was surprised that she so rarely saw anybody she knew, but then probably there were a lot of people from outside the town.

At last the house lights dimmed. There was a murmur of anticipation as the stage was illuminated. The simple lighting transformed the room. Everything was focused on the stage. At last, four figures walked in to applause and struck up their first number. Laura loved that moment, when the band played. She could just focus on them and the music. In some ways it didn't matter how bad they were; they cast a kind of spell over her. It was too loud to talk so it was just a case of losing yourself. This group were not bad. The vocalist had a reasonable voice. The lead and bass guitarists worked well together. The music had a thumping beat. She didn't know any of the songs, but she could just listen to the words and move to the beat and forget about everything else. She was surprised when the lead singer said they were taking a break. They'd played for about an hour.

The lights came on and destroyed the magic. She turned to Lottie to ask if she fancied fighting the queue either for a drink or the loo, when a voice from behind, made her turn round.

"Can I buy you two ladies a drink?"

The owner of the voice was tall, with blonde hair and a blonde beard. He was smiling at them.

"That's really kind of you," said Lottie, "but the queue is massive."

"Don't worry," he said, "I can shortcut the queue, I'm the sound engineer. What do you want?"

"In that case," Lottie said, looking quickly across at Laura, "we'd both have a white wine."

"Be back in a minute. By the way, I'm Mike. Don't go away."

"We certainly shan't," they both said together.

"Where did he spring from?" said Lottie, watching him as he made his way through the crowd.

"I guess somewhere backstage," Laura replied. "I wonder why he asked us?"

"Because we are the only two beautiful women in the room," replied Lottie, extravagantly.

Before they could continue, Mike was back with two white wines.

"That was quick," said Laura admiringly, "how did you manage that?"

"I have an arrangement with the barman. If I manage to sneak out at the interval he serves me at the side of the bar. I don't have time to queue up."

"Sounds a good arrangement," Lottie said.

"So what do you think of the band?"

"They're not bad," Laura said. "Are you one of their crew?"

"No, I work here at the Corn Exchange. I do the sound each Thursday and for anything else, normally. Do you like rock?"

"Yeah," said Lottie. "We come most Thursday nights to see what's on. It's better than the rubbish they play at the discos round here."

"Sure," Mike said. "Are you locals then?"

"Depends what you mean," replied Lottie. "If you mean were we born and bred here, then certainly not, but we live in the town."

Laura was happy to let Lottie do the talking. She studied Mike carefully. He was taller than she was. His blonde hair fell almost to his shoulders, but his beard was neatly trimmed. The black tee shirt he wore was stretched tight across his chest, revealing a well-built figure with little trace of fat. He looked as though he had made an effort to keep in shape. There was a quiet confidence about him, though he did not seem arrogant.

"Me too," he said. "It's not a bad place to live, for a small town." He stopped for a moment. There was an awkward pause, then he spoke again. "I've got to go back to my desk in a minute, the band will return soon for the rest of the gig. I know it might seem a bit of a cheek because I've only just said hello, but do you fancy coming for a drink afterwards?"

Lottie looked across at Laura, who shrugged. "Okay, if it's not for too long. We've both got to work tomorrow, so we can't be too late. Or I won't have the energy to contain my little darlings."

Mike looked puzzled.

*"I'm a teacher," Lottie said.

"Oh, I see," he grinned. "Great. If you hang on here when everyone goes, I'll only be about ten minutes."

"We won't move an inch," Lottie said, giving him a slightly quizzical look.

"Okay," he said, "see you in a bit." He gave them a final grin and disappeared into the crowd that was beginning to fill up the hall.

"Well, what do you make of that?" Lottie turned to Laura with an enquiring look. "I must say, you were a bit quiet."

"I don't know, really." Laura thought for a moment. She genuinely wasn't sure what to make of this man who'd suddenly appeared. "He seems okay."

"Do you want to stay? We could just go, you know," Lottie asked.

"Why not? At least he's someone different. We don't have to stay long. It'll be closing time pretty soon after they finish anyway."

"Okay, as long as you promise to do a bit of talking."

"I will," Laura said, "as long as you let me get a word in."

Lottie opened her mouth to reply, but was drowned out as the band started up. Instead, she made a face at Laura, who stuck her tongue out in return. Then they turned back to the music. The second half of the gig seemed to drag. Laura felt uncertain. The encounter had been so brief. In some ways, it was so odd he'd come up to them like that. She supposed that if he was stuck at his controls every Thursday, he never really got the chance to meet anyone, even though the hall was full of people. He'd seemed okay, whatever that meant.

At last the band finished and the hall emptied. They stood together, feeling slightly awkward and conspicuous. Lottie looked at her watch. They talked about the band. The drummer had seemed a bit over the top. The lead singer was good, but had sometimes tried to hit notes that were too high for him. Lottie looked at her watch again. She was becoming impatient and was about to suggest they go when Mike appeared, hurrying across the hall with a denim jacket over his shoulder.

"Sorry," he said, "just had to sort out a slight problem. Let's go this way." He led them to a side door they hadn't really noticed before. "Where do you fancy?" It opened onto a small street beside the Corn Exchange and then down an alley that brought them out further down the high street. "The Lamb or the Royal Oak?"

"Not the Lamb," Lottie said. "They serve under age and I don't want to meet any of my little or not-so-little darlings."

"Okay," he said. "The Royal Oak it is. I think they have an extension to eleven thirty on a Thursday." He turned left and they followed him along the street, walking quickly to match his pace. The one thing the town had, like many English small towns, was plenty of pubs. They had once tried to have a drink in every one, but had got rather drunk and had to get a taxi back to Laura's. Within a couple of minutes they were going into the Royal Oak. It wasn't a pub they went to often. Taking its cue from its name, it was oak panelled and rather dark. It was moderately full but they managed to find a table.

"What can I get you?" Mike asked. "White wine again?"

"No, it's okay," said Lottie with determination. "We'll get you a drink. What do you want?"

"But I invited you and you waited for me," Mike protested.

"Yes, but you bought us a drink at the Corn Exchange. We would never have got served without you because of the queue." She gave him one of her looks.

"Okay." He put his hands up in mock surrender. "A pint of best would be great."

Lottie went off to the bar.

"Very determined, your friend," Mike said, looking across the table at Laura. "I'm not surprised she's a teacher."

"Lottie is very determined," Laura laughed. "She doesn't take any prisoners, so watch yourself, and she's fiercely independent."

"So that's Lottie and you're…?" he asked. The conversation at the gig had been so short that they had never told him their names.

"I'm Laura," she said, smiling at him.

"The two Ls, eh? Lottie and Laura. Are you a teacher too?"

"No, I work for social services."

Lottie returned with two glasses of wine and a pint of beer.

"Thanks," Mike said, "cheers." He raised his glass. They raised theirs in return. He drank deeply, emptying about half of it, then looked at them apologetically. "I'm really thirsty," he said. "It gets pretty hot backstage with the lights and all the people." He put the glass down and grinned at them across the table. "So, where do you teach?" he asked Lottie.

She started to describe the secondary school, embarking on one of her wonderful picturesque monologues about flaking walls, leaking roofs and stroppy teenagers, which soon had them both laughing. Laura had heard it countless times before, although it was never entirely the same. Lottie had always been more confident than Laura when it came to talking. Even on that first day at secondary school, when they had met, it was Lottie who had walked across the room and introduced herself as Laura had stood there, feeling alone. She could talk in a way that was interesting and amusing. It made her the centre of attention. Laura didn't really mind; she was normally happy to sit back and observe. She loved watching people. They had always fascinated her, which was why she had been drawn to sociology and psychology at school. Tonight, though, for the first time she envied Lottie. Suddenly she would like to have been funny and interesting and able to capture people's attention. Yet, as she watched, it seemed to her that, although Mike was listening to Lottie and appeared absorbed by what she was saying, he was actually studying her. She suddenly found him looking at her. Their eyes met for a moment, then he looked away.

They had finished their drinks and Mike was standing up, offering them another one.

"No, I'd love to, but I really do have to go to work tomorrow. If I go now I'll just catch the last bus."

"Me too," Laura said.

"Well, why don't I give you a lift? My car's just at the back of the Corn Exchange," Mike said. They looked at him doubtfully. "It's okay, I've only had this pint to drink, so I'm well under the limit. I never drink when I'm doing the sound. You can't take the risk of getting it wrong."

"But we live on opposite sides of the town," Lottie said. "I live out towards Seddon Road while Laura lives off Beech Avenue."

"That's okay," Mike said. "I live a bit further out than Laura. I'll drop you first, Lottie and then Laura. It won't take long; anyway, I don't have to be up as early as you two."

"That's really kind of you," said Lottie, "but I'd still like to go now, if you don't mind. If Laura wants to stay I can get the bus."

"No," said Laura, "I really need to make a move too. I've got a busy day tomorrow."

"Let's go, then," Mike said and led the way out onto the street. "It's been really nice to have a conversation. You don't know what it's like being stuck backstage all night, plugged into the earphones while you lot are leaping up and down and having fun. Maybe we could meet up for a drink or a meal sometime, when I'm not chained to the sound system."

"Do you work full-time at the Corn Exchange?" Laura asked.

"No, it's not a full-time job. Two or three evenings a week, sometimes more if they have a production. Occasionally during the day. I work part-time at Andy's Records as well. Now and again I get asked to do sound for a band."

"You mean when they're on tour?" Laura asked.

"Yes. Then I can be away for two or three months or longer." They reached the car park at the back of the Corn Exchange. "Here we are." He indicated a red Ford at the far end. "I'm afraid it's not very stylish, but it goes." He unlocked the car. Lottie got in the back as she was going to be dropped off first and Laura sat in the front with Mike.

"So, do you go on tour much, then?" Lottie asked, leaning forward and putting her head between them.

"Not so much now." Mike started the car and pulled out of the car park. "When I started out I spent most of my time touring. You'll have to direct me; although I've lived here for a while I'm not that good at street names. I sort of know where most things are, but not what the streets are called outside the centre." Lottie directed him to turn left at the next traffic lights.

"What is it like to tour with a band?" Laura asked.

"You really want to know? What do you think, four or five lads and three or four roadies, all cooped up together? Living in a truck or staying in cheap motels. Absolute hell." Mike laughed. "I mean, I never got to go with any of the really big bands, at least not when they were big, so there weren't any luxuries."

"Next right," said Lottie, "then it's the third house on the left."

He pulled up and got out to open the back door for her. "Nice to meet you, Lottie. I think it's the first time I've spoken to a schoolteacher since I left school myself. Maybe we can meet up again for a drink."

"Yes, okay," said Lottie, "give Laura your number and we'll arrange something."

"What about Saturday? I've actually got it off, because they've got some sort of dinner and they don't need any sound."

"Sorry, it's my Nan's birthday and I'm going down to my parents'. Maybe next weekend. Talk to Laura about it. I've got to go."

"Okay. Hope the kids don't give you a hard time tomorrow. Bye."

"Thanks, bye." Lottie turned and walked up to the house where she rented a flat. Mike got back in the car. He drove on, then turned left and then right so he could go back across town to where Laura lived.

"Was it really that bad? On tour, I mean," she asked. "I mean, surely the gigs and the audiences and things were exciting?"

"Sure. It was good to feel part of something. I mean it's not as glamorous as actually being up on stage. Being backstage you don't really see much of the audience, although you can sense how the gig is going. You do get that buzz when it starts. You can feel the excitement. But then you hear it all through the earphones and in a way you don't hear it as a concert. Not like when you go to one. You're focusing on the system, on keeping the balance right, or dealing with any feedback. You are sort of seeing it from a technical point of view, I guess."

"But you like the music?" she asked. She was trying to imagine him with his earphones on, hunched over the control desk, looking at counters and twiddling dials.

"Oh, I love rock and roll." The words came with a passion that surprised her. "Where now? As I said, I'm not great on street names."

Laura directed him and soon he was pulling up in front of her house.

He turned his face to hers. "Can I have your number?" He leant across and opened the glove compartment. "I'm sure I've a pen and some paper in here somewhere."

"Do you want to come in for a minute?" The words came without thinking. "I've got some paper indoors. I can give you Lottie's and my numbers."

He looked at her. "Are you sure? I know you've got work tomorrow. I don't want to keep you up."

"It's okay," Laura heard herself saying. "It'll just be for a moment."

They got out and he followed her to her front door. She unlocked it and let him in. He looked round the room.

"Do you rent this?" he asked.

"No, It's mine. I bought it about a year ago." Laura couldn't keep the pride out of her voice.

"You've got it really nice." Mike's tone was full of admiration as he inspected the room carefully.

"It's nearly there. It took a lot of scrimping and saving. Getting the furniture has been hard. I tend to go to auctions and look for bargains and then do them up. I reupholstered the settee and the chairs."

Mike walked further into the room. He ran his fingers over the settee.

"Very nice. It's a real home. It's got that feeling. I don't know, comfortable. You must be very proud of it."

"Oh, I am." There was real pleasure in Laura's voice. "Sit down. Would you like a drink while I find my address book?"

Mike chose one of the armchairs and sat down, still looking around the room. He seemed to be studying every aspect of it with great care. His attention to detail and his sense of the homeliness of the room pleased her. "Well, I'm not really staying."

"I'm sorry, I don't have any beer. It'll have to be wine or Scotch, I'm afraid." Laura ignored his faint protest.

"Scotch, please, but only a small one. I've still got to drive and I don't want to be over the limit."

Laura went through into the kitchen. She returned with a glass of wine in one hand, a whisky in the other and her address book under her arm. Putting the glasses down on the table, she sat down on the settee at the end closest to him and opened her address book.

"What's it like working for social services?" he asked.

"Shit," she said without looking up, surprising herself with the feeling she put into it.

"How do you mean?"

Laura paused for a moment and thought. Why had she invited him in? She wasn't normally so impulsive. How could she explain to him, a complete stranger, what her job was really like? She wasn't witty and clever like Lottie, and it wasn't a job that lent itself to humour, although it had its grim comic moments. Looking up, she saw that he was watching her intently. Again, their eyes met and she felt a strange warmth. There was a look of concern in his face that touched her.

"Oh, it's hard to explain, really." Laura sighed, as the recollection of the day came back to her and she suddenly felt weary. "It's supposed to be about helping people who cannot be helped."

"Go on." His voice was supportive.

"No," she shook her head. "It's too late at night. Some other time."

"You're tired. I'd better go." Mike started to get up, but she put her hand on his arm.

"You haven't given me your number yet. And what's your name? I can't really just put it under Mike."

"Pearce." He grinned at her and gave her the number.

She wrote it down in her book, then began to write out Lottie's number and her own on a loose piece of paper. As she wrote, Laura asked, "Well, Mike Pearce how did you end up as a sound engineer touring the world?"

"When I was a kid I loved rock and roll. I loved mucking about with technical things, fixing things. I'm afraid I wasn't much good at school. I just wasn't interested, only in rock and roll."

Laura neatly folded the paper and handed it to him. For a brief moment their hands touched.

"But it's a long story, too. You've got work tomorrow and perhaps it will give us a reason to meet again." They both stood up and walked towards the door. Halfway there, he stopped and turned to face her. They were standing very close together.

"Laura, it's been great to meet you," he began. It was the first time he had spoken her name. For some reason it sent a thrill through her. She looked up at him, blonde, bearded, smiling. Her impulses took over. She put her arms round him and kissed him full on the lips. It was not a polite peck, but a full passionate kiss. Her tongue forced itself between his lips. She could taste the whisky he had been sipping. Desire filled her. She felt him respond to her. His tongue touched hers. She closed her eyes, holding onto the moment. His left arm encircled her and pulled her closer to him. She felt his chest against her. Tentatively, as if uncertain as to what would be acceptable, she felt him place his right hand on her left side, below her shoulder blade. The touch of his fingers increased her desire. She enjoyed it for a moment and then, opening her eyes, gently pushed him away. Mike looked at her, about to say something, when she reached down and pulled her top over her head, revealing the ivory bra that she had chosen with such care. She saw his eyes widen, then he pulled her towards him and they were kissing again. His right hand explored her bra and then slipped inside it, cupping her breast. The feel of his hand against her flesh made her gasp slightly. Then his hands were behind her back, finding and undoing the clip of her bra. She moved away from him and removed the bra, dropping it on the floor. As she did so, he pulled his tee shirt off, so when they embraced again, her breasts were against his chest. For an instant, Laura wondered what she was doing. This was not her. But the thought was lost as she felt his body against hers and they kissed again. His hands slid down her back and touched her bottom, pressing her against him. Laura reached behind her and took his hands in hers, pulling them round in front of her and pushing him away. She took each in turn and kissed them. Then she let them drop. Quickly she went to the front door and locked it. Then she returned to him and, taking one of his hands in hers, led him, without speaking, across the room and to the stairs. She paused to switch off the light and took him in the darkness upstairs and into her bedroom. Once inside, she kicked off her shoes and embraced him again, kissing first his lips and then his chest. Her hands felt for the buckle on his belt and undid it.

The alarm woke Laura. It was Friday and work. She lay, trying to make sense of the body next to hers. Then she got up and went to the bathroom to shower. The water woke her and she stood thinking about the night. This was not her. She did not normally throw herself at men and drag them upstairs to her bedroom. Confusion and embarrassment filled her. What must he think of her? She dried herself and, suddenly self-conscious about her nakedness, wrapped the towel tightly around her before going back into the bedroom.

Mike was already dressed and sitting on the bed. He got up and came towards her. Laura didn't know what to say.

"I'll go and get out of your way," he said quietly. "I know you've got work."

"What about breakfast, coffee?" Laura felt even more confused. She didn't know whether she wanted him to go or to stay.

"No, honestly, I'll be fine. I'm sorry, when I came in I didn't mean to stay."

He seemed as embarrassed and confused as she did. Maybe he thought she was a slag and was desperate to get away. Laura wondered if she would ever see him again.

"Look, I don't normally go to bed with someone I've just met. You must think I'm a tart," she blurted out.

Mike came close to her and put his finger against her lips. "Ssh," he said. "I don't, either. It just happened; it seemed natural. I don't think you're a tart." He kissed her, not a hot kiss of desire, but with warmth and gentleness. "I think you're great. You're the best person I've ever met."

"But you don't know me," Laura protested.

"No, but I want to." Her pulled her against him and kissed her again. She felt the towel beginning to slip. "I want to see you again," he went on. "You're working today and I'm working really late tonight. What about Saturday? Can I take you out for a meal?"

"Okay, yes. That would be nice."

"Good, I'll come round about seven. Is that okay?"

"Yes."

"Great." He released her and moved towards the door. "Till Saturday." Just as he was about to leave, he came back and kissed her again. "You're great. I've never met anyone like you before." Then he was gone. Laura heard him go down the stairs and let himself out through the front door. She sank down onto the bed. Her world seemed to be spinning round her. His car started and drove away. Then there was silence. Looking round her empty room, she wondered if she had imagined it all.

A glance at her watch brought reality back. She needed to hurry or she would be late. Dressing for work was easy; blouse and trousers or blouse and skirt. Soon she was downstairs with coffee and toast. Going through to draw the curtains back in the front room, she saw their glasses on the table. Well, it certainly wasn't a dream.

Before she left, she texted Lottie: "Enjoy meal. I am staying here." Then after a pause she added "Other fish to fry."

The day seemed endless. There were the interviews to do with the two little girls. There was a meeting with a single parent whose partner was beating her up. There were case notes to write up. Laura found it hard to focus. Her mind kept returning to Mike and to last night. Even in the interviews, she suddenly realised that she had not heard what had been said and had to ask for it to be repeated.

At last she was back at home, sitting in the front room, but that was worse. Laura kept going back through what had happened and her own extraordinary behaviour. She was normally a bit reserved, shy even. There had been relationships before, but they had often been slow to start and quick to finish. She'd been with Lottie to discos, where middle-aged men had tried to grope them and been revolted by it. Yet last night she had stripped off for a complete stranger and taken him to her bed.

She poured herself a large glass of white wine, ran a bath and lay soaking in it. The sex had been okay. It didn't always work the first time she did it with someone new. He had struggled to take her stretch jeans off and in the end gave up and let her do it for him. She smiled at the thought of it. He had been gentle and considerate. She felt that he had touched her like a person, not just a piece of flesh.

Laura had felt conformable with him. There was something almost familiar, as though she already knew him. But she hadn't ever met him before. And the whole thing was very odd: to be approached out of the blue. She wondered if he had been watching them; sitting there at his controls, cut off from the crowd. Could he see the hall and the crowd? Maybe he'd been planning to approach them for weeks. The thought sent a bit of a shiver down her spine. Mike seemed normal though, not that sort. He was quite good-looking and interesting. There was something about him that made him different from most of the men they'd met in the town.

She gave up thinking and relaxed, stretching out in the warm water. Suddenly she sat upright. Would he actually come tomorrow night? Was he just being polite? Anxiety filled her, but then she went through the events of the morning and felt reassured. Most men who had no intention of seeing you again just said they'd phone you. Arranging to go out for a meal was a bit elaborate.

When she went back in the bedroom there were two messages on her phone. The first said, "Good frying Lottie." The second said, "looking 4ward 2 2morrow Mike." Laura looked at the second one for a long time, feeling a sense of excitement growing, then texted back, "me2 Laura."

Saturday dragged too. She went to the gym early and spent a couple of hours working out. Then she showered and did some washing, including the sheets. After that it was time to go to the auction, as she had planned. She managed to get a small bookcase for the spare room. It looked dreadful; someone had painted it yellow, but the wood was sound and, once it had been stripped down and varnished, it would be fine. Laura had also bid for a rather nice watercolour of the market square that had caught her attention. The bidding had gone too high, so she'd given up. There had been no desks she could afford, so that would have to wait for another day.

All day she had tried to keep focused on what she was doing and to avoid thinking about the evening ahead. She spent some time at the computer, typing up the week's case notes. There was supposed to be time to do it during working hours, but there never was. At four she decided that it was time to begin to get ready. Laura's first task was to decide what to wear. She felt like a schoolgirl on her first date. The contents of her wardrobe hung before her eyes in all its glory. A dress, a skirt, trousers? She wanted to look attractive, though not over the top. He'd said a meal out, which could be anything from posh to a fish and chip café. Although she sensed that with Mike it wouldn't be a fish and chip café. A skirt and blouse were too boring, too much like work. Laura took great care with her clothes. She made some for herself and scoured the sales and saved to try to buy really nice things. Her black cocktail dress was definitely OTT, and after her performance as a scarlet woman on Thursday night, she decided red was not a good idea. In the end she chose a simple dress in pale blue. It was sleeveless, low enough at the front to reveal a hint of cleavage and caught in at the waist with a skirt that fell to her mid-thigh. She took it out of her wardrobe and hung it on the door. Next she chose a blue set of bra and panties and laid them on the bed. This time, her choice of underwear had more purpose. She took a pair of tights from her drawer, then rejected them in favour of a suspender belt and sheer stockings. Happy with her choice, she went downstairs and inspected the state of the wine in the fridge. There was a little left in the bottle, so she poured it into a glass. There was a bottle of Pinot Grigio in her cupboard that filled the empty space. The sharp, dry taste always refreshed her.

Taking her wine upstairs, she ran a bath and put in some of her special bubble bath. It was an expensive birthday present to herself and was kept for special occasions. In among the lilac bubbles she closed her eyes, letting the scent of flowers rise around her, feeling it permeate every pore of her skin. Her thoughts returned to Thursday night. It seemed like a dream, a set of jumbled images. Mike sitting in her front room. The moment when he stood to leave, when she was very close to him. His lips against hers; his hands touching her. The memory aroused her. And then it had gone so quickly out of control. Even on her own in her bath, the memory of it brought a flush to her cheeks. It was so unlike her. She tried to visualise the evening ahead, but couldn't. He would come to her front door, then what? What would it feel like when she saw him again? On Thursday she had found him attractive, but she had had a bit to drink. Would he seem different when she was sober? Would she seem different to him? But then, he had not been drunk. Like a schoolgirl on her first date, she was filled with a mixture of excitement and anxiety, of desire and fear of the desire. Her first date; that was not a memory lane down which she wished to wander, so she quickly dismissed the image. Opening her eyes, she looked at the bubbles that covered her. A shaft of sunlight came through the curtains, throwing up a line of colour on the wall. For a few moments she did the thing she'd learnt in the meditation classes. She pulled herself inside her body and then thought herself into every individual part. The bath was safe. It was like being in limbo, while she was there she didn't have to do anything. It was simple and uncomplicated. The thought of his touch returned to her and desire triumphed over uncertainty. Laura sat up and began to wash her hair.

After her bath Laura took her time to dry her hair, dress and put on her make-up. This was different from the rush of Thursday nights – coming in late from work, needing to eat, shower, dress and be out. And for the first time for a while she was dressing not just to make herself feel sexy. She agonised again over the blue dress, but eventually returned to it.

By half past six she was ready and sitting downstairs in her front room. It was ridiculously early. She needed to do something to pass the time, so she poured herself a half-glass of wine. Having had one glass slowly while she dressed she decided she'd better not overdo it. Picking up the novel she was reading, she tried to lose herself in it, but every few minutes she would check her watch to see that the minute hand had not moved as much as she had hoped. Increasingly nervous, she drank some wine to steady herself, then got up and looked at herself in the mirror. What she saw looked pretty good, to her anyway. The dress was simple and showed off her figure well. Heels gave her that extra bit of height. She wasn't short and often didn't bother with them, but Mike was tall.

At five to seven she panicked. Suppose he didn't come? She would feel really stupid sitting there, made up to go out. At two minutes to, she panicked again. Suppose when she saw him this time she thought he was completely repulsive? Suppose he thought she was an easy lay. Suppose?

Dead on seven a car pulled up outside her house. She resisted the temptation to stand up and go to the window. The car door closed and footsteps approached her front door. She remained seated; she did not want to appear to have been waiting for him. The doorbell rang. For a moment she sat still, then, taking a deep breath, she got up, crossed the room and opened the door.

Mike stood there, smiling at her. He had a bunch of flowers in his hand.

"Hi," he said, "these are for you."

They looked at each other, unsure whether to kiss or embrace. Neither seemed to have the confidence to take the lead.

"That's so kind of you," Laura said, feeling genuine pleasure. It was an old-fashioned gesture and she appreciated his thoughtfulness. "Come in for a minute while I put them in a vase." She took them and he followed her into the front room, shutting the door behind him.

"How's your day been?" he asked, standing slightly awkwardly.

"Okay. I bought this at an auction." She gestured to the bookcase that she had left in the corner of the room. "It looks pretty dreadful, but once I've stripped it down and stained it, then it'll be fine." Mike walked over to look at it while she went through to the kitchen to find a vase for the flowers. They were freesias. She loved the delicate yellow and blue flowers and the soft intoxicating scent.

"You're pretty keen on buying things and making them your own," he said from the front room.

"Yes." She brought the flowers back and put them on the coffee table. "It's the best way if you haven't got much money and you want to furnish a house with real things not rubbish from MFI. Thank you for the flowers. They're lovely."

"That's my pleasure," Mike replied. "Shall we go?"

"Okay." Laura picked up her handbag.

"What do you like to eat?" Mike asked as they went out to his car. He went round to the passenger's side to open the door for her. His slightly formal courtesy flattered her. He was wearing an open-neck shirt, a dark blue jacket and white chinos. She felt pleased that he had made an effort.

"I don't really mind," she said from the passenger seat.

"Have you been to the Lion and Fiddle? It's out in the country, about a twenty minute drive. The food's quite good and it won't be too busy on a Saturday, unless you'd rather go to somewhere in town."

"No, the Lion and Fiddle sounds fine. It's a nice evening for a drive."

"Okay, then." Mike started the car. They drove for a while in silence. It was a beautiful evening, Laura thought. Although it was mid-September, the sun was shining with a warmth reminiscent of summer. Despite that, the air already had a chill and the sun had that honey light so typical of early autumn.

"Were you working very late last night?" Laura was keen to break the silence. She always found it too easy to retreat into her own thoughts, and tonight she wanted to make an effort.

"Yes, till about three," he laughed. "There was a function, a dinner dance for some local club or society. Maybe it was the football club, I don't remember. They had a disco and a band so they needed me to sort out the sound."

"Was it pretty rowdy?" She wanted to keep the conversation going.

"I've helped with worse. It actually finished at two; it was three by the time we'd got everything packed away." They were leaving the town behind them and driving between green fields with scattered houses. Laura noticed the confidence with which he handled the car.

"So, a late night?" Laura was struggling to find something different to say.

"Yes, but I didn't need to get up too early. What about you?"

"No, I was the opposite. An early night and then up early to the gym."

"You go a lot?"

"I like to keep fit and I'm not keen on jogging. I like swimming. Do you exercise?" It was a relief that they had moved onto a different topic. He turned left off the main road and down a country lane. There were trees on either side of the road now. The sunlight flashed between the branches.

"I work out a bit when I can, not really enough. I used to play football, but I found it hard to make the training. Are you keen on sport?" The road began to climb steeply, the trees on either side were thicker and for a while they lost the sun.

"No, not really. I played netball at school, and hockey. I was never great at team games. I just like to try to keep fit."

Mike concentrated on the road, which began to wind its way up the hill in steep bends. Although she'd made one or two drives out into the country, Laura had never been this way before. They reached the top of the hill and the road levelled out. There were woods on either side. Here and there, there were parking places and paths.

"Do you like walking?" Mike glanced across at her.

"Yes, sometimes," she replied. Her parents had dragged her out for walks on Sundays and of course Boxing Day. It was never something she'd really done. Going for walks on her own didn't really appeal to her. But he seemed interested in it and she felt awkward. She wasn't sporty and didn't go walking. Perhaps she would find just how little she had in common with this blonde, bearded stranger.

"There are lots of nice walks in this part," he said. "It's easy walking. There are plenty of different paths you can follow. In May when the bluebells come out it's really beautiful."

Laura looked out of the car window at the woods. She tried to imagine them filled with the delicate blue flowers. He surprised her with this interest and knowledge of the countryside. She felt a bit of a townie. They came out of the woods and over the crest of the hill. The valley was suddenly revealed below them. Trees and farms were spread out like a picture.

"What a lovely view," she said.

"Yes, isn't it?" He pulled off the road into a parking space so they could both look. They sat in silence, watching the scene bathed in the autumn sunshine. "Not far now." Mike slid the car back onto the road and they followed it until they came to an old stone building with a sign. Mike turned off into the car park, which was half full.

"It's a pretty place," Mike said as they walked through a garden to the pub. "It's great to come for lunch in the summer and sit out here in the garden." He led her through the side door into a dark room with wooden benches and stained beams. She followed him into a conservatory that looked out over the garden and down to the valley below.

"It's probably best to sit in here. The bar's a bit dark. It's better in the winter. What do you want to drink; let me guess, white wine?" Laura nodded. "Any particular kind? They have a range here."

"Pinot Grigio or Sauvignon Blanc," she replied. "Not Chardonnay, if you can avoid it."

"Right." He turned and disappeared back into the bar. Again, as on Thursday, she was struck by his quiet self-assurance. It was beginning to relieve her feeling of awkwardness. In a few minutes he was back with a glass of wine, a lemonade and two menus.

"No beer?" she asked.

"No, I try not to drink if I'm driving. I saw too much of it when I was touring. People who thought they could drive when they couldn't." A serious look crossed his face, like a shadow, as though he was remembering something that upset him. "Do you want a starter?"

"No, I'll just have a main, thanks." She glanced down at the menu. It was good, but not cheap.

"Are you sure? Go on if you want."

"No, it's okay. I've got to think of my figure."

He grinned at her. "There's nothing wrong with your figure, as far as I remember." Their eyes met and she blushed at the reference to Thursday night and looked away. She wanted to say that she didn't normally sleep with strangers, but it wasn't the kind of thing you could say in a restaurant in front of other people. Instead she looked down at the menu, trying to hide her embarrassment. For a while she said nothing and studied the menu in silence, trying to focus on what she was going to eat. Mike reached out and gently touched her hand holding the menu. Laura looked up and, meeting his eyes again, was surprised by the look of concern in them.

"Sorry," he said "that was unfair. I didn't mean to upset you."

"It's okay." She pulled the menu back towards her, breaking the contact. "I'll have the trout." She forced a smile.

He said nothing and went to the bar to place the order. Laura tried to make sense of her feelings. Embarrassment made her want to withdraw and distance herself from him, while at the same time she felt drawn to him. When he came back he scanned her face, carefully looking for clues to her feelings. "Laura, tell me about yourself. Tell me the story of your life." She knew he was issuing her an invitation, a way of moving forward.

And so she did. How she was born in an average, semi-detached house, of average parents in a village on the edge of an average English town and had lived her average life. Laura didn't really like talking about herself because she didn't really think that she'd ever done anything extraordinary or exciting. She wasn't like Lottie, who could make even mundane things entertaining. Mike listened intently, his eyes watching her. Now and again he would stop her and ask questions, with a tone of real interest. As she talked and as he listened, she felt herself warming towards him. He bought her another glass of wine. Laura offered to pay, but he insisted that he had invited her out. She resolved to make sure they split the bill even thought it might be a battle. The food came and they ate while she continued talking. Mike seemed especially interested in her time at university. He made her tell him about the lectures, where she lived, how she studied. Behind his questions seemed to be a real admiration for what she had done. The idea that someone might find things in her mundane life to admire or be interested in came as a surprise to Laura. Again, when she told him about how she saved up to buy her house and hunted down her bits of furniture, he seemed fascinated. He asked her to explain how she had stripped down and reupholstered her settee. It was as if he wanted to know and absorb every practical detail of what she had done

By the time she had finished they had eaten the dessert, which he had persuaded her to have, avoiding any further reference to her figure.

"Laura," he said, looking at her with his blue eyes. "You are a remarkable woman."

She blushed again, unused to such a compliment. "Not really, it's all pretty ordinary."

"And you're lovely when you blush." He grinned at her, which made her blush even more.

"Now it's your turn. You made me do all the talking and you've heard the unremarkable story of my life. I still know nothing about you, except that you are a sound engineer and you work at the Corn Exchange."

"Okay," he put his hands up in mock surrender, "but let's go. I'll tell you on the way back."

So they paid. Laura lost the battle to divide the bill and realised that Mike had a stubborn streak in him. Soon she was sitting next to him in the dark as they drove back. He chose a different route that was quicker and more on main roads.

"Unlike you, I left school as soon as I possibly could. The only thing I was interested in was rock music and mucking about with equipment. I used to save up and skive off, either days or afternoons, to see bands. My dad walked out when I was ten and my mother just couldn't really cope. She so wanted me to do well, but she couldn't get through to me. I got good grades in Electronics and in Science and scraped something in English and Maths. When I left school I got a job in a factory and a part-time job in a music shop. I could work night shifts in the factory and in the shop in the afternoons. It was easy because nobody else wanted to work nights. It was okay for a while. When I'd earned some money, I went to London and hung around the recording studios. I slept rough for a while. I got to know this sound engineer and he would let me come in and help him. One day he was ill and I filled in for him. The drummer in the group doing the recording thought I was good and asked me if I'd tour with them."

"How old were you then?" Laura asked, understanding now his fascination with her time at university.

"About seventeen. I was dead lucky, it was just the break I needed. I went with them all over. England, Scotland, France, Germany. And it was great. I was being paid to spend my time listening to rock music."

They were entering the outskirts of the town. He glanced across at her.

"Would you like to come back to my flat? It's not as palatial as yours."

Laura stiffened. This was the moment she'd been dreading. "What happened the other night," she said. "I'm not normally like that."

"I know," he said gently. "Look, I'm not asking you to stay, but I would like you to see it. It'll help me to finish my story." He paused. "Laura, I really like you and I really want to get to know you properly. I wouldn't do anything to upset you. I'd like you to come in and see it, you don't have to stay. I'm happy to drive you back to your place afterwards."

Laura was quiet. She felt a warmth and affection in his voice. Despite what had happened already between them, he had treated her with a respect and courtesy that did not make her think that he just thought of her as an easy lay.

"Okay," she said. "I'll come in. But just for a bit."

He looked across at her. "Thank you," he said.

They were quiet then as he drove, finding his way through the different streets. He parked the car outside a three-storey Victorian terrace.

"You know," Laura said, almost thinking aloud, "actually you live much closer to Lottie than to me."

"Yes," Mike said, "but I wanted to be alone with you, not with Lottie."

As they walked to the front door, Laura thought about that. It was the first time anyone had ever actually wanted to be with her rather than Lottie. Mike let her in and led her up to the first floor.

"It's just a two-room flat, I'm afraid. But it is home for me" He unlocked the door and switched on the light. As she entered the room, Laura stopped and gasped. The room was simply furnished with a settee, a chair and a coffee table. In one corner, were a small dining table and two chairs. What took her breath away was music. Apart from the corner where the table was, the walls were lined with music. Records, CDs, cassettes, were stacked literally from the floor to the high Victorian ceiling. Some were on a proper bookshelf, some on makeshift shelves supported by bricks and others just in piles on the floor.

"You certainly like your music." She was looking around the room in awe.

"It's my life," he said simply. They stood in silence for a moment. Laura thought for the first time in the evening that Mike seemed to have lost his self-assurance. It was as though this time he was baring something of himself to her and he was nervous about what she would think.

"Let me take you on the grand tour," he said, breaking the silence. "It is not grand and it will not take long." He showed her the tiny kitchen with its cooker and fridge, an alcove off the main room. There were two other doors in the living room. One led to a bathroom and the other to his bedroom. It was simply furnished: a double bed, a chair, a wardrobe, a mirror, and again, stacks of music.

"Now you've seen my estate, would you like me to take you home or would you like a glass of wine?" Laura thought she could sense a nervous tremor in his voice. She could not just go. That would be to reject him; besides, she was curious and she was beginning to feel something for him.

"A glass of wine would be lovely," she said, sitting on the settee. "Then you can tell me the rest of your story."

"Great," Mike replied and went into the kitchen. Laura looked around the room. She had never seen so much music before. At first it all seemed a jumble, looking more closely, this wasn't the case. There were labels stuck on shelves showing that everything was in fact precisely arranged; every record, CD or cassette was in its allotted space.

Mike joined her on the settee with a glass of wine for her and a whisky for him. "It's okay," he said, seeing her eyes go to the tumbler. "I've been drinking lemonade all night, so even with this I will still be fine to drive you back."

"I know." Laura tried to sound reassuring to him. "Are you going to put on some music?"

"Of course." Mike stood up. "What would you like?"

Laura's impulse was to say "What have you got?" but she realised this was absurd because he appeared to have everything that there was to have.

"You choose."

"Okay." He stood for moment, thinking. Then he walked to the far wall, pulled out a record and crossed to the other side of the room, where there was a turntable and all other imaginable ways of playing music. The room was filled with a sudden flood of sound. It was a warm, happy sound with an urgent, infectious rhythm that immediately made Laura's feet begin to tap. She took a long drink of her glass and stood up.

"Do you dance?" she said, kicking off her shoes and walking across the room to him.

Mike looked confused. "Who, me? No, never. Not if I can possibly avoid it."

"How can you love music and not dance? Can't you feel it tugging at you and wanting you to move?"

"I suppose so." He sounded uncertain.

"Come on, let me show you." Laura took his hands in hers and started to move him round the room. She tried to lead him in time to the music, but Mike seemed unable to move to its rhythm.

"You're hopeless," she said, looking up at him. He grinned at her and then, putting his arms round her, drew her close to him.

"It's much better like this," he said, and they continued to move to the music. Then he bent and kissed her on the lips. All evening Laura had been aware of his physical presence and it had excited her, but she had carefully kept her distance. Now suddenly his body was against hers. The desire she had felt on Thursday night returned. She parted her lips and let his tongue explore her mouth. They stood for a moment like that. Then his hands began to explore her back, finding the zip on her dress, and her bra strap beneath the thin material. She did not resist or push him away. His touch aroused her, and all her resolve to avoid intimacy with him disappeared. Her fingers reached for the buttons on his shirt and began to undo them. His hands slipped down to her thighs and then up under her skirt until he found the place where the suspenders joined her stockings. Simultaneously they both took a sharp intake of breath, as his hands came in contact with the bare flesh of her upper thigh.

Laura woke to find him watching her, his chin propped on his hand. His blue eyes had a strange intensity. When he saw her eyes open he bent over and began to kiss her gently; first her mouth, then her neck, her nipples, her stomach. This time their love-making was slower, more deliberate, without the sudden rush to gratify desire of the previous night. Already Mike seemed to know how to arouse her and keep her aroused so she teetered on the brink of orgasm, until they came together. Afterwards, Laura lay in Mike's arms, dozing until his voice woke her.

"A coffee, or do you have tea?"

"Coffee would be great." She smiled at him. He took a red silk dressing gown from the back of the door and went into the next room. Soon he was back with two coffees, then took his into the bathroom.

Laura propped herself against the pillow and listened to the shower. Here she was, lying in his bed. It seemed strange and at the same time natural. Her eyes travelled round the room as she sipped the coffee. It was plain, really rather bare. The furniture was old fashioned, in a heavy looking wood: a chair, an ugly wardrobe in the corner and a dressing table with a mirror. They sort of matched and probably came with the flat. There were a few photographs on the dressing table. They seemed mainly to be of groups of young men. Probably some of the bands he had toured with. Not much that told her anything about him. Mike came back from the bathroom, a towel round his waist.

"Here," he said, handing her another one. "Have a shower or a bath. I'll go and sort some breakfast out. There's a shirt of mine if you want something to wear."

She lay propped up on pillows sipping her coffee and watched him while he dried himself and pulled on a tee shirt and jeans. Looking up, their eyes met; he came over to the bed and kissed her.

"You're great," he said, then disappeared into the next room. Once he had gone she got up and went to the bathroom. At first she couldn't work out the shower. It came on with a stream of cold water that made her shiver. Eventually she got the temperature right and let the warm water play over her.

Back in his bedroom, she investigated his shirt but decided instead to retrieve her blue dress and underwear from where they had been discarded. She put her stockings and suspenders together in her handbag. When she came into the living room the sun was streaming in through the windows. In daylight his vast collection of music looked even more impressive than ever, and the room was filled with the gentle sound of an acoustic guitar. Mike had laid the table in the corner with plates and glasses. There was a jug of orange juice, butter, jam. "Do you like croissants?" he asked from the little kitchen.

"Yes." Laura suddenly felt hungry. "What's the time?"

"Just after eleven. Some more coffee?"

"Yes, please." Laura had lost all track of time. "I hadn't realised it was so late."

Mike came back with coffee and a plate of croissants. "Time goes quickly when you're enjoying yourself." Laura blushed, dropping her eyes to the table.

"No offence," he said quickly, noticing her reaction, as if remembering the way she had been at the restaurant. He reached over and placed his hand on hers. She looked up at him and met his eyes. They were full or concern and kindness. "Look, Laura," Mike said softly. "I think you're fantastic. You're intelligent, attractive, funny and very sexy." Laura could feel herself blushing again, but she could not take her eyes from his. She wondered who this great bear was who was turning her life upside down. Mike continued, "I never want to do anything to upset you or hurt you, I really don't."

Laura was quiet for a moment, holding his gaze steadily. "OK, I think you're great too." She paused. "But it's all happened so quickly. Before Thursday I'd never met you. Now I've spent all night in your bed. I'm not sure what you really think of me." Laura paused again and then continued blushing, even redder than before. "When you say things like you just did, it makes me feel, I don't know, a bit like a whore."

Mike came round the table and knelt before her on the floor. He took her hands in his and looked up at her earnestly. "Look, Laura, I know I've only met you twice but I feel a special chemistry between us. The sex is fantastic and I find it really hard to keep my hands off you, but it's much more than that. I feel as though I have found something I've been looking for. It's not just about wanting to make love to you, I want to spend time with you and get to know you properly. Believe me."

Laura looked down at him. It was all happening so fast, how could she be sure that she could trust him? But he was right; she felt something more between them. She had surprised herself by how easily they had made love and how relaxed and uninhibited she felt with him, right from that first night. His kindness and sensitivity made her feel safe.

"Okay," she said. "I believe you."

"Honestly?" Those blue eyes were staring up at her.

"Honestly. Now get up before those croissants go completely cold."

Mike got up and went back to his seat. There was silence for a while as they ate the croissants. Mike was the first to break it.

"It's a beautiful day. Do you fancy going for a walk?" He gestured out of the window to the sunlit streets.

Laura felt torn. The day was beautiful, but she knew she needed to do more work on writing up her case notes. Sunday afternoon was normally her quiet time. She would complete her case notes from the previous week and look through her diary to prepare for any meetings in the week ahead. This calm, methodical preparation meant she could start the week organised and confident. With this done, Sunday evenings could be spent relaxing with a book, or in front of the TV, or working on a piece of furniture. It was an important part of the weekend. The thought of a walk, though, of spending more time Mike, was really appealing.

"I'd love to, but..." she began.

"But what?" Mike interrupted, looking at her pleadingly.

"Well, I've got work to do, case notes to write up and other stuff."

"We won't be long. I promise. I don't want to disrupt your work, but you can't sit inside on a day like this. We won't get many more. It's probably the very last of summer."

Laura gave in. "Okay, only if we're not too long. I'll have to go back to my place and get some clothes. I can't really go for a walk in this dress and certainly not in those shoes." She gestured towards her high heels, lying where she had kicked them off the night before.

"No problem," Mike said, grinning with pleasure. "Have another croissant."

They finished their breakfast quickly and were soon on their way to Laura's house. Mike was talking about a walk he knew along the river. It was on her side of the town, not far out in the country. He seemed so confident and full of knowledge of the area and the best places to go. At her house she went upstairs and quickly changed into jeans and blouse, picked up a sweater and put on her trainers.

Mike parked beside an old bridge in a small village about four miles from the town. He led her a little way up a lane and then turned off onto a footpath that took them down alongside the river. The grass was still wet with dew. The sun was warm against her. Although it was September, everything was still green and seemed almost unbearably bright. His hand naturally found hers and so they walked hand in hand through the fields by the winding river. Laura felt happy, almost like teenagers on a first date, she thought. Actually, better, because there was no angst or gaucheness. Mike was a comfortable person to be with and he was so considerate, opening gates for her and helping her over stiles. As they walked, he talked. He told her his story, the story that she had interrupted when she had made him dance last night. How he'd been asked to go on tour with different bands to operate their sound system. His travels to France, Germany, other European countries and even the United States. She listened, enthralled by the quiet, matter-of-fact way in which he talked about the places he'd been and the different things he'd seen. In some ways it made her own conventional journey through life seem even more unremarkable. Yet he told his story with such modesty and with no obvious intention to impress her, so this feeling soon went.

She asked him questions about different places and things he had seen. At times he would stop and point things out to her – trees, or plants, or birds, or a particular view. As a town girl, she was impressed by his easy knowledge of the countryside, how observant he was. The path took them into woods and then it forked. Without hesitating he took the right fork. It led them to a small clearing, along one side of which ran the river. They called it a river, although here it was narrow, more like a stream, really. Mike led her to the bank.

"I come here sometimes," he said. "I find it a really peaceful place. Shall we sit down for a bit?" Laura nodded and he put his jacket on the grass for her to sit on. They were sitting right on the bend of the river. To their left there was only a short stretch that disappeared into the trees growing thickly on either side. To the right, however, it went upstream, ascending a number of small waterfalls. The sun was on their backs and caught the water as it tumbled down towards them.

Laura was immediately drawn in by the peace and beauty of the spot. "How lovely," she said and moved closer to him so their shoulders touched. He put his arm around her and drew her gently towards him. They sat in silence, listening to the river and watching the sun flashing on it. Gently he released her arm and lay back on the grass, looking up at the sky. Laura turned and looked down at him.

"Do you ever feel that there are moments when time stops?" He was looking up at her. "Moments which are fixed points that stay in your memory?"

"Perhaps," Laura replied. "Perhaps there are some moments that you don't want to end. Ones that are so peaceful or so beautiful that you want to try to hold onto them." Then she said, "Thank you for bringing me here, Mike," and bent and kissed him.

He reached up and pulled her down beside him and returned her kiss. This was not a kiss of sexual desire, but one of pure affection. They lay in each other's arms. She closed her eyes and listened to his breathing, and beyond it the sound of the water.

Laura had no idea how long they lay there, floating on the soft combination of those sounds. Then she felt him get up; she opened her eyes and looked up at him standing over her. "Come on, Miss Laura, I need to take you back because you've got your case notes to write."

"Hang my case notes." The strength of emotion in her voice surprised her, yet it was suddenly the way she felt.

"That will not do," Mike said, reprovingly. He reached down, took her hands and pulled her to her feet, and embraced her.

Laura parked her car on her drive. The cold November wind whipped her scarf across her face as she walked to her front door. She heard the van draw up next to the kerb. This was Mike's moving-in day. It was a Saturday, exactly seven weeks since he had taken her out for that first meal. It had quickly become obvious that the best thing was for Mike to move in with her. She was no longer surprised by the speed with which she had reached this decision. Her possessiveness of the home she had worked hard to buy and furnish and her love of the independence that living alone had given melted away before her desire to spend as much time with him as possible. There was no question of her moving into his rented Victorian flat, so there was only one alternative. Now here he was, driving the van he had borrowed with the first of the loads of his possessions. Laura went to help him unload the boxes of what she knew would fill the van – records, cassettes, CDs.

They had had to wait until the month he had needed to give as notice on his flat had expired. So she was looking forward to helping him arrange his stuff. She had planned it all very carefully. Actually, he didn't have very much, apart from his immense collection of music. Most of that was going to go in her spare bedroom. She had spent the last few weeks looking with him for the right shelves so that it could all be fitted neatly inside. His record, CD and cassette player would sit in the corner of her front room with a set of shelves to house his current favourites.

Mike insisted that he would pay her a reasonable rent and his share of electricity, water bills and council tax. The extra money would make it easier for her to manage, and what he would be paying was far less than his current rent, so financially they would both benefit. Most importantly, she would have him around all the time, without having to trek to his flat. Since that first weekend they had quickly settled into a pattern of life. She still went with Lottie to the Corn Exchange on Thursdays. Mike would meet them afterwards, take them for a drink and drive them home. He normally worked either Fridays or Saturday nights which gave her a night to herself. The other night they would do something. Sometimes it was just the two of them, sometimes they went out with Lottie, who seemed readily to have accepted Mike's arrival. They had a good relationship which meant that, unusually, it did work when they went out as a three. On Sundays, if the weather was good they went for a walk together. Mike was making her familiar with the local area and beginning to teach her to know and recognise the trees, plants and birds that they saw on their walks. His moving in would really set the seal on their relationship.

They both put their boxes down in her front room. He grabbed hold of her and lifted her off her feet, kissing her while he swung her round until he put her down again, giddy and laughing.

Laura lay curled up on the settee, her head on Mike's lap. She stared into the open fire, feeling warm and relaxed. Outside there was deep snow and it was bitterly cold, but her front room was cosy and snug. She watched the red glow of the fire and the flames licking around the logs. The mellow sound of the saxophone filled the room. She had never listened to jazz before she met Mike; he had introduced her to it and now she loved it. The music seemed to seep through her and sweep her away. Gazing into the fire she could imagine shapes, fiery mountains, dark castles, strange figures. It was a game she had played as a child. She loved sitting or lying and staring into the fire in her parents' front room; turning all of the lights off and watching the shadows flicker on the walls, she would make up stories to herself of the things she could see. Now she found her mind wandering, and she began to slip in and out of consciousness.

"Laura, there is something I need to tell you." Mike's voice had a sudden urgency about it, though it seemed to come from a long way away. "Laura, I need to tell you something." He gently, but firmly squeezed her shoulder, dragging her out of her reverie. She sat up.

"Mike, what is it?" She looked at him curiously. There had been an edge in his tone, very different from the usually relaxed and laidback one.

He looked into her eyes and then turned away, staring into the fire. "I need to tell you about something that happened ten years ago. It is something I have never told anyone about, but I feel that I need to tell you."

"Is it something terrible about you? Something you've done?" She was suddenly nervous. He was so nice, almost too good to be true. Was there another side to him that she didn't know?

"It is terrible in a way and strange, but not like that." Mike hesitated for a moment, as if overcome with uncertainty. Then he took a deep breath and began to speak. "Ten years ago I was a sound engineer for a band on a tour of the States."

"Yes, I remember you telling me."

"We did a gig in New Orleans in the summer. It was incredibly hot." Mike paused, as though picturing it for himself. "After the gig some of the local guys took us to a jazz club. It was the first time I'd ever heard jazz. It was great, really magical. There was a strange woman there dancing, she was wearing charms. She moved round the room as though she was looking for someone. Every time she came close to people, they looked away from her and wouldn't meet her eyes. The guy who was with us said that it was to do with voodoo and that she was bad news. I didn't know that when she came to our table, and so I didn't turn away. I looked straight at her and our eyes met. It was as though," he paused, "I know it sounds silly, it was as though she looked right into me. Then later I went to the men's room. On the way back I met her in the corridor and she pulled me into this room and..." He stopped and looked at Laura. She felt his embarrassment.

"And, go on," she said. He looked away from her. "And I had sex with her, or I think I did."

"What do you mean you think you did?" Laura smiled at his embarrassment. "Surely you know if you did or not?"

74

"As I came she kissed me, and there was almost like an electric shock and I passed out. When I came round she had gone and I was sitting on the floor. I had had a lot of beer to drink and I thought I might have imagined it all and passed out. Then when I went back into the main room she was dancing again. Then these three guys came into the club. At that point our local friend said it was time to leave. It was as though they knew there was trouble coming. I was so fascinated that they had to pull me away." He stopped again, picturing the scene in his mind.

"What happened?" She prompted him gently, fascinated, but dreading his response.

"They held her arms and cut her throat. Right in front of everyone they curt her throat. It was awful." Laura put her arm round him and hugged him gently.

"It must have been horrible," she said.

He looked at her. "I've never seen anything like that. I just could not believe what I was seeing." He stopped again, as though even now the image was too much for him.

"What happened afterwards?"

"We ran back to our truck and hit the road straight away. Then, when I woke up I found this in my pocket." He held up the small ivory figure. "It is one of the charms that she was wearing round her neck. I found it in the pocket of my jeans. She must have put it there."

Laura took it and examined it carefully. It was a figure of a woman, carved intricately in ivory.

"Then the dreams came. Every night I dreamed about what happened. It was always the same dream; I was in a corridor and she was at the end. I was always trying to reach her, but before I could get there they would come and cut her throat."

"You must have been in a state of shock because of what you'd seen. It's not unusual. I read about cases like that when I studied psychology."

"Then the dreams changed. One night we stayed at a motel. I dreamed I saw a woman in the room who took an overdose. The next day at reception I found out that it had actually happened."

Laura looked at him. "Are you serious?" Her psychology told her nothing about this.

Mike gave her a strange look. "I am absolutely serious. Laura, you have to believe me. I am not making this up. I've never told anyone before because I never thought anyone would believe me. And there is more. I gave the receptionist at the motel a ticket for our gig in Philadelphia. Then I dreamed that she would be killed in a car crash. I tried to contact her to tell her not to come, but I couldn't reach her. She was in a multiple pile-up on the freeway and was killed instantly." For a while there was silence in the room; the only sound was the crackling of the fire.

Laura was sitting on the edge of the settee. She had turned and was staring intently at him. She tried to make sense of what he had said. She looked down at the small carved figure lying in the palm of her hand. "So, what you are saying is that after the incident you began to dream. Your dreams tell you both about the past and about the future. Have you had other dreams like that?"

"That's right. Whenever I stay somewhere where something has happened, like a death, then I dream about it. Afterwards I find out that what I dreamed about actually happened."

"And the future too?" Laura restated what he had said to be sure that she had understood it. All her social science training told her that everything had a rational explanation.

"Yes." Mike paused, took a deep breath and then, looking straight at her, said, "I dreamed about you."

"What?"

"I dreamed of you. I dreamed that we were going to meet. That's why I was so confident; I'm not normally so confident with women. That's why I had no interest in Lottie, why I pretended I lived on your side of town. I knew that we would meet and I knew that we would get along. I dreamed it."

Laura was silent, astonished. "Are you making this up?"

"No, I promise. I've never told anyone else before. It has been my burden." He held his hands up, palms open. Then he leant towards her and took her hands in his, pressing the ivory figure into her palm. "I love you, so I had to tell you, otherwise it wouldn't be fair. I've thought about it for months. I didn't know when or how to do it. I kept putting it off, trying to find the right moment. You need to know about me, about this thing I suffer from, even if it means you don't want to see

76

me again." Mike looked at her and then looked down, as if waiting for a verdict from her. Suddenly all his confidence and good humour had gone. He looked strained and tired.

Laura felt a mixture of emotions. She found it impossible to comprehend what he had said and what it really meant for him and for her. But he was so vulnerable and all the warmth of feeling that had built up in her over the last few months seemed to fill her. She took her hands from his, the ivory figure slipping silently onto the settee, and hugged him. Her lips found his. "Don't be silly. You're the best thing that has ever happened to me. I have no intention of walking away from you, or asking you to move out. If some strange power has brought us together then maybe it cannot be entirely bad."

"Maybe." His voice sounded uncertain and he held her close and for a while they did not speak.

Then, gently, Laura disengaged herself. "You are right to tell me. Maybe I can help you understand what this all means. But I'm curious, tell me what you dreamed about me?"

"It started two years ago. That's sometimes the way the dreams work. I can have the same dream for months. I dreamed I saw two girls dancing, a blonde one and a dark one. I dreamed that we went for a drink and I saw the name of the pub. I dreamed of sitting here in your front room. Then I dreamed of the moment on the night we met when you pulled off your top and embraced me." Mike blushed and so did Laura. She vividly remembered that night and the inexplicable behaviour.

"I looked out for you for months and then when I finally saw the two of you dancing, I knew it was you. But it was so difficult to find a way to meet you; until we met and talked I wasn't really sure that the dream would come true. I never dreamed such a personal dream about the future before. But everything I saw in the dream was right – what you were wearing, your hair, what you drank. As soon as we started to talk, I knew it would be as I dreamed it and it was."

Laura listened intently; she was quiet for a moment, then asked the question that had formed in her mind. "So, have you had any dreams about us, about the future?" There was a slight tremble in her voice.

"No, since we met I haven't dreamt at all. For the first time for ages

I have slept without dreams. I have had periods like that before when the dreams stopped, but they never lasted so long." He seemed happier now that he had told her. The old, confident, reassuring Mike was back and the strain had gone from his face as though he had indeed shared his burden.

Laura reached across and took his hands in hers. She looked at him for a long time. When she spoke her voice was calm and serious. "Mike, I do not understand what you have told me. My training is in the social sciences and I believe in rational explanations. I don't know what this strange power is or what it might mean for you or for me. I do know I care about you very deeply, and I don't want to lose you. It's the opposite; I want to help you to understand what happened to you, to make sense of your dreams and to try to use them for good. You must promise me one thing though." He made as if to speak, but she put her hand to his lips. "If you start to dream again and you dream about us, you must tell me what you see, however bad or good it may be."

Laura's eyes met his.

"I promise," he said. "Whatever I dream I will tell you, however good or bad. To be honest, it is such a relief to be able to talk about it. It has become a weight. I am glad that you have the strength to help me understand it." They kissed to seal the promise that had been made.

Laura sat on the settee, surrounded by piles of books. Mike was out working at the Corn Exchange, so she was on her own. Since he had told her about his dreams she had gone over his story again and again in her mind. He had spoken with such certainty that she did not doubt that he believed what he said. But was it true? Could it possibly be true? Laura was neither religious nor superstitious. Her study of the social sciences had reinforced her natural scepticism. Her experience as a social worker had taught her that people could be strange and do strange things, but that there was always some kind of social or psychological explanation. So she had become determined to try to understand what had really happened to him. It wasn't that she doubted him, or what he thought he had experienced and the strange power he said he had. But she needed to understand it. Once she could truly understand it then she thought she could help him to come to terms with it.

So, following her academic training she had turned to research. The day after he had told her, she had sat at the kitchen table with a blank sheet of paper and brainstormed a number of lines of enquiry – dreams, post-traumatic stress syndrome, precognition, retrocognition, voodoo. She had begun with voodoo. To her, the most fanciful explanation was that some kind of power had passed from the woman to Mike. He had said that they had called her a "voodoo woman". Then there was the little carved figure. Was it some kind of charm? Did it have some kind of symbolic power? She always thought it was best to start with the least likely explanation, so that it could be ruled out. Using both the internet and books, Laura found plenty of information.

Voodoo, or voudou, was a kind of folk magic. It had been brought originally by the slaves from West Africa to the Caribbean and to the southern states of the US. They had kept their original beliefs alive and had added to them aspects of Christianity and any other beliefs they came across. The result was a bizarre mixture of different things. It seemed to be especially strong in Haiti and in Louisiana. It certainly involved the use of charms of different kinds. Most of it was benign white magic, designed to heal or protect, but there was also mention of it being used to curse or for revenge. There were only vague references to this darker side and no details. It was this side that had caught the popular imagination, with tales of devil dolls and zombies. This seemed to be entirely fictional, found in novels or B-movies. Women did play a prominent part in it. There were references to voodoo queens, especially to a Marie Laveau, who had lived in New Orleans in the late nineteenth century. Her influence appeared to have been more benign than evil. There was nothing more recent. There were pictures of dolls and charms, though none like the ivory figure. In the end it did not really help. Voodoo did exist in New Orleans and it could have a dark side. The killing could just as easily have been about jealousy or money, a jilted lover or an angry pimp. She needed to find out more about this darker side, but there were no references she could find to it. Laura sighed. Social science now seemed so much more straightforward.

Next she had turned her attention to the dreams. Here her knowledge of Freud was of some help. The recurring dream after the incident was fairly easy to explain. Mike had witnessed a brutal killing, sudden and unexpected. It had shocked and traumatised him and his mind kept replaying it, again and again. It accentuated his sense of guilt at not being able to do anything to stop it. That's why he was always struggling to reach the woman, but never could. This was not unusual in people who had witnessed such events. She was familiar with this from the work she had done in several unpleasant cases of domestic violence or child abuse. There was a large and growing literature of research on post-traumatic stress syndrome, which she intended to come to later.

The idea of dreams that could predict the future or retrieve experiences from the past was far more problematical. It went way beyond the bounds of Freud and was directly contrary to the established laws of science. This was her current focus and she was really struggling with it. She was amazed at the vast amount of material that there was. It ranged from popular accounts of people's claimed experiences, of which there were lots, to formal research programmes carried out mainly at American universities. What Mike had described seemed less unusual then she had first thought. Some claims had been subjected to rigorous scientific examination of the evidence that normally debunked them. The issue, of course, was that conventional science rejected the validity of any such experiences because they went against all scientific laws. By default, any claimed experiences, therefore, had to be fraudulent and most of them, it seemed, were. She had now focused on two ideas that seemed central to Mike's mysterious powers. The technical terms for them were precognition and retrocognition.

Precognition was the idea that someone could see into the future and predict events that would happen. Mike's claim that he knew that they were going to meet and that she would be attracted to him would be seen as an example of precognition. An enormous amount of research had been done about this, mainly in the United States, asking subjects to record their dreams and then matching them against future events. A different approach was where people predicted what patterns would be created by randomly generated sets of shapes. Most of the scientific studies seemed to have been inconclusive.

Laura put the book down for a moment and drank some wine. She frowned as she struggled to grasp the concepts. If every event is caused by a pre-event, how could someone have knowledge that an event would happen before the things that caused it had themselves happened? But some scientists, who were influenced by relativity, believed it might be possible. They had put forward what they called the theory of resonance. She picked up the book and tried again to grasp the meaning of the passage.

"It relates to the neuronal spatio-temporal patterns that are activated in the brain. For example, a precognition would occur when the pattern activated at the time of the future experience of an event resonates with any similar pattern that is spontaneously activated in the present. This might enable the present activation to be sustained until it produces the conscious awareness of an event similar to the one that would be experienced in the future."

So, if Mike met someone in the past, it might trigger the same pattern as meeting me in the future, which might be replayed in a dream. She wasn't entirely convinced, but she was aware that relativity had fundamentally changed the paradigm that underlay physics and led to scientific explanations for the inexplicable. She also knew that most of what was currently known about the way the brain operates had been learnt in the last ten years. Who knew what future discoveries might reveal? The denials of science and scientists were sometimes the product of vested interests. Perhaps what she was dealing with came from something different from the underlying chemical structures of life. Perhaps the dreams were in some way a different dimension of knowledge or reality. Just as in the social sciences, the apparently contradictory approaches of positivism and interpretive theory could be seen not as opposites, but different perspectives on the same thing.

Laura sighed and took another drink of wine. She was not sure where any of this was getting her. However, she decided to try the other concept – retrocognition. The first book she picked up was an account by two Edwardian ladies about how they were wandering in the park of Versailles, became lost, and thought they had met Marie Antoinette. This was apparently called a time slip. It was charming though not really relevant. And of course, it had been highly criticised. Laura put the book down and thought for a moment. It was impossible, easily or quickly, to test precognition. You would have to wait for something sensed in a dream to come true. But it might be possible to test the ability to recall some event from the past that you could not have known about. The start of an idea began to form in her mind.

Mike drove down the winding country lane as the light began to go. It was early March and daffodils were beginning to come out with the promise of spring. Already the nights were lighter. She had wanted them to arrive in the light, but she had had to attend a serious case review, which had dragged on into Friday afternoon and made leaving early impossible. Her mind strayed back to it briefly. It was the case of the two girls that she had had to take into care. It was the day on which she had first met Mike. That thought had distracted her from the case for a moment. The father had hanged himself in his prison cell. She had had to be there to give evidence of the breaking down of the door and the removal of the children. For once it was not social workers who were in the dock accused of not acting quickly enough. In fact, their whole course of action and the way they had carried it out had received praise. The question was whether the police had been negligent in not keeping the father under proper surveillance in the cells. The girls had not been present and she had wondered vaguely what had happened to them. She believed that they had been fostered in separate families, but once they had been allocated a specific social worker she had not had further involvement.

Mike paused at a crossroads. "Which way now?"

Laura looked at the map. There was just about enough light for her to read it. She found the name of the village on the signpost. "Go left," she said. "The pub is in the next village, it's only another five miles."

"Great," he replied, taking the car down what seemed to be an even narrower lane. "I'm really beginning to feel hungry. I hope their food is as good as you said it was."

"An idyllic country pub with its own independent brewery, the Pheasant Inn offers food that uses local produce cooked to the highest possible standards," Laura recited the brochure from memory. Finding exactly what she wanted had taken some time. She needed something that Mike would go for without asking questions. This seemed almost perfect. Real ale, good food, quaint surroundings and a weekend of exploring nice country walks in the spring weather. He had fallen for it straight away and had never questioned the idea of a surprise weekend away at a cut-price rate. When she'd asked if he knew the place he said he'd never even heard of it. And if nothing happened then they would simply have had a lovely weekend together. She wondered if she should have said something more, but that would have defeated the whole object. Was it in some way unfair? Perhaps, but she needed to know. She needed some kind of proof. It would help her to understand which would help him. That was her justification to herself. Laura had been through this train of thought a hundred times before and after she had made the booking. She had always come to the same conclusion and she was determined to carry it through.

Mike turned the headlights on and they swept the hedges as they followed the winding road. They drove in silence as she watched the hedges and banks go past. At last they came to the sign she was looking for.

"This is it," she said. "Carry straight on until you come to the green with a church on one side. The pub should be on our left. I think the car park is at the back."

The green quickly came into view on their right. Or she assumed it was the green; it was an area of open space, as far as she could see. Almost at once the pub was there, with a sign pointing to the rear. As they turned off the road she had the impression of a rambling, half-timbered building. There were only three other cars in the large car park.

"Doesn't seem very popular," Mike said, as he chose the nearest place to the building.

"It's only just after six," Laura replied. "Besides, you said you wanted a peaceful weekend."

Mike took their bags out of the boot and they walked across to a door with a light over it that said "Reception". Mike had to bend his head as they went through the door into a low-beamed corridor. This led them to a lobby with a small counter signed "Reception" which had a notice "Please ring for service". Laura rang the bell. They heard it ring, presumably in the bar, and a blonde, middle-aged woman appeared.

"Can I help you," she said, smiling at them.

"We booked a room for the weekend," Laura said. "Laura Watson."

The woman checked the book. "Ah yes, here we are. Could you just fill this in?" She pushed a form towards them over the counter. "If you can put your address and car registration number and sign here. I need to swipe a credit card for any meals and drinks." Laura took it and filled it in while Mike looked round the lobby. She always filled the forms in because he seemed so hopeless. "I see you're booked in for dinner, bed and breakfast. Dinner is served from half past seven in our restaurant just to the left of the bar. Breakfast is served in the same place from half past seven to half past nine in the morning." She swiped Laura's credit card on the machine and reached for the key for room twelve. "Would you like an early morning call? I am afraid we cannot offer you a paper, we don't get them until nine."

Laura looked at the key in alarm. This was not right. She glanced over her shoulder. Mike was at the far end of the small lobby looking at a photograph on the wall. She leant over the counter and said quietly, but firmly. "There must be some mistake. I specifically asked that we have room twenty-one."

The woman looked at her. "Oh, yes," she said, consulting her book again. "I just thought you would prefer room twelve as it's not so far from reception."

Their eyes met. "No, thank you," said Laura. "I want room twenty-one. That's the room I booked."

The woman gave her strange look. "But," she began, and then stopped as she saw the look of determination in Laura's eyes. "Okay, if you're sure that's the room you want."

"I'm sure," Laura said firmly. The woman replaced the key and took down the one for room twenty-one.

"Right at the top of the stairs," she said. "It does have a fine view over the green. Do you need a hand with your bags?"

Laura took the key. "No thanks, we don't have much." She turned away. "Come on, Mike, let's go and find our room."

They followed the sign to the stairs. "Was there some kind of problem with the booking?" Mike asked.

"Not really," Laura said. They went through a door and then began to climb the stairs. There were beams and plaster on both sides, with photographs and paintings. "This place looks genuinely old," she said, keen to change the subject quickly. "Look, some of these photographs show what it looked like in 1900." She stopped on the landing in front of a black and white photograph. "Look, they covered all the half timbering with plaster. What a shame. Here are the different stages of the restoration that was done in the 1990s."

Mike paused and looked at the photograph. "So what did the guidebook say about it?"

Laura thought back. "I think originally it was a set of sixteenth-century cottages. Then in the seventeenth century they were knocked together to make a coaching inn."

"I would have thought it was a bit out of the way as a coaching inn," Mike said, moving onto a photograph showing the thatched roof being redone.

"Not originally, but in the late eighteenth century they built a new turnpike road and that took the traffic away. Come on, our room is up on the next floor." Laura picked up her bag and began to climb the next flight of stairs. At the top they followed a low corridor with rooms on both sides. Room twenty-one was right at the end.

Laura put the key in the lock and turned it, opening the door and switching on the lights. Mike followed her in, put his bag down and looked around. They were in a large room with a low ceiling. It looked as though it had been recently redecorated, the walls a new white and the beams stained dark brown. It ran across the whole width of the building, so the roof sloped to windows at both sides. Facing the door was a large double bed; to the right of it was a door that Laura guessed must lead to the en suite. She crossed the room and opened it. The en suite also went the length of the house, with a bath and separate shower against one wall, a toilet at the end by another window, and then a washbasin. The room had been tastefully tiled in a blue and white Delft style. It was spotlessly clean. She came back into the bedroom. It was spacious, with a wardrobe, a dressing table and chair and two armchairs. Each piece looked as though it were antique, possibly restored, Laura thought. It had obviously been chosen with care to fit in with the beams and the low ceiling. The overall impression was of age combined with modern comfort.

Mike closed the door. He came towards her and put his arms round her. "You are clever," he said, and kissed her on the mouth. "This is really brilliant. I just know we're going to have a great weekend." He drew back from her and looked at her quizzically. "What time did they say dinner was?" he asked.

"Seven thirty."

He glanced at his watch. "It's only twenty past six, so there might just be time, mightn't there?" He gave her a big grin. "But you look so severe and professional I'm not sure I dare even ask."

Because she had been late there had been no time to change, so Laura was still in the clothes she had worn for the serious case review. A plain white blouse, black skirt and black tights with her hair tied up. She laughed and put her hands up to undo her hair so that it fell loose over her shoulders. As she did so Mike stepped forward and put his hands on her breasts.

"I've always wanted to make love to a social worker."

Laura threw her arms round his neck and kissed him. Breaking away from her he bent, and in one quick movement he picked her up and placed her gently on the double bed.

There were three other couples in the restaurant and the bar, empty at first, steadily filled up over the evening. The food was everything the brochure had promised. There was local trout, pheasant and even rabbit pâté. Laura was glad that she wasn't a vegetarian though, because that fashion had obviously not made it yet to this part of rural England. The waitress was a young girl, obviously from the local school, doing her Friday night job. The restaurant itself was not large, but the tables were not too close together. The low ceiling and the beams gave it an intimate and relaxed feel. Despite the fact that it was spring, the log fire still burned in the large fireplace, which looked as though it was probably original. Over the meal they talked about their plans for the next day. Laura had bought an OS map with the village on and a book of walks for the area. She was keen that they try not to use the car and suggested a circular walk that would take them across to another village, where there was also a good pub, and then back a different way. Mike was enthusiastic. He liked walking and being in the country and the chance of a good lunch added to it. "Mind you," he said, pausing for a moment over the dessert menu, "if breakfast is like this we'll need a good walk and I'm not sure about lunch." As he wasn't driving he had insisted on ordering a bottle of wine with the meal. Laura loved wine, but she tried to be careful. She wanted to be sober enough to be clear about what happened during the night, if anything did.

After dinner they sat in the bar for a bit, taking in the village life. It seemed a mixture of genuine local people and those out from the city. They had chosen a corner from which they could watch the other customers and talk quietly without being conspicuous. At one point though, Laura was sure that they were being discussed. The receptionist, now serving behind the bar, was talking to an old man with a white beard. She suddenly glanced in their direction, leant across the bar and said something. He looked over at Laura and then turned back, shaking his head.

Laura had a coffee whilst Mike began to sample the local beer. The place claimed to have its own small brewery that was at the back somewhere. She had noticed a set of outbuildings on the other side of the car park and supposed that that must be where it was. They could have a good look around tomorrow in daylight. Laura wasn't sure whether Mike drinking a lot would be a good thing, but there was no point in trying to stop him, it would only make him suspicious. Eventually, she enticed him upstairs by putting her hand on his thigh under the table and asking him if he fancied a bit more social work.

She led him up the two flights of stairs to their room, fending off his attempted amorous attention on the way. In the bedroom she let him undress her. He said it was like unwrapping a present. After they had made love they talked for a little while about where they would walk. Then Mike fell asleep. Laura could hear his breathing become regular. She waited a few minutes, trying not to fall asleep herself.

When she was sure that he was in a deep sleep, she gently slipped out of bed. First she found her nightdress. She shivered; it was only early March and the bedroom was cold. Perhaps the cold would help to keep her awake. Then she went to her bag and found her notebook, pen, the Dictaphone and a small torch. She moved quietly round to the other side of the bed so that she would have a good view of him. She pulled one of the armchairs over so that she could sit beside the bed. As she still felt cold, she went to the wardrobe and took out one of the spare blankets. Then she settled in the chair, drawing her feet up and wrapped the blanket round her. She looked at her watch. It was just after midnight.

Opening her notebook, she turned on the torch and wrote a heading – the place, the date and the time. Then she settled herself to wait. What she was waiting for she was not quite sure. Nothing she had read had given her any clue as to what it looked like if someone was having an experience of retrocognition. Gradually her eyes became accustomed to the darkness of the room. A shaft of moonlight came through a gap in the curtains. That helped. She looked at him intently. His face looked relaxed and peaceful as he slept. She wondered what she should look for if he dreamt. Would his face reveal that he was seeing something, or would his hands tense or his breathing change? To begin with she felt alert and focused. Nothing happened. She moved in her chair to try to find a more comfortable position; the blanket slipped a little and left her foot exposed to the cold. She rearranged it. Somewhere she heard a clock strike. She guessed it must be the church. She wondered why she hadn't heard it before. That made her listen, but there was nothing to hear. The night was still, without any wind. No cars passed along the road. Their room was at the far end from the bar. It was probably closed by now, or was restricted to a few locals or residents drinking quietly after hours. She listened carefully. There was no sound. Then somewhere she heard a door slam, then nothing.

She realised that she had been so busy listening that she had stopped watching Mike. So she focused again on his face. She thought how boyish he looked as he slept. She had never really watched him sleeping before. It felt odd, almost as though she was taking advantage of him. She wondered how he would feel about it. In a sense, she had deceived him. But there had been no choice. It would only mean something if he was completely unaware. So she focused intently on him for a while. But nothing happened and nothing changed. She yawned. She looked around the room. In the half-light the beams seemed dark and brooding. She wondered what the room had been like then. She tried to visualise it, wondering if the furniture had all been in the same place. The newspaper article had not had pictures of the room, only of the inn and of the couple. She wondered if the woman had sat over near the window. She closed her eyes for a moment to help her to imagine what it might have been like.

Laura woke suddenly. It took her a moment to remember where she was. She must have dozed off. The church clock struck three. The shaft of moonlight had moved, so now it fell across Mike's face. She looked at him. Something was different. He was no longer boyish and relaxed. His forehead seemed furrowed with concentration. She noticed that his hands were clenched into fists. She felt for her notebook and pen. Carefully she opened it and began to write notes. The moonlight was bright enough now for her not to need the torch. That made it easier. Balancing the notebook, whilst holding the pen and the torch had been difficult. She looked at Mike and in a series of bullet points described what she saw. He seemed to become more agitated and his lips began to move as though he was speaking but no sounds came out.

Laura watched, fascinated. She felt a mixture of emotions. In one way it was good. Her plan had worked and now she was able to record evidence of what Mike had described. Yet there was also something unnerving about it. She didn't know what was happening to him or what he was seeing. It was as though he was not in control of himself. How could something like this happen? What did it mean? She watched and took notes for about twenty minutes. She realised that she didn't know how long he had been dreaming before she woke.

Gradually Mike's face began to relax and his hands unclenched. His eyes opened. He seemed confused, as though disorientated. Then he saw her. "Laura," he said. "I have been dreaming."

Laura bent towards him and took his hand in hers. "I know," she said softly.

"Why were you watching me?"

She paused for a moment. "I needed to know that what you said was true." Mike opened his mouth to speak but she put her hand up. "No, we can talk about why later. First you must tell me about your dream." He looked at her uncertainly. "Please," she took his hand again. "It's important. If you tell me about your dream then maybe I can help you."

"Okay," he said. He lay back for a moment, trying to recall it clearly. Then he turned towards her and began to speak:

It was like when I dreamed in the States. I saw this room. It was as though I was here and yet not here. The room was different. There was a dressing table by the window and a desk over in the corner. A man was sitting at the desk typing on one of those old portable typewriters. He had black hair and he was unshaven. He would type furiously for a while and then stop. Every now and then he got up from the desk and walked across the room. Paced rather than walked. He would go to the window and look out. It was grey and wet outside. Then he would return to the desk and type again. After a while he stopped and looked at his watch. He said something to himself and drummed his fingers on the desk. Then he got up again and crossed to the window. He looked out across the green to the church. Then he spoke in a louder voice. It was a tense, angry voice.

'She's late. She should be back by now, damn her. Where is she, the vixen?' He stared out of the window and across the green. There was no sign of anyone. The rain swirled against the window. He turned and began walking back to the desk, then on impulse crossed and looked out of the other window, the one that looks down at the yard and the brewery.

As he did so a woman dressed in a blue raincoat came out of a door in one of the outbuildings and crossed the courtyard. She seemed to be in a hurry.

'There she is, the slut.' There was an air of triumph in his voice. 'What the hell has she been up to? I'll worm it out of her.' He turned and stood facing the door of the bedroom, his arms folded across his chest. His face was contorted with anger. There was the sound of feet hurrying up the stairs.

The door opened and the woman in the raincoat came in. She had long, blonde hair falling down over her shoulders. She was tall and slim but seemed small beside him. Her face could have been pretty but now it had a look of fear. Despite the rain her coat seemed dry. She took three steps into the room, letting the door close behind her. 'Where the hell have you been?' His voice was loud and harsh. 'You're more than ten minutes late.'

She looked nervously at the floor, not meeting his eyes. She was trembling.

'Yes. I know, Frank, I'm sorry I did not realise the time had gone so quickly.' He took two steps towards her.

'Take off your coat,' he said. The voice was lower and full of menace.

'Yes, of course.' She fumbled with the buttons. He watched her in silence. Eventually she managed to undo the coat and take it off. He took it and inspected it carefully, then with sudden violence threw it on the bed. Beneath the coat she was wearing a dress with red and white flowers on it. It was buttoned up to her neck and the skirt fell to below the knee, like they used to wear in the 1950s.

'It's raining outside,' he said.

'Yes,' she said. He walked round behind her.

'But your coat isn't wet?'

'No,' she mumbled.

'If it's raining outside, then why isn't your coat wet?'

She suddenly looked up and made an attempt at confidence.

'Because I went into the church. It was raining so I went into the church. It's fourteenth-century and very beautiful. You would like it. Perhaps tomorrow.'

'Then why did you just come from the brewery? I saw you just now from the window.' He walked round in front of her and stood looking down, his face very close to hers.

'The brewery is old, too,' she said quickly. 'It's as old as the pub. It was so interesting that I forgot the time.' She looked up at him pleadingly. 'I'm really sorry I'm late. I promise I'll make it up to you.'

She stood up on tiptoe as if to kiss him. As she did so he drew his fist back and punched her hard in the stomach. She fell to her knees, gasping for breath. He leant down, grabbed a handful of her hair and pulled her to her feet. She cried out in pain.

'You've been a bad girl,' he said. 'You were late and lateness deserves to be punished. But what else have you been up to? He gave her hair a sharp tug.'

'Nothing, I promise you, nothing,' she sobbed. 'Please don't hurt me anymore.' He put his face very close to hers again.

'Have you been with a man?' He tugged her hair again.

'No, I promise.'

'Can I smell man on your body?' He sniffed at her neck.

'No, you know I would never go with anyone but you.'

He let go of her hair and began to unbutton the front of her dress.

'I promise you, I promise you,' she said, the tears falling down

91

her cheeks. 'Please don't hurt me.' He unbuttoned her dress to her waist and then pulled it open to reveal her bra. He bent his head again and sniffed her neck and her breasts.

'Can I smell a man? Can I smell a man?' He walked behind her and pulled the dress off her shoulders and arms. She stood trembling. He sniffed the back of her neck and her shoulders. 'What do I smell, I wonder what I smell?' All the time his voice was low and dangerous. He paused and stood in silence for a while. The only sound was of the woman crying. Then he grabbed hold of her wrists and forced them up behind her. He pushed her across the room towards the bed and then forced her to bend down over it. He quickly changed his grip, holding both her wrists in one hand and leaving the other one free. 'I don't smell a man this time but I smell a bad girl. A bad girl who has been late and what happens to bad girls? They need to be punished.' He pulled up her skirt to reveal her bottom in a pair of white knickers. He drew back his hand and slapped her hard three times on the bottom. Then he pulled down her skirt and pulled her to her feet. 'Now the bad girl has been punished, she has to ask for forgiveness.'

She knelt down in front of him on the floor. 'Please forgive me, Frank, I promise I will never be late again.'

'Good girl, and how will you make up for your lateness?' She threw her arms round his knees.

'I will be very nice to you. I will do whatever you want me to.' He pulled her gently to her feet.

'The bad girl is all forgiven and the good girl is back again,' he said and took a big handkerchief from his pocket and wiped her face. Then he kissed her on the lips. 'I think you better go and wash your face.' As she moved across towards the bathroom, he held onto her hand. As she stepped to the full length of her arm, he suddenly pulled her back to him.

'But if I catch you with another man I will squeeze the life out of you.' He let her go and she disappeared into the bathroom. He crossed the room and stood looking out of the window, down at the brewery. Turning, he walked to the bed. He picked up her coat and felt the outside. Then he went through the pockets but found nothing. He flung it down again and went back to his desk, where he sat frowning and looking at the typewriter.

Mike paused.

"Then I lost it for a while, I don't know why. When I saw the room again it must have been later."

The woman was sitting at the dressing table in her underwear putting on her make-up. Hanging on the handle of the door was a dark red dress. The man had shaved and changed. He was standing on the other side of the room putting on a tie.

Once he had finished he crossed the room and stood behind her with his hands on her shoulders.

'How nice. You are making yourself look pretty, just for me.' There was a touch of sarcasm in his voice. 'I've been thinking,' he paused and put his head on one side, 'there is something I don't quite understand.' He paused again. The woman continued putting on her make-up. 'It wasn't raining when you went out. It only started raining later on. So how did you get from the church to the brewery without getting wet? It must have taken at least five minutes and it was raining really hard.' He gripped her shoulders hard with his hands.

'Stop it, you're hurting me.' She looked up at him over her shoulder. He released her shoulders.

'What a beautiful neck you have,' he said. He bent to kiss the back of her neck. 'How white and smooth and elegant.' He slipped his hands on either side, caressing her neck gently with his fingers. She sat completely motionless. 'Perhaps you never went to the church at all. Perhaps you spent all your time in the brewery.' His fingers closed around her neck. 'Is that what happened?' He tightened his grip upon her throat. 'Did you meet someone in the brewery?' He continued to tighten his grip on her.

'Please,' she said, lifting her hand to touch his.

'Did you meet someone in the brewery? Tell me.' He pronounced each word with great emphasis and began to squeeze her neck more and more tightly. 'Did you meet someone in the…?'

The woman was struggling for breath. Her right hand reached out onto the dressing table, searching for something. She found a pair of scissors, picked them up and with all her strength brought them back up above her head into his face.

He screamed in pain and released her. The scissors had caught him on the cheek just below his eye. He staggered back, clutching his face and trying to stop the bleeding with his hand.

'You bloody bitch,' he shouted. 'How dare you mark me? You whore.' She stood staring at him, her face was ashen. She held the scissors out in front of her. He took a step towards her. 'I will make you suffer for this, you whore. Wait till I get my hands on you. I am going to wring that pretty white neck of yours.'

She backed away from him, still holding the scissors with both hands out in front of her. 'Keep away from me.' Her voice was hardly audible and she was trembling.

He laughed at her. 'I'm not scared of your little scissors, slut. I'm going to enjoy making you scream for mercy.' He launched himself at her, reaching for her throat again. He caught her off balance and she fell backwards. Losing his balance too, he fell on top of her. As they fell, she held the scissors out in front of her and his weight drove them deep into his chest. He cried out as the point entered him and writhed, and then he was still. She lay motionless, pinned to the floor by his weight. Then with a great effort she pushed him so that he rolled over on his back. The scissors were sticking out of his chest. She looked down at him as if dazed. There was blood on her breasts and bra. She turned and picked up the raincoat from the bed and put it on, buttoning it up. She found some keys and went out of the room, locking it behind her. I heard her footsteps on the stairs. Then the room was silent. The man lay on his back, blood slowly staining his shirt.

After a little time I heard footsteps coming up the stairs. Two sets of footsteps. The key turned in the lock. The woman came in followed by a young man with brown hair and a beard. He walked across and looked at the dead man.

'My god, Anne,' he said, 'I didn't really believe you.' He looked at the blood oozing onto the carpet. 'What a mess.'

'Robert, I had no choice. He was going to strangle me. He had his hands round my neck. He knew. Somehow he knew that I'd been with someone.' She started sobbing and then she looked up at him. 'You've got to help me. I don't know what to do. I just can't think.

He stepped towards her and put his arms around her, holding her to him. 'You've got to call the police. You've got to tell them what happened. What's been happening? How he hit you and hurt you.'

She looked up at him. Her tear-stained face was frightened and desperate. 'But nobody will believe me. They will say I am a murderer. They'll think I did it for you. They'll lock me up for years. Don't let me down, Robert. I need your strength.'

He took her gently by the shoulders and kissed her. 'I am not going to let you down. But we must think about it carefully. You told me that he's beaten and punched you ever since you were married. Surely somebody else must know, must have seen something?'

She shook her head. 'He was so clever. He never hit me in the face where it would show. If I had bruises on my arms then he made me wear dresses with long sleeves. I was too afraid of him to tell anyone. You are the first person I've told. Nobody else will know. Nobody cares anyway what happens between a husband and wife. Even the police don't think any of it is their business. If we call the police I will be tried for murder.'

'But a jury would believe you. You could tell them everything that happened.'

She shook her head. 'I can't, I just can't. I would have to give evidence. I would have to be cross-examined. I can't do it. Please take me away. Being with you gave me the courage to fight for my life. For the first time I had something to live for. Otherwise I would probably have just let him strangle me, because it would have meant an end to the pain and the misery.' She looked up at him pleadingly and put her hands in his. 'Please take me away. I just want to escape. I want to be with you. Take me away somewhere they can't find us.' He looked down at her uncertainly. 'Please,' she said, 'don't let me down.' She turned away from him and stood for a moment. The room was silent. Then she walked over to her dead husband. She stepped over him and pulled the scissors out of his body. Then she turned and faced the young man she called Robert. She held the scissors up with the bloody points against her chest.

'Either take me away or leave me alone now. I will kill myself. I would rather be dead than in prison or apart from you.'

He crossed to her and took the scissors from her. 'You know I'm not going to let you down. You're right, we'll go away together. I have a little money. If we take his car we can drive to the coast, from there we can take a boat to Ireland. If nobody finds him until morning, it should give us time to get away. You must pack a bag. Is there blood on your clothes?' She nodded and undid the coat, showing where the blood was on her underwear.

'You must clean yourself up.'

'What about him?' She gestured towards the body. Robert stood thinking for a moment.

'We need to get him into the bed. Turn down the bedcovers.' Anne did as he told her, pulling the sheets and blankets right down to the bottom of the bed. Then together they managed to lift him into the bed. He got a towel from the bathroom to staunch some of the blood and then pulled the sheets up to his neck. He tried to mop up some of the blood from the floor. Then he picked up one of the chairs and put it over the stains so that they weren't obvious.

'Now listen carefully,' he turned towards her and took her hands, 'go into the bathroom and take a bag with you. Take off your bloodstained clothes and put them in the bag. Then wash yourself and put on clean clothes. Pack a few things in a bag. Take any money of his you can find. I've got to go back to the kitchen. You must go down to dinner.' She looked at him in horror. 'You must. If you don't come down at all they will start to wonder. You must go to the restaurant and have your meal. Tell them Frank is feeling ill, that he's got a temperature or something. Take your time and try to act normally. Then ask them to make some soup and bread to take up to him. Insist that you take it up yourself. Also tell them that you think he is overtired. He's been writing too much. Say you probably won't be down for breakfast, but you don't want to be disturbed. After you've eaten, come up to the room. When I've finished in the kitchen I'll go back to my room and pack. Once everyone's gone to bed and it's quiet, I'll go out into the yard and throw some gravel up against this window. Then take your bag and come down the stairs. Be as quiet as you can. Make sure you bring the car keys. We'll take the car. If nobody sees us then hopefully they won't discover him until midday. That should give us time to get away.'

Anne threw her arms round him and kissed him. 'You're so clever,'
she said. 'Thank you, you have saved me.' She kissed him again. He
gently pushed her away.

'There will be time for that later. Now I must go. Do exactly as
I've told you. Be brave and try to keep calm. Everything depends
on you.' He walked towards the door, then stopped and came back.
He took her face between his hands and kissed her. 'I love you and
I want to spend the rest of my life with you.' He went to the door.
'Lock it behind me,' he said. Then he was gone. She stood for
a moment, alone in the middle of the room. Then she looked at her
dead husband and smiled. She took off her raincoat and took a bag
with her into the bathroom.

Mike stopped. He seemed completely drained.

"That is where the dream ended." He lay back in the bed for
a moment and closed his eyes. Laura bent down and opened the blue
cardboard wallet file. She took out some photocopies of news cuttings.
She found one and passed it across to Mike.

"Look at this," she said. "Do you recognise any of these?" He
opened his eyes and sat up. He took the piece of paper and looked at it
carefully. It was part of a front page. There were three photographs and
a headline. "Promising writer murdered by wife's jealous lover".

"Yes," he said. "That's them. That's the man at the typewriter, the
husband. I think she called him Frank. That's the woman and that's
the other man, the one who came afterwards."

"You're sure these are the people you saw in the dream?"

"Yes, absolutely. The dream is fresh in my mind and retelling it
to you now has made it seem fresher." His voice was tired, but full
of conviction. He looked down at the article below. "This isn't what
happened."

"What do you mean?" Laura asked.

"This article says that Frank was murdered by this other fellow,"
he looked at the article, "this Robert. It says that he went to his room in
the inn and stabbed him to death with a pair of scissors. But that isn't
what happened. The woman, his wife," Mike looked down again at the
paper, "Anne. She killed him in self-defence."

97

"How do you know?"

"Because it's what I saw in the dream. Frank had his hands round her neck. He threatened to kill her." There was silence then Laura spoke again.

"That is what she claimed in her defence. She said he had become jealous of her and attacked her. She said that he had tried to strangle her and that she had picked up the scissors in self-defence and in the struggle he was killed."

"That is exactly what happened," Mike interrupted her.

"The jury wouldn't believe her. Robert's fingerprints were found on the scissors and the prosecution maintained that the two had planned to murder him and run away together."

Mike's voice was agonised.

"That happened afterwards. She went to get Robert because she didn't know what to do. He tried to get her to phone the police, but she refused. She threatened to kill herself. That is when he took the scissors from her. That's how his fingerprints got on them."

"That's as may be; the problem was they tried to cover it up. They stole Frank's money and his car and tried to escape. That was enough to convince the jury that it was pre-planned."

"How did they get caught?" Mike asked. "In my dream I just heard them making plans."

"Somebody saw the car leave and went to investigate the room. When they got no response, they unlocked the door and found the body. They phoned the police. Anne and Robert were picked up in Liverpool trying to get the ferry to Ireland."

"He treated her very badly, her husband. I saw him hit her and make her grovel in front of him. She seemed terrified of him."

"Anne said that in court. It was part of her defence that he had treated her very badly. But there was no evidence. She had never told anyone about it. Nobody had ever seen any sign of it. She claimed that this was because he was clever. He never hit her in the face or on the arms or legs anywhere that anyone would see, but the jury just didn't believe her. The barrister for the prosecution kept asking her why, if this was happening, she didn't tell anyone and she had no answer. They thought that it was just an excuse. You've got to remember that this was forty years ago. There was no awareness of domestic violence as there is today. What a husband did to his wife in the home, behind closed doors, was not regarded as anyone else's business. The police hardly ever intervened in these situations. Even today, it is hard to get women to come forward about it. I know, it's one of the areas I work in."

"So the jury found them both guilty?"

"Yes. They were sent to prison for life. They were lucky they weren't hanged. We still had capital punishment in the 1950s. But Anne couldn't cope with life in prison. It seems some of the other prisoners gave her a hard time and she committed suicide."

"How terrible," Mike said gloomily. "What a miscarriage of justice. And poor Robert. He never did anything. It's so sad."

"But it's so exciting." Laura got up and took his hands. Her voice was full of feeling. "Don't you see you've proved to me that you can see things that have happened in the past? I don't know how. It goes against science and psychology, but you can. I set this as a kind of a test." He looked at her. "It isn't that I really doubted you, I just couldn't see how it could happen. I thought you might have convinced yourself, but it is real. Oh, Mike." She kissed him. "You have an amazing power and you can use it for good."

"What do you mean?" He sounded uncertain.

"You can tell the true story of what happened here. You can set right that miscarriage of justice by telling people the truth. I can help you write it up. You can use your power for good." Laura felt such admiration and affection for him. She pulled off her nightdress and slipped into bed beside him. "Oh Mike, I love you so much." She kissed him again on the mouth and ran her fingers over his chest. Somehow the power he had and the story he had told attracted and aroused her despite her tiredness. The warmth of her body and her touch overcame his tiredness too. So they made love again. As they came together, Laura almost felt as though his power had entered her and touched her deep inside.

Afterwards they lay back, exhausted. As she looked up at the ceiling and thought about what had happened in this room, a thought struck her. I wonder what happened to Robert? If he's still alive, he might be able to corroborate everything Mike dreamt. Then she fell asleep.

*

99

Mike parked the car in front of the row of terraced houses beside the village green. Number nineteen was the second from the end. They went up to the blue front door and Laura rang the bell. It rang inside and they heard the sound of footsteps. The door opened. A tall man opened it. He was the same height as Mike, but much thinner. His hair was completely white and his face was brown and weathered with deep lines on it.

"Robert?" Laura asked.

"Yes." His voice was soft and had a kind of strength that she had not expected.

"I'm Laura. We spoke on the phone." She held out her hand. Robert looked at her in silence, then shook her hand. The handshake was as strong as his voice and his hand was hard from outdoor work.

"Please come in," he said and opened the door wider. He shook hands with Mike and then led them down a dark corridor. He opened the first door they came to and led them into a small room with lace curtains.

"Please sit down." Robert gestured them to the settee. "Would you like a cup of tea?"

"That would be lovely," Laura said, "and thank you so much for agreeing to see us."

"I'll just make a pot of tea. I'll with you in a minute." Robert disappeared back into the corridor without waiting for any response. Laura looked round the room. It was simply furnished, with a settee, an armchair and a coffee table. There was a gas fire against the wall that was unlit. Either side of it there were shelves filled with books. There was a single painting above the mantelpiece. It was a print of a painting by Corot of a road with trees. The colours were deep greys and greens. It had a gloomy sense about it. The room was chilly and had a feeling of being unused. Laura guessed that this was a "front room", set aside for visitors and special occasions, neither of which there appeared to have been many of. She looked at the furniture. It was plain and simple. It looked as though it had been bought from second-hand shops. But it had been restored with a care that provoked her admiration.

Robert returned with a tray of cups, a teapot and a plate of plain digestive biscuits which he put down on the coffee table. He poured them out cups of tea and offered them milk, sugar and biscuits. When all this had been done he sat back in the armchair opposite them and looked at them in silence.

"Robert, it's very kind of you to give us some time."

"It's a diversion," he said. "I don't get many visitors."

"As I said on the telephone, we'd like to talk to you about Frank's death." Laura carefully avoided the word murder.

"Ah, the murder, it was a long time ago and in a different life." There was a touch of melancholy in his voice. It suggested that this was a life perhaps he did not wish to return to.

"We've read the newspaper articles and the transcripts of the trial and we're keen to hear from you what really happened. I know it may be a bit painful for you, but it would really help us to understand what seems to have been a miscarriage of justice. Do you mind if I record you?" Laura produced the tiny machine from her bag.

He sighed. "Alright, but it won't do any good." He was silent for a moment, as though thinking back. "I was working as a chef at the Pheasant in the village. I trained in catering when I did my national service. It was my first job as a chef. I worked as an assistant to start with in London in one of the Quality Inns. I wasn't really happy in the city. I grew up in the country, in the next village in fact. My mother knew I wasn't happy and sent me the advert when she saw it in the local paper. A new couple had taken over the Pheasant and wanted to operate it as a small hotel, offering breakfast and dinner to guests and dinner to local people. It was quite a new thing at the time, so I applied and they interviewed me. My references were good and I got the job. I loved it. We used mainly local produce and tried to offer something really good. They wanted traditional English food, but they didn't mind putting other things on the menu as well. I did part of my national service in Malaysia and I became interested in Far Eastern cookery. They were happy for me to experiment and try things, it was really great. I'd been working there for three years when Anne and Frank came to stay. He was a writer and he had come to finish his novel in the peace of the countryside." Robert was silent for a time, picturing it in his head.

"How did you come to meet Anne?" Laura prompted.

"The afternoons were my time off. I would do all the preparation for the evening meal and lunch for any guests that wanted it, then I had three hours off. I used to walk or fish. Frank wrote in the afternoon and Anne had to go out. Frank had told her that he couldn't write with her in the room. So in the afternoon she had to find something to do, whatever the weather. To begin with, she had tried sitting in the bar reading, but it was gloomy and she got bored. Anne didn't really know how to spend her time and she started to go for walks. One afternoon she saw me fishing in the stream beyond the wood and stopped to talk. Anne was a city girl and felt unsure of herself in the country. When she told me that, I offered to show her around and take her for walks."

"What did Frank think about this?" Laura asked.

"He never knew. Anne said that he was insanely jealous. She said that if Frank knew, he would lose his temper. He would beat her up and probably me too. So we were careful. We never left or came back together. We never walked down the street together. We had a place where we would meet. It's a stile at the corner of the wood. We used to meet there at half past two every day. Both of us had to be back by six. It gave us time to walk and talk." Again, Robert was silent. "It was a good time. I showed her the different paths and the woods. I taught her to fish and how to set snares. I introduced her to the different plants and how to recognise the different birds from their singing. Anne was a fast learner and I think she came to love the country." There was a note of sadness and regret in his voice.

"You fell in love with her?" Laura asked gently.

"She was pretty – so pretty. I had never met a woman like her. Everything she wore made her look beautiful and stylish. She was intelligent. She'd been to university and read a lot of books; she knew so much more than I did. But she wasn't arrogant about it. She didn't laugh at my ignorance. She was kind and she valued what I could teach her and in return she taught me."

"Did you become lovers?"

"She was so unhappy. At first I didn't understand. I thought that she was just sad to have to be on her own and to spend so much time each day away from her husband. Then she began to tell me about how he treated her. They'd met at university. He swept her off her feet. He was handsome and glamorous, a writer with real talent. It was only after they were married that she discovered his dark side. He was very cruel to her. He had hundreds of ways to hurt her and humiliate her. She showed me the bruises and burns on her body. But he was clever. He never made marks on her where other people could see." Robert sighed again. "I felt sorry for her. It was so unfair that someone so pretty, so kind, so gentle should be treated in such a way. I couldn't bear the fact that she was so sad. I just wanted to make her happy. I tried to persuade her that she should leave him. I wanted her to come with me. I was ready to leave my job for her. I was a good chef, I could work anywhere. But Anne was afraid. She said that he would never let her go. She was terrified that if he suspected she was going to leave him he would kill her. She used those very words. Then there would be the disgrace and the scandal. She said it would destroy her parents. She was their only daughter and they thought that Frank was such a good son-in-law and that she was so happy. I tried to convince her. I told her we could go abroad together. But she said that wherever we went Frank would find us. He was clever and he was implacable. He would never give her up. All the time it seemed to be getting worse. From what Anne told me, Frank found more and more ways to torment her. He seemed to get some kind of pleasure from it. Eventually she agreed that when he finished his book we would run away together."

"What happened on the day Frank died?"

"The weather was foul. It was raining hard and far too wet to walk, so Anne came to my room. I had a room in the brewery, it was part of my contract to live on the premises. She'd come before sometimes but it was dangerous. She had to cross the yard and the yard was overlooked by one of the windows from their room. She said that she had waited until she could hear him typing furiously and then had run down the stairs and across the yard. Anne said that the book was nearly finished. They would be leaving in about a week. I begged her again to leave with me.

We made love, but we had to be careful. Anne said that Frank always inspected her when she came back, to see if there was any sign or smell that she had had contact with another man. We lost track of time and suddenly it was after six and she was late. She was terrified of what would happen. Whenever she did anything that Frank thought was wrong he punished her. It was just another excuse to hurt her and make her suffer. I was worried about her, but I had to let her go.

Then at about a quarter past seven Anne was outside the kitchen window. She seemed upset and obviously wanted to speak to me. I signed to her to go into the brewery. Then I made an excuse and left the kitchen to meet her. She was in a terrible state. She told me that Frank had tried to strangle her, and in defence she had stabbed him with a pair of scissors. I went up to the room with her. Frank was lying on the floor bleeding from his chest. I checked for a pulse, but he was dead. I told her that she must phone the police at once and explain what had happened. Anne wouldn't listen. She became hysterical. She said nobody would believe her that she'd be sent to prison. She picked up the scissors and threatened to kill herself if I wouldn't help her. I had to think quickly, I couldn't be away from the kitchen for long. We picked him up and put him in the bed and pulled the sheets and blankets up to his face. I told her to wash and change. She had blood all down her front, where he had fallen on top of her. I told her that she should go down to dinner as though nothing was wrong. She was to tell them that Frank was ill and then take a tray up for him. Then she was to pack a bag and wait. When everything was quiet I would throw gravel at her window. I would meet her by his car and we would drive away together. I hoped that nobody would suspect anything until morning. My plan was to drive to Liverpool and then cross to Ireland."

"But it didn't work out." Laura said.

"No," Robert sighed again. "Somebody must have seen her go down the stairs or heard us drive off in the car. The police stopped us before we could get to Liverpool. With a bit of luck we could have reached Ireland and started a new life together. Instead they arrested us. I was never alone with Anne again."

"You were kept in custody until the trial?" Laura asked.

"Yes, the prosecution opposed bail, not that I had enough money for it anyway. We tried to explain what had happened, but nobody would believe us. The prosecution accused us of planning the whole thing. They said that I had gone to the room deliberately to kill Frank. My fingerprints were on the scissors. I'd taken them from Anne when she threatened to kill herself with them. They made me out to be the cause of it all. I had seduced Anne and then planned with her to murder

Frank and steal his money. Anne told them the truth, but there were no witnesses. There was no evidence of the way he treated her. Everyone saw Frank as this kind man, a real gentleman and a promising writer. The jury lapped it up and the papers loved it. Anne couldn't bear it. Her parents disowned her and she went to pieces completely during the trial. After the verdict we were both taken away to prison. I asked for a moment with her, but my request was refused. I never saw her again."

"Did you know that she committed suicide in prison?" Laura asked gently.

Robert was silent. "I only found out much later. They never told me at the time. I wasn't surprised. Prison is hard. Anne was too gentle, too kind, she would never have been able to stand it. Probably it was the best thing for her. I hated to think of what it would have been like for her."

"But you served your sentence?"

"They gave me life, then after twenty-five years of good behaviour I was released on parole. That's when I found out that Anne was dead. I had sort of hoped that she might have survived, that we might be together again. But I had not heard from her. I only got one letter from her, then nothing. In that letter she begged me to forgive her for ruining my life. It was so like her to take all the responsibility upon herself. I wrote back to her telling her that there was nothing to forgive. I said I was not sorry for what I had done. Given the chance I would have done it again. I told her that she must be strong, that eventually we would both be free and we would meet again. I never got a reply. I just kept hoping though deep down I knew that I would never see her again." Robert stopped talking. He seemed to be deep in his own thoughts. For a long time there was silence in the room.

Eventually Laura spoke. "So, what did you do when you were released?"

"By then everyone had forgotten about it. My mother was dead. Anne's parents were dead. It was a crime committed a quarter of a century ago. The world had moved on and nobody remembered it or me. I couldn't go back to the village though, or to my home village. I went to London and tried to pick up my old career in catering. It was all different. I got a job in a fast-food restaurant, but it wasn't the same. I stuck it out for a while and then I moved down to Torquay. I worked in a pub and after a couple of years became their main chef. I enjoyed that. It was nice being by the sea and the people were friendly. I saved up my money and bought this place. It was very run-down. The previous owner was an old lady who had lived here till she died. Her family wanted a quick sale without having to clear the house, so it was cheap enough for me to afford. I spent my holidays doing it up to make it habitable. When I retired I came to live here. It's not a pretty village, but it's quiet and private. I have a garden and I rent an allotment. I grow lots of my own fruit and vegetables. I play darts for the local pub once a week. I cycle a lot and walk. It keeps me fit."

"You never married or met anyone else?"

Robert shook his head. "It's not easy to find someone in your fifties. Besides, all those years in prison I think I grew inside myself. It's hard to explain. I tried to keep the memory of Anne fresh in my mind. I knew I was innocent of any crime apart from trying to help a woman I loved. But over time memories fade. I didn't even have a photograph of her or anything to remind me of her. I just became empty inside. I'm not sure I could have had the capacity to love anyone else. Besides when you don't particularly want to meet someone it's easy not to." He smiled grimly.

"Do you still have the letter? The last letter that Anne wrote to you?"

"Of course." He seemed surprised that Laura might think that he would not have it.

"Could we see it? Would you mind?"

"If you want." Robert didn't move. He looked across at them curiously. "But why are you so interested in what happened? It's nearly fifty years ago."

Laura looked across at Mike. He spoke for the first time. "I had a dream and in the dream I saw what happened in the room."

Robert looked puzzled. "I don't understand."

"We went to stay at the Pheasant. We booked the room where Frank and Anne stayed. Mike told me that he has a strange power. I can't explain it. He can dream about things that have happened in the past. Things he doesn't know about. I wanted to see if this power was real. I read about the murder and I took him to stay at the Pheasant to see if he would dream about it. He did, and what he saw fits exactly with what you've said. He saw Frank try to strangle Anne. We wanted to come and hear your story of what happened. We'd like to write about it and to set the record straight. I know it won't make any difference, but we want to tell the truth about the murder."

Robert looked at them for a while before saying anything. "I don't know. It seems very strange. But it would be nice to feel that the truth is known, even though anyone it mattered to is dead."

"Could we see the letter? Please."

"Okay." Robert got up and left the room.

Laura turned to Mike. "It all fits, it is exactly as you dreamt it. Everything he's said supports it. This will help our retelling of the story."

Robert came back. He held in his hand a faded envelope. He handed it to Laura as though it was something immensely precious to him.

Laura took it. With great care she removed from it a sheet of folded paper.

"Do you mind if I read it out?" He shook his head but said nothing. As Laura reread the letter aloud she found it hard to keep the emotion out of her voice.

My dearest love,

I am so sorry for the pain and suffering that I have caused you. I know that I have destroyed your life and caused you to be imprisoned for a crime you did not commit. The guilt of this rests heavy upon me. I know that there is nothing that I can do to set this right.

How I wish now that I had listened to your wisdom when you told me to call the police. How I wish I had left Frank as you begged me to do and gone away with you. I am sorry that I did not have the courage to do so.

Thank you for all the time you spent with me and all the things you taught me about the woods and the fields. I am a city girl and you opened my eyes to a beauty I had not seen. Thank you for all your gentleness. You showed me what making love is, something I did not experience in the hell of my marriage. I can truly say that the time I spent with you – those stolen afternoons – were the happiest of my entire life. It is those memories that I cling to now. They are the only things that help me to bear this place.

I am afraid, though, that the torment I suffer here is too great for me to endure. I know that I will never see you again. I only ask that you forgive me and know that I love you.
Anne

Laura fought hard to stop her voice from trembling and felt tears welling up inside her. Robert turned his face away and she could sense that he was crying.

"I am sorry," he said at last. "To hear you read it and to talk about it to you has brought it all back to me. I think perhaps you'd better go."

Laura crossed the room and knelt in front of him, taking his hands in hers. "I am sorry to have caused you such grief. But thank you for helping us. We will tell the truth of what happened. Perhaps in some way, that may make it easier for you."

He looked down at her. Then he gently removed his hands from hers and got to his feet. "Perhaps," he said. "Now I want to be alone." They stood up and he led them to the door. He did not offer to shake hands, but as they left he stood in the doorway. Finally he said, "Good luck with what you are doing. Perhaps it will make a difference." He looked at Mike. "This is a strange power you seem to have. I don't envy you having it. Be careful how you use it." Then he shut the door.

Laura stood looking out at the street. It was a beautiful June evening and she had opened the windows to let what little breeze there was blow through the house. She had changed after work and was in a loose-fitting red and white summer dress. Her hair, released from its daily restraint, flowed down to her shoulders. She stood motionless, staring out of the window. In one hand she held a white A4 envelope. Behind her on the coffee table was a glass of iced water. She was waiting for Mike, who was late. Typical of him to be late today, she thought. It was just over three months since they had stayed at the Pheasant and she had three important pieces of news for him. One was in the white envelope that she held in her hand. It was a letter from a television company inviting Mike to take part in a television programme. It was called *Spooky Places* and it was about ghosts and haunted houses. The invitation, the result of a letter she had written to the producer about the murder at the Pheasant and Mike's dream, represented a major breakthrough in their attempt to make good use of his extraordinary power. An appearance on the programme would bring him publicity and could launch him into a new career as a psychic medium. The title made her smile. It offended all of her social science training, but it was the label given to those who claimed to have the powers that Mike undoubtedly possessed.

The second piece of news lay on the coffee table beside the iced water. It was another letter, this time an offer of a contract from a publisher. Laura had worked hard in her evenings and at weekends to write an account of the events at the Pheasant using Mike's dream and Robert's interview. They had made visits to two other places where Mike had also been able to describe tragic events from the past. They were interesting, but without the same compelling nature of the first, with its sad story of tragic love and a miscarriage of justice. Laura's idea was to put them together into a book. She hoped to have ten or twelve stories in the end. After talking to Lottie she had produced a draft of the outline and the first three chapters and sent it to a number of publishers. One had replied enthusiastically, offering a contract. Laura wanted to try to get it published around the time of the programme. That should be possible. The invitation to appear was in two months' time, but it wouldn't be screened until the spring of next year. She hoped that that would be enough time to do the remaining visits and write them up. She already had a list of possible places.

And the third piece of news. That was different. The first two were unmistakeably good. They provided an opportunity for them to earn some money and give Mike a new direction. He had been reluctant at first. He was uncomfortable about exploiting something he didn't really understand. Eventually, Laura had managed to persuade him that there was nothing wrong in trying to make some good out of something that had caused him so much suffering. She had said that the more he used his power, the more they could understand and try to control it. That still remained her main objective, although the chance of making some money from it had become more important in the short term.

That third piece of news was much more difficult. Laura wasn't sure how he would react to it. She wasn't even sure how she felt about it herself. It had been a surprise to her because she had tried to be careful. But she knew exactly when it had happened. She knew absolutely. Like so much else that had changed their lives, it could be dated back to that night at the Pheasant.

Mike's car drew up outside. He saw her standing in the window and waved. "Isn't it a beautiful day?" he called. "Do you fancy going out for a drink?"

"Maybe." She turned to meet him as he came in through the door. Suddenly she felt nervous and tried hard to keep the tremor out of her voice. "You might well want to celebrate," she handed him the envelope. He opened it and read it.

"That's brilliant," he said and crossed the room. He picked her up off her feet and swung her round. "You are so clever."

"That's not all, but you'll have to put me down before I tell you."

With exaggerated gentleness he placed her back on her feet. "Well?"

"I've had a response from a publisher. They like the idea of the book and they're offering us a contract." Laura gestured towards the letter on the table.

Mike picked it up and read it then turned to face her. "Even better, we must definitely celebrate."

"And..." she said breathlessly.

"And?" He looked at her questioningly. "What more good news can there possibly be?"

"I'm pregnant." Laura said.

4

England, June 2006 – August 2009

Mike sat back in the seat of the car. The hood over his head kept him in complete darkness. He had given up trying to make conversation, so there was little for him to do but think.

His mind went back to that day, when Laura had taken a deep breath and told him she was pregnant. For a moment he stood, completely taken aback. Then of course he had hugged her, lifted her up in the air, and said it was wonderful. All the time he was trying to think. His relationship with Laura was comfortable. He liked being with her. He liked living with her in her house. But children? They had never talked about it. He had never thought about it. She always seemed to be in control in that area and he had left it to her to take precautions.

Laura had let him hug her, then pushed him away and looked at him steadily. "Do you really feel like that?" she had asked. "It was a mistake, I don't really know how it happened. It must have been that night at the Pheasant. We've never talked about children. I don't know if it is what you want? Is it a commitment you are ready for? If it isn't then you are free to go."

He had kissed her and taken her in his arms; assured her that he was really excited by it; told her that he was happy that she was bearing his child; that he was looking forward to being a father; after years of wandering now it would be good to settle down. All the time there was a tiny voice inside him asking whether this was really right. As he had tried to convince her, he was also trying to convince himself. After that day things had changed. When the book was published it did sell and made some money for them. But he had felt uneasy about it. The power that he had was not something that he understood or could control. He wasn't sure about exploiting it for gain. Laura didn't seem to feel like that. Her focus had shifted, from trying to make sense of what had happened to him, to gaining some benefit from it.

For Laura there had been no such shift. Using the power was about confronting it and learning to control it. She did not share Mike's sense of unease and had little sympathy with it. Now that she was convinced he really did have the ability to see into the past, she wanted him to make use of it. This caused tension between them.

Mike had found the other visits she arranged increasingly hard to cope with. The spontaneity of the time they had stayed at the Pheasant had gone. Instead he felt under pressure to deliver. Seeing the tragic events of other people's pasts was harrowing and exhausting. Witnessing what happened meant experiencing it. The tragedy of Anne and Robert had moved him and left a sadness gnawing away at him. The other stories mounted up, one after the other, until he felt he was carrying a burden of sorrows. After the visits, the dreams would sometimes return, leaving him feeling disturbed and upset. Laura was too preoccupied with the work she was doing on the book to notice the effect upon him.

The television programme had turned out to be a bigger challenge than he had expected. From the start Mike had felt that it was a circus. To him the programme was deeply flawed because of its central contradiction. The producer was keen to appeal to a mass audience by pandering to the popular fascination with the supernatural and serving up stories of ghosts, if at all possible spiced up with sex, violence and high tragedy. At the same time it adopted a pseudoscientific approach, challenging and attempting to debunk as elaborate frauds the very stories it presented. The scientific strand was championed by Ellie, a striking red-haired presenter. Her attitude to Mike was as contradictory as the programme. She seemed to spend part of her time crucifying him for being a conman and the rest trying to get into bed with him.

The first programme focused on the Pheasant and the story of Anne and Robert. Laura had taken part, which had given Mike confidence. They had gone through the story of the dream, using extracts from the tape and dramatic reconstructions shot in the actual room at the Pheasant. The programme also included some key moments from the trial. The production team had tried to get Robert to take part. He had refused point blank, though they were able to use bits of Laura's tape of their interview with him. The final part of the programme consisted of an interview with Laura and Mike, conducted by Ellie. Here she had tried to show that the whole thing was a set-up and that Mike had carefully read up on the trial and made it up as a publicity stunt. Ellie gave them and Laura in particular, a really hard time. There was an aggressiveness in Ellie's questions to Laura that seemed to come from more than scientific scepticism. Laura had done most of the talking and had remained calm and unruffled, carefully setting out in detail why this was not a fraud. Mike was surprised by her quiet determination and felt really proud of her. Ellie refused to be convinced. Afterwards she had tried to question Mike again off-set and on his own. She had trapped him in a corridor on his way to removing his make-up. Standing so close to him that their bodies were almost touching, Ellie tried to coax Mike into admitting that Laura had put him up to the whole thing. Mike had been very conscious of her physical proximity and the way she was making herself available to him. But he had just repeated the same story as in the interview and escaped as quickly as he could. Overall the programme had made good television and the producer was pleased with it. Mike was invited to come back and do another one later in the series.

Laura wanted him to do a programme about the incident in New Orleans, but Mike refused and had deliberately not mentioned it to Ellie or anyone in the production company. Instead, they decided to try to film Mike actually having a dream. He was to be taken to a place which was associated with some kind of dramatic happening and stay there until the dream came. The plan was to record the whole process. Mike hadn't liked the idea from the start. Dreams simply came to him and he had no control over them. He wasn't sure that he could just deliver a dream to order. Laura talked him into it. She persuaded him that if he could do it for her then he could do it in front of the cameras. So, reluctantly, he agreed.

Then the day before, Ellie persuaded the programme director that Laura should not be present at the filming. Ellie's argument was that there could then be no possibility of any collusion between them. Mike wanted to refuse at once. Having Laura with him gave him so much more confidence. She seemed at home in front of the cameras, in a way that he wasn't. Besides, Mike felt that Ellie had other reasons for not wanting Laura to be there. Again, Laura persuaded him that he had to agree. She felt Ellie was trying to test their credibility and, if he refused, it would do even more to convince her that the Anne and Robert story was a fraud.

So here he was, sitting hooded in Ellie's car. The production team were going to meet them at the location. Ellie had insisted that Mike should be blindfolded so that he had no idea at all of their destination. Ostentatiously she had put the hood over his head before he even got into her car. Mike had protested, but Ellie said the location had to be a complete mystery. So they had driven off together. It seemed a long drive, especially as he was in complete darkness, and Mike found it hard to keep conversation going. Ellie was curious and asked him lots of questions about his background and upbringing and how he came to have the strange power he claimed. Mike again avoided any reference to the events in New Orleans. For some reason, he felt even more reluctant to share them with Ellie. So they had lapsed into silence and he had sat replaying the last year of his life.

The car began to slow. "Nearly there," Ellie said cheerfully. It juddered as it went over what sounded like a cattle grid. Mike heard the sound of gravel beneath the wheels. The car stopped and the door opened. Hands reached in and helped him out. Ellie took his arm and led him up some steps into a building. He sensed they were in a large room, a hall possibly. Then they went up two flights of stairs onto a landing. There was carpet beneath his feet and he seemed to be walking along a corridor. A door was opened; they passed through it and stopped. The hood was abruptly pulled off his head and Ellie was smiling, saying, "Here we are at last." Mike blinked for a few moments to adjust to the light. He was in a large room with a high ceiling. At one end against the window there was a solid mahogany desk and chair, suggesting that the room was perhaps a study. The curtains had been drawn over the windows so he could not look out, although it already seemed dark outside. In the middle of the room there were two settees with a low table between them and at the far end a single bed. Mike guessed that it was not normally part of the room and had been brought in especially for him. The production crew had set up and focused their cameras and sound equipment on the bed.

They were standing around waiting in anticipation.

"This is it," Ellie said, putting his bag down by the bed. "Make yourself comfortable. I've arranged for some food. I don't know if you want it downstairs in the dining room or on a tray up here?"

"If I've got to wear a hood downstairs then I'll have it up here," Mike said. "Are this lot going to stay all the time?" He gestured to the production team. "If they are, then I'm never going to get to sleep, let alone dream."

Ellie followed the crew downstairs after telling Mike that he was allowed to explore the floor he was on but nowhere else.

Mike went out onto the landing. It was a large rectangular space around the stairwell, which descended to the first and then the ground floor. The house seemed late-Victorian. Looking over the banister, he could see a large hall with a tiled floor partly covered by rugs. The room he had come out of was at one end, facing the top of the staircase. There were two doors on either side of the landing and another one facing him. He walked around the landing and looked in the different rooms. Four were bedrooms furnished with heavy wooden furniture. One had its bed missing and Mike supposed it was the one that had been moved into the study. The other room, the one facing him, was a large old-fashioned bathroom. Mike used the toilet and then washed his face.

As he returned to the study he met Ellie coming up the stairs with one of the team. They were each carrying trays with plates of food. Ellie also had a carrier bag looped over her wrist which clinked as it swayed. Mike opened the door for them and they put the trays down on the small table between the two settees. Ellie thanked the other man, who Mike recognised as one of the camera crew, and he left them. She took a bottle of red wine out of the carrier bag, opened it and poured two glasses. Then they sat down opposite each other and began to eat.

"I'm sorry it's only cold food," Ellie said, "but we had to bring it all with us." Mike nodded his thanks. He suddenly realised that he was hungry. They ate in silence, until they had both finished. Ellie put their plates on one tray and then carried it over and put it down beside the door. Then she sat next to him and filled up his glass with wine to the top. "Now we need to relax you," she said, turning to face him and putting her hand on his thigh.

"That's going to make me excited, not relaxed," Mike said.

"Really?" Ellie looked at him with interest and moved her hand up his thigh to his crotch. "Are you slipping out from under Laura's thumb?"

Mike looked at her. Ellie's green eyes held his. Her red hair was cut and styled in the fashion of the flappers of the 1920s and she had a large gold loop earring in each ear. Her face was pale with a high forehead, fine cheek bones and a slightly upturned nose that added a touch of mischief to what was otherwise a look of refinement. She was half turned towards him, her knee touching his and, as in the corridor after the first programme, Mike was acutely aware of the closeness of her body, the tight blouse stretched over her breasts, the slimness of her waist and the curve of her hips.

He placed his hand over hers and removed it from his crotch. "Look, Ellie, I'm here to make a programme. How am I going to make it work if you distract me?"

Ellie laughed. "But that's it; I don't want it to work. I want to expose your cheap little fraud for what it is. I just don't see why it should be a completely wasted evening."

Mike got up and walked to the window by the desk. He needed to put some space between them. Looking out into the darkness, he felt exposed and under pressure and wished Laura was with him. The most important thing was to try to relax and focus, so that he could dream. To do this he had to resist Ellie's sexual advances. But he knew that the more he rejected her, the more determined she would be to prove that the whole thing was false. This experiment had been deliberately set up to achieve that end. If he accepted her overtures then he would have betrayed Laura and be compromised. Ellie would find a way to use this against him as well. After a long silence, he turned to her. "It's ten o'clock, I'm going to try to settle down so that I can sleep. I know you've got to stay in the room, but can we turn the lights down?"

"Suit yourself. I'll sit at the desk, it's got a very low light."

Mike picked up his glass of wine and went over to the bed. He took off his shoes and lay down. Ellie took her glass and the bottle and went over to the desk. Once she had put the light on she crossed to the door and turned all the other lights off. Mike stretched out and closed his eyes. He tried to blot out the feeling of there being someone else in the room. The journey and the tension had made him tired, although he still felt on edge. He tried the deep-breathing exercises that he had learnt. At the Pheasant everything had happened naturally; on other weekends it had been harder and so he had tried to develop some strategies to relax and sleep. The room was becoming chilly so he pulled a blanket over himself. Mike visualised Laura. He so much wished that she was with him. He tried to imagine her lying next to him; the pressure of her lips against his; her skin warm and soft beneath his hand. Mike woke to find he was indeed caressing a body. Ellie had undressed and was lying under the blanket next to him. Mike recoiled from her. "What are you doing?" he whispered.

"I thought you might be cold. You certainly seemed to be enjoying the warmth of my company." She took his hand and put it on her breast.

"I was dreaming, I thought you were…"

"Laura," she interrupted. "How sweet, but I bet I can give you a better time than she does. Especially at the moment." Ellie pushed her body against him and planted her lips firmly over his.

It was true that because of Laura's pregnancy they had not made love for a while. The feel of Ellie's body was beginning to arouse him. Mike knew he had to be resolute. He pushed her away and turned his back to her. "Stay if you want but I'm going to sleep," he said.

"You're such a spoilsport," Ellie sighed. She snuggled up against his back and kissed him on the neck. Then her hand reached over and tried to touch him between the legs, but he had placed his hands there in anticipation of such a move. Mike closed his eyes and tried to shut her out. Eventually she got tired of being ignored and left. He heard her feeling her way in the darkness across the room and started his deep-breathing exercises again.

Mike was standing in the room. It must have been morning because sun was streaming through the windows. A man sat at the desk writing. His back was towards Mike so all Mike could see was black hair and that he was wearing a waistcoat. Mike watched him for what seemed a long time. The man was working his way through a pile of papers on his left. He would pick each one up and read it. Occasionally he signed one, at other times he made notes on the paper or in a red-backed ledger in front of him. There was a knock on the door. The man turned. For the first time Mike could see his face. His forehead was lined with creases and his neatly trimmed black beard was speckled with grey. "Enter," the voice was deep and mellow. The door opened and a woman came in dressed as a maidservant, carrying a tray upon which lay a white envelope. She crossed the room and held out the tray to the man at the desk. "Thank you," he said. She inclined her head to him, then left the room. The man picked up a paper knife from his desk and carefully slit the envelope open. He took out a sheet of white paper and unfolded it. The man got up from his desk and walked to the centre of the room, reading. Suddenly he stopped staring at the paper in his hands. He put his other hand on his forehead, then walked back to the desk. He sank into the chair, dropping the paper in front of him and sat staring out of the window.

"Wake up," a hand was shaking him. Mike opened his eyes to find Ellie staring down at him. Behind her were the production team.

"You were dreaming?"

"Yes."

"I thought so, that's why I called the team. You've been asleep for ages."

"Why did you wake me?"

"To see if you were dreaming."

"You interrupted it. You broke the dream."

"Tell us what happened."

"But you broke the dream."

"So?"

"It wasn't finished."

"Tell me what you dreamt. We need to record it."

So Mike told them what he had seen, but he felt uncomfortable looking into the lights and talking to the cameras.

"That's not much," Ellie said when he had finished. "That's not enough to make a programme out of."

"You interrupted me. The dream wasn't finished."

"Well go back to sleep and dream the rest."

"I don't know if I can do that." Mike felt angry and frustrated.

"Why not?"

"I've always followed a dream through to the end, until it finishes. I've never broken it and come back to it. I am not in control of it like that."

"I bet you're not." Ellie was smirking at him.

"What do you mean?"

"You know what I mean. It's all a big con. You don't dream at all. This is just an excuse."

"And you are doing everything you can to make sure I don't."

"Of course, what do you expect? Leave him," she said to the team, "let's see if he can re-find this mythical dream and tell us what's happened." So they left. Mike closed his eyes and tried to focus, but he felt too angry. Although he tried to picture the man and the room again he couldn't even get back to sleep. For what seemed like hours, he lay there until the darkness began to turn to grey. Getting up, he went to the window. The house was surrounded by parkland. In the distance there was a faint streak of dirty yellow. Wind blew rain against the window. Ellie was asleep, slumped over the desk. Mike quietly left the room and crossed the landing to the bathroom. He ran cold water and splashed his face with it. When he returned to the study, Ellie was awake.

"Where have you been?" she demanded.

"Just to the bathroom."

"So did you recapture your precious dream?"

"I didn't even sleep."

"What a surprise!" Her voice was full of sarcasm. "Still, we can always try again tonight." She got up and walked over to him. "Perhaps you might be a little bit friendlier." She put one hand up and ran her fingers through his hair.

"What's the point? You've already made your mind up." Mike stepped away from her.

"If you want me to change it, then you're going to have be more persuasive, aren't you?" Ellie gave him a meaningful look.

Mike had had enough. He felt tired, frustrated and angry. "I'm not staying here another night. Take me home."

"If you do that, then the programme will be scrapped. I'll tell the producer what a fraud you are and he'll pull the first one as well."

Mike hesitated. If that happened, Laura would be furious, but he just wasn't strong enough to resist Ellie for another night. Ellie saw his indecision and pounced upon it like a cat. In an instant she was beside him, one arm around his shoulder, her cheek pressed gently against his, her other hand over his crotch. "Come on, be a good boy. Let's be friends, you won't regret it." Her voice was soft and persuasive. She gave her final word added emphasis by giving his testicles a gentle squeeze.

It was too much for Mike. "I don't care." The words came tumbling out as he broke away from her, strode over to the bed and picked up his bag. "If you want me I'll be by the van, I think it would be better if I travelled back with the team. I won't have a blindfold so I don't want to have to spend three hours looking at your face." He walked out of the room, slamming the door behind him and went down the stairs.

"Temper, temper," he heard Ellie say in the room behind him.

Once he reached the ground floor Mike stopped and looked around. His guess had been right when he had looked over the banister the day before; this was a large entrance hall with paintings on the walls. He scanned them curiously and stopped in front of one of a tall bearded man. It was the man from his dream.

"That's him," he shouted, "That's him."

One of the production team came out of one of the rooms. Ellie looked over the banister from the second floor. Mike looked up at her. "That's him, the man in my dream, the one sitting at the desk."

"So?" She came slowly down the stairs and stood next to him, looking at the portrait. "So?" she repeated.

"It proves I did dream."

"You could be making it all up."

"But I'm not."

"Then stop being such a bloody prima donna, stay and see if you can prove it." Ellie's eyes met his; the challenge in them was clear.

Again, Mike hesitated. He was tempted to accept and try again. But he had never attempted to return to a dream in this way and he wasn't sure if he could. Ellie was determined to seduce him. She knew he found her attractive and he was sure she could sense he was weakening. If she succeeded and he was unable to recapture the dream, then her triumph would be complete. It just wasn't worth the risk.

"No, thanks. Whatever I say or do, you won't believe it. Let's just call it a day and go." Mike walked towards the front door.

"Fraud," Ellie called after him. "You don't even believe in it yourself."

So they went back. Laura met him at the front door, when they dropped him off.

"How did it go?"

"It was awful." Mike pushed past her and dropped his bag.

"What happened?"

"Ellie happened. She was in my face the whole time, needling me, challenging me. I managed to get to sleep and I had a dream, but she woke me up in the middle of it. I tried to go back to it. I just couldn't."

"So?"

"We came back. Ellie wanted to stay and try again tonight. I just couldn't face it?"

"Why not?" Laura's eyes searched his face for an answer.

Mike swallowed hard. He couldn't face telling Laura how Ellie had tried to seduce him. She might not believe that he had been able to resist. "I just couldn't stand being with her for another night."

"Really?"

"She got under my skin."

"You should have stood up to her."

Mike could tell that Laura thought he had given in too easily. "I just couldn't," he tried desperately for some way to convince her. Laura gave him a long look. Mike could tell she was wondering what exactly had gone on between them, in what other ways had he given in to Ellie. "Look, I'm sorry."

Laura turned away from him. "It doesn't matter." The flatness of her voice said that it mattered a great deal, that she felt he had thrown away all her hard work. There was nothing he could say and they never spoke about it again.

Ellie was furious. That programme had to be scrapped. She tried to convince the producer to pull the first one as well. In the end he refused; it was too good and probably the best one of the series. She was able, though, to persuade the producer that Mike was too unreliable to work with and it was made very clear that they wanted nothing more to do with him.

By this time Laura was seven months pregnant. She became increasingly preoccupied with the baby and grew more and more distant from him. At times she seemed to resent both him and the baby. The closer her due date approached, the more agitated Laura became. Several times she shouted at him that she wished she had had it aborted and that it didn't feel part of her at all. These outbursts upset Mike, but he supposed that it was because she was frightened of giving birth. It terrified him, and all he had to do was watch.

Laura's fear was justified. Her labour was long and painful and the consultant had to assist the final stage of the delivery with forceps to drag their screaming baby daughter, Alice, into the world. Mike was with Laura the whole time, talking to her and holding her hand. He had hoped that this would in some way help to re-establish the warmth of their relationship.

After two days Laura was home and her mother came to stay. Mike had met Laura's mother a few times and he was never really sure that she approved of him. This feeling of disapproval had increased when Laura became pregnant. Her mother seemed to have assumed that they would get married. Mike had sort of expected that too; after all it was what most people did. He had even bought a ring and asked her properly. Laura would have nothing to do with the idea. She said that they had never thought of it before, so why should they now? Marriage would not strengthen their relationship or make them better parents. So Mike had put the ring away somewhere safe in case it was needed in future. Alice did seem to bring Laura and her mother closer together, and Mike saw real warmth between them that had not been there before. The downside to it, however, was that he felt almost completely excluded. He accepted it patiently, thinking that it would change once Laura's mother went home. After a long two weeks she left.

Laura remained withdrawn. Alice did not sleep well. Laura was tired and seemed depressed. Mike tried to help by changing nappies, giving Alice a bottle, getting up in the night and keeping the house tidy. None of this seemed to be enough. There was tension between them and for the first time they argued. Laura said it was obvious to her that he didn't want the baby and she was sorry that she had ever had it. Mike protested vigorously, pointing to all the things he was doing. As soon as he had finished, Laura continued as though she had not heard a word, saying it was a terrible mistake and she wished she had had an abortion. Mike opened his mouth to speak, but she went to her bedroom and would not let him in. Deep inside him that tiny feeling of unease began to grow bigger.

Mike shivered. Although it was July it was early morning. Mist sat heavy over the landscape and its dampness chilled him. He pushed the pram along the pavement past the line of semi-detached houses. It was just after six and they were all quiet with their curtains drawn. There was nobody else on the street. No cars, no pedestrians. Only the birds, but even their song seemed muted and dulled. Alice had woken early after waking several times in the night. Laura was exhausted and he had said he would take Alice out to the playground. He didn't have to be at work until ten so there was plenty of time and it would give Laura a chance to sleep. It suited him anyway.

At the corner of the street he paused. He was not going to the playground just round the corner. Alice was cooing in her pram and a longer walk would be better for her. Nearly eight months old, she could sit up and crawl and was just starting to pull herself up on things. He was already able to put her in a swing or on a small slide. For now though, being taken out for a walk was still what she enjoyed best. The fresh air and the motion of the pram calmed her down and would soon send her off to sleep. Mike often took her out for walks, especially in the morning. He was gradually exploring each of the playgrounds within a reasonable walk from Laura's house. He told himself that he was looking at each to decide which one Alice would enjoy best. But he knew that this wasn't really true. In reality he was looking for the playground in the dream.

This was not one he had been to before. It was in the middle of a housing estate and should take between twenty minutes and half an hour to get there. Following the route he had memorised from the map, the way seemed easy until he entered the estate. Then it was confusing. All the houses looked the same – neat semis and some rows of modern terraces. So he stopped at the corner of the street, uncertain which way to go, trying to remember the directions and wishing he'd brought the map with him. It should be right, cross the road and then down a little alley. Just when he was beginning to think he'd gone wrong, he found the alley on his left and turned down it.

There was a hedge on one side and a brick wall on the other. A tabby cat with green eyes watched him silently from the wall. At the end of the alley he came out into an open tarmacked space with garages on three sides. In the left-hand corner there was another alleyway. It led down beside the garages and crossed another alley that ran behind them. He had not realised what a maze of alleys the estate was. It was somewhere he'd never been before and some parts of it had a bit of a reputation. Suddenly he came out into another open space. He recognised it immediately. Right in front of him there was an old-fashioned roundabout. That's what made him certain it was the playground in his dream – roundabouts were rare now, for health and safety reasons. There hadn't been one in any of the other playgrounds he'd been to. Beyond the roundabout there was a large metal slide and beyond that, three swings. To his surprise one of them was occupied by a girl in a black hoodie. She was gently swinging herself backwards and forward. Beyond her was a patch of grass with one set of football posts. It all had an air of neglect. The council had a policy of redoing its playgrounds to conform to those health and safety requirements. It had obviously not got as far as this one yet. The playground was exactly as he had seen it in his dream. It seemed even more lonely and deserted in the mist. On his right there was a wooden seat. He pushed the pram towards it and sat down. Alice was fast asleep. He looked down at her peaceful face and watched her little chest rise and fall as she breathed. The mist showed no sign of shifting, although the air was not as chilly and he was warmer now from the walk, so he sat and looked out over the playground, thinking about the dream.

This dream was always the same. It was early morning; he was in a playground, standing by an old roundabout, idly spinning it, watching as it slowly turned round and round. Suddenly he looked up across the playground. On the other side a woman stood staring at him. He knew her at once – her golden brown skin, her reddish blonde hair falling in curls. It was the woman from the jazz club. He recognised her immediately. It made him start. She saw him and walked across the playground towards him. Her clothes were different from when he had seen her last. She was wearing a sleeveless blue dress, buttoned to her neck that clung to her, revealing the curves of her body. Gracefully she came towards him and taking his hands in hers, pulled him to her. His eyes caught the necklace of carved ivory figures that stood out white against the blue dress. He looked at her face and into those blue-green eyes. "I've waited so long for you to come." Her voice was husky with emotion. "Where have you been? Why have you taken so long?" Stepping closer, she put her arms around him and kissed him. He closed his eyes and felt her body against his, the softness of her breasts through the thin dress, the warmth of her thigh against his leg. Her tongue explored his mouth. Suddenly he was falling, falling. Then he woke full of desire, her image so vivid that when he closed his eyes he could see her again.

Once the dream had started it came every night without fail. He had promised to tell Laura whatever he dreamt, but how could he tell her about this? She was tired, tense and depressed. So he said nothing. The dream was driving him insane with desire. Logically he told himself that it was just a fantasy caused by Laura's withdrawal into herself. They had not made love for months. If he tried to touch her she would shrink away from him and then become tearful and say she was sorry. She told him that it was difficult for her and she needed time to adjust after the birth. So then he had started to look for the playground. He wasn't sure if he was really trying to find it or just trying to prove to himself that it didn't exist so he could pull himself together. Taking Alice out for a walk was an easy excuse. He had visited lots of playgrounds, but none had been right. He had almost given up until he'd seen this one on the map.

Now here he was. There was no question; this was definitely the place. It was just as he had seen it in the dream. But there was no woman in a blue dress walking towards him. Only a girl on a swing. He looked at his watch. He hadn't realised how long he had sat there. It was time to go back. Well, at least he'd found it and perhaps that would dispel his fantasy for good. He wasn't sure whether he was disappointed or relieved. As he stood up to go, the girl got off the swing and sauntered towards him across the playground. She was taller than he had thought; her hood covered her head and kept her face in shadow. Reaching the pram she looked down into it, saying nothing. Then she turned to look at him and her hood fell back. With a start, he saw golden brown skin, reddish blonde hair falling in curls and a pair of blue-green eyes. Mike couldn't focus for a moment. He turned away and walked quickly, pushing the pram down the alley without looking back

It was only a girl. A girl on a swing. And yet, when he saw her face, he saw the woman from his dream. That wasn't possible. Ten years ago he had seen that woman murdered in a New Orleans nightclub. He had seen her throat cut. It had been easier when he could have simply dismissed his dream as a sexual fantasy, now he didn't know what to think. He wished he had never set out to look for the playground. Why hadn't he given up when he did not find it? He couldn't explain what had made him keep searching. Now he knew it existed he didn't know what to do. Maybe he was losing his grip. Perhaps the tension in the relationship was getting to him, too. That must be it. It was just a little girl in the playground. It was his imagination that had turned her into the woman from his dream. By the time he reached home he had dismissed it as pure imagination. He would pull himself together, focus on the realities of his life. He would never go to the playground again.

The mist was beginning to clear and the sun to shine as he opened the front door. The house was quiet. He tiptoed upstairs and looked into their bedroom. Laura was still fast asleep. A shaft of light fell across her. She looked relaxed and at peace. He could see the beauty that was there when they first met. This was reality. He must hold onto it. Mike went downstairs and made up a tray of tea, toast and half a grapefruit. As he brought it into the bedroom, her eyes opened and she smiled at him.

For three weeks Mike stuck to his resolution not to go back to the playground. But he could not stop thinking about it. He kept going over what had happened again and again. The playground was the one in his dream. There was no doubt about that. It wasn't just the roundabout; the way it was laid out was right too. The girl on the swing was not the woman in the blue dress. She could not be. When the hood had fallen back, her hair, her face, her eyes, the colour of her skin, was that all his imagination? He wasn't sure. The uncertainty was hard to bear. It kept gnawing away at him.

His dream continued to come almost every night. Now it was subtly different. The woman in blue waited for him on the other side of the playground. She beckoned for him to come. He found it hard to move, as through the grass was like a bog that sucked his feet in so that each step required an enormous effort. She would meet him halfway. She would reach out her hands to him as before, but there was sadness in her eyes. When she spoke, her voice was full of sorrow. "Why won't you come to me? Why do you make me wait so long? Don't you want me any longer?" When he tried to touch her she would draw back, teasing him and before he could reach her he would wake.

Mike couldn't continue like this. It was distracting him from his efforts to rebuild his relationship with Laura. He felt that if he went once more, he would know for certain. Either there would be nobody there or he would see the girl again and she would be just that, an ordinary girl. Whatever happened, it would mean that he could push it all to one side and then perhaps the dreams would stop.

Once Mike had made the decision he had to wait for an opportunity. Again it came early in the morning. Alice was suffering from colic and had had a particularly bad night. So he took her out for a walk. He told Laura that he might be longer if Alice didn't settle and promised to stay out as long as possible so that she could get some sleep. She kissed him goodbye, then turned over gratefully and was asleep before he had even gone downstairs.

Unlike the first time, this was a beautiful summer morning. It was already warm so he was wearing a short-sleeved shirt and shorts. The sun was bright and he was glad that he had put on his sunglasses. He walked steadily, sure of the way and did not get confused by the maze of alleys. Alice gurgled away for a while and by the time he reached the playground was fast asleep. It was just as last time. He came out abruptly from the alley and found himself in front of the roundabout. In the bright summer sunshine it seemed less mysterious, though even more dilapidated. At first he thought that it was empty, then he saw the girl. She was swinging lazily to and fro on one of the swings at the far end. He stopped for a moment, unsure what to do, whether to approach her or not. She took no notice of him and appeared not to have seen him. So he sat down on the seat and waited.

He studied the girl carefully, watching her through his sunglasses, trying not to appear to stare at her. This time there was no hoodie. She was wearing a flimsy yellow top with straps over her shoulders and a very short blue denim skirt. As she swung to and fro it revealed the brownness of her thigh far above her knee. Her hair was reddish blonde and fell down in curls to her shoulders, just as he remembered. There seemed to be some kind of jewellery round her neck though he couldn't tell what it was. She was exactly as he had seen her when her hood had fallen back. She was not the woman from the jazz club. There was a resemblance, a remarkably close resemblance. This was a girl. And she was not wearing a blue dress. So that should have been enough. He had come and seen her and she was not the woman in his dream. Mike knew he ought to go. He had done what he had set out to do. But he didn't move. He sat and watched the figure on the swing as she moved backwards and forward.

Then the swing slowed to a stop and she looked across at him, as though noticing him for the first time. She slid smoothly off it and walked across the playground towards him. Her movements were lithe and graceful. It reminded him at once of the dancer in the club. She had the same natural, unselfconscious freedom about her. As she reached the pram he stood up, suddenly feeling all the self-consciousness that she seemed to lack. Now he could see that around her neck hung a string of carved ivory figures. His head began to spin again. He put his hand on the pram to steady himself.

The girl looked down at Alice in the pram, ignoring him completely. She stared intently at the baby for a long time. Then she looked at him and her blue-green eyes met his. He had to focus. This was a girl, not a woman.

"I waited for you, but you didn't come." Her voice had that same huskiness as in the dream.

He struggled to speak. "What do you mean?" he finally managed.

The girl ignored his question. Then she took a step towards him and held out her hand. "Come." Her tone was gentle, but firm. This was a command, not a request. Without hesitating he obeyed and took her hand. It was cool and soft. The girl began to walk and he walked beside her, pushing the pram with his other hand.

128

She led him away from the playground and down an alley between some garages. Then she turned left along another alley that led between the backs of two more rows of garages. Each garage had access from this alley by a door. The girl stopped by one of the doors and released his hand. She took out a key. The key turned easily in the lock. She opened the door and gestured for Mike to go in.

Mike blinked as he stepped out of the sunlight into the darkness of the garage and took off his sunglasses. Behind him the girl turned on a switch and a long fluorescent tube hanging from the ceiling flickered and then came on. He heard the girl close and lock the door behind him. Mike looked around. He was in a single garage with a low roof and no windows. It smelt cool and musty. Along one side were shelves lined with tins and bottles. On the other was an old wardrobe, its door hanging open. He could dimly see clothes hanging up. Next to it on the floor was a double mattress covered with a duvet, blankets and pillows. By the door where they had come in there was a sink with a single tap. In the far corner there seemed to be some objects propped up. He turned to face the girl as she came towards him from the door, taking his hand off the handle of the pram. She stood in front of him and looked up at him. Mike's heart was racing and he found it hard to breathe. He kept trying to think this is a girl, not a woman.

She reached up and kissed him on the lips. Her tongue was suddenly inside his mouth; the taste excited him. He was losing his focus, he needed to get out of here. Her fingers were undoing the buttons on his shirt. With an unexpected knowingness, her hands were caressing his chest. She stood back and slipped the straps of her top over her shoulders so it fell to her waist. Reaching down without looking, she unzipped her skirt and let it drop to the floor. Then she pressed her body against him and he could feel the nipples of her small breasts against his chest through the flimsy bra. Her tongue was inside his mouth again and he closed his eyes. He breathed in and could smell her – a mysterious, exotic perfume that made him reel. Her hands were undoing the buttons of his shorts, slipping inside the waistband and pushing them and his boxers to the floor. Her thighs pressed against his. She led him to the mattress and pulled him down onto it. Mike felt as though he was in a trance. What was happening did not seem real. He tried to think this is a girl, not a woman; I must not do this; I must leave. But she was not behaving like a girl. Her mouth and her fingers were all over his body, making him hot with desire for her. She seemed to know exactly how and where to touch him. He was intoxicated by her and the pent up frustrations of months of rejection by Laura took control. He closed his eyes and surrendered to a world of sensations and jumbled images. At one point she sat astride him, taking him inside her, leaning back while he reached up and cupped her breasts in his hands. Then he was on top of her, thrusting deeper and deeper, as though searching inside her for the elusive sensation that would provide the climax to his ecstasy.

Afterwards Mike lay panting, his senses reeling. The girl was beside him on the mattress. There was silence in the musty garage. Once his breathing had become more regular and his head had cleared, Mike raised himself on one elbow and looked down at her. "Who are you?" he said.

The girl looked up at him. "It doesn't matter."

"But you must have a name."

"I'll tell you another time."

"Why were you at the playground?"

"I was waiting for you."

"But how did you know I would come?"

"Why did you come?" She threw the question back at him. Mike was silent for a while.

"I came to the playground because I saw it in a dream."

She looked up at him and smiled. Her eyes flashed. "I was there because I saw in my dream that you would come."

Mike stared at her. "So you dream too. And you dreamt of me?"

"Yes, I dream too. I saw you in my dream and saw that you'd come, but for a long time you didn't come. The first time I saw you, you turned away. I wasn't sure that you'd come again. The dream said you would come and you did." Her tone was matter-of-fact, as though what she was describing was completely obvious.

Mike looked down at her. "In my dream I saw a woman. A woman I met a lifetime ago. You're not her, though you look like her. How can that be?"

"Dreams are strange things. You ask too many questions. Now

your baby is waking and you must go." Alice was stirring in her pram. The girl got up and began to dress. She found her skirt and shoes and put them on. Then she went over to the pram and bent over it. "Your baby is very pretty, what's her name?"

"Alice," Mike said. He scrambled to his feet, retrieved his clothes and quickly put them on. The girl was bent over the pram, cooing. She had given Alice her finger and Alice held it in her little hands, gurgling with delight. As Mike approached, buttoning his shirt, she straightened up and turned to look at him.

"You'll come again." Mike wasn't sure whether this was a question, a statement or an order.

"Perhaps," he said uncertainly.

"You will come again." This time her tone made the meaning clear. "I'll wait for you in the playground. The early morning is a good time. Bring the baby, then your girlfriend will not be suspicious." The girl crossed to the garage door and unlocked it. She opened it and looked up and down the alley. There was nobody there. Mike pushed the pram out through the door into the bright sunlight. Just outside he stopped and looked at her. The girl stood in the doorway. He saw again the golden brown skin, the hair falling to her shoulders. Her blue-green eyes met his. She took a step forward and reached up and kissed him, putting her tongue inside his mouth and whispered to him. "You'll come and I will be waiting." Then she closed the door and he heard the key turn in the lock.

Mike walked away quickly down the alley, trying to remember his way back to the playground. Alice was gurgling; at any moment she might become fractious. He reached the playground. It looked the same as when he'd come, except that it was empty. The summer's morning was also the same, only the sun was hotter. The sky was just as blue. The alleys and roads were just as deserted. But everything was different. Things were no longer the same. He had betrayed Laura. This girl had taken him into a garage and seduced him. How could she behave like that? Perhaps it was a dream. Perhaps it hadn't happened. Perhaps he had just fallen asleep on the seat. After all, he'd not slept much last night either. Maybe this was just another sexual fantasy. But Mike knew that it wasn't. The image of the girl was in his mind. When he closed his eyes he could see her. He smelt that mysterious scent that seemed to hang around her; he could still taste her in his mouth, where she had just kissed him. And she had dreamt of him. What did that mean? He'd set out to put an end to the dream, to shrug it off, to discard it. Now it was as though the dream had stopped being just that and had become part of his reality. Mike didn't know what to do. He did know that he must never go back to the playground again, but he also knew that he would.

Mike managed to stay away from the playground for nearly a month. For the first two weeks his resolution was strong. To begin with he felt guilty and scared. He had betrayed Laura. Would she sense that he had been with someone else or would he somehow give it away? He felt as though it was written all over him. But Laura did not seem to notice anything. To make up for what he had done he was attentive to her, trying to rebuild their relationship. Laura didn't seem to notice; she was too preoccupied with her own thoughts.

July turned into August and the weather broke. It rained solidly for a whole week, so going to any playground was completely out of the question. Alice grew and developed all the time. Her crawling was now determined and confident, and often she pulled herself up onto her feet by anything that would support her. She had a more regular sleep pattern. This helped Laura, who was less tired and started to show signs of her old self. There were still times when she was depressed and withdrawn and she would sit for hours in the front room just staring out of the window. Before Alice was born she had converted the spare room into a nursery. They had searched the auction rooms for a nice cot and Laura had stripped it down to the wood and sealed and stained it. Now she seemed to have lost all her enthusiasm.

Mike wondered what she would do when her maternity leave finished. He had tried to talk to her about it, but she had refused. His earnings were not much. They could manage, though it would be a struggle. He felt again that if he had not bottled out in the second TV programme then he would have earned some decent money. In the second week in August the town had an arts festival. Mike was very busy during the day as well as in the evenings. It meant he was earning more money, but he was working most of the time and there were no opportunities to take Alice out.

He had not dreamt at all for three weeks, though he had often woken in the middle of the night feeling guilty. He lay watching the shadows on the ceiling and listening to Laura's breathing. Part of him felt that he ought to tell her what had happened, but he knew he couldn't. Laura still would not let him make love to her. She said she was sorry and she became tearful if he suggested it. She said she just didn't feel ready yet and begged him to be patient. So he stopped asking and just said that she must tell him when she felt differently. Perhaps because of this, Mike could not stop thinking about the girl. He kept replaying in his mind what had happened. She looked so much like the woman from the jazz club it unnerved him. What surprised him even more was the raw force of her sexuality. A girl she might be, but she was no naive innocent. The way she had touched him showed an experience and a knowingness that you would not have expect. This combination of youth and a complete lack of any inhibitions had made the sex powerful and exciting. The memory of it was enough to arouse him and make him long for more. As the guilt and fear subsided and Laura continued to be remote, his desire for her grew and grew, until he became desperate to see her again.

At the start of the fourth week he dreamt about the playground again. Now it was different. He was in the playground and the girl was on the swing. She looked across at him and smiled. She beckoned him to come over to her. She was wearing the yellow top and the short denim skirt. As he reached her she smiled at him again. "I'm waiting for you. It's time to come again." He stood watching her. She reached up and pulled the straps of her top down over her shoulders, as he remembered her doing. "I know you want me. So come." Then she laughed, walked the swing backwards and then let herself go. She swung lazily past him and as she did she hitched the skirt up higher and higher. After he woke her image stayed with him and the room seemed filled with her scent. Sleep was impossible. Thoughts filled his mind. Was this latest dream just a projection of his desire for her? What had she meant by saying that he was in her dream? Her answers were so enigmatic. If it was true then perhaps they were linked together in some strange way.

As dawn broke Alice began to cry. Laura half woke and turned to him. "Oh, no. Mike, I'm feeling so grotty." She began to get up but he put a hand gently on her shoulder.

"It's okay. I'll see to her."

"Would you? You're such a dear."

"Maybe I'll take her out for a walk," Mike heard himself say as he got out of bed. "I haven't done that for weeks." That doesn't mean I'll go to the playground, he told himself. But he knew he would.

"I'm sure she'd like that," Laura murmured. Then she went back to sleep. In her room Alice was wide awake and beginning to cry. Mike changed her and dressed her and took her downstairs to the kitchen. Once there he put her in the high chair and made up some food from a jar. She was just beginning to start on solids and was often hungry in the morning. He played with her, making the spoon into an aeroplane which made her gurgle with laughter. Then he made up a bottle of water and a bottle of milk, picked her out of the high chair and put her in the pushchair. Alice had now graduated from the pram to a pushchair so that she could sit up and watch the world as it went by. She immediately began playing with the different-coloured shapes on the bar across the pushchair in front of her. He left her in the hall and went upstairs to say goodbye to Laura, who was fast asleep.

Outside it was already warm and the sun was beginning to rise. At the gate he paused. There was no need to go to the playground. The park was nearer. Turning left he started off in that direction. As he walked, the girl's image came into his mind and her words, "You know you want me". He heard her musical laugh and smelt her scent. He crossed the road and turned right instead, heading away from the park. One more time, he thought, it will definitely be the last. He would go to the playground. If she wasn't there he would turn around and go straight to the park. If she was there he would tell her that he could not come again. That it was a mistake. Above all he would not let her take him to that garage. He would not let her kiss him and seduce him again. But the thought of her touch and the brownness of her body made his pulse quicken.

He found himself emerging from the garages into the playground. The girl was as he had imagined, sitting, on the swing. As before, she ignored him. He thought about taking the initiative and walking across to her, but it would have been awkward to cross the playground with the pushchair. In any case, Alice was already struggling to get out. Mike undid the restraining straps and carried her over to the slide. He put her on the top and gave her a gentle push so that she slid down to the bottom. The girl came over and joined them. This time she was wearing a pair of green shorts and a tight black tee shirt. She caught Alice as she reached the bottom of the slide for the third time. "Hello, Alice," she said, picking her up and holding her high in the air. "My, how you've grown. Would you like a go on the swing?" Mike followed as the girl carried Alice and put her in the baby swing. She began to push Alice to and fro gently. The little girl chattered away, full of enjoyment.

Mike stood and watched. Alice accepted her instantly and the girl seemed to know just how to amuse the toddler. He moistened his lips. "I think we need to talk," he said. "I don't understand who you are or how you know me?" The girl turned her head to look at him, still gently pushing Alice. The first two buttons of her shirt were undone and he could see the ivory figures resting against her skin. Her eyes looked into his, seeming to draw him in.

"Later." Her voice was soft. "First we need to play with Alice until she's tired. When she sleeps, then we can talk." Then she turned her attention back to the little girl. So they played with Alice for the next twenty minutes on the swings, on the slide and the girl even took her on the roundabout while Mike pushed it round. At last Alice pointed to the pushchair. The girl brought her over and Mike strapped her in. Then he knelt down beside her and took out the bottle of water. Alice drank and then looked around sleepily. The girl rocked the pushchair to and fro until Alice's eyes closed.

"Come with me," the girl said, "I have something to show you. Something that will help you to understand."

"Can't you bring it to me here? It's better for Alice to be outside." Mike tried to keep to his resolution, even though he was desperate to be alone with her.

"She's asleep now. She won't know. If you don't want to come, then go away." The girl looked at him and when he did not reply began to walk away down the alley. Her hips swayed as she walked.

Mike followed her. "Okay, I will come, but not for long."

"It won't take long," she said, without looking over her shoulder, and continued walking.

"Wait," he said and, taking the brake off the pushchair, began to follow her. She stopped and waited for him and he put out his hand for hers; she took it and walked beside him to the garage door. When she reached it she took out her key and unlocked it. Mike paused for a moment, caught between desire and guilt.

The girl switched on the light and turned and looked at him. "Come," she said, "or go away. If you want to understand you must be brave." Mike pushed the pushchair into the garage. The girl closed and locked the door behind him.

"Why do you lock the door?"

"I don't want us to be disturbed."

Mike looked around, trying to take more in this time. The shelves had a mixture of bottles on them. Some were large like wine bottles and others small, as though they held medicine. There was the wardrobe full of clothes that seemed to be mainly dresses; the sink with the single tap; and over in the far corner, the collection of things he could not really see. "Do you live here?"

The girl laughed. "What do you think I am, a gypo?" The word sounded strange and somehow unnatural in her husky voice. "No, I don't live here. But it is my place, my special place. I come here when I want to be alone, when I want to be private."

"So where do you live?"

"Close by."

"What is it you have to show me?"

"Later," she said softly. She pulled off her tee shirt and tossed it aside. She kicked off her shoes. Then she undid the buttons on her shorts and let them drop to the floor. She walked towards him and took his hands. "Come," she whispered and, taking his hands, led him to the mattress. "It's what you want."

This time she was slower and more deliberate. Gradually, step by step she moved him from one sensation to another, teasing him and prolonging his pleasure until he longed for the final moment of fulfilment.

Afterwards Mike turned to look at her as she lay naked beside him. "Please tell me your name."

"Why do you want to know?"

"Because I can't keep thinking of you as the girl on the swing."

"Why not? Mystery is important. It fuels desire. Sometimes mystery

136

is better than knowing. It's exciting, when knowing is often trivial and boring."

"But I want to know who you are. I want to understand why I dream of you and you dream of me."

"Knowing my name won't tell you who I am. It won't help you to understand."

"But it's a step."

"Perhaps." She shrugged her shoulders. "If you're so desperate, then my name is Marie."

"That's a French name. So are you French?"

"It's a French name, but I'm not French. I told you that knowing my name wouldn't tell you who I am."

"So who are you?"

"That's not for me to tell, it's for you to discover. Knowledge comes by searching."

"Where should I look?"

"Everywhere?"

Mike paused. The conversation seemed to be getting him nowhere. "Marie," he said aloud, listening to the sound it made and trying to fit it to her. "Marie, Marie." But he wasn't sure that it did fit. His eye fell on the necklace of ivory. He put his fingers inside it and held the figures up to the light. They were exactly the same as the figures he remembered seeing in the jazz club, exactly the same as the single figure that he still had at home. "Where did you get this?"

"It was my mother's."

"And where is your mother?"

"She died a long time ago."

"How?"

"Too many questions. Now Alice is waking and we must get dressed." She was right; he could hear Alice stirring. They dressed. Marie went across to the shelves. "I have a present for Alice." She held out a wooden doll.

"But her mother will wonder where it came from."

"You'll tell her that you bought it somewhere." Marie bent down and gave the doll to Alice. She took it with delight and began to explore this new toy with her hands and to put it in her mouth. "See, she likes it.

She won't be happy if you try to take it away from her now." Mike knew she was right. Alice was already possessive of things that were given to her. If he tried to take the doll away she would scream and cry.

"You promised to show me something that would help me to understand."

"And I have. Now you must go." Marie was already walking to the door.

"But what?"

"That's for you to see. Sometimes we're shown things but we don't see them."

"Marie, why do you talk to me in riddles? Why can't you just tell me what all this means?"

"Because I don't know what it means to you. Only you can decide that. If you don't see what's shown to you, then there's no meaning. Now you must go. Soon her mother will wake and want you by her side." Marie unlocked the door and opened it. She looked both ways down the alley.

Mike pushed the pushchair out of the door. Then he turned. "Marie, shall I come again?"

"If you want me you'll come. If you want to understand then you'll come. So I think you'll come again."

"So are you always at the playground?"

Marie laughed at him again. "First you think I am a gypo then you think I spend my life on a swing. No, I'm not always in the playground."

"But then how will I find you?"

"You must come early in the morning, like today, and you must bring Alice. Then I'll know that you're coming and I'll be waiting."

"Why must I bring Alice? Wouldn't it be easier if I came without her?"

Marie sighed. "No. As I told you before, you must bring Alice so that her mother doesn't suspect. Why would you come to a playground on your own as a man? It would be suspicious." She closed the door and he heard the key turn in the lock. Mike turned away and began to push the pushchair slowly down the alley. He tried to think about what Marie had said to him, to try to make some sense of it. Something was nagging at him. There was something obvious, he was sure, but he hadn't seen it.

Mike looked down at Alice, who was still happily playing with the doll. In the daylight he was able to see it properly for the first time. The doll had skin painted golden brown, long curly reddish blonde hair, her eyes were a blue-green and she was dressed in a blue summer dress.

Mike tried to see Marie as often as he could. She had become like a drug that he couldn't do without. The pattern was always the same; he would go in the early morning when Alice woke; they would play with Alice in the playground until she became tired and went to sleep; afterwards they went to the garage and made love until Alice woke again. Marie was brilliant with the little girl and Alice soon began to become attached to her. The sex was always exciting. Marie was both uninhibited and unpredictable. She seemed to know what Mike's fantasies were and how to satisfy them. Making love with Laura had always been good, but this was something different. Mike did things with Marie he had never done before. She drew him across boundaries and into new territory. Always, though, it was she who led, she who set the pace and she who was in control.

Mike knew that he was betraying Laura. He kept telling himself that his relationship with Marie didn't mean that he loved Laura any less. Marie was connected to him by the dream; she was a being from a different world. It was almost as though she had been sent to gratify his desires at a time when Laura couldn't. Somehow that made it alright. His initial sense of guilt became submerged by the insatiable desire he felt for Marie.

After they had made love, Mike continued to try to find out more about her, with little success. Marie was evasive and often Alice would wake and cut short his questions. All that he knew was that her mother had died when she was very young. He still felt that there was some connection that he was not seeing, but perhaps it wasn't important.

Summer ended and autumn began. One morning at the start of October Mike returned to the house after being with Marie. Alice had fallen asleep again on the way back, so he left her in the pushchair in the hall and went upstairs to see Laura.

She was still in bed, her head propped up on her pillows. "You're so good to me," she said. "I really don't deserve you. Come here." He sat on the edge of the bed and looked at her. Her face was pale with tiredness. "Kiss me." He bent and kissed her on the lips. She returned his kiss. "I'm sorry I've been such a cow. It's just, I don't know how to explain. Sometimes it seems having Alice was all my fault and you don't really want her."

"Shush," he put his hand to her lips, "that isn't the way I feel." He stroked her hair with his hand.

"You say that but it's not the feeling I get from you. There are moments when I wish I'd never had her. Then I feel guilty. Can Alice sense in some way that I don't love her, that you don't love her either? I couldn't bear her to feel like an unwanted child."

"She won't, because it isn't true. Look, I know it's difficult for you, but I just want to help you through it." He bent and kissed her gently on the lips.

"I know, that's the strange thing. I know you love her and so do I. Part of the time I wish she wasn't here. Part of the time she's the most precious thing in the world. I'm afraid for her. I can't bear for her to be out of my sight. I'm concerned that something terrible is going to happen to her. That someone is going to come and take her away from me." Laura stared out of the window. "I have this nightmare."

I'm sitting in the front room with Alice. She's sitting up and playing on the floor. The doorbell rings. I get up and open the door. There's a couple there, a man and a woman. They're smartly dressed. The man's in a suit and a tie, the woman in a white blouse with a grey skirt and black tights. She carries a leather briefcase. I ask them what they want. The woman looks at me and speaks.

'We're here to collect Alice.'

'What?' I hear myself say. I feel afraid.

'We've come to collect Alice. We have the papers, they're all in order.' She speaks to me patiently as though I am a child.

'Alice is mine. I'm her mother. You can't take her.'

'You may be her mother, but you really don't want her. We know that and so it's all been arranged. As I said, the papers are all in order. So please open the door so that we can collect her. She knows we're coming. She's waiting.'

I shout at her, 'No. Go away. You can't have her.' I try to shut the

140

door in their faces, but the man puts his foot in it. He pushes me out of the way and they walk past me into the front room. Alice is there, she is bigger now. She must be five or six. As soon as she sees them she backs away against the wall and cries out.

'Mummy, Mummy, please don't let them take me.'

The woman walks slowly and calmly towards her. 'Come with us, Alice. You know she doesn't really love you. She never wanted you to be born. It was us that made you, not her. Now you must come with us. There's work for you to do.' She steps forward towards Alice. Alice backs away from her.

'Keep away from me. I don't want to go with them. Mummy, stop them.'

I step into the room to help her. The man grabs my arms; he forces them up behind my back until they hurt and pushes me against the wall. I turn my head. Alice is standing with her back to the wall. The woman has put her briefcase down on the coffee table. She opens it and takes out a bottle and a handkerchief. She unscrews the top, pours some liquid onto the handkerchief and closes the bottle. Then she turns to Alice and takes a step towards her.

'Mummy, help me,' Alice screams. I struggle to try to help her, to try to say something. The man pushes my arms up higher against my back. The pain is intense and I cry out.

'Alice is being a silly girl.' The woman's voice is calm and soothing, but there's no feeling in it. 'Alice is getting hysterical. She needs a little something to make her calm again so that she does as she is told.' Suddenly the woman moves forward. She grabs hold of Alice's arm so that she can't move. With the other hand, she places the handkerchief over Alice's nose and mouth. Alice tries to scream and struggle, but the woman holds the handkerchief firmly in place. Alice's movements slow down and she goes limp. The woman picks her up and lays her on the settee. She puts the handkerchief and bottle back in her briefcase and takes out some papers and a pen. Then she turns towards me.

'Why do you cause such trouble?' she says in a stern tone. 'It's what you want, so now you must accept it. Bring her here.'

The man pulls me away from the wall, he forces me to walk across the room and then to sit in the chair.

'Now you must sign the papers and we'll go.' She pushes the papers and the pen towards me across the table.

I push them away. 'I'm not signing anything. I don't know who you are. Get out of the house now or I'll phone the police.'

The woman looks at me and sighs. 'Why must you make it so difficult for yourself? You know it's what you really want. It's what you've always wanted. You never intended to conceive her in the first place. That was our doing and so that makes her ours.'

'I don't care what you say, I'm not signing.'

The woman sighs again. 'Are you good with pain? I don't think so. You couldn't even manage the birth without painkillers. What kind of a mother are you?' She nods to the man. He takes two straps out of his pocket and before I can move, he's strapped my arms to the sides of the chair. Then he crosses to the briefcase. He opens it and takes out a scarf, a small hammer and what looked like a pair of pincers.

'What is he doing?'

'He is an expert at this.' While she speaks, the man ties the scarf across my mouth so that I can't cry out. 'He'll work on your left hand. First with the pincers he'll pull out each of your fingernails. Then with the hammer he'll break each of your fingers. Then he'll start on your left foot and then the right foot. The pain is excruciating. Sooner or later you'll sign the document. If you're sensible you'll sign it now. The longer you wait, the more pain you'll suffer. There is another thing; he's very systematic and he doesn't like to be delayed. Once he starts, even if you sign, he may continue to complete the job. He doesn't like to leave a hand or a foot missing only one or two nails; he likes it to be complete. You have only to nod to tell us you wish to sign right now and the pain will stop.' She looks at me in silence for a long time, letting me think about what she's said. 'Are you ready to sign the paper?' I shake my head. I see the man pick up the pincers from the table. He holds the thumb of my left hand and with the pincers grasps the nail. Then he pulls hard. The pain is unbearable.

"The last time I dreamt it, I woke up covered with sweat and I was shaking. The dream was so real I had to get up and go and look to check that Alice was in her cot. It was terrible. The worst thing of all wasn't the pain, but that they were going to take Alice away from me. That Alice cried out to me for help and I could do nothing. I felt so guilty." There were tears rolling down Laura's face.

Mike put his arms round her. "Why didn't you tell me about this?"

"Because it was just a silly dream; it's not like your dreams that mean something. It's the mixed up way I feel about Alice. That's obvious. It's my guilt about feeling that I didn't really want her."

"It was real for you and it upset you. You should have told me about it. After all, you made me promise to tell you if I dreamt." But I haven't, Mike thought to himself. He paused. "How often do you have this dream?"

"Perhaps two or three times a week. It's not always the same, although it always begins in the same way with the man and the woman ringing the doorbell. They're always the same and dressed the same. Sometimes the ending is different. Sometimes there's no torture. The woman just grabs hold of Alice and picks her up, kicking and screaming, and carries her out to a car. The man holds me until she's in the car. Then he pushes me on the floor and goes outside and starts up the engine. I run outside and shout for help. I try to stop the car. I hold onto it, but he gets out and pushes me to the ground. I see Alice at the window, still calling for me to help her as they drive off. It's so real that I can't stop thinking about it. When Alice wakes me in the night I get so tired, then I fall asleep and have this terrible dream. I wake up again in a panic and can't go back to sleep. I've become afraid to sleep in case the dream comes." Laura sank back on her pillows; the effort of telling him had exhausted her.

"No wonder you seem so tired and withdrawn." Mike kissed her. "You must tell me about your dreams. When I tell you about mine it's like shifting a burden. It really helps and you must let me do the same thing."

Laura hugged him. "You're right, and just talking now has made me feel better. It was just you seemed to have drifted apart from me. I know it was hard for you when my mother was here. Giving her time and Alice time meant there was no time left for you. That must have been difficult. I could tell that you resented her being here, but I needed her. It was a way of making my peace with her. I know she's disappointed that we didn't get married."

"And she doesn't really like me."

"I'm not sure that's true. She doesn't know you."

"But she thinks that I don't deserve you. I'm undedicated and I don't have a profession. And I came along and seduced you and made you pregnant."

"Well, maybe something like that. But none of that is true. You know it isn't and you know I don't think that about you."

"Perhaps." Mike was sometimes not at all sure what Laura really thought about him.

"Well, it isn't what I think." She hugged him. "You have strengths that I don't have. I think we make a good team. It's just that by the time my mother left we'd grown so far apart I didn't really know how to bring us together. And I feel so mixed up about Alice."

"Do you think you should go to the doctor? Lots of women suffer from post-natal depression."

Laura's face hardened. "No, absolutely not. I'm not depressed and I do not need some insensitive male giving me drugs."

"What about some sleeping pills? It might at least help you get some sleep without dreaming."

"No." Laura hated going to the doctor. Her GP was a rather brisk young man with no bedside manner, who tended to dish out prescriptions as if he was on commission from one of the drug companies. There was an awkward silence. "I will look for something homeopathic, though. You're right. I do need to get some sleep. But the dream, as I said, it's because I'm so mixed up about Alice."

As if on cue, there was a wail from downstairs as Alice began to wake. Laura made to get up.

"No," Mike said. "I'll see to her. Have your breakfast and have a bath, relax a bit. I'm not due at work for another couple of hours." He went to move, but she put her arms round him and kissed him.

"Thank you," she said. "I do love you."

"And I love you too." Mike meant it. As he went downstairs to feed Alice he thought about Laura's dream. It had never occurred to him that she might dream too. He was so immersed in his own dreams that he had never thought about her or anyone else. There were things about her dream that disturbed him deeply. She was probably right that it was due

144

to her sense of guilt and mixed up feelings about Alice. But who were the people who came to take her away? What did they mean by saying that Laura had never wanted Alice and that they had created her? Laura was sure that Alice was conceived that night in the Pheasant, after he had told her his dream. It had not been planned and in that sense the conception had been unwanted and a mistake. But it didn't mean that someone else had created Alice. He shrugged his shoulders, unable to make any sense of it.

After their talk, the tension seemed to have gone out of their relationship. She was prepared to let him touch her again, although she made it clear that she wasn't ready yet to have sex. She did go to the health-food shop and bought some homeopathic medicines. This helped her to sleep better and the dream seemed to come less often. As he had hoped, talking to him about it really seemed to have helped her. He enjoyed the role reversal. Being a listener rather than a talker was different and, although he still felt responsible, there was less pressure.

Later in October, Laura went in to see social services about returning to work. She had begun to feel that it would help her to establish herself again. They agreed that she could come back for three days a week and start at the beginning of November. Three days suited Laura fine. She had found a nursery that Alice could go to on a Wednesday. She would look after Alice on Mondays and Tuesdays and then go to work from Wednesday to Friday. Mike would look after her on Thursdays and Fridays. It suited Mike too. These were days when there was a chance he could see Marie, especially now the mornings were too dark to take Alice anywhere.

Autumn turned into winter. In December, two weeks before Christmas, Alice had her first birthday party. It was a small affair. Laura baked a cake that had a single candle on it. Laura's friend Lottie came round. She was Alice's informal godmother. The three of them sat round in the kitchen with Alice in her high chair. They sang happy birthday and then got Alice, with Laura's help, to blow the candle out. By then, Alice had moved from crawling to tottering around on two feet, sometimes at great speed. Her curiosity was boundless, so Mike had spent a number of weekends carefully fitting child-proof locks to all the places she would like to go, but Laura felt she shouldn't.

Alice chattered away continuously and, like all doting parents, they felt they could already hear those random sounds begin to take on some meaning.

Later that evening, after they had eaten and Alice was asleep, Laura opened a bottle of white wine and poured herself a glass. Mike realised that this was the first time she had drunk any alcohol since she had discovered she was pregnant. She had taken that aspect of pregnancy, like all others, very seriously. Laura came into the front room where he was sitting with the glass of wine in her hand. "Come upstairs," she said, and reached out her hand to him. He took it and she led him upstairs into the bedroom. Laura put her glass down and drew the curtains. Then she put her arms round his neck and kissed him. "I'm sorry," she said. "I just haven't felt like making love for so long." Mike opened his mouth to speak, to say that it didn't matter, but she kissed him quiet. "You know that the whole pregnancy and birth was difficult for me and how I felt. Now we need to move on. It's as though there's something stopping me from making love, some obstacle. I've got to overcome it and you have to help me. You need to be gentle."

She stood back from him and reaching behind, unzipped her dress, pulled it off her shoulders and let it fall to the floor. Mike saw that she was wearing her old sexy underwear again. He kissed her and pulled her against him. Then Laura lay down on the bed while he took off his shirt and jeans. He started to move towards her then stopped. "Would it be best if I used a condom?" When they were not making love he had not worried about his contact with Marie. Now suddenly it was an issue. Mike had no idea whether Marie slept with other people as well and they never used a condom. He knew he had betrayed Laura, but he didn't want to infect her as well.

"Probably," she said. "We don't want any more little accidents. Well, not just yet."

Christmas came and went. Alice didn't really understand it. She was at the stage when the wrapping paper and the boxes were as much fun as the presents. The weather was cold and Mike did not see Marie for over a month.

In February, because of vandalism and reports of underage drinking, the council fitted CCTV to both the playground and the surrounding garages. It was the first stage in the intended complete refurbishment of the playground. The cameras were well placed to record everything that happened in the area.

The council had been thorough because of the damage to some of the garages. They had placed cameras to record access to the garages from both the front and back. Some were obviously there to act as a deterrent. Two cameras were damaged very quickly and had to be replaced, so the council had placed other cameras that were more discreetly positioned. Every movement around the garages was, therefore, carefully recorded. It was not streamed to a control room, but stored in case it was needed to follow up acts of vandalism or illegal drinking.

The next time Mike went to see Marie, it was not early in the morning, and he came alone. Laura had decided to go and stay with her mother for a long weekend. It seemed an ideal opportunity; Mike was beginning to feel uncomfortable, as Alice got older, about making love while she was sleeping in her buggy. It would also be a chance to spend longer with Marie and perhaps have a proper conversation with her.

Mike arrived at the playground just after five in the afternoon. Without the pushchair he had reached it much more quickly. It was February and so it would be dark by six. He had a bottle of wine in his hand, wrapped in a carrier bag, a sort of a peace offering in case she was cross with him. A little alcohol might help get past Marie's clever and ambiguous answers.

There was no sign of Marie, only the deserted playground, looking even more run-down in the fading light. Mike was surprised. He had assumed that she would be there waiting as usual, that even though he had come at a different time, she would know. He thought for a moment. Marie had said she lived nearby, but he had no idea where. The only thing to do was to go to the garage. Over the months he had been coming, he had learnt the way there from the playground. Even so, on his own in the gathering darkness, it was suddenly confusing. Mike took the alley at right angles to the roundabout. Then another alley crossed it. He paused for a moment and turned left. It was one of the doors on the left-hand side he was sure. It did not have a number, it was blue and he thought it was the fifth one. He counted the doors and the fifth was blue.

Mike knocked softly on the door. There was no response. Suddenly he felt uneasy. Perhaps he shouldn't have come. It was a different time and he hadn't brought Alice. But he needed to try to assert himself. He knocked again more loudly; still there was no answer. Carefully he put his bottle of wine down on the ground next to the door. He tried the handle; it was locked. Marie always locked it when they were inside and locked it again when they left. Mike tried to peer through the lock to see if the light was on. He knocked again and called softly, "Marie, are you there?" There was no response and he felt stupid. He began to wish that he hadn't come.

"What you doing, man?" The voice came from behind him and made him start. Four youths were standing behind him in the alley. Two were African Caribbean and two were white. They were all wearing hoodies pulled down over their faces. He guessed that they were aged between fifteen and eighteen.

"What you doing nosing around here, man?" One of the African Caribbeans spoke again. His voice was soft, but it had an edge to it.

"I'm looking for someone." Mike's feeling of unease had suddenly increased.

"Oh, yeah, who?" This time it was one of the white youths. There was no mistaking the aggression in his voice.

"A girl."

"What girl would that be?" It was the African Caribbean again.

"I think she's called Marie."

They all laughed. "Marie, I think! What would Marie want with you?"

"I wanted to talk to her."

There was silence for a moment. The other African Caribbean spoke for the first time. "Police?" It was a question.

"You think?" The first replied.

"Maybe." They looked at Mike suspiciously. Then, without any warning the white one kneed Mike hard in the groin. Mike did not see it coming and doubled up in agony. Two of them grabbed hold of his arms and pulled him upright again, pinning him to the wall.

The first African Caribbean, who appeared to be the leader, stood in front of him. "Camera," he said. At this the fourth stretched up. For the first time Mike noticed that there was a CCTV camera mounted inconspicuously on one of the garages opposite. A youth put a woollen hat over the camera, blocking its view. The one standing in front of Mike punched him hard in the stomach. Mike doubled up again but was pulled upright by the two holding his arms. As soon as he was upright again one of them kneed him hard again in the groin. Mike cried out in pain as they pulled him upright again,

The leader spoke. "Now, Mr Policeman. You tell me what you are doing poking around here?"

"I'm not a police..." Mike began; he was interrupted by another punch to the stomach. Mike doubled up, retching. Once more he was pulled up straight.

"Don't give me no shit, man. Don't tell me you're looking for some girl." To reinforce his words there was another hard punch to the stomach followed by an equally hard knee in the groin.

Mike's head was spinning; he felt dizzy and sick. The pain in his stomach and his groin was almost unbearable. He gasped out, "But it's true. I'm nothing to do with the police. My name's Mike, I'm a sound engineer."

The leader searched his pockets, found his wallet and fished it out. Rifling through it he removed twenty pounds and Mike's credit card and stuffed them in his own pocket. The he came across the driving licence. "Mike Pearce," he read aloud, then he laughed. "Pearce, that's a good name for a policeman." He threw the wallet and the driving licence on the ground and, reaching behind him, pulled out a knife. Stepping very close to Mike, he held the knife up. When he spoke, his voice was as smooth as silk.

"Now, Mr Policeman, Mr Sound Engineer, you're going to start to make some sound. You're going to sing to me like a bird. The first thing you're going to sing is the number of your credit card. Then you're going to sing to us why you're here nosing around. If you don't sing I'm going to cut you. First I'm going to cut your cheek. Then I'm going to cut your eye. If I don't like your song I'm going to cut you into little pieces and flush you down the drain. You understand?"

Mike nodded. He was trying to think. They had him pinned against the wall. He was strong. Perhaps if he timed it right he could break free, but there was a fourth and he was unlikely to be able to get away in the maze of alleys that he didn't know.

The soft voice continued. "Just to show you I'm serious, I'm going to start by making a little cut then I'm going to ask you for your PIN number." Mike stiffened and the pressure of the grip on his arms increased. He saw the point of the knife rise towards him and felt a sharp pain on his right cheek. He could feel the blood begin to run down it. "Policeman, you bleed like a pig." The others laughed at the joke. "Now you start with your PIN number. This is only a little cut. If you don't tell me I will make it bigger. Then I will take out your eye. So sing to me."

"Okay, I just need to think."

"You get it right. I will send my friend with it to the cash machine. If you trick me I will also cut your cock off."

"Okay, okay." Mike tensed himself to make an attempt to get free.

"What game are you little boys playing?" Marie's voice had a hint of derision in it. The youths froze. She walked down the alley and looked at each of them in turn. Then she said something to the leader in a kind of Pidgin English that Mike didn't understand. He began to answer her back, but Marie interrupted him. She faced him, one hand on her hip and spoke long and forcefully. It was obvious she was telling him off. He shrugged his shoulders and muttered something. She delivered another torrent of invective. He bowed his head, put the knife away and signalled to the two youths to release Mike. Then Marie saw the wallet and the driving licence on the floor. She picked them up and waved them at him. He produced the credit card from his pocket and gave it to her. She looked in the wallet, spoke again and he shook his head. Again she gestured to him. Reluctantly he produced the money he had taken and handed it to her. Marie then spoke to him angrily. He shrugged, gave Mike a long hard look, then turned away and walked off down the alley followed by the other three. One of them stopped, came back and took the hat off the camera. Marie stood with her hands on her hips and shouted after them. Then she turned to Mike.

"Why are you here? I told you to come in the early morning. Where is Alice?" Her voice was angry.

"Laura has taken Alice to her parents for the weekend. I thought it was a chance to see you."

Marie glared at him. She seemed about to launch into a tirade against him, then noticed the blood on his face. "They cut you." She reached up and touched his cheek, which was still bleeding. "Are you okay?"

Mike moved gingerly away from the wall. His stomach and groin were a mass of pain. Every movement was agony, he felt dizzy and leant against the wall for support.

Marie put out a hand and steadied him. "Little boys with their games," she snorted. "You're hurt." There was real concern in her voice.

"I'll be okay. It's lucky you came when you did, though. They seemed to think I was a policeman. He threatened to cut me into little pieces." Mike swayed a bit on his feet. He was shocked by what had happened. "Can we go into the garage and sit down? I'll be alright in a minute." Mike gestured to the door.

Marie shook her head. "No, that's not a good thing to do. You need to get away from here. It's better for me to walk home with you. I'll help you." She slipped her hand under his arm and round his shoulder to support him. They had taken a couple of steps when Mike remembered the wine.

"I brought you something. It's only a bottle of wine." He pointed to the carrier bag beside the garage door. "I thought it might help us to relax and talk."

She picked it up and looked at it. "Wine, you are funny." She came back and took his arm. He walked slowly and she led him through the alley and away from the playground. It took more than half an hour to walk back to Laura's house. Mike felt sore and dizzy. He had to stop several times. Marie dabbed at the cut but it continued to bleed. By the time they reached the house he was exhausted. He unlocked the door and then sank into a chair in the kitchen.

"Do you have a first-aid kit?" He pointed to the cupboard to the right of the sink. Laura had insisted that they create a good first-aid kit before Alice was born.

"Babies are always falling over and hurting themselves," she'd said. "I did and I'm sure Alice will, so we better be prepared." Mike was in too much pain for this thought to spark any guilt. Marie found cotton wool and TCP. She cleaned the wound, which made him wince. Then she got him to hold a piece of cotton wool against it to try to stop the bleeding.

She looked at him seriously. "You really need stitches, I think."

Mike shook his head. "I can't face the thought of the hospital and I don't think I could drive there. Anyway, they might ask awkward questions. You obviously know these people. I don't want to make more trouble for you. Have a look, I think there should be some Steri-Strips in there somewhere. Let's try those first." Marie rummaged in the cupboard. Eventually she found them. She got him to try to hold the sides of the wound together and then stuck four strips across it. Then she put some gauze over the top and used tape to keep it in place.

"I think that has stopped the bleeding, but you mustn't move your head quickly and you must be careful when you talk." Mike nodded. "Especially you must try not to laugh." Mike didn't feel he had much to laugh about, though he slowly nodded anyway. "Where else did they hurt you?" Mike pointed at his stomach and between his legs. "Let me guess," she sighed. "They punched you in the stomach and kicked you in the balls. I think I ought to have a look to see that there is no real damage. It would be better if you could get upstairs." Mike made to get up, but Marie put her hand on his shoulder. "Wait." She went out of the kitchen. He heard her go into the front room and close the curtains. Then she locked the door. She went upstairs and drew the curtains in the bedroom. He looked at his watch. He needed to phone Laura. He always did when she went to her mother's, to check that she had got there okay. If he didn't phone she might be suspicious. Marie came back into the room.

"I must phone Laura. She'll be expecting me to."

"Okay." Marie found Mike's mobile in his pocket, pulled it out and gave it to him. Then she went back into the front room. Trying to keep his head clear and ignore the pain, he dialled the number. Almost at once, Laura answered.

"Hello. Where have you been? I tried to phone you earlier, but your mobile was switched off and you didn't answer the house phone."

"It was such a nice night I just went out for a walk. I lost track of time and I'd forgotten my mobile was turned off, sorry." Keeping his voice normal was a struggle.

"Oh." There was silence on the other end of the phone. He wished he had thought of something more convincing.

"How was the journey? How is Alice?"

"The journey was fine. We hit a traffic jam on the motorway, but it didn't last long. Alice slept all the way, bless her. I'm afraid she's wide awake now, though and full of energy. Do you want to say hello to her?"

Mike said "Hello, Alice" into the phone and heard some almost recognisable sounds from the other end. Alice was definitely beginning to learn to talk. Then he asked after Laura's mother. Laura reminded him of a prescription he had to collect, told him to do some washing. He said he would phone the next evening and then told her he loved her. As soon as he had put the phone down, Marie was back in the room.

"Now we must try to get you upstairs. Put your arm round my neck and let me help you." Mike did as he was told. The stairs were narrow and it was not easy going up them together. He was aware of Marie's body next to his and her scent. Her strength surprised him. They reached the bedroom and he sat on the corner of the bed. "Now take your shirt off." She helped him undo the buttons and pull his arms out of it. Bending down, she undid his laces and pulled off his shoes. "Stand up, so I can get your jeans off." Gingerly he stood up, swaying; it hurt every time he moved his stomach. Marie undid his belt and gently pulled his jeans and boxers down over his ankles so he could step out of them. She turned the duvet back to one side. "Now lie down on the bed on your back." Mike lay down and looked up at the ceiling. Marie knelt beside the bed and ran her fingers over his stomach. They were cool and smooth, but he winced as she gently pressed his stomach muscles. Then her fingers moved lower down. As she touched his testicles he couldn't help reacting despite the pain. She stood up and looked down at him, smiling. "Your stomach is badly bruised and sore though there's no internal damage. The other part of you is also bruised though seems in full working order. So there's no permanent damage down there either. You've been lucky. It could have been much worse."

Mike made as if to get up. "No. You should lie there." She pulled

153

the duvet over him and then went downstairs. She came back carrying the bottle of wine and two glasses. "As you brought the wine for me I think we should drink it." She put the glasses down on the dressing table and filled them. Then she came over to him. "Sit up." As he did so, she moved the pillow up behind him. Once he was propped up she handed him a glass of wine. She took a glass herself. He took a deep drink and felt the wine flow into him. Marie turned on the light beside the bed and then switched the main light off. She walked round to the other side of the room and put her glass down on the little table. She turned her back to him. He watched as she undressed and then slid into bed beside him, propping herself up on a pillow. Mike found it hard to take it all in. Marie was here beside him, in Laura's bed, in Laura's house. How had that come about? He took another deep drink of the wine and tried to think about what had happened. His stomach and groin ached.

"You know those yobs?"

"Sort of."

"What does that mean?"

"They hang around our estate. They're little boys who try to play big boys' games. They pretend they're hard men. Little gangsters."

"They certainly knew you. What did you say to them to get rid of them so quickly?"

"I told them that you weren't a policeman and that you were my friend, to leave you alone and stop being so silly. I told them to go and play somewhere else."

"And they did it. Just like that?"

Marie sighed. "They know not to mess with me." There was the same determination and strength in her voice that he had heard when she had spoken to the youths.

Mike turned to her suddenly. "Thank you, you probably saved my life or at least, you saved me from an even worse beating. I was about to try to escape when you came. But four against one, the odds weren't good."

Marie shrugged. "You were lucky." They were silent.

"What language did you speak to them in? I couldn't understand what you were saying."

"It's a kind of patois. A mixture of English and other words. It's common in many black communities."

"But you're not black."

"No. I'm mixed race. My grandfather was black. My mother was mixed race like me. I think my father may have been black, but I never knew him."

"Didn't your mother tell you about him?"

"My mother died when I was very young. I never knew her either."

"That's sad."

"Life can be sad. I was brought up by my aunt, my mother's sister, so I've always thought of her as my mother. She treated me well so my life hasn't been so bad. Because I never knew either my mother or my father, I've never really missed them."

"Do you live with her still?"

"Sometimes."

"What does that mean?"

Marie sighed. "You ask too many questions. I'm tired of talking." She took Mike's wine glass and put it on the side table. Then she turned off the bedside light and disappeared under the duvet. Her lips kissed his bruised stomach then moved lower down. The presence of her body next to him and the touch of her lips was so powerful, that it made him want her despite the pain.

"Be gentle," Mike said. "I'm still really sore."

When Mike woke it was very early. Outside the curtains it was still dark. The bed next to him was empty. In the bathroom the shower was running. Marie, here in Laura's bed, in Laura's house. Was this the ultimate betrayal? He tried to sit up and flinched with the pain of his stomach and groin. Reaching up, he touched his cheek where the dressing was still in place. He was going to have a lot of explaining to do when Laura came back. Perhaps he ought to go up to the hospital today and get the cut properly stitched.

The shower stopped. After a few minutes Marie came into the bedroom, a towel wrapped around her. Mike watched her as she dried herself. She didn't seem to mind or even notice his gaze. She had a kind of uninhibited innocence. Her body had the beauty and shapeliness of

155

youth. The gold of her skin, the curve of her breast, the flatness of her stomach and the smoothness of her thighs – there was a natural litheness about Marie, something almost feline. Despite the pain, he could feel his desire for her begin to rise. It was not surprising, he thought, that he had never been able to keep any resolution he had made not to see her. He wanted her too much to be able to stop seeing her and she knew that. Her blue-green eyes met his.

"It's early," he said.

"I must go before any of your curious neighbours start to peer through their lace curtains. I don't want to be seen leaving your house. It's important that Laura doesn't know about me."

"I know." Mike felt both guilt and desire. Marie finished drying herself and laid the towel over the chair. She turned to face him. Mike took in every aspect of her naked body. Once again, desire triumphed over guilt.

"Are you still sore?"

"A little, but not too much."

"Let's see," she said. She pulled the duvet off him.

Once Marie had gone, Mike started to clear up and remove any trace of her. He stripped the bed, put the sheets and towel on to wash and cleaned the shower. It was slow work because it hurt him whenever he moved. Then he made a coffee and sat down to think. Marie, too, had thought he ought to get his cut looked at properly. She had put another makeshift dressing on it before she left. He needed an explanation, a convincing story of how he had come by his injuries, both for the hospital and for Laura. Even if she didn't return for a couple of days, the cut would not have healed, nor would the bruising have faded. And it would leave a scar. Mike was not very good at making up stories. Any kind of assault should have been reported to the police. That was out of the question. He had promised Marie that he would do nothing to make trouble for the youths. It might make it difficult for her and also for him when he wanted to meet her at the playground. So the story had to be an accident. He sat and thought for a long time. Eventually he went out into the small back garden. There was a piece of guttering that was loose. He had promised Laura that he would mend it. Mike looked up at it. If he was up the ladder and it wasn't secured properly then it might slip. If, when it slipped, the ladder got caught up between his legs then it could bruise his groin and stomach. It would be possible for him to fall and catch his cheek on something sharp. There was nobody about because it was still early. It would be better to wait for another couple of hours. A witness, at least to the results of the fall, would be very useful. He went back inside and made himself breakfast.

Once he felt the time was right, Mike went outside and put the ladder up against the wall. He climbed up it and looked at the guttering. He went back inside and carefully removed the dressing and the Steri-Strips from his cheek. Back outside, he checked that there was nobody in the gardens or in the downstairs rooms. His witness needed to find him after the fall, not see the fall itself. He carefully tilted the ladder until it was a few feet from the ground. Then he dropped it, shouted and fell on top of it, tangling his leg in it. Getting unsteadily to his feet he swore loudly. As he had hoped, the cut in his cheek had opened again and was bleeding profusely. Pauline, who lived next door, came rushing out into the garden and looked over the fence as he got himself up.

"Are you okay, Mike?"

"My own bloody fault. I should have secured the ladder properly."

"You've got a nasty cut on your cheek. Let me come round and help you." She went out of her back gate and in through Laura's. Soon he was sitting in the kitchen while she tried to stop the bleeding. "I think the cut will need stitches. You'd better go to the hospital. Do you want me to drive you?" Mike reassured her that he thought he would be okay to drive in a minute. Pauline patched him up and made him a cup of tea, then she sat with him until he felt able to drive, offering again to take him if he wanted. Mike told her that he felt he could drive and thanked her. It was Saturday and he wasn't working in the evening so there was no hurry.

After an hour's wait at the hospital he was seen by a nurse. She cleaned the cut on his cheek and put four stitches in it – ironically, the same kind that Marie had used the night before. After another twenty minutes, a female doctor came to examine the bruising on his stomach and groin. She was satisfied that there was no internal damage, but expressed surprise that the bruising had come out so quickly and was so severe, simply from contact with a ladder. Mike fended off the question by saying he did tend to bruise easily, feeling unconvincing. The doctor had been on duty since six and had a queue of other patients to see so she didn't pursue her doubts. Mike walked out with a prescription for painkillers and an outpatient's appointment in a week's time.

Mike felt pleased with himself. He had created a story that had a witness and medical verification, one he almost believed himself. In many ways it was far more plausible than being beaten up and stabbed by a gang of youths. He felt sure that he would be able to tell Laura what had happened without stuttering or losing confidence. Suddenly he felt hungry and realised that he hadn't eaten since the early morning. After making himself beans on toast, he rang Laura. She was sympathetic and concerned and offered to come back straight away. Mike persuaded her that there was no point. He had been to hospital; he was now fine, just a bit sore.

Laura agreed to keep to her plan and stay with her mother until Monday. He talked to Alice, who was full of something that he didn't quite understand; it seemed to be about a dog. Before she hung up, there was an awkward silence. Then Laura said, with real, "Are you sure you're alright? I know it's been difficult, but you are very precious to me."

Mike told her he loved her and was looking forward to seeing her. Then he rang off. For a long time he sat in silence, staring at the phone. A mixture of relief and uneasiness filled him. He didn't like telling lies; it wasn't in his nature. Laura's concern touched him and reawakened a niggling sense of guilt. As long as he kept these two worlds apart, the world of Laura, of Alice, of reality, and the world of Marie, of his dream of fantasy, then everything would be okay. As soon as they touched, as they had last night, then it became complicated. It brought him face to face with his betrayal of Laura and the guilt he normally managed to suppress.

Eventually he got up and, picking up the half-empty bottle of wine and a glass, went through to the front room. He put on a record and stretched out on the settee. The light was already beginning to go. Taking a large drink, he lay back and closed his eyes. The music swept over him. It was one of his old jazz records, music he had listened to so often it was like an old friend. The mellow sound of the saxophone filled the room. He tried to get some kind of perspective on things. Marie had told him to stay away for a while, until the situation settled down. She would let him know when it was okay to come again and had given him a phone number. If he needed to contact her, he was to ring and leave a message on an answerphone.

Last night's events had changed their relationship. It seemed to have become more real, more definite. Mike wasn't sure that was what he wanted. He loved Laura and his dream had brought her to him. His dream had also brought him to Marie; so young, so confident, so passionate and at the same time, so controlled. Perhaps she was right about it being better that she remain a mysterious puzzle. Some of that mystery had lifted last night.

Images flooded his mind; Laura pulling her tee shirt over her head; Marie standing naked before him in the bedroom; a doll in a blue dress, slowly turning into the dancer from the club who came towards him laughing. He walked towards her, but then suddenly he was held. Hands grabbed his arms and pinned him to a wall. Somebody grabbed his hair and pulled his head back. A black youth stood in front of him with a knife. The woman in the blue dress suddenly turned into Marie; she was trying to reach him, trying to say something, but she couldn't. The youth with the knife laughed. He turned to Mike and looked at him. In his eyes there was nothing, no hatred, just an absence of feeling. He raised the knife and smiled. Suddenly Mike understood. This time, it was his throat that was going to be cut. He tried to struggle but couldn't. The hands held him tight. His head was pulled back. The knife was raised.

Mike woke in the dark. He sat up and grimaced with pain, wondering where he was. Then he realised that he was in the front room. He must have fallen asleep on the settee. Outside it was dark. Slowly he got up and drew the curtains. Moving gingerly, he went upstairs, undressed and got into bed. His sleep lasted until dawn, without a single dream.

By the time Laura came back, Mike was feeling physically much better. He had not dreamt again and he dismissed the dream about having his throat cut as the impact of shock and of his experience of being beaten up.

The "accident" brought Laura closer to Mike. It was as though, as she said, she had taken him for granted and the injury had made her realise how precious he was to her. It did strike him as somehow ironic that this was all built upon a lie. And yet, perhaps, good things could come out of bad. The new warmth that had started on Alice's first birthday blossomed with the spring. They began to make love again regularly, although Mike insisted that they should continue to use a condom and Laura agreed.

Late March suddenly burst into a week of glorious weather. The days were sunny and warm, with clear blue skies. Alice at sixteen months was walking with increasing confidence and chattering away. They realised that she was no longer a baby and had grown into a little girl. To make the best of the weather they had a day at the seaside. It was a three-hour drive, so they started early and returned late. Alice discovered sand for the first time, which fascinated her. Mike bought a bucket and spade and made sandcastles, which Alice delighted in walking over and levelling to the ground with shrieks of amusement. It was a day when Mike felt that they were a real family. When they got back, Alice was sound asleep and did not wake when he carried her upstairs and put her in her cot. They took a bottle of wine upstairs to their bedroom and made love and talked till late.

There was no contact at all from Marie. Mike began to wonder whether she might disappear from his life as quickly as she had come into it. What frustrated him was that he felt that he had most of the pieces of her jigsaw, but just couldn't see how they fitted together. He thought he saw her once in town, walking with an older black woman and a younger girl, who looked very much like her. She walked past him as though he didn't exist. Mike had also seen the four youths. It was a Friday evening and he was on his way to work at the Corn Exchange. They were hanging around outside a takeaway. He looked up and recognised the one with the knife. Their eyes met. Mike looked away. As he passed them, he heard one of them call, "Wanker," and they all laughed. He just kept his head down and continued walking. Inside he felt a mixture of fear and anger, but he tried to put it out of his mind.

It was mid-April when he finally got a message from Marie. The March sunshine had given way to gales and rain. Then the weather had calmed down, the sun was warmer and the nights and mornings were lighter. The trees were beginning to come into bud. He came out of work one day to find a piece of paper wrapped round one of his windscreen wipers. The message was written in neat, precise writing. It was short and to the point. *"Come tomorrow or Friday. Come early. Bring Alice. I will be there."* He read it twice, looking curiously at the writing, then screwed it up into a ball and tossed it into a nearby litter bin. Mike felt a sense of excitement. He had half thought that he wouldn't respond, that he would make a clean break. Part of him had hoped that no message would come. Now it had, he knew he would go. It was Wednesday today, so he would see her tomorrow morning. He suddenly felt that he should take Marie a present of some kind to thank her for helping him. He wasn't sure what to buy her. Flowers didn't seem right and would be far too conspicuous. A piece of jewellery, some earrings perhaps? He couldn't remember if Marie wore earrings. The only piece of jewellery he had seen her wear was the necklace of ivory charms. A ring was no good, it was far too suggestive. He looked at his watch. It was just before five. There might be time to go to the jewellers if he was quick.

Mike bought a pair of simple silver earrings with a single pearl. He wasn't sure if they were Marie's style, but then they were only a token. A token of what, he suddenly thought? He reminded himself that they were a token of thanks, of gratitude for the way that she had intervened and helped him. The assistant said how pretty they were, put them in a small box and gift wrapped them. Mike put them self-consciously into his pocket and went back to his car.

Thursday morning was bright and sunny, with heavy dew on the grass in the gardens he passed. Alice sat in her buggy, wide awake, pointing and chattering at things as they walked along. It was a long time since she had been to a playground so she was full of excitement and tried to wriggle out of the buggy as soon as they arrived. Marie was waiting for them, sitting on her swing, wearing blue jeans and a black sweater that clung to her body; she came straight across to meet them.

"Hello, Alice," she said cheerfully, bending down to the buggy. "Would you like to go on the swings?" Marie undid the safety belt. Alice was out of the buggy at once and set off towards the swings and Marie began to push her. Mike followed with the buggy, then left it to one side of the swings and went to join her. Marie's focus was entirely on Alice. She pushed her to and fro, talking to her all the time. The little girl was giggling with delight. Mike watched in silence, feeling excluded. He wanted Alice to be asleep so that they could go to the garage. Desperately he tried to think of something to say. The CCTV cameras watched, discreetly recording the scene for future analysis.

"It's been a while," he said finally.

"Yes." Marie spoke without looking at him. "It was better to wait a bit and let things settle down." She paused, then looked across at him. "I'm sorry. I would've liked to see you sooner, but it wasn't possible." There was a warmth in her voice that surprised Mike. Normally she was so matter-of-fact. "How are you? How's your cheek?"

Mike instinctively reached up to touch the scar. "It's healed. I'm okay."

Marie turned her attention back to Alice. They played on the swings for a while. Then she took Alice to the slide and pushed her down it. Mike caught her at the bottom and handed her back to Marie. Then Marie stood on the roundabout holding Alice, while Mike pushed it round. Alice loved all of it, but showed no signs of being tired. After half an hour he gave her a drink of juice and put her back in the buggy, although she was still wide awake.

"Can we go to the garage now?" Mike asked.

"Okay. But I don't think Alice's going to sleep." She led the way down the alley and Mike followed with the buggy. They reached the garage and unlocked the door. She turned to face him.

On impulse, he left the buggy and kissed her on the lips. She pushed him away. "Not here," she hissed at him. She turned and went inside. The moment was preserved by another CCTV camera. Mike followed her inside and closed the door. Alice looked round the garage and pulled at her straps. This was an exciting new place. She wanted to get out and explore it. Marie picked up a small carved cat from one of the shelves and bent down and gave it to Alice. The little girl was fascinated and began stroking it and talking to it.

"I have something for you." Mike felt in his pocket and handed her the little package, feeling awkward. "It's just to say thank you for stopping those lads and patching me up." Marie took it and looked at it, holding it in her fingers without opening it.

"Thank you." She led him behind the buggy so Alice couldn't see them and kissed him. She reached up and touched the scar on his cheek with her finger, tracing its shape gently. Suddenly Mike really wanted her. He put one hand on her breast, feeling the shape of her nipple through the sweater. Alice, having lost interest in the cat, began to struggle with the strap again. Marie stepped away from him. "It's not possible. Alice isn't going to go to sleep, she's older now. We must be careful what she sees. You must go now."

"But…"

"I know you want me." Marie stood close to him, her hand casually resting on the top of his thigh. "Come again next Thursday. I'll ask my sister to come. She'll play with Alice while we…while we come here. But you'll need to bring money so I can pay her." She let her hand linger for a moment.

"Okay. I'll try. How much?"

"Five or ten pounds, whatever. Now you must go." Marie broke away from him and turned to Alice. "Hello, little one. You want to get out, don't you, but not today. Daddy's got to take you home." Then she unlocked the door.

Colin Morris was a police officer with a responsibility for community relations. His area included the large council estate to the west of the town. Part of his job was to check regularly what had been recorded on the new CCTV cameras that weren't yet linked into the control room. The idea was that it would give them some additional information about what was happening on an estate that was beginning to be considered a problem area. It also meant that if there were reports of incidents or complaints from residents, there was a chance that there might be evidence to support an investigation. The cameras had been put in at the end of January and he was supposed to check them every month. But he'd been on leave, then busy and so now in mid-April he was doing it for the first time. It meant that he had nearly three months to check. He didn't see really why he had to do it. You would have thought that the private security firm that had installed the cameras could look through and would have enough sense to spot anything important. His superintendent didn't agree and felt it needed Colin's particular knowledge of the area to be able to see anything of significance. So he had set aside this afternoon and sat in the small room in the police station with the playback machine and the pile of tapes. He sighed. It was a small, windowless, claustrophobic room and he disliked it intensely. But the work had to be done. It involved fast-forwarding through the tapes until there were any images. Anything of interest was to be copied and retained at the police station. The tapes were then to be returned to the security firm to be wiped and reused.

There were eight different cameras and he had sorted the tapes into groups by camera and by month. From experience he knew that it was better to take a month and look at each camera in turn. That way he could pick up quickly anything of interest that came up on a number of cameras. He knew most of the people on the estate he was likely to be interested in. So he set to work on February. The first two cameras covered two of the alleys. There was nothing on them at all. Then he turned to the two cameras that covered the playground. There was more here. Some parents brought children, children played on their own. In the evenings a group of half a dozen youths gathered. He knew them well and spent some time looking at them, but he couldn't see anything criminal. A man he hadn't seen before came to the playground in the early evening. He seemed to be looking for someone, though the playground was deserted. The man was carrying something in one hand, wrapped in a plastic bag. It looked like a bottle. He waited for a while in the playground and then went off down the alley, walking slowly and uncertainly, as if trying to remember the way.

By a garage, the man appeared again and knocked on the door. He put the plastic bag down by the door and knocked again. Then suddenly he was surrounded by four youths. Morris knew them. This was Charles and his gang. Charles was black and sassy and always had a smart answer. Morris never understood why West Indians gave their children such classic English names. Charles had been done for assault once and they suspected him of dealing in drugs. The little group of youths that gathered in the playground in the evenings were very much his gang. In fact, they were one of the reasons for putting in the CCTV in the first place. Morris watched closely. There was some conversation between them. Then suddenly one of the youths kneed the man hard in the groin.

He was not expecting it and doubled up in agony. Two of the youths grabbed his arms, pulled him upright and pinned him to the wall. Charles stood in front of him. Then someone put something over the camera. The screen went black.

Morris cursed. He had guessed that they knew where some of the cameras were. He fast-forwarded. Suddenly the darkness lifted. The man was leaning back against the wall. The youths were going off down the alley. There was a girl there, what was her name? She was Charles' cousin. There was no evidence of her doing anything criminal yet, although Morris thought it was only a question of time. She was certainly attractive. Now she was in the alley, shouting something after the gang of youths. Then she turned to the man. He looked in a bad way. Taking out a handkerchief, she pressed it to his cheek, which was bleeding. Then she took his hand and helped him walk slowly off down the alley. They stopped and she came back and picked up the plastic bag and then they went off again.

Colin copied this incident to the tape for future reference. It was clearly a criminal assault, but he was not aware of an incident of this kind in February. Anything involving Charles, he would know about it. So then perhaps the man hadn't reported it. That was often the case with things involving Charles and his gang; they were very good at intimidating people. Morris made a separate note of it and the date and time. He would run a check, just to make sure.

Morris went back to going through the tapes. There was nothing of any interest in March. In April the same man who had been assaulted made an appearance in the playground. This time it was early morning and he was pushing a buggy with a child in it. The same girl, the one who was Charles' cousin, met him. They played with the child for about twenty minutes or so then they disappeared. Morris picked them up in one of the alleys. They stopped, the man kissed the girl, but she pushed him away. After that they went into a garage. A few minutes later they came out again and went off in different directions. There was nothing criminal or even suspicious, but Morris copied it too. It might just be useful. There was nothing else in April, so he packed up the tapes, left the office and locked the door behind him.

*

Mike set out again for the playground the following Thursday morning. Luckily, the weather was still fine, although it had gone colder. He was full of desire for Marie, though he felt uneasy about the idea of leaving Alice on her own with a strange girl. The closer he got to the playground, the more his misgivings increased. He didn't really see why he needed to bring Alice at all.

Marie was sitting on the swing next to another girl. Mike recognised her as the girl he had seen with Marie in town. She had the same gold skin and long reddish blonde hair falling in clusters of curls. Her hair was longer than Marie's and she was slightly shorter. Marie was wearing a short coat with her denim skirt and knee-length black boots. Her sister was wearing jeans, a hoodie and trainers. Mike watched as they came towards him. Marie's sister must be one or two years younger, he thought. Marie behaved in such a way that Mike no longer really thought of her as a girl or considered her age at all. Her sister didn't seem to be as well developed, though it was difficult to tell because the hoodie masked her figure.

"This is my sister, Yvette." Marie gestured to the girl.

"Hello," the girl said, looking at Mike with interest. He saw the same fine featured face and a pair of dark eyes, different from Marie's blue-green ones.

"Another French name, but not a French girl."

"That's right," Marie said, smiling at him. "Now let's introduce Alice to Yvette." Marie bent down and released Alice from her buggy. The two girls took her over to the swings. Soon Alice was swinging to and fro and talking happily. Mike watched the two girls curiously. They were very alike in the way they moved and held themselves. Once she was happy that Alice was settled with Yvette, Marie came over to Mike. "Alice will be fine with Yvette. If she starts to cry or becomes unhappy, then Yvette will come and find us. Do you have the money?" Mike nodded, took the two five pound notes from his wallet and handed them to Marie. She put them in her coat pocket. "Good. Let's go."

Mike stood for a moment, suddenly reluctant. "You're sure she'll be okay?"

"Of course, Yvette is good with little children."

"I'll just go and speak to her in case she suddenly realises I've gone."

"If you wish, it isn't necessary."

Mike walked over to the swings and bent down next to Alice. "I'm just going with Auntie Marie to get something, I won't be very long. Auntie Yvette will look after you. Okay?" Now Alice could talk, he had started to introduce Marie to her.

Alice looked at him. "Okay," she said, more interested in being pushed by Yvette.

Marie had already turned and walked away towards the alley. Mike looked back at Alice, who was playing happily, and then followed her. Inside the garage, Marie slipped off her coat and turned to face Mike. Under it she was wearing a thin white cotton tee shirt, cut low at the front, and the short denim skirt. He wondered whether she was cold. She came towards him. "Let me see." She turned his cheek up to the light and ran her cool finger along the scar. "I'm afraid you have a mark for life." Mike nodded and shrugged his shoulders. She reached up and kissed his scar. Then she kissed him on the lips. Her fingers were busy undoing the buttons on his coat. She stepped back so he could slip it off his shoulders. He shivered involuntarily. The garage was cold and damp. Marie bent, unzipped her black boots and kicked them off. Mike stood uncertainly for a moment, thinking suddenly about Alice. Marie took his hand and led him over to the mattress. As she turned, something caught the light in her hair and he realised that she was wearing the pearl earrings. The sight gave a strange feeling of satisfaction, as though in some way it showed that she acknowledged him. They lay down on the mattress and pulled the duvet over them. Marie took off her tee shirt and skirt and felt for the buckle on his belt. The smell of her body filled his nostrils. Her hands were inside his boxers, Mike pushed up her flimsy bra and pulled her towards him.

Afterwards they lay together under the duvet. Mike felt the warmth of Marie's body against him. Together they inhabited a cocoon that protected them from the cold of the garage. It seemed as though time had stopped. He looked down at her head on his chest and gently stroked the mass of her hair. Marie looked up at him, her eyes full of light. For a while they just looked at each other.

"Did I cause you much trouble?" Mike broke the silence.

"Nothing I couldn't handle." Marie's voice was cool and assured.

"It was just better for you that you didn't run into the little boys again. You haven't, have you?"

"No, I haven't seen them at all." Mike didn't think his encounter in town was worth mentioning.

"Good. It's better that you don't. You must only come when I leave a message. If you want to see me, then phone, as I told you."

"Okay, it's more difficult now that Alice is older."

"That's not a problem. Yvette's happy to look after her as long as I give her notice and you pay."

"But as she gets older she'll notice things. She'll talk about you and Yvette."

"That doesn't matter. You can just say that we're people who use the playground. Make something up; say we have our own children too."

"Wouldn't it be better if I came on my own?"

"No, that would be far more suspicious. Anyway I like Alice, I like to see how she grows and changes."

"But..."

Marie sat up and looked down at him. "You come with Alice or you don't come at all. That's your choice." Her eyes and voice were serious.

"You know I want you." Mike pulled her down against him and kissed her. "I don't know why. I shouldn't want you, but I do. I shouldn't be here, but I am. It's just..." He stopped.

"You're betraying Laura." Marie pushed herself up and looked down at him again. It was strange to hear Marie speak the name. In the past, she had always referred to her as Alice's mother.

"Yes."

"The dream brought us together and keeps us together. There are lots of other girls you could fuck if you chose, but you want me." The harshness of the word shocked Mike. He never liked to think about sex in that way. "I know how to set you on fire, to make you long for me." Marie reached out and touched him. Mike immediately felt his body responding to her. "You have free will. You come because you choose to. If you were strong enough you could choose not to. But you aren't strong enough to resist, so we're bound together until there's a change." She sat astride him and put her hands on his chest. Then she leant forward until he could feel her breasts against him and her lips found his mouth.

There was a knock on the door. "It's time. Alice wants her daddy and wants to go home." They heard Yvette's voice softly from the other side. Marie looked down at him.

"Remember, it's your choice," she said. Then she got off him and began to look for her clothes. Mike watched for a moment, without moving. The strange light of the fluorescent tube reduced the golden brown of her skin to paleness. He suddenly wanted Marie and felt like pulling her back under the duvet. But he knew that it would be pointless, so he began to dress too. He was still doing up his shirt when Marie went to unlock the door. She turned and looked at him. "I'll send you a message when you should come. Only come if you want to." Her voice was slightly mocking. Then she opened the door. "Hello, Alice. Have you been a good girl?"

Mike hurriedly finished dressing and put his coat on. Yvette watched him curiously over Marie's shoulder as she bent down to Alice in the buggy. Mike felt her appraising him in a way he didn't expect. He moved towards the door.

"Thank you, Yvette. Has Alice been okay?"

"No trouble." Again, he felt her eyes on him.

He bent down to speak to Alice, who immediately began talking as soon as she saw him. "Time to go home now," he said. He took hold of the buggy and turned to say goodbye to Marie and Yvette, but they had already gone into the garage and he heard the key turn in the lock. The CCTV camera recorded remorselessly.

Mike walked back feeling frustrated from that final interrupted contact. He knew Marie was right, that it was his choice, and he wanted her too much to stop seeing her.

At the end of May when Morris checked his tape again, there was a lot more to interest him. The cameras had picked up a car being driven into one of the garages at night. Figures in hoodies appeared, unloading packages. The next afternoon, a number of young people seemed to gather in the playground, but then the camera had been smashed. Morris made careful notes and transferred the images. To him this looked like drugs; he would need to talk to his superintendent and see if they could do some undercover work on the estate.

The man cropped up again. He came to the playground in the morning with the child in the buggy. Marie, he had remembered her name now, met him and this time she had her sister with her. They met and the man gave her something that could have been money. Marie and the man left the playground and appeared again going into a garage. After some time the sister took the child to the garage. Afterwards the man went away with the child. This wasn't as interesting as the car and there was no obvious sign of anything criminal, but Morris found it suspicious, so he added it to his collection. He came across the same scene twice more before the end of the month. Each time, the younger girl looked after the child while the man went away with Marie. Something he needed just to keep an eye on, Morris decided.

In June, Mike took Laura and Alice to the seaside again. This time then went for a long weekend and stayed in a bed and breakfast on the seafront. The weather was lovely when they arrived, a hot sun blazing in a cloudless blue sky; they were grateful for the slight breeze that came in from the sea. Alice loved it. She ran on the sand and for the first time paddled in the sea. Laura and Mike each took one of her hands and lifted her over the small waves that came in onto the beach. Mike had brought the bucket and spade and Alice quickly remembered that the best thing she could do with his sandcastles was to knock them down with shrieks of laughter. They had ice creams and fish and chips for supper. Alice was asleep as soon as she lay down on the little folding bed that had been put up to make their room a family one. Mike bought a bottle of wine from a supermarket and he and Laura lay on the bed and drank and talked. Although Alice was sound asleep Laura didn't feel comfortable making love with her in the same room, something that gave Mike a twinge of guilt. The next two days were idyllic in the way the English seaside can be. They picnicked on the beach and went for a trip along the coast in a fishing boat. On the last day the weather broke and it poured down. That forced them to explore the indoor entertainment that the town provided. After a visit to a small aquarium, they felt they had exhausted what there was and set off for home early.

The rest of the summer passed slowly and uneventfully. They had days out to local attractions and went further once, to take Alice to the nearest zoo.

When he could, Mike went to the playground. Alice and Yvette seemed to have struck up a real liking for each other, although Mike had to be careful that Alice didn't talk too much about Yvette at home. Mike still asked questions, but increasingly lost himself in his short, passionate encounters in the garage. Eventually the leaves turned and began to fall as summer became autumn and then autumn became winter.

They spent Christmas at Laura's parents. Mike was reluctant to go, but Laura had insisted – she felt that she had to go and she wouldn't leave him to have Christmas on his own. It turned out better than he had anticipated. Alice was the centre of attention and loved every minute. It was easy for him to fade into the background. Even so, he was glad to be able to leave after Boxing Day. He had a couple of evening jobs he had to do, which made a good excuse. Laura decided that she would stay on until New Year's Eve, when he would come back and collect her and Alice.

So at ten o'clock on the 27th of December, he set out to drive back. It had been grey, mild and wet over Christmas, now it turned cold. The morning was bright and sunny, the fields white with frost and he enjoyed the drive back along the empty roads. Although he missed Laura, he felt a great sense of relief at not having to be on his best behaviour. There was another thought at the back of his mind. He had only seen Marie once since November. He had been busy and the weather had been poor. She had sent him two messages and one meeting hadn't been possible. Now he had four nights at home alone until Laura came back. It might be possible for Marie to come on one of those nights. Even though his relationship with Laura seemed now to be back on track and he was sure that he loved her, Marie excited and fascinated him. The two women inhabited parallel universes, separate dimensions of his existence. They were different people with whom he had different relationships. Laura was his rock and he felt that he could spend the rest of his life with her; she was the dimension of reality. Marie was a mystery, a puzzle. He felt he needed to see her in order to understand it. Each time they met, it was as though he might find another piece of the jigsaw. Or perhaps Marie would hand him another piece? The trouble was, he still couldn't fit the ones he did have together. She was the dimension of the dream. He was surprised that he had so easily come to accept having these two women in his life. Again he had the feeling that as long as he could keep them apart, things would be fine. Fortunately, Marie seemed as eager as he was that Laura should know nothing. So in that sense he felt secure.

By the time he reached Laura's house he had made up his mind. He took the crumpled paper with the number that Marie had written down for him in her neat writing. Although he'd never used it, he knew the number by heart. Taking out his mobile he looked at it, feeling awkward. The fact that he knew that it would be an answerphone made it easier. He rehearsed carefully the message he would leave. He took a deep breath, picked up the phone and put in the number. The phone rang for a long time. He tried to imagine it in a room somewhere, ringing, but he couldn't. When he rang Laura he could picture the phone on the table in her parents' hall or her taking her mobile out of her handbag. He had no idea where this phone was. Eventually the answerphone clicked in with a voice he didn't recognise. He spoke his message into the phone and pressed the key to end the call. Then he sat for a while, thinking. He had bought Marie a Christmas present. It was a pearl necklace that matched the earrings he had given her before. In a way, it was a silly thing to do. He was treating her like some conventional girlfriend, which she certainly wasn't. Still, perhaps now he would get a chance to give it to her.

The next afternoon a note appeared, folded round his windscreen wiper. The message was simple and direct as usual. "*I will come tomorrow night.*" He read it carefully, then folded it and put it in his pocket. Tomorrow was good because it was one of the nights he wasn't working.

Mike came back late that night, had a sandwich and a coffee. Lying alone in Laura's bed, he thought about what preparations he should make. It was dark by four, but he had no idea what time Marie would come. He didn't know whether to prepare a meal for her or not. In the end he decided he would cook enough for two. If she came, she could eat, if not, he could always finish it the next day. Mike tried to think what he could make. He didn't know what she liked or if she was a vegetarian. In the end he decided on paella. He could make it vegetarian and then add prawns and fish just before he served it. The prospect of seeing Marie excited him and he found it hard to sleep. Eventually he dozed off at about two in the morning. He didn't dream at all and woke late. The weather had changed again. The bright frost had gone and the sky was grey and overcast. Even by ten it hardly seemed to be light and by half past three it was already dark.

The day passed slowly. He had had a lazy bath and made himself a cooked breakfast as a treat. That suddenly made him think. Would she stay for breakfast? Did he need to get something else in? At mid-morning he went out and did his shopping. He took his time and bought the ingredients carefully, including two good bottles of wine, one white and one red. Once back at the house, he made himself a sandwich for lunch. Then he sat and listened to music for a while. Normally this calmed him, but not today, he remained restless and on edge. After that he prepared the paella. He worked in the kitchen, leaving the front room door open to hear the music playing. By five o'clock everything was ready. He had drawn all the curtains as soon as it was dark, making sure that there were no gaps that might allow prying eyes to see into the house. The food was made and just needed heating up and the table was set for two. He sat in the front room and waited. The television didn't attract him so he picked up a book and looked through it idly. Mike had never been a great reader unless it was music related or technical. This was a book that Laura had bought in the first days of her research. It was about charms and symbols. He took out the small ivory figure, which he still carried with him, wrapped safely in his pocket. Looking at it again it seemed to him as though the carved female figure resembled Marie. And yet there had been a time when he had thought he could see Laura in its features. Tonight it was definitely Marie it reminded him of. He leafed through the pages, looking at the pictures and found nothing quite like it.

Six o'clock passed and then seven. There was no knock at the door. He decided that he would eat at eight. The time came so he heated up the paella, adding some of the prawns and smoked fish. Eating alone at the table set for two felt strange and rather forlorn. He thought about opening one of the bottles of wine, but decided against it. Afterwards he cleared away the unused cutlery and plates, leaving only the wine glasses out. At nine o'clock he returned to the front room and put on some rock music. Mike began to wonder whether Marie was going to come at all. She normally kept arrangements that she made. Perhaps something had happened to her. The memory of the four youths was still raw with him. He ran his finger ruefully down his scar. Mike began to worry, but there was nothing he could do. He thought of walking out towards the playground and quickly dropped the idea.

At twenty to eleven there was a soft knock at the door. He opened it to find a figure swathed in a scarf and hood standing on the doorstep. For a moment he didn't recognise Marie. Then he opened the door and let her in, locking it behind her. Once inside she took off the scarf and coat. She was wearing a black polo neck jumper and a pair of jeans. "It's really freezing outside." She turned to look at him.

"It's good to see you," Mike said, suddenly feeling awkward.

She kissed him. "Let's go upstairs," she whispered in his ear.

Mike stepped back, surprised as always by her directness. "Would you like some wine?"

"Okay."

"White or red?"

"I don't mind." Marie was already climbing the stairs. Mike collected a bottle of red wine and two glasses from the kitchen and followed her. By the time he reached the bedroom she had already undressed and was lying with the duvet pulled up her chin. "Come and thaw me out," she said.

After they had made love they lay together enjoying the warmth of each other's bodies. It was such a luxury, Mike thought, not to have to worry about being interrupted. Suddenly he remembered the present. "I've got something for you," he said and went downstairs. The house was already cold and he shivered as he came back to the bedroom with the small package in his hands. He got into bed and handed it to her.

"What is it?"

"It's a Christmas present, so Happy Christmas." He kissed her. She examined it tentatively, turning it round in her hands. "You can open it if you like."

"Do you want me to?" Again, her directness startled him. He thought for a moment. His first instinct was to be polite and say that it was up to her. But actually he did want her to open it. He wanted to know if she liked it.

"Yes."

She tore off the paper and opened the small box. She took out the necklace and held it dangling from her fingers so that it caught the light. "It's pretty."

"It matches the earrings." He had noticed that she was wearing them.

"Yes."

"Are you going to put it on?"

"Maybe." As always, she had around her neck the string of ivory figures.

"Perhaps you could take this off." Mike touched one of the figures.

Marie shook her head. "No. I never take this off."

"Why?"

"Because it was my mother's. It's the one thing she left me. So I never take it off." Mike held an ivory figure between his finger and thumb. As he did so, he noticed that there was a broken link on the necklace, as though there was a figure missing.

"It's very unusual. Do the figures have some special meaning?"

Marie gave him an odd look. "Maybe. As I said, it was my mother's, so that makes it special to me. It links me to her. Look, I'll put it on as well." She unfastened the pearl necklace and then refastened it. The pearls lay white against her brown skin.

"Tell me about yourself."

"What do you want to know?"

"Anything, everything. I know so little about you."

Marie sighed. "You know what you need to know. It's better that we're strangers."

"But I want to know you better."

"That mightn't be a good thing."

Mike was exasperated by her blocking. The wine made him bold.

"Do you go to school?"

"Sometimes. School has little to offer me. I learn from the world and from people."

175

"Do you sleep with other men?" The question came out without him really thinking about it.

"Why do you want to know?"

Mike shrugged his shoulders. He didn't know why he'd asked the question. It was something he'd had thought about it a number of times. Marie was a girl, and yet as experienced and worldly as a woman. She had certainly not been a virgin when they had first made love.

"I suppose I'm curious."

"Would you be jealous if I told you I did?"

"I don't know." The answer was honest. He didn't know how he would feel about it, about the thought of someone else touching her. Mike paused for a moment. "Well, do you?"

"It is none of your business."

"That means yes, then?"

"It means it's none of your business. If you continue to ask, I shall leave." She sat up, the duvet falling to her waist. Mike put his hand on her shoulder.

"OK. I won't ask. It doesn't matter to me anyway." Marie lay down again and turned away from him, pulling the duvet up over her shoulders. She lay there rigid and apart from him. For a moment there was silence. Then he leant over and kissed the back of her neck. "I'm sorry, I didn't mean to upset you. I'm just interested to know about you." For a moment she didn't respond. He stroked her back gently under the duvet, feeling the smoothness of her skin.

"I understand that you're curious about me, but I'm serious. Our lives are mostly separate and that's how they have to be. The relationship between us isn't of the usual kind. It's not permanent and it won't last. The more you know about me, the more you may want to make it normal. Like giving me Christmas presents. So really, the less you know the better. In the long run you'll understand. When our relationship ends it will be less painful for you."

Mike thought for a moment. He knew that she was right. He had known that buying her a Christmas present was a stupid, conventional thing to do. Her talk of their relationship ending took him by surprise. He was not in control of it and never had been, so he had never thought about it finishing. "I understand, but I would still like to know just a little more about you and where you came from."

"Alright, I'll tell you what I know. As I said, my mother died when I was little. I was probably about two years old. Yvette was only a baby. We were sent to my aunt who lived in London. I say my aunt, I'm not really sure whether she is my aunt or just a friend. She took us in and brought us up. Then about two-and-a-half years ago we moved here. I'm not sure why. I think there was some trouble."

"Thank you." It was the most that Marie had ever told him about herself. "It must have been hard growing up not knowing your parents."

"My aunt was kind. I don't complain."

"It's odd you came to live here about the same time I did."

"Maybe, maybe not. Perhaps it is what ties us together."

"You mean the dream." Marie nodded. "Then tell me about your dream."

"Not now. I'm tired of talking." She moved closer to him and ran her hands over his chest.

Mike woke to find Marie already dressing. He sat up and pulled on a tee shirt. "Going so soon?"

"It's best. At this time nobody will notice me."

"What about breakfast?"

"I don't eat breakfast."

He followed her downstairs. "When will I see you again?"

"Not for a while. I have to go to London to stay with friends. It may be a month or so. I'll send you a message." She put on her coat and began to wrap the scarf around her. Mike stopped her for a moment and kissed her on the lips. She returned the kiss briefly, then continued to cover her face. "I have to go." There seemed to be a touch of urgency in her voice. Before he could say anything else, she'd unlocked the door. As she went through it she turned, almost as an afterthought. "Thank you for the necklace." Then she had gone into the darkness. Mike stood thinking. Then he went upstairs and took his ivory figure out of its place. It was exactly the same size as the ones that Marie wore round her neck, and one of them was missing.

Month by month Morris continued with the tedious job of monitoring the CCTV footage. Over Christmas there had been some underage drinking and vandalism in the playground, which had brought complaints from the residents who lived nearby. The footage had helped to identify the times and the main culprits. They had put a uniformed officer there a few times and given the youngsters a good talking to. This had put a stop to it so he could think of that as a win. The man with the toddler continued to visit the playground regularly, always following the same pattern. Morris was uneasy about it. He was beginning to suspect some kind of sex-related racket, but there was nothing obvious. He decided to keep his eye on it and so kept transferring the relevant clips. Once, he looked back at it and saw he was building up quite a file. There was a rumour that in the New Year they might get some of the new Police Community Support Officers. If they did, he'd mentally earmarked one to spend a bit of time at the playground to try to find out what was going on.

It was early March before Mike heard anything from Marie. He had begun to wonder whether she'd gone for good. It was quite likely that that was the way their relationship would end. She would just disappear and he would be left wondering if she'd ever really existed. He'd thought a lot about their last conversation and also about the missing figure. It had given him a key to the puzzle and he was keen to try it out. He also missed her. Although his life was less complicated without her, it was also duller.

The weather suddenly turned warm and sunny. For weeks it had been grey and overcast, with hard frosts. The cold had given way to pouring rain and strong winds. Then suddenly it had changed. There were daffodils everywhere and a feeling that the winter had gone and spring had begun. The next day, there was a note on his car inviting him to meet the following morning and as usual telling him to bring Alice. At the mention of the word playground Alice was by the buggy and ready to go. It was a beautiful morning. Mike felt exhilarated by the weather and the thought of seeing Marie again. This time though, there was something more than the prospect of sex with her, there was a question he wanted to ask.

Alice, too, was in a good mood. She insisted on walking and skipped along as he pushed the buggy. Sometimes she walked beside him holding his hand. Sometimes she ran ahead and then stopped and waited. Once she wasn't looking and he was afraid she would fall and there would be tears. She was completely fearless and often overreached herself in her enthusiasm. Then she would come crashing down on whatever surface she was on and tears would follow. Luckily she righted herself.

When they reached the playground, Yvette came to meet them. She was wearing a short red skirt and a white blouse. There was no sign of Marie. Mike asked Yvette where she was. Yvette shrugged her shoulders. "Maybe she'll be here in a minute. Let's play with Alice till she comes." The little girl loved it. Mike helped her up the steps of the small slide and Yvette caught her at the bottom. They did this lot of times. Then they put her in the swings. There was still no sign of Marie. After about forty minutes, Alice had had enough. She walked slowly over to the buggy, climbed into it and announced, "Home time."

Mike strapped her in and turned to Yvette. "Where is Marie? Isn't she coming?"

Yvette shrugged her shoulders again. "I don't know. I thought she was. Maybe she's in the garage, let's go and look."

Mike followed her. Alice started yawning and by the time they reached the garage she was asleep. Yvette knocked and there was no reply. She took out a key, unlocked the door and beckoned him inside. Mike pushed the buggy in after her. She turned on the light. Mike left the buggy and looked around. There was nobody there.

Yvette came close to him. "You can fuck me instead if you want." She began to undo the buttons of her blouse. Mike looked at her, seeing her properly for the first time. She was no longer the little girl in jeans and a hoodie. In that year she had begun to turn from a child into a woman. Her skin was the same golden brown as Marie's. Her hair was the same colour too, with the same natural curls, but it was longer and fell down below her shoulders. She had the same high cheekbones, although her eyes were dark, not the blue-green of Marie's. Mike stared at her. For a moment he was speechless. The directness of her offer had taken him completely by surprise.

"I don't think that's a good idea," he managed to say.

Yvette ignored his comment. She finished undoing the buttons of the blouse and pulled it off, revealing a dark red bra that matched her skirt. She took a step closer to him. "I'll give you a good fuck." Then, as if she

179

guessed his thoughts, "Marie won't mind. She said if she didn't come that I should fuck you." She reached out her hand for the buttons on his shirt.

Mike stepped back, struggling to find something to say. There was no doubt that, just like Marie, Yvette aroused him. He could smell her. He could see her small breasts in the red bra. But something wasn't right about it. Marie had seduced him and he had surrendered to her. It was as though she had stepped out of his dream with her uncanny likeness to the woman in New Orleans. Yvette was different, just an attractive young girl. He repeated his words. "I still don't think it's a good idea."

"Don't you like me? Don't you think I'm as pretty as Marie?"

"It's not that." Mike was thinking desperately of an excuse that would not offend her.

"You think I'm too young?" Yvette moved very close to him; her hands were unzipping his fly. "I'm more experienced than you think. I know how to give you a good time." She slipped her hand inside his trousers and gently cupped his testicles. Mike felt himself responding to her touch. He grasped at an idea.

"We played with Alice for a long time in the playground. I mustn't be too long. Her mother might become suspicious." She held him for a moment, feeling his response to her touch, then she withdrew her hand.

"Okay," she said, her voice full of disappointment.

Mike took her by the shoulders and pulled her towards him. "Yvette, I think you are really pretty." He put one hand on her breast. "It's just I have to go, maybe next time."

"Maybe," Yvette said and stepped away from him. "You'd better go. I'll tell Marie you came." She turned and unlocked the door. She looked outside in the alley and then let him out. In the alley he remembered the money. He took it out of his jeans pocket and walked back and gave it to her.

"You'd better have this. Thank you for playing with Alice." She took it and locked the door.

"I hear you turned down my little sister." There was a tone of mockery in Marie's voice. It was ten days later and they were lying under the duvet in the garage. Yvette had given him a meaningful look when he had reached the playground. She had managed to brush against him when she came to help Alice out of the buggy, "She was very disappointed," Marie continued. "When Alice fell asleep and I didn't come she thought it was her chance." Mike sighed. Marie propped herself up on her elbows and looked down at him. "So why didn't you? She's an attractive young girl."

"I don't normally go for young girls."

"You did for me."

"That was different."

"How?"

"I don't know. You were in my dream, you reminded me of someone." There was a question Mike needed to ask, but not now. "You made me lose control."

"You came because you wanted to. You fucked me because you wanted me. Don't you want to fuck my sister?" Mike didn't reply. The conversation made him uncomfortable. "Do you think I would mind, that I would be jealous?"

"I don't know."

"Well, I wouldn't be."

"It didn't seem right." Mike was struggling to explain himself.

"Though it is right to fuck me like you just have."

"No. I don't know. Look, life is complicated enough. Having sex with your sister would make it more complicated."

"But you'd like to. She'd certainly like you to. I saw the way she brushed against you. Shall I go and get her now so that we can swap places? Perhaps you'd like to fuck us both at the same time, a threesome?"

"Why are you talking like this? Are you angry with me? Are you jealous?"

"No. It's just you pretend to be moral and it irritates me. You're still so inhibited. You let go a bit with me, but not enough. You need to follow your desires. You really wanted her and you held back. You made an excuse about time, when really you wanted her."

"Now it's my turn to say you're talking too much," Mike said. He pushed Marie over on her back and put his mouth over hers. But there was still the question he wanted to ask her.

*

181

Two weeks later Mike went to meet Marie again. Alice was skipping beside him as usual. As soon as she saw him Marie came to meet him, wearing a pair of very short black shorts and a plain white tee shirt. She scooped Alice up in her arms, saying, "What shall we play on first?" Alice pointed to the slide which had now become her favourite. Marie had not said a word to Mike but the message was clear. Yvette came and stood next to him. She was wearing the same short red skirt and white blouse as she had been when she had been alone with him.

"Come," she said simply. They walked together to the garage. Mike felt uneasy, but knew he had no choice. To refuse would have offended both her and Marie. He didn't want to do that.

Once inside the garage Yvette kissed him on the mouth. She undid the buttons of his shirt and ran her fingers over his chest. Mike pulled her close to him. He smelt her hair and her body. The smell was different from Marie's. Despite still feeling that this was not right, her physical presence soon aroused his desire for her. He touched her small, firm breasts and her thigh under the short skirt, and felt her respond. He surrendered himself to the moment.

Later Mike heard the key turn in the lock. Marie pushed the buggy into the garage. Alice was fast asleep. Marie looked at them for a moment, then undressed and slipped under the duvet next to him.

Morris stared at the clip of video and replayed it again. The girl opened the door of the garage wearing only a bra and a skirt. She was Marie's sister, and Morris guessed that she was probably thirteen. The man came out with the toddler in a buggy, then he stopped, went back and gave the girl money. Morris wasn't sure what it meant, but he didn't like it. Why, he wondered, had they delayed the deployment of the PCSOs? He needed one on the ground to find out what was happening. There was no chance of that until August, and Morris didn't have the time to follow it up, so he added it to the file.

Spring turned into summer. What had been an unconscious *ménage a trois* became a *ménage a quatre*, of which three were aware and one was not. Looking after Alice for two days a week, made it easy for Mike to take her out to the playground. Attendance at school never seemed to be an issue for Yvette or Marie so they would meet every two weeks, sometimes even every week. Mike never knew which one of them would come with him to the garage to have sex. He sometimes wondered if they tossed a coin for it. He never felt as comfortable with Yvette as he did with Marie. He couldn't escape the feeling that sex was wrong with Yvette in a way that it wasn't with Marie, but he accepted it in the same way as he had somehow accepted his unfaithfulness to Laura. Sometimes, if Alice fell asleep, they would both be there with him together. That was almost too much to cope with. It seemed like some sexual fantasy that was too bizarre to be true. Two beautiful teenage girls, young and yet immensely experienced, devoting themselves to having sex with him. It was unbelievable and miraculous. He thought that it must be a dream and one day he would wake up and find that none of it was real.

So he took it and enjoyed it as something ephemeral to be grasped while it was there, and he didn't ask his questions. In no sense did it reduce his love for Laura or his fondness for Alice. It didn't ever occur to him that by taking Alice with him and using her as an alibi he was putting her at risk. Both the girls seemed to be as fond of Alice as he was, and they were very good with her. Sometimes he wondered if Laura and Alice were also fantasies, and he would wake up one day in a dreary bed and breakfast in a nondescript town and have to get on with the rest of his life.

In August it became incredibly hot in the way that summers are supposed to be. One day Mike got a note from Marie asking him to come to the playground, this time for late afternoon rather than early morning. Laura was at work and had said that she had to stay for a meeting, so getting away was easy. By the time he reached the playground Mike was thirsty. He wished he'd thought to bring some water for himself as well as Alice's drink. Yvette met them and took Alice away to play on the swings. Oddly the place seemed deserted. Mike supposed that the heat had driven people indoors. The garage was cool. Marie looked at him and laughed. "You look hot," she said. "Would you like a drink?"

"Oh, please." Mike was grateful. It seemed as though she had read his mind. He sat down on the mattress and pulled off his tee shirt. She went over to the far corner of the garage where he noticed there was a small fridge. "Beer?"

"Please." He lay back, enjoying the coolness. Marie took two bottles out of the fridge and closed it. She turned her back on him and he heard the sound of the bottles being opened. After a moment she turned and walked towards him with a bottle in each hand. Her short blue summer dress swirled around her brown thighs. He sat up. She held out one of the bottles to him and he took it. It was wonderfully cold in his hand, and he put it to his lips and drank. The cold beer was just what he needed.

"Thanks," he said and drank again. Marie watched him, took a sip from her own bottle and then sat down next to him on the mattress. He put his arm round her shoulders and pulled her towards him. "You look lovely."

She pushed him gently away. "Drink," she said. "First deal with your thirst, then I will deal with your hunger. There is plenty more beer in the fridge." Mike raised the bottle to his lips again and drank until it was empty. Marie watched him while sipping from her own bottle. He put the empty bottle down and turned, putting one hand around her waist. With the other he gently caressed her breast through the thin summer dress. Marie murmured and kissed him, her tongue exploring his mouth. He could taste the beer on it. Her kisses were slow and deliberate. He moved his hand down onto her thigh and up under the short skirt.

Mike began to feel dizzy, as if the drink had gone straight to his head. The room seemed to be moving around him. He stopped and tried to steady himself.

"What's wrong?" Marie whispered, taking his head between her hands. Her hands were cool, his head suddenly felt hot. Mike tried to speak, but although his lips moved no words came out. Blackness began closing in on him.

"Ssh." Marie's voice seemed to come from a long way away. "Lie down and close your eyes. You will feel fine in a moment." Obediently Mike lay back on the mattress and closed his eyes. It felt as though he was spinning and he gripped the mattress to stop himself falling. Marie's cool hand stroked his forehead. Her lips brushed against his.

Mike tried to open his eyes again, but his eyelids seemed too heavy to move. A great weariness filled his body. He just wanted to sleep.

Mike woke with a start, wondering where he was. His head was pounding. Trying to sit up he was overcome by nausea and sank back onto the mattress. His watch showed quarter past four; he'd been asleep for over two hours. Slowly he struggled to sit up, trying to remember what had happened. The heat of the day; the beer; the dizziness. Something was trying to force itself up through the nausea into his consciousness. Something wasn't right. Where was Marie? She had been there with him, but as he peered round he saw that he was alone. And Alice, where was Alice?

Alice had been with Yvette. The thought made Mike panic. Alice wasn't in the garage, so where was she? Had they taken her away? He tried to stand and fell back on the mattress. Where were they? Why had they left him here alone? Again he pushed himself up on to his feet, and this time he succeeded. Slowly he walked, swaying, towards the door, concentrating hard on each step he took. He had to get out. He had to find Alice. Reaching the door, he turned the handle. The door did not move. He pulled at it. He banged on it. Marie and Yvette had locked him in the garage. Why? What were they doing with Alice? He tried to push aside the dizziness and think for a moment. One of the knacks he had developed when he was with the band was to open doors that weren't meant to be opened. He looked around the garage for what he needed: a thin screwdriver or a piece of wire. The lock was old. If he could just think straight he would soon open it. Staggering to the other side of the garage he reached the wardrobe. A metal coat hanger would do. He pulled a dress off a hanger and it fell on the floor. With the coat hanger in hand he moved slowly back to the door. Once there he leant against it for a moment, gathering his strength. He manipulated the end of the coat hanger until it was straight and inserted it into the keyhole, trying to catch the lock. A wave of nausea rose up. He stopped and rested his head against the door, then he tried again. This time he was successful and slowly managed to move the lock. Click. He turned the handle and the door came open.

Mike walked out into the dazzling sunlight. His head immediately began pounding again. Where could they be? He made his way to the playground, but it was empty. Returning to the garage he could smell smoke. On the other side of the garage he came to a gap between it and the next one. Although it was overgrown, the grass had been recently trampled down. He followed the makeshift path and came to a small open space surrounded by the backs of garages. He'd never even realised it existed.

What Mike saw in front of him made him stop. At the far end of the space a fire was burning. The smoke was mixed with the sweet smell of incense. Marie and Yvette had their backs to him. They were swaying and chanting. Yvette was beating time on a small drum. Between them stood Alice, her head crowned with a circle of flowers. Her arms and face were covered in blood. Mike froze in horror, then he realised that it wasn't her blood. On the grass was a dead chicken. Its neck had been cut, and beside it was a bowl filled with its blood.

Mike gathered his strength and stepped forward. "What are you doing to her?" His voice was loud and hoarse. He hardly recognised it. Marie and Yvette turned to face him. Mike could see that their arms and faces were also smeared with blood. They stared at him in surprise, then he stepped forward again, his anger rising. "What are you doing to her?"

"Go back." Marie stood in front of him. "We must finish the ceremony."

Mike pushed her to one side and picked Alice up, holding her close to him. He could smell the sweet sickliness of the blood. It made him feel nauseous again. He turned to leave the open space, but Marie was blocking his way. She held a large knife, covered with the chicken's blood. Yvette stood beside her.

"Stop." There was a force in Marie's voice that he had never heard before. "You cannot take her." These were not requests but commands, spoken by someone who expected them to be obeyed. Mike remembered how she had spoken to the thugs who had attacked him. The force of her words made him stop.

"What is all this? What are you doing to Alice? Why did you lock me in the garage?"

"It was time."

"What do you mean, it was time?"

"It was time for the ceremony, time to make Alice truly one of us. You must go and let us finish." Marie raised the knife. "We locked you in the garage so you wouldn't see. So you wouldn't interfere."

"But she is not one of you." Mike felt the anger in his voice. "She is my Alice, my daughter, and I'm taking her home." Alice began to cry. She was frightened by the loud voices and the anger. Mike held her close and stroked her back to reassure her. "You are frightening her," he said in a lower voice.

"She wasn't frightened until you came. Give her to me." Marie stretched out her arms.

"No. She's my daughter and I'm taking her home." Mike held Alice closer to him.

Marie laughed. "Your daughter? You don't understand. You are just an instrument, a tool of the spirit. Power was given to you, the power of dreams. Alice will have far more power than you. She will be a spirit queen, but she must be inducted into the spirit. It must be done at the right time and in the right way. Now give her to me. Once the ceremony is done you can take her. She'll come to no harm." Marie stretched out her hands again.

Mike stood. Despite the nausea and the thumping in his head things suddenly began to make sense. He asked the question he had wanted to ask since Marie had come to Laura's house in January.

"Were you born in New Orleans?"

Marie smiled. Her voice softened. "Yes, I was born in New Orleans. The woman you met was my mother."

Mike understood. With his free hand he pulled from his pocket the ivory figure, and held it up. "This is the missing figure from you necklace?"

"Yes, she gave it to you as a sign."

Mike stood looking at her. Marie saw his hesitation, and her manner towards him changed. "Listen, Mike, you know we would never hurt Alice. She is as precious to us as she is to you, but we need to complete the ceremony. Alice has reached the age when she must be initiated into the world of the spirit. She must learn to be its servant and its medium. Please do this for me. Work with us and let the spirit truly enter you, then I'll tell you the truth. I'll answer all your questions.

You can help us to make Alice realise her destiny. The next time you come we will reward you. Yvette and I can give you pleasures you've never tasted before. What we've given you so far is nothing compared to what you'll have now." Marie moved very close to him. She touched his bare shoulder and turned her face up to his, searching for his lips. He felt Yvette press herself against his back and begin to kiss his neck. Mike was confused and dizzy. His nostrils were full, not with the scent of jasmine, but the sickly, cloying smell of the chicken's blood. Alice squirmed against his chest and whimpered. She didn't know what was happening and she was afraid. Mike recoiled from Marie, suddenly feeling disgust. Marie sensed it and her face changed. When she spoke again her voice was still quiet, but it was full of menace.

"If you take her away now that is the end. You'll never enjoy me again. It will be finished. I could try to stop you. I could cut you with this knife." She raised the knife until the point touched Mike's right cheek. "I could give you another scar to match the one you already have, but that would frighten Alice. If you leave I'll cut you in a different way. I shall put the curse of the spirit upon you. It will cut you in places and in ways you will not expect. Whatever you do you won't escape it. And if you leave here it'll make no difference, Alice will still be ours. Her future is marked out in the blood and the ashes. I have seen it. So choose. Become one of us and you can lose yourself in pleasures you cannot even imagine. Be one of us and honour the gift that my mother gave you before they killed her. Or go, and suffer."

"Your mother, why did she choose me?"

"She knew they were going to kill her. She saw it. She needed to pass on her power. She needed someone with the courage to carry it. You looked her in the face when all the others turned away, so she gave the gift to you. Do you have the courage to pass it on?" Mike stood. The jigsaw was complete.

Marie mistook his silence for surrender; she thought that she had convinced him. "Now give me Alice, and go and wait for me in the garage." Impatience made her voice uglier and more dismissive than she'd intended. It was enough to give Mike a glimpse of a different, crueller side of her.

"No." Mike said only that one word. He held Alice close to his chest and pushed past them. He took the path out of the open space. Behind him he heard Marie screaming something in a language he didn't understand. He felt the knife cut his shoulder, but he did not look back.

5

England, September – October 2009

Laura sat in the front room sewing. Alice was on the floor playing with large brightly coloured blocks of Duplo. Outside the rain fell steadily. It was only the second week in September, but the weather had moved straight into winter and summer seemed like a distant memory. Laura smiled as she thought of the few days they had spent at the seaside. They had seemed like a proper family then. Mike had been brilliant with Alice, and Laura had felt that she loved both of them.

Alice came over to Laura and held up the strange construction she had made. Laura took it and looked at it carefully. "Well done Alice. Can you tell me what it is?" Alice began, words tumbling out as jumbled as the bricks of Duplo. Then the doorbell rang. Laura put down her embroidery. She had been so engrossed with Alice that she hadn't noticed anyone come to the door. As she went through to the hall, she suddenly remembered her nightmare and hesitated. The bell rang again with a loud urgency, so she hurried to open the door.

Outside were two policemen. "We're looking for a Michael Pearce." It was the taller one who spoke. "We believe he lives here." Laura thought the policeman looked familiar, which was quite likely because as a social worker she often had contact with the police.

"Yes he does, but I'm afraid he's not back from work yet." There was an awkward pause as they stood looking at each other. "Why don't you come in?" Laura opened the door for the police. "He shouldn't be long."

"That's very kind of you." Again it was the taller one who spoke. The other one, younger and dark haired, said nothing.

Laura led them through to the front room. "Please have a seat." She gestured to the settee. They sat down, perching on its edge, their bodies angled forward. "Excuse the mess. I'm afraid Alice is in building mode."

Laura indicated the Duplo that Alice had strewn over the carpet. Alice stood looking at the two visitors with interest. "Come and say hello, Alice." She came over and offered each her tiny hand. They laughed and shook it gently.

"Would you like a cup of tea while you're waiting?" asked Laura.

"No thank you, Mrs Pearce." It was again the taller one who spoke. Laura studied him carefully, trying to place him. The silence was uneasy. Both men seemed embarrassed.

"What do you want with Mike?" Laura said with a cheerfulness she didn't feel. "Is it anything I can help you with?"

"I don't think so, Mrs Pearce. We just need to ask him a few questions."

"What about?" She tried to keep the anxiety out of her voice.

"We'd rather discuss that with Mr Pearce himself." The response was firm. The question seemed to have increased their embarrassment. Laura smiled to herself at the second use of Mrs Pearce. People always assumed that she and Mike were married. Her stubbornness was the reason that they weren't. At the seaside she had started to feel that she should relent and agree. Mike had tried to persuade her several times in the past.

"Sorry?" She realised that the tall policeman had asked her a question. "Have you been married long?"

"Well, we're not actually married," she said, smiling a little to herself at the policeman's increased embarrassment, "but Mike's lived here for nearly three years." The uneasy silence returned. Laura felt she needed to do something so she knelt down on the floor next to Alice. "Come on, Alice, time to tidy up. Daddy will be home soon. We don't want a mess for Daddy, do we?" At the word "Daddy" Alice went over to the window and stood leaning against it, looking out expectantly.

"I'm sure I know you from somewhere." The taller policeman's comment took Laura by surprise. She looked up at him from the floor.

"It's quite likely. I'm a social worker. I used to be full-time, but since having Alice I only work three days a week. I've worked together with the police quite a lot. It's always been a good partnership." Laura felt that when she said "social worker" the dark haired policeman had given her a funny look. A look of surprise.

191

"That's what it must have been. Were you..."

"Mike's here now." Laura interrupted as she saw Mike park outside her house. She stood up and was about to go into the hall when the tall policeman motioned for her to stay in the room. The policemen both stood up as they heard Mike opening the front door.

"Hello Laura," he called cheerily as he came into the room, then he stopped in surprise when he saw the police.

"Michael Pearce?"

"Yes."

"Mr Pearce, we need to ask you a few questions. We would like you to come down to the station with us."

"Okay, but can you tell me what it's about?"

The tall one looked meaningfully towards Laura. "We'd rather discuss that at the station with you, sir, if you don't mind."

"No, of course not." Laura looked enquiringly at Mike, who shrugged his shoulders. Then the police ushered him out of the house and down the drive to their car. In a few moments they had gone.

Laura stood staring out of the window at the empty road. A little hand reached up and touched hers. "Daddy gone," Alice said sadly, looking out of the window too. Laura bent down and hugged her.

"Shall I read you a story? I am sure Daddy will be back soon." But Laura wasn't sure. In fact, suddenly she wasn't sure of anything. She didn't understand what was going on. There had been something curious about the attitude of the two police officers, as though whatever they knew made them pity her.

Recently Mike had seemed preoccupied and tense. Only last week he had said, "I'm tired of living here. Why don't we move somewhere else? Let's go and live by the seaside." Laura had looked at him, stunned. The thought of leaving the house that she had worked so hard to buy and furnish and the job she enjoyed had been too much for her. She liked working part-time. It kept her in touch and still left her time with Alice. It all seemed to work so well, Mike looking after Alice for two days a week then Alice having a day at the nursery. Alice had settled in very well and had already made friends. The three of them had become a real family. Mike had seen the disappointment in Laura's face and had quickly said, "Well maybe not. It was only an idea. It was just so nice by the sea." He hadn't brought the subject up again, and Laura had dismissed it as him getting itchy feet. He'd told her from the start that he did from time to time. After all, he'd always moved around, and this was the first time that he'd lived in one place for so long. Now, however, she wondered if there was something else bothering him; if he was in some kind of trouble.

A little hand pushed a book into Laura's, and a voice said, "Story." Laura took Alice on her lap and read to her. Reading helped Laura to stop thinking and it helped the time pass, but she remained uncertain and unsettled. Alice sensed this. Every now and then Alice would get down from Laura's lap, go to the window and look out at the empty road. Then she would turn, look at Laura and say "Daddy not back" in her sad little voice.

Laura didn't know if it was a question or a statement. Each time she hugged Alice and said, "Soon, Daddy will be back soon."

After over an hour of reading there was still no sign of Mike and Laura felt it was time to make Alice's tea. She prepared it in the kitchen and then, as a special treat, let Alice eat in the front room watching one of her favourite children's programmes. Just as they were finishing the phone rang, making Laura start. She hurried to the phone and picked it up nervously.

There was silence for a moment, then Mike spoke. "Hello Laura."

"Mike, what's going on? When are you coming back? Do I need to come and fetch you?" The questions came out all in a rush.

There was a long pause, then Mike spoke. "It's complicated. I can't explain over the phone. They want me to stay longer. Can you put together some overnight things and bring them up to the station?"

"Mike, what's this all about?"

"I'll explain later." There was a funny flatness in his voice.

"Are you in trouble?" She couldn't keep her anxiety out of the question.

Again there was a silence. At last he said, "There are some things I need to sort out. I'll try to explain when you come up." He paused once more, then added, "don't worry, I'm sure it'll all be okay."

"You're sure?"

"Yes, I'm sure, honestly." The conviction he injected into his tone seemed artificial. It was intended to reassure her, but it didn't.

"Okay. I'll ask Pauline to look after Alice. I'll be with you as soon as I can."

"Thank you," he said. "I really do appreciate it." And this time she knew he meant it. She put the phone down and looked at it.

"Daddy?" Alice was standing watching her.

"Yes, Daddy. He's going to be a bit longer than we thought. He needs me to take him some things."

"Daddy not coming." Alice's voice was sad, and Laura could see the tears forming. She hugged her daughter.

"Not just yet, but he'll come soon. How would you like to go and play with Auntie Pauline for a bit?"

"Cat," Alice said brightening up. Their next door neighbour had a tortoiseshell kitten that Alice loved to watch.

"Yes, cat. Now go and get one toy to take with you and I'll find a drink and a biscuit. I'll just go and see that Auntie Pauline is okay about it."

Laura went next door. She didn't know quite what to say, or whether Pauline had seen the police car parked outside and the two officers usher Mike into it, so she just said, "Mike's out, and I've got to pop out for about an hour. Could you look after Alice for me?"

"Yes, of course" was Pauline's cheery reply. Her own children had grown up and left home and hadn't produced any grandchildren yet. Pauline adored Alice and was very good with her. Alice adored the cat, so it was a perfect arrangement. Once Alice was safely next door Laura found an overnight bag and put a change of clothing, pyjamas and a wash bag in it. Her head was spinning. She didn't really know what else Mike would need. Soon she was driving to the police station, the bag beside her on the passenger seat.

As she drove the questions came crowding in. Mike was clearly in some kind of trouble. He'd said it was complicated and he would sort it out. She tried to think what it could be, but her mind was blank. Maybe it was something to do with work. Perhaps it was a health and safety issue. Maybe something had gone missing and someone had accused him. These things did happen. It must be something like that.

*

Mike looked at the pile of photographs in front of him on the table. The top one showed Yvette in a red bra and short red skirt. The one below showed Mike clearly handing money to the scantily clad Yvette.

"Well?" The question came from the tall policeman sitting opposite him. In the background he heard the whirring of the tape recorder. The silence was long. "Do you have anything to say?" The policeman stared at him.

"It's complicated."

"How is it complicated?" The policeman picked up the top photo and looked at it. "Here is a thirteen-year-old girl coming out of a garage with you, wearing only her bra and a very short skirt." He picked up the next photograph and held it up. "Here you are giving the same girl money. You paid a thirteen-year-old girl to have sex with you."

"I didn't have sex with her."

"Then why did you pay her money?"

Mike sighed. This wasn't going well. "I usually paid her money to look after Alice while I was with her sister."

"So you paid a thirteen-year-old to look after your child while you had sex with her fifteen-year-old sister?" There was a touch of incredulity in the police officer's voice.

"Sort of."

"I will take sort of to mean yes. But on this occasion the sister wasn't there, so why did you pay a thirteen-year-old girl money?"

"I felt I ought to."

"Why? Could it be because you had sex with her?"

"No, I didn't. She wanted me to, but I refused. I paid her the money because I didn't want to upset her."

The policeman looked at Mike. "She wanted to have sex and you refused?"

"Yes."

"Why did you refuse?"

"Because I thought she was too young."

"But you had sex with her sister."

"Yes."

"She is also under the age of consent."

"Yes, but it was different."

"How was it different?"

Mike shrugged his shoulders. How could he explain? It hardly made sense to him, so how could anyone else understand? The policeman paused for a moment and looked at Mike, waiting for a comment. Then he went on.

"It seems pretty clear from the evidence of the photographs and the testimony of the two girls that you have persuaded them to have sex with you. In fact, you have paid them money to have sex with you. That you did this while your own child was there is not only illegal, it is pretty awful."

"But it wasn't like that," Mike said stubbornly. "I didn't persuade them. They offered themselves to me. I didn't pay them for the sex."

"Why should they offer themselves to you? How do you come to know them?"

Mike sighed again. "It's a long story."

"That's okay, we've got all the time in the world."

"Okay. It started over ten years ago in New Orleans."

"Go on."

So Mike told the story of what had happened to him, and how he had come to meet Marie.

Laura sat in the police station holding the overnight bag. She had explained to the sergeant behind the desk why she had come. He had told her she could leave the bag and he would make sure that Mike received it, but she'd said that she wanted to see Mike. The sergeant had told her that Mike was still being interviewed and she could wait if she liked. So Laura sat and waited. She had already been there for forty-five minutes, and she kept looking nervously at her watch. She didn't want to leave Alice with Pauline for too long. At last the tall policeman who had come to the house appeared in reception. The sergeant said something to him and pointed to Laura, then the tall policeman came over to her.

"Hello. You've brought some things for Michael Pearce? You can give them to me if you like."

Laura held tightly on to the bag. "I really wanted the chance to speak to Mike and find out what is going on."

"I see."

"I can't stay too long. I've left my little girl with a neighbour." The policeman looked uncertain. "When Mike phoned and asked me to bring the things he said it would be possible to talk to him."

"Okay. I'll see what I can do." The tall policeman got up and disappeared. A few moments later he came back. "Mrs Pearce, if you'd like to follow me I have arranged a room where you and Mr Pearce can meet, but you'll have to give the bag to me I'm afraid. It will need to be searched and checked before we can give it to him." The officer stretched out his hand and she gave him the bag. "Please follow me." He led her out of reception and down a corridor. He stopped by the third door on the left and opened it to a small room in which there was a table with a chair on each side. A WPC sat at right angles to the table.

"Please have a seat here, Mrs Pearce. Michael Pearce will be here in a moment."

The tall policeman turned and went out. Laura looked around the room. It was completely bare apart from the table and three chairs, and it had no windows. Light came from a fluorescent tube on the ceiling. There were no pictures and the walls were painted a nondescript cream. She'd never been in a police station in her life before, and certainly never in an interview room. She looked at the WPC who was younger than she was. The WPC's hair was fair and she wore a short-sleeved white blouse. Her face was expressionless and she avoided Laura's eyes. There was no clock, and the only sounds were footsteps and talking from the corridor. The room seemed to be in some curious kind of limbo. It was disconnected from reality, even the reality of the reception. Laura wondered vaguely if this was what hell might be like, not that she really believed in it.

At last footsteps came down the corridor and stopped outside the room. The door opened and the tall policeman appeared with Mike. The policeman gestured to the chair facing Laura.

"You've got ten minutes," he said, nodding to the WPC.

Mike sat opposite Laura and looked down at the table. Laura waited for him to speak. Eventually she broke the silence. She tried to keep her voice even; she was very conscious of the WPC sitting and listening. This was not what she'd been expecting.

"Mike, what is all this about?"

He sighed and then looked at her. He seemed to have difficulty in meeting her eyes. "They have accused me of having sex with girls under the age of consent."

"What? But that's ridiculous!" Laura almost laughed with relief. The idea of Mike having sex with other women was so completely unthinkable. "There's got to be a mistake. They must have mixed you up with someone else." Laura's voice trailed off as she saw the expression on his face.

"I'm sorry," his voice was heavy and dull, "but it's true."

Laura stared at him. She sat back in her chair. "How can it be true?" Everything suddenly seemed unreal. What was happening in this windowless room under the glare of the fluorescent light was so different from the life she thought she'd been leading. She had come into the police station anxious and uncertain, but she had not expected this. The room became airless and oppressive; she struggled to breath.

Mike reached across the table to touch her hand but she pulled it away, feeling repelled by him.

"How could you?" Laura spoke the question that stood for all the questions running through her mind: how could you have sex with someone else? How could you do it and I not know? How could you do it to me? How could you do it to Alice? How could you do it and say you love me? How could you betray me?

"It isn't the way you think it is."

"How is it then?"

Mike looked at the WPC. "It's hard to explain here and now."

Laura leant forward in her chair, suddenly urgent and animated. "Mike, I have to know. You have to explain. I thought you loved me."

Mike looked at her, his expression wounded. He too leant forward and his face was close to hers across the table. For the first time he met her eyes properly.

"But I do. This has nothing to do with my love for you. Trust me." Again he tried to reach out and touch her. Again she moved her hand away and her chair back from the table to increase the distance between them.

"How can I trust you when you have betrayed me?" Her voice was full of anger. "You have betrayed me and you have betrayed Alice."

198

"But I haven't betrayed you. If I had betrayed you then you wouldn't know and I wouldn't be here." He paused as though trying to explain something that was impossible to explain. "I mean, I know I betrayed you at the beginning, but I didn't mean to. When there was a choice, when I could see the threat to you and Alice, I chose you. That is why I am here." His voice was no longer flat and heavy with guilt. It was desperate.

Laura heard what he said but it made no sense to her. How could he admit he had betrayed her and then say he hadn't? She looked at him. "I'm sorry, Mike, I don't understand."

"I know it doesn't make sense. Please trust me." He leant forward, his eyes pleading with her. "Believe me, I do love you."

Laura didn't move forward. She stared at him. "Mike, I don't know what to think. I don't know if I can ever trust you again." She turned to the WPC. "Please, I want to finish this."

The WPC stood up. "If that's want you want. Please wait here while I take Mr Pearce back to the cells." She indicated to Mike, who stood up.

As he reached the door he turned and looked at Laura. "Please believe me. I never intended to hurt you. This is all to do with my dreams. Please try to trust me." Then the door closed behind him. Laura sat staring blankly from his empty chair to the cream-coloured wall. She felt nauseous. The WPC came back into the room, looked at Laura and put a hand on her arm.

"Are you alright, Miss? You look very pale. Would you like to sit here with a glass of water for a while?"

"No, thank you," Laura said politely. She wanted to get out of the room as quickly as possible. The WPC took Laura down the corridor and into reception, again asking her if she was okay. Laura thanked her and left. She walked across to where she had parked the car, got in and burst into tears. Laura didn't normally cry, and the tears had come without warning. Now she bent over the steering wheel and sobbed uncontrollably. Her world, the one she had built up with such care, had fallen apart completely. Except for Alice. Untypical, unplanned Alice. Laura had surrendered herself to a moment, just as she had the first time she met Mike. The thought of Alice made Laura look at her watch. She had been away for nearly two hours. She needed to get back. Thinking of Alice made her wonder what she was going to say. There would be Alice's look of expectancy when Laura parked and the disappointment when she saw that Laura was on her own. Then the questions would start: "Where Daddy?" Laura didn't know what she would say. What could she say? She would have to tell some lie about him being busy and that he would be back tomorrow, but he probably wouldn't be back tomorrow. And if he was, did she really want him in her house?

Colin Morris looked at the pile of photographs and papers on the desk in front of him. He sat in the windowless room with the video machine and the television. Something wasn't right. Something didn't quite add up. He'd thought to begin with that this would be a simple and straightforward case. Now he wasn't so sure.

There was a knock on his door; a middle-aged bespectacled man stuck his balding head round it.

"Morning, Colin. Can I come in?"

"Of course, Richard. Have a seat." The man came into the room. He was wearing a light grey suit and a striped tie, and carried a black briefcase. "Thanks very much for coming over. Would you like a coffee?"

"Tea, please, milk and no sugar." Morris picked up the phone and asked for a tea and a coffee.

Richard Sibthorpe settled into his chair and looked at Morris expectantly. "So, what can I do for you?" Sibthorpe was a qualified psychologist based at the local hospital. He also worked with the police occasionally, giving them advice or carrying out assessments when necessary. The police didn't really need their own full-time psychologist, so Sibthorpe filled in when there was a need. He got a little extra pay for it, and the hospital was happy for him to do the work.

"It's this case here," Morris said, gesturing to the pile of papers. "Michael Pearce. He's been accused of propositioning two underage girls and paying them to have sex with him."

"Sounds straightforward enough. Do you have statements from the girls?"

"Yes, their aunt brought them into the station two days ago. They made full and detailed statements."

"Does Pearce admit guilt?"

"Well, yes and no."

"What do you mean?"

"He admits to having sex with both of the girls, but denies that he initiated it and that the money he paid them was for the sex."

"Surely it's academic then. Whether he initiated it or they initiated it, he has had sex with girls below the age of consent. That is illegal. It counts as statutory rape, and you have enough to put him away for a few years."

Morris nodded. "You're right, of course. It's just that..." He stopped.

"Just what? You're normally keen to get these types behind bars and out of the community."

"Well, the sex has been going on for nearly two years, but the girls have only just come forward now."

"Presumably they were too scared to do so before."

"That's exactly what the aunt says. She says she knew nothing about it because they were too frightened to tell her. As soon as she knew she brought them straight to the police to make a statement."

"Sounds reasonable."

A constable came in with two cups and put them down in front of Morris and Sibthorpe. Morris picked his up and took a sip, then continued.

"It does, but not necessarily for these two girls. They're not little innocents. We've had suspicions for some time that they've been working for the aunt as prostitutes, we've just never been able to prove it."

"Tell me about them."

"I don't know much. The girls are both dual heritage of some kind, and strikingly attractive." He passed a photo of them across the table. Sibthorpe looked at it.

"I see what you mean. I should think that they'd both be highly desirable."

"They live with their aunt. Apparently the mother is dead, and they've no idea who their father was. They moved from London two years ago. I don't know where they were before that. The aunt's son is a really nasty piece of work. He runs a little gang on the estate. We believe he's into drug dealing, assault, petty crime, possibly burglary. It's very difficult to prove anything he does because the estate people are too frightened to talk to us for fear of a reprisal."

"So with that background, it isn't likely that the girls would be frightened of anyone?"

"Exactly."

"What about the man, Michael Pearce did you say? Has he got any form?"

Morris passed a photograph of Mike over the table. "None at all. He also moved here a couple of years ago. He works as a sound engineer at the Corn Exchange. Lives with a woman who is a social worker. They have a small daughter. We checked his background and he has no previous convictions for anything, not even a speeding ticket. I've had an initial conversation with the Corn Exchange. They say he's great. Very talented, very reliable. They didn't think he'd stay here long because he's worked for some quite big bands, but it seems he met this girl and decided to settle down."

"Did she know anything about it?"

"Not a thing. She is completely shaken by it, especially because she's worked in child protection. In fact, I've worked with her. She always seemed very bright and very professional."

"So what does Michael Pearce have to say for himself?"

"Well that's just it. He told me some long and fantastic story about seeing a woman murdered in New Orleans. Now he thinks that she was the mother of the two girls. The elder one, Marie, looks just like her. He says it's all to do with voodoo. Pearce claims to have had dreams that led him to Marie, who seduced him. He thinks that they're trying to get some sort of power over his daughter. He claims he interrupted a kind of ceremony in which they had daubed the girl with chicken's blood. Apparently he lost his temper and took the child away, and that's why he thinks they've suddenly come to us and made these accusations against him. I know it sounds fantastic, that's why I wanted to talk to you about it. Voodoo and dreams aren't really my area."

"They're not mine either. I'm a social scientist, not a witch doctor."

"I know, but you do deal with things of the mind. Because of the kind of girls they are and the family they come from, it seems to be a bit of a set-up. I want to be sure before I throw the whole book at him. If you could have a chat with him it would help. I don't know if he's delusional or just a liar. If it turns out that he is delusional and they have exploited him in some way, there could be mitigating circumstances. It might also give us the kind of lead we are looking for to take some action against the whole family. Frankly I think the girls' cousin is a bigger threat to the community than Michael Pearce."

"I see where you're coming from." Sibthorpe thought for a moment. "Are there any independent witnesses or evidence?"

"No witnesses, but there's a lot of CCTV footage. That's where the still photos are taken from. At the start of last year we put cameras on the estate to try and get a handle on what was going on there. It didn't really work, but we've lots of film of the happy couple. They tended to meet at the playground on the estate, and then go off to a garage owned by the aunt. This is where the sex took place."

"And what does the footage show?"

"Well, some of it is obvious." Morris passed the photos of Yvette over the table. "Here's the younger girl coming out of the garage in her bra and skirt. Here is Michael Pearce paying her money. The rest is less clear."

"What do you mean?"

"Take a look at this video clip. When I began to notice clips of them meeting I saved them on a disk just in case something came of it." Morris turned on the television and then pressed the play button on the recorder. "Look, this is the first time they appear on camera." He showed footage of Mike and Marie playing with Alice in the playground. "All completely innocent. They play with the little girl and then go to the garage, but not for long. After that they go their separate ways. There is no sign of any payment, although it could have happened inside. There are other clips where they leave the little girl with the sister and then go off to the garage. You can see Pearce paying the sister. He maintains this was only for looking after the child." Morris found another clip. "This is the odd one, though." The clip showed Mike on his own outside the garage. "This is the cousin Charles and his gang. They pin Pearce against the wall, then something is put over the camera." He fast-forwarded the tape. "When it starts again Marie is there shouting at her cousin, and Michael Pearce looks in a pretty bad way."

"There's certainly no sign of him intimidating her. If anything it looks as though her cousin beat him up. Was the incident ever reported?"

"No, but as I said that's not unusual when the cousin is involved."

"Why did Pearce go to that playground in the first place?"

Morris sighed. "He says he dreamt about a specific playground, one with a roundabout in it. He kept visiting playgrounds until he found it. And he's right, this is the only playground in the town with a roundabout."

Sibthorpe thought for a moment. "Interesting," he said. "Yes okay, I'll have a chat with him. Where is he now?"

"He's in the cells. I have charged him initially. I'll keep him in custody because of his potential danger to other girls in the community, although I don't really think he is a danger."

"Okay. Can I take all the documents, photos and tapes? I'll have a look through them, then come and chat with him. It won't be until Thursday. I'm really busy tomorrow."

"That's not a problem. He's not going anywhere. The trial won't be for months, and although I will need to put him in front of the magistrate's there isn't a slot for at least a week. I just need to make a decision by then about whether I keep him on remand or let him out on bail."

"Good. As soon as I've seen him I'll let you know if I think it's worth pursuing."

"Richard, I really appreciate that." Morris stood up.

"Not a problem. I don't get a case involving the supernatural every day." Sibthorpe laughed, and then added, "Thank goodness."

Mike lay on the bed and looked at the ceiling. It was exactly a week since he' been taken to the police station. In the first twenty-four hours there had been a lot of activity. There had been two interviews, then the police had charged him and kept him in custody until he could appear before the magistrate. He'd been told that the magistrate would decide on whether he would be kept on remand or bailed.

For the first two days after his meeting with Laura he'd felt depressed and frustrated. He wanted her to know exactly what had happened and needed her to understand that, although he had let her down, in the end, it was his refusal to put Alice at risk that had created this situation.

Morris, the policeman in charge of the investigation, had told Mike about the statements made by Yvette and Marie, and had read out some parts of them. It was a very different story from what he knew had happened. According to them, Mike was a paedophile taking advantage of two young girls, intimidating them and paying them for sex. It hadn't been like that. Mike wasn't sure he could have intimidated Marie even if he'd tried. This was his punishment for refusing to go along with them and let them finish their initiation ceremony. He understood now that he wasn't important. It was Alice they wanted. They had used him as a way of getting to her. He remembered how insistent Marie had been that he should always bring Alice with him, saying that Alice gave him an excuse to leave the house. It also gave Marie access to Alice. The little girl knew and trusted her. However, proving it all was impossible. The story seemed so far-fetched that nobody would believe it. They were two innocent girls and he was a predatory man, who had even taken his own child with him, as he took advantage of them. Mike had watched the policeman's reaction when he'd tried to explain. He could tell that Morris didn't believe him.

But Mike needed Laura to know. She had seen him dream; she knew it was real. The day after he'd seen her he thought she might come back, then he realised that she wouldn't. The look on her face and the way she had recoiled from him made him feel sick inside. Even if she did come, how would he explain with some WPC sitting there listening? He decided to write her a letter. The police would read it, but it was no more than he was already telling them so it didn't really matter. He asked for a pen and writing paper and made a start. It wasn't easy. He wasn't much good at putting things down on paper unless they were technical specifications, so it took a long time.

By the third day after his arrest he had finished. The letter ended with three pleas. The first was that Laura look after Alice. Mike was worried that somehow Marie and Yvette might try to snatch her away. The second was for Laura to come and see him. The last was that she try to forgive him and understand that he'd never intended to betray her. He asked for the letter to be posted or delivered to Laura. The WPC said that she would make sure it was done.

Since then nothing had happened. Mike seemed trapped in a regime of sleeping, eating, exercising and lying on the bed in his cell staring at the ceiling, like he was doing now. He was the only occupant of the police station. One night a drunk had been brought in, arguing and swearing. All night there had been banging and shouting, then in the morning quiet returned. It was almost as if Mike had been forgotten by everyone. He kept track of time by crossing the days off on a piece of paper. Music would have made the time pass more quickly, but the only thing he could do was lie on the bed, close his eyes and imagine he was choosing a record or CD from his collection. He knew some of them so well that he could almost hear the music in his head.

Today, though, Mike couldn't do it. He felt hopeless and depressed again. He'd hoped he would've heard something from Laura. She must have had his letter by now, but there was nothing. He just lay there waiting, not sure what it was he was waiting for.

Ever since the disagreement with Marie, he'd had the same dream every night. He had gone to the playground to look for Alice. Marie was playing with her. She had put Alice on the swing. Mike tried to get to Alice, but each time he tried to cross the playground it was as though his feet were stuck. Marie saw him and laughed. She kept pushing Alice higher and higher into the air. To begin with Alice enjoyed it and was giggling and laughing; as Marie pushed her harder and higher she became frightened and started to scream. She looked at Mike, asking him to help her. He tried to reach her, but he couldn't. Marie kept laughing and pushing. Alice kept screaming. Then Mike would wake. Whether the dream was a prediction or the result of his anxiety he didn't know.

A face looked through the grill in the door, a key turned in the lock. "Come on, Pearce," the burly PC said, "there's someone who needs to see you."

Mike got off the bed and stood up. Laura, he thought. It must be Laura. She has read the letter and wants to speak to me. He felt excited and nervous as he was led down the corridor to the interview room. As soon as the door opened the nerves and excitement vanished. Sitting across the table was a bald, bespectacled middle-aged man in a suit.

"Come in and sit down, Michael." The man's tone was friendly, but Mike sat opposite him feeling let down and resentful.

Laura lay in the bath and thought. It was early evening and Alice was asleep in her room. Now she slept through the night things were much easier. Of course she was awake early in the morning, but early mornings had never bothered Laura or Mike. Laura now had this time in the evening to relax, which was very precious.

She thought about Mike's letter. For two days after she'd seen him at the police station she had felt completely numb. She could hardly even bring herself to think of him. How could you know someone and not know them at all? That's what she had kept thinking. How can someone you trust do something so terrible? How can you not know or sense that it is happening? She knew all about child abuse and paedophiles from her job. She had seen enough victims to know the damage it did. How could she have had a child with a man like that? If he'd had an affair with another woman it would have been bad enough, to have sex with young girls was unforgivable.

Of course the police had come back to interview her, but there was nothing she could tell them. No, she hadn't had any idea what was happening. Yes, Mike had taken Alice out to the playground a lot. No, he'd never behaved inappropriately to Alice in her presence. Yes, she knew all the signs. For God's sake, she had done the child protection training. But there had been no signs, or she had missed them. Could she really have been so stupid? So unobservant? Laura felt the unspoken judgement of the police.

Yes, there had been a cool period between her and Mike after Alice had been born. Laura had been depressed and unsettled, and she remembered that she wouldn't make love with him for a long time. She had felt so guilty and mixed up about both wanting and not wanting Alice, though she hadn't told the police that. There were some things that they really didn't need to know, but it had made her think. Was it during that period of coolness that it had all started? Was it in some way her fault? Mike hadn't seemed frustrated or angry by her coolness. The opposite, in fact he'd been kind, gentle and reassuring. How could he be so different?

Then the letter had come. Pages of it, written on lined paper in Mike's untidy scrawl. She'd read it last night, drunk a whole bottle of white wine and then gone to bed. Exhausted, she'd fallen asleep at once, and only woke when Alice tugged at her arm, saying, "Mummy up." Since then she'd thought of nothing else. Now, sitting in the bath, she went through it again.

The whole thing sounded fantastic. Nobody could possibly believe it. The account of the dream that had brought him to the playground gave her an explanation. Before that there had been nothing, but shock and disgust. Mike did dream, she knew that. She knew by heart the story of New Orleans. Was it possible that this girl, this Marie, was the daughter? At least from Mike's account these were not the innocent young girls that Laura had been imagining, but she needed to know more.

Mike's letter reassured her and it also frightened her. If he was right that Alice, her precious Alice, was the target, then that was far worse than anything. Was it possible the girls would somehow try to take Alice from her? From the sound of it, this Marie knew people who were capable of great violence. Or was the plan more subtle than that? If Mike was convicted as a paedophile, there would be a question about whether Alice was safe in this house, and whether Laura was a suitable mother.

Children who were taken into care were then put in foster placements. The thought of that sent a chill through Laura. If Mike was right and there was a threat to Alice then Laura needed to do something. She wasn't going to stand passively by and have her daughter taken away from her. There were a lot of things she needed to know. She had spent too long in a state of shock, simply not knowing what to do. Now it was time to take action. She would begin tomorrow. She didn't know if she would or could forgive Mike, but she needed to talk to him. Above all, she would fight to protect her daughter.

At eight thirty on Friday morning, Colin Morris had just entered his little office when there was a knock at the door and Richard Sibthorpe came in.

"Well, what did you make of him?"

"Interesting," Sibthorpe said. "I'm sorry, I'd hoped to speak to you yesterday, but I had to dash back to the hospital, so I thought I would try to find you first thing."

"Well?"

"I don't know. I didn't go through the whole story, just asked about a couple of things. The idea is ridiculous of course and yet he seems very convinced, which in turn makes him convincing."

"So?"

"So I'd like some time to go into it in more detail."

"Really?" Morris sounded surprised.

"Yes, I think it deserves proper examination."

"Okay."

"But I don't want to do it here. I need him more relaxed than he will be in a police cell. I also want to be able to observe him properly. If I move him to the hospital, we have a special section where we can keep patients under observation for twenty-four hours a day if necessary. One-way mirrors, that sort of thing. I'm very keen to have the chance to observe him if he has one of his dreams."

"Okay. But will you need a constable to keep an eye on him? I don't think the inspector would agree to that."

"He has no track record so I don't think he's going to go berserk. He's hardly likely to flee the country, especially if he thinks that we are taking him seriously."

Morris thought for a moment. He looked doubtful. "It's a bit irregular."

"No, it isn't actually. It is quite common, if there are potential mental-health issues, to transfer a prisoner to a hospital for observation. I will take full responsibility for him. You can sign him over to me. After all, you're the one who wanted me to give an opinion."

"Okay." Morris grinned. "I agree, but I'll need to run it past the inspector. When?"

"As soon as possible. This afternoon if we can manage it. I've already asked them to make preparations at the hospital. The area I want to use is currently available."

"That soon? And for how long?"

"How long can I have? A couple of weeks? You said the trial wouldn't be for months."

"No, but the hearing in front of the magistrate will be sooner. I need to know by then what attitude to take to bail. Two weeks maximum."

"Fine."

"Oh, and you might find this interesting." Morris held out a sheaf of papers. "It's a photocopy of the letter he wrote to his partner."

"Thanks. Is it okay if I speak to her too?"

"Yes if you like, but you'll be lucky if you can get anything out of her. She either didn't know anything or didn't want to tell us anything. I really think she didn't know. She seemed shocked and mortified by the whole thing. She works as a social worker, so for her own partner to do something like this has been very hard for her to take."

"Yes," Sibthorpe said thoughtfully, "but she is the only person who has witnessed one of his dreams."

"What?"

"She has witnessed one of his dreams."

"If you believe it. Hang on here a minute, I'll see if I can catch the inspector now. Once he's agreed you can go ahead."

Laura sat in the front room watching Alice play. There was a notebook in front of her on the table. She was trying to make a plan. The first thing to do was to find out much more about what had happened. Before Mike's letter she hadn't even wanted to think about it, now she needed the details, however painful. The chances of talking to Mike on his own were minimal. The key was to find out more about the two girls who had made the complaint against him and she couldn't do that without talking to him. Going direct to the police and asking them for details about the girls was a possibility, but she would need to be very careful. Any attempt by her to approach the girls could be seen as interference, or even perverting the course of justice. If she were to end up in prison too that would be a disaster.

It was difficult to know where to start. Probably with Mike, but how would she go about trying to see him? Ring the police station and ask, that was the obvious answer. Mike hadn't spoken to a solicitor yet because he hadn't asked for one. Perhaps that was a way forward. A solicitor would have the right to ask for copies of the girls' statements, and any other evidence. Laura was just thinking how to get a solicitor when her phone rang. She picked it up and heard Mike's voice.

"Laura?"

"Yes."

"Can you be in between three and four today?"

"Yes. Why? Are they releasing you? Has something happened?" She felt a surge of hope.

"I'm being transferred to the hospital."

"Hospital. Why? Are you alright." She remembered how she had reacted to him in the police station.

"They want some psychologist to keep me under observation. I think it's to do with the dreams." Laura felt relieved that he wasn't ill. There was silence for a moment, then he said, "Did you get the letter?"

"Yes."

"Well?"

"I don't know." Now it was her turn to be silent. "Why didn't you tell me about the dream?"

"It was a difficult time for you." There was silence again, as though he was waiting for her to say something, to give some indication that she did understand, but she had been honest when she'd said she didn't know how she felt. Laura wished she could give him some reassurance, and tried to think of something to say, but couldn't.

"I need to come round on the way to the hospital to pick up some clean clothes." He was trying to sound brisk and businesslike. It didn't quite work.

"I'll be here."

"Okay." Mike put the phone down without saying anything else. Laura stared at it, wishing she could have said something more.

Alice was standing there, looking at Laura. "Daddy?" she asked. Laura wondered if she could have known, but Alice asked the same question whenever anybody rang.

"Yes, Daddy. He's going to come and see us this afternoon. Only for a little bit, then he's got to go away again."

"See Daddy afternoon." Alice smiled happily and went back to her toys.

Mike was right, of course. From his letter, Laura knew that she had been preoccupied and depressed when his dream had started. She understood why he'd not felt able to talk to her about it, but he had promised to tell her whenever he dreamt. It was also a time when they were not making love. Again the thought struck her, was it her coldness that had pushed him into this relationship? It must have made him more vulnerable, but to what? To being seduced by a thirteen-year-old girl because she looked like someone he'd seen murdered? That sounded too fantastic.

At ten to three the cell door was unlocked, and Dr Sibthorpe was waiting. Mike picked up his bag and walked to reception. The tall policeman (Mike thought his name was Morris) was there too. Dr Sibthorpe signed some papers, then Morris walked out with them to the car park. He turned to Mike.

"I am sure that Dr Sibthorpe has explained to you why you're being transferred to the hospital. I'm entrusting you to his care. This is rather unusual, but we don't see you as an immediate risk to the community." He gave Mike a searching look. "Don't let me, or yourself, down. If you cause any trouble it'll make it worse for you when you come to court."

"I won't," Mike said, meeting his eyes. Morris said nothing more to him, just warned Dr Sibthorpe to take care and then went back into the station.

Mike found it strange suddenly being in the outside world again. He got into the passenger seat next to Dr Sibthorpe.

"Michael, you'll need to give me directions. I understand we're going to pick up some of your stuff on the way."

So Mike gave directions to Laura's house, which replaced the need for conversation. As they drove, Mike looked out of the window. It was a beautiful day. He knew it was a Friday, but he'd lost track of the date. He wasn't sure if it was already October. Certainly some of the trees they passed were beginning to turn, their leaves showing patches of brown and yellow.

At last they drew up outside the house. "I'd like to come in and meet Laura," he said. "I need to arrange a time to talk to her as well."

"Of course." Mike hid his disappointment. He'd been hoping he and Laura might have a little time alone together. They got out of the car and walked up the drive. Laura opened the door and let them in.

Alice immediately ran towards Mike, calling, "Daddy, Daddy, Daddy."

He picked her up and swung her round, replying "Alice, Alice,

Alice" and giving her a big hug. Dr Sibthorpe watched them, then introduced himself.

"Hello Laura. Can I come in for a moment?"

"Of course." Laura opened the door and showed him into the front room. She was thinking of the day when the policemen had come. "Would you like some tea or coffee?"

"No, it's alright," Dr Sibthorpe said, "we won't stay long."

Mike had taken Alice over to her toys and was playing with her. Dr Sibthorpe sat down opposite Laura. His manner was very different from the police. He was much more informal, and his use of her first name hinted at a friendliness that did not, in fact, exist. Laura wondered if it was natural, or part of the manner he'd developed in dealing with his patients. She could sense him watching her, and suspected beneath his apparent warmth was someone with the ability to observe and analyse in a way the police could not.

"Laura, I don't know if Michael has been able to explain to you what's happening."

"Not really."

"There are some rather unusual features in his case, so the police have asked me to do a psychological assessment of him. For this reason, he is being transferred to the hospital where I can keep him under close observation for a week or two."

Laura looked over to Mike, who was still playing with Alice.

"Do you think he is in some way unbalanced then?" She spoke quietly, hoping that Mike couldn't hear her question.

Dr Sibthorpe looked at her. "Perhaps. That's what we need to find out. What do you think?" He too kept his voice low. Laura hadn't been prepared for such a direct question. She was aware that he watching and noting her reaction.

Laura shrugged her shoulders. "I don't know. I didn't think so." Then added. "Would it be better for him if he was?"

Dr Sibthorpe continued to study her. "Possibly." He paused. "I would like to have the opportunity to talk to you about Michael in more detail. I'm particularly interested in his dreams. Would you be prepared to come and see me at the hospital? Or, if you prefer, I can come here."

"Of course." Laura thought. "I work Monday, Tuesday and Wednesday. It's difficult at the moment because Mike used to look after Alice on those days. Possibly Thursday. I'll have to see if Pauline, our neighbour, could look after Alice for a while."

"As I said, I could come here if it would be easier."

"I think it would be better at the hospital, or at least without Alice."

"Whatever you like. Here's my card. My mobile number is on it, so you can ring over the weekend if you like."

"Thank you."

Dr Sibthorpe stood up. "I'm sure you two could do with a little time together. I'll go and wait in the car. Michael, I can give you half an hour, but no more. I'm not sure Morris would approve at all." He laughed. Laura got up to show him to the door. "Don't worry." He waved her away. "I can let myself out. Better make the most of what little time you've got." He disappeared out of the room and they heard the front door open and close.

Mike had stood up at the same time as Dr Sibthorpe. Now he looked at Laura uncertainly, not knowing what to say. When he'd come in he'd immersed himself in the joy of seeing Alice. Laura turned to face him across the room. She thought he looked pale and tired. Neither knew how to cross the divide that separated them, until Alice grabbed Mike's hand and pulled it hard.

"Come, Daddy, Mummy," she called out, pulling him towards Laura. Seeing Alice's desire for them to be together moved Laura. She came across the room and hugged Mike. He held her without speaking. Alice wrapped her arms around both of them at knee height.

"Oh Laura," Mike said, and Laura realised he was crying. She cried too. She found his lips and they kissed, then he pushed her gently a little away.

"Laura, I'm so sorry. Can you understand? Can you ever forgive me?"

She looked at him, tears still rolling down her face. "I want to understand. I don't know if I can forgive you. Perhaps, perhaps when I understand more, but not yet. Mike, I need to know about what happened. I need to know who those girls are, and what they're like." The words came out in a rush. He led her over to the settee and they sat next to each other.

"Listen," he said, "because we don't have much time. I only know their first names and the estate they live on. I know nothing else, but be careful. Look after Alice. I'm sure that it's her they want. Now I need to go upstairs to get some things." He stood up and took his bag with him.

"I understand." She followed him up the stairs, with Alice trailing behind. "What do you think about this doctor?"

"I don't know. Maybe they're taking the whole business of the dream seriously." He went into the bedroom and started putting his things together.

"Or maybe they think you're deranged." Laura sat on the bed and watched him.

"Perhaps I am. Perhaps it would be better to be mad than bad."

"Don't be too sure. Even today mental hospitals can be as unpleasant as prisons, and they might keep you locked up for longer. I'm not sure I trust Dr Sibthorpe."

"Being in the hospital can't be any worse than being locked up in a police cell. In hospital I might not be locked up all the time. There may be opportunities either to prove my story or to escape. Who knows? Whatever happens, you have to take Alice away from here. It isn't safe for her. She's what they want. This is all about her, I'm sure. Go and stay with you mother for a few days."

"I don't want to go without you." The words and the stubborn determination of her tone surprised both of them. "We need to get away together."

Mike held Laura close to him again. "Let's see how the observation goes. They might believe my story."

"They might." Laura's sounded doubtful. "But what if they don't? What if you go to prison? What if they take Alice into care? I just couldn't bear that." Laura expressed for the first time the thought that had been nagging at the back of her mind. "That might be the girls' plan, to try to be her foster placement."

Mike was silent. He hadn't thought of that. His worry had been that the girls would try to snatch Alice; kidnap her somehow and make her disappear.

"Then we have to be ready to go, to leave the country. If they don't know where we are then none of that can happen."

"But where?"

"I don't know, Spain perhaps. Isn't that where all the criminals go?"

"I learnt Spanish at school and I can still remember some of it. There are plenty of flights, and it's cheap to get there."

"That's it then. If it goes wrong we'll go to Spain. Disappear and start a new life."

"Alright, I'll check out the flights."

Mike thought for a moment. "We might have to go quickly. You'd better have your things ready to pack." He took out his wallet, which the police had given back to him with all his other possessions. "Here's my credit card. I'll write my PIN number down. Start to take money out of the account. Not large sums, just fifty pounds at a time. Do the same with yours. Build up some cash that we can take with us."

"I'll buy euros too. What about the house?" Laura looked around her. She would be devastated to leave all she had built up, but she would do anything to protect Alice.

"Talk to Lottie about it. Better her than Pauline. Arrange to leave the key with her, or post it to her. Ask her to look after it for you. You'll need to tell Pauline that you're going away. Say you're so upset by the whole thing that you're going to stay with your mother and you're not sure when you'll be back."

"Yes, that's a good idea."

They heard the beep of a horn from the road. "That must be Dr Sibthorpe telling me that time is up."

"Oh, Mike." Laura hugged him and they kissed. She felt positive and determined. Her uncertainties had been brushed to one side. That didn't mean she had forgiven him, she told herself. They were merely united in their desire to protect Alice. She was the only thing that mattered.

They separated, and Laura asked, "Do you know anything more about the girls?"

"No. Like I said on the phone, I only know their first names and they live on that estate. I don't even have a photo."

"I need to find out more. I need to see them."

Mike looked at her with concern. "Be careful Laura, they're bad news. Stay away from them." He thought of the gang of four yobs. The horn sounded again. "I've got to go."

216

Laura hugged him and kissed him again. "Take care."

"Daddy going." Alice had stood silently, watching them talk. Mike picked her up and hugged her.

"It won't be for long this time, I promise," he said. "Be a good girl for Mummy. You take care too." He looked at Laura. "Stay away from those girls." Then he went down the stairs. Laura heard the door close. She crossed to the upstairs window, and watched as he got in the car and Dr Sibthorpe drove away.

Mike inspected his new home carefully. It was very different from the cell in the police station. In some ways it was like a hotel room. At one end there was a large window. Mike immediately crossed to it and looked out. His room was located at one end of the hospital. The outlook was across the grounds to the perimeter wall. As the room was on the second floor, he was high enough to see over the wall to the woods beyond it. There were no bars on the window, but he noticed that it was securely locked and there was no key. Beside the window was a single bed that had been made up with blankets and crisp white sheets. Mike sat on the bed and looked around. Next to the bed was a desk against the wall and a chair, then a dressing table under a large wall-mounted mirror. On the opposite side there were cupboards with sliding doors. The room narrowed to a passage as it led to the door. Just before the door there was a small en suite with a toilet, washbasin, shower and another large mirror. This would be real luxury after the communal facilities of the police station.

Mike got off the bed and unpacked the few clothes and toiletries he had brought. Dr Sibthorpe had explained that he would give Mike time to settle in. He had said regretfully that the door would have to be locked. That was part of the deal with Morris. However, there would be no police guard. Dr Sibthorpe would try to arrange for Mike to be taken out each day to walk in the grounds, if he wanted to. Meals would be brought to his room. There was a bell he could press if he needed anything else. A nurse would come eventually if Mike rang, although the hospital was a little short staffed at the moment, especially over the weekend so he would need to be patient. Dr Sibthorpe would be back on Monday morning to carry out a longer interview, which would help him to plan the period of observation. He would also want Mike to do some assessments and take a number of medical tests. He apologised that there was no television, and said he would see if he could get hold of one. Finally he had left a pad of paper with pens and pencils and invited Mike to think back over what had happened and write down anything that might be useful.

Once he had unpacked, Mike moved the chair from the desk to the other side of the bed and sat looking out of the window. It was so nice to be able to see something other than a patch of artificial light. It was six o'clock and the sun was sinking. The hospital grounds were well kept. There were lawns, flower beds and groups of trees – oaks, a silver birch and a large horse chestnut. The hospital was on the edge of the town, situated close to open countryside. If Mike could get out of his room and the building, leaving the grounds wouldn't be a problem. The wall wasn't high; it was there more to mark the hospital's boundary than for real security.

Mike wondered idly what observation actually meant. Interviews, assessments, tests and what else? He looked round the room again, unable to see what he was looking for, but sure it must be there. This was a new suite, purpose built for clinical observation. Somewhere there would be a concealed video camera. And the mirror? Mike got up and walked across to it, looking at his own reflection staring back, and wondering. Was it really a mirror? Was Dr Sibthorpe sitting on the other side of it right now, watching him? Mike couldn't tell, though it was certainly possible. He went back to his chair by the window. Yes, this room was certainly better than his cell, but he was going to have to be on his guard.

Over the weekend Laura began to make preparations. The sense of unity she had felt when she'd seen Mike had stayed with her. She still believed that there were issues to be resolved between them, but these could be put to one side for the moment. There was a purpose and a plan. This was so much better than the shock and uncertainty that she'd felt after their first meeting in the police station.

There was nothing Laura could do about finding the girls over the weekend. Looking for a solicitor no longer seemed such a good option either, so she concentrated on preparations for the possible escape. She rang Lottie and arranged for them to meet for lunch in town. She hadn't seen Lottie for a couple of months. After Laura had started her relationship with Mike, she and Lottie had inevitably drifted apart. They'd tried to see each other a bit, but when Laura had discovered she was pregnant their meetings became less frequent.

On her way to meet Lottie, Laura used Mike's card to draw out fifty pounds. Then she went to a different cash machine and drew out a hundred pounds on her own card. After that she went to the post office and bought two hundred pounds worth of euros, paying for them with her debit card. She'd been on the internet already that morning, looking for possible destinations. There were two airports they could leave from. The closer one was quite small and might be too obvious, so she'd gone for the one that was further away. It had a range of flights, and once they were in the EU they could move freely between countries without having to use their passports. She went down the destinations in Spain. Madrid, the capital, was a possibility. Malaga and Alicante were both holiday destinations and might not be busy during the autumn and winter. A British family might stand out there, although she knew both places had large expatriate communities. Palma on Mallorca and Mahon on Menorca she quickly dismissed. These were holiday islands, and islands might be harder to move on from quickly if they needed to. Barcelona stood out. It was a large city on the coast and somewhere that Laura had always wanted to visit. Its cosmopolitan population should make it an easy place to disappear. There were plenty of flights and they were not expensive. To fly somewhere else and then travel on to Barcelona might be the clever thing to do, that would depend on whether there was time. Laura was pleased with her morning's work and, despite everything, felt in a good mood when she met Lottie in the Crown.

Laura had deliberately taken the bus in to town and had left Alice with Pauline, playing with the cat. She and Lottie bought drinks, ordered food and went to sit in a quiet corner, just as they used to do. With a jolt Laura realised that it was almost exactly four years since she'd first met Mike.

They chatted quietly while they waited for their food. Lottie told

Laura about her holiday in Crete and the brief romance she'd had there. Term was in full swing and the students seemed to be as challenging as ever. Lottie was thinking that it was time she moved on to another school. Every time she mentioned it, though, her boss seemed to find something attractive to offer her, so she stayed. Now she was Head of English and being groomed for senior management. She admitted that she'd done well, but it was a mistake to stay too long in the same school. Laura listened, enjoying Lottie's company and regretting that they hadn't seen more of each other.

Laura said that she would be sad if Lottie moved on, then a sudden thought struck her.

"You don't have a couple of girls at your school?"

"Probably lots." Lottie laughed at her. "We do have over twelve hundred, you know."

"I know, but are you the only secondary school in the town?"

"Yes, we are."

"Their names are Marie and Yvette. I don't know their second names, but they are very distinctive. Dual heritage, long hair, very attractive."

Lottie thought for a moment. "Could be Marie Cameron. I think she might have a sister who's a bit younger. I actually taught her in Year nine last year, or I tried to. She was so frustrating. Really bright, charming and, as you say, an absolute stunner, but she was never there and never did any homework. Yes, Marie Cameron I think. I'm not sure that's her real name. I remember when I asked her tutor about her attendance, she said Marie lived with an aunt or something. There's a cousin too, but he's African Caribbean. He's very nasty."

"Where does she live?"

"Not sure. On the Hawthorns I think." The Hawthorns was the estate where the playground was. Laura had the lead she wanted.

"Thanks Lottie. That's really helpful." Laura took a deep breath and leant forward towards her friend. As she spoke she lowered her voice. "Look Lottie, Mike's in a bit of trouble. I won't tell you what it is because it's better you don't know. He is being set-up by some people, so if it's in the papers don't believe what you read."

"I'm sorry. What can I do to help?" That was typically Lottie. She was Laura's friend, and her first instinct was to offer her help.

"We may have to leave in a hurry. I'd like to drop round a few things from my house. They're not really valuable, just a bit special. I won't be able to take them with me. Could you look after them till we come back?"

"Of course. That's not a problem. "

"I'll leave you a spare set of keys. Just keep an eye on the house now and again. I'll leave some keys with Pauline too."

"Okay. Is this something to do with the two girls you mentioned?"

"Possibly, but honestly it's better that you don't know."

"Okay."

"Lottie, thanks. You've been a real help." They chatted on for a bit, then Laura looked at her watch and said she needed to go and collect Alice. She arranged to drop off the things on Sunday night. Before they parted she gave Lottie a hug.

"You're a real friend, you know."

"You know I'll always do my best. Take care, and come back soon."

Just after nine on Monday morning Mike heard the key turn in the lock. The door opened and Dr Sibthorpe came in, greeted Mike and asked him how he was settling in. Then he asked Mike to come through to his office for the first interview. They walked a little way along the corridor and then turned left into what seemed to be a suite of interview rooms.

Dr Sibthorpe had a spacious office. A large desk with a computer on it stood against the window. Around the room there were filing cabinets and bookshelves. There was also an area with four easy chairs around a coffee table. Dr Sibthorpe motioned for Mike to sit down and asked him if he'd like a drink. Mike asked for a glass of water. Dr Sibthorpe took a bottle from a small fridge and handed it to Mike along with a glass, then he picked up a cassette recorder, which he placed on the table.

Dr Sibthorpe sat opposite Mike. "Michael, before we start, and before I turn on the tape, I want to explain the purpose of my observations. There are certain unusual things about your case. My job is to investigate them and see if they help to explain how you behaved, and why you committed the offences you did."

Mike stared at him. "Do you believe my story?"

"If you mean do I believe that when you dream you can see both the future and the past, then probably not."

"Oh." Mike felt disappointed.

"Scientifically, events in the future are the result of a chain of other events. Logically and scientifically, you cannot predict the future. If an event in the present occurs differently, then the future event will be different. Many people have claimed to have the power of precognition, but none of these claims have ever been scientifically substantiated. However, it is possible, by acting in a certain way, to make the things you think will happen in the future actually take place. It's a kind of self-fulfilling prophecy. Do you follow me?"

He paused and looked at Mike, who nodded.

"The mind is a very strange thing. We don't even fully understand the physical workings of the brain, and what we do know we've learnt mainly in the last ten years. Our knowledge is increasing all the time. I do know that a highly traumatic event can put an individual into a profound state of shock. In this state of shock, they may convince themselves of things that are not actually true. The brain can be very good at telling us what we want to think."

"So you think I may be suffering from some kind of state of shock?"

"According to your story, over ten years ago you witnessed a terrible event. Seeing such an event may well have put you into a profound state of shock that has affected you ever since. That's what I need to try to establish."

"I see." Mike sounded, and felt, uncertain. Dr Sibthorpe looked at Mike, and there was a kindness in his expression.

"Look Michael, you have a blameless record and yet you have committed some serious criminal offences. We need to understand why. For yourself, you need to be able to understand and make sense of what happened to you."

"Okay." Mike nodded.

"Now I'm going to start this morning by asking you to talk me through what happened in New Orleans." Dr Sibthorpe got up. "I am going to attach these two pads to you, one to either side of your chest. They will provide the machine with readings of both your heart and your breathing." Dr Sibthorpe gave Mike sticking plaster to fix the pads in place, then switched on the machine. Mike saw it begin to draw a sort of a graph. One line was in red and one in blue.

Sibthorpe sat opposite Mike again. "As you talk, this will help me to see if what you're saying has any emotional impact on you. Later on I want to take what's called a CAT scan of your brain. It may be that I'll want you to retell your story while connected to the scanner too, as I would then be able to see what's going on in your brain while you're talking.

"So, if you're ready Michael, I'm going to turn on the tape recorder. All I want you to do is to tell me the story of what happened in New Orleans. Sit back and relax. Close your eyes if you want to. Try to visualise exactly what happened. To begin with I will just listen, but when you've finished I may want to go back and ask you some questions. Are you ready? You can start as soon as I turn on the tape."

Mike took a drink of water, then sat back in his chair. "Okay, I'm ready."

Dr Sibthorpe turned on the tape. He sat facing Mike, a notebook on his lap and a pen in his hand. Mike heard the tape start and began to talk. He thought back to that night over ten years ago and described what he remembered of it. Trying to forget about the pads taped to his chest, he spoke for a long time. Dr Sibthorpe interrupted once to change the tape in the cassette recorder; apart from that he said nothing. At last Mike was finished, and suddenly he felt very tired. Leaning forward he took a drink of water.

"Thank you, Michael. That was very helpful." Dr Sibthorpe wrote a few notes down, then he looked up at Mike. "Tell me, Michael, how did you feel when you saw her being killed?"

"I couldn't believe what I was seeing. I wasn't expecting it. The others seemed to know that something was going to happen. They tried to pull me away, but I turned and I saw."

"What did you see?"

The images were as vivid as ever. "I saw the men hold her. One stood on each side of her. They held her arms so she couldn't move. They pulled her head back by the hair to expose her throat. Then the third one cut. The knife caught the light. He brought it across her neck.

As he cut, a red mark appeared. The others let go of her head and it fell forward onto her chest. Then my companions pulled me away and we ran out of the place."

"How did you feel?"

"I don't know. Just devastated. Like I said, I'd never seen anything like it before."

"You had been drinking?"

"Yes, we'd had some beer."

"A lot?"

"A bit, but I wasn't drunk if that's what you think. Maybe a bit tipsy."

"Michael, do you take drugs?"

"I've tried cannabis. It went with the band. Not since."

"Were you smoking cannabis that night?"

"No. The others were, I didn't."

"When you went to the toilet?"

"Yes?"

"You had sex with the dancer?"

"I don't know."

"What do you mean?"

"Well I thought I did, but I came to on the floor. Perhaps I fantasised it, but then how did I get the figure?"

"Do you still have it?" In response, Mike took the figure out of his pocket and placed it on the table between them. Dr Sibthorpe picked it up and looked at it carefully. He went to his desk and fetched a magnifying glass to examine the detail of the carving. Then, with a small camera, he photographed the figure from a variety of angles.

"Very interesting," he said, handing it to Mike who put it back in his pocket. "So, this dancer had a necklace of these figures?"

"Yes."

"And Marie, the girl in the playground, also wore such a necklace?"

"Yes." Dr Sibthorpe made some notes. Then he looked up at Mike again.

"I think we'll take a break now." He switched off the tape. Mike looked at his watch. It was just after twelve. The interview had lasted nearly three hours.

"What do you think?"

Dr Sibthorpe looked at him. "It is too early to tell. From the sound of it you witnessed a very disturbing incident. What effect that has had on your mind I don't yet know. That's really all I can say at this point." Dr Sibthorpe packed up his things and took Mike back to his room. "I'll see you again tomorrow. I have other patients to attend to this afternoon."

At work on Monday, Laura managed to schedule her day so that she was in the office over lunchtime. Most people went out for a break so the place was fairly empty. She waited until she was alone, then took the key to the locked filing cabinet marked "Confidential" and opened it. First she took out the file of a boy whose case she was working on, then she looked for Cameron. There were two files: a bulky one for Marie, and a much thinner one for Yvette. Laura lifted them both out, locked the cabinet and took them over to her desk.

Laura placed Yvette's file under the one for the boy and opened Marie's. She had hoped to photocopy the file, but there was far too much. She didn't dare take it away because the police could ask to see it at any time, so she went through it quickly. First she found Marie's address and made a note of it. Then she took out the initial assessment, the latest reports from the school and the social worker. She photocopied them and put the copies in her bag. Yvette's file was much slimmer so Laura was able to skim through it quickly and copy the necessary documents. After this she replaced both the files in the cabinet. By the time others started to come back from lunch Laura was reading through the file for the case she was working on. The afternoon dragged, until at last it was time to leave and collect Alice from the childminder's.

Mike's arrest had made work more difficult; someone in the office had recommended the childminder. Luckily there had been a place as another child had just left. Laura had been worried to start with, but Alice seemed to have settled into the new routine well. It had meant that Laura needed to change her working days; fortunately it hadn't been a problem to the rest of the team. Laura didn't know how much they knew; she had just said to her line manager that her circumstances had changed and that she hoped it would only be temporary.

At home Laura made tea and played with Alice. Once Alice was safely asleep, Laura poured herself a glass of white wine from the bottle in the fridge, took the photocopies out of her bag and sat with them on the settee.

Marie Cameron lived with Aunt Rose. Her date of birth was noted as 25 April 1994. Place of birth was unknown. The identity of her parents was also unknown. A note indicated that Rose Cameron had fostered Marie as a private arrangement, being the only surviving family member. The family had moved from London in 2004. All this information was on the first assessment, dated 2006. The assessment had taken place because a neighbour had contacted the police. The neighbour was especially concerned about the number of men who came, at different times, to a house where there were two young girls. The social worker had made a home visit in order to assess the situation. She'd reported that the house was clean and well kept. There seemed to be no shortage of money, although Mrs Cameron was out of work at the time and claiming benefits. When questioned about the apparent wealth Mrs Cameron had explained that, when Marie and Yvette's mother had tragically died, a trust fund had been set up to pay the costs of bringing them up. This fund was entirely devoted to the girls. Rose had indicated that she did not claim benefits for Marie and Yvette, except child benefit. The other benefits were claimed to support herself and her two sons. She had said that she was very good at managing the money. When questioned about the different men who came and stayed at the house, her response had been that she had five brothers. Her brothers and their children often came to visit since they had moved from London.

Marie was described as very mature for her age. At twelve going on thirteen she dressed and behaved like a girl two or three years older. The social worker had written a confidential note that she suspected Rose was selling Marie for sex, but there was no evidence to support this. She'd talked to the neighbour, and found they were no longer prepared to say anything. They had claimed it was all a misunderstanding and they now realised the visitors were all family. Again, the social worker had written a note that she suspected this sudden change of opinion might be due to intimidation.

The social worker had continued to monitor the situation. In 2007, Marie had twice been picked up by police patrol cars out on the streets late at night, dressed in what the officer had described as an inappropriate manner for a girl of her age. Again there was the suspicion of soliciting, but Marie had maintained that she was coming back from a party at a friend's. This had been an explanation her aunt had strenuously supported. After the second time, Rose had made a complaint that the police were unfairly harassing them because of their race.

Following this, the police and social worker seemed to have backed off for a while. Laura sighed. All this certainly showed that Marie was no innocent little girl being exploited by an older man. It looked as though she was highly experienced and knew exactly what she was doing.

Laura turned to the school report. That simply bore out what Lottie had said. Marie Cameron was identified as being bright with great potential, but no motivation or interest. Her behaviour in class was good, her effort poor, homework seldom done and her attendance record dire, so much so that there had been a referral to the educational welfare officer. After this Marie's attendance had improved, though not her motivation.

It all seemed to fit with what Mike had said, but why should Marie want a relationship with him? Could he be right that her mother was the woman he had seen murdered in New Orleans? Marie's mother was certainly dead, though there was no evidence anywhere that she had come from America. The papers made Laura even more curious. She wanted to see this Marie and talk to her. How to do that, though, she wasn't sure.

Dr Sibthorpe didn't appear on Tuesday until mid-afternoon. He had already sent a message to say that Mike wouldn't be given lunch today because he intended to do a brain scan in the afternoon. A male nurse came and collected Mike, taking him further down the corridor to a room that seemed to be like both an operating theatre and a laboratory. The room was divided in two by a glass panel. In one part there was a bed attached to a gleaming white machine. In the other there were computer screens, chairs and a table. Mike was taken into the room with the computers, where Dr Sibthorpe was waiting for him. He greeted Mike with enthusiasm.

"What do you think of it?" Dr Sibthorpe gestured through the glass to the gleaming white machine.

"Impressive," Mike replied.

"Yes. We've only had it six months. It's brand new and very expensive. I persuaded the hospital to get it. You are looking at the future of psychology. With this machine we can look inside your head. We can watch what your brain does while you're actually thinking."

"Mmm." Mike sensed that this was Dr Sibthorpe's new toy, and that he was desperate to play with it.

"We're still discovering how to get the best out of it, but I thought it would be especially useful in your case. Now you're going to need to get gowned up." Sibthorpe turned to the nurse. "Geoff, take Michael next door so that he can change into a gown." The nurse led Mike to a room divided into cubicles, and handed him a white gown.

"Go in there and get undressed to your pants, then put on the gown. Hang your clothes up and leave your shoes there. You'll need these for your feet." He handed Mike a pair of white fabric flip-flops, like the ones provided by expensive hotels for their guests. Mike went into the cubicle and undressed as he was told. He came out wearing the white gown and slippers, and the nurse took him back into the other room.

"Now Michael, I want you to go next door and lie on the bed," said Dr Sibthorpe. "First we'll do a straightforward scan. Then we'll show you a set of images and scan your reactions. Finally I'll ask you a few questions. I won't be in the room with you, but I'll be able to see and hear everything."

"Will it hurt?" Mike asked.

"No, it's completely painless and has no side effects."

Mike went next door and swung himself onto the bed. He looked up at the pure white tiles of the ceiling. He heard Dr Sibthorpe's voice asking him to move up the bed a little and to the right because he wasn't quite in the centre. Again, Mike did as he was told.

"Okay, here we go," Dr Sibthorpe boomed.

The bed slowly slid backwards until it stopped under what seemed to be a large camera, with two others on each side. Mike was aware of a sensation that reminded him of a chest x-ray he'd once had. Then the bed moved him back out into the light.

"Was that okay?"

"Yes," Mike heard his voice reply. It seemed somehow separate from him.

"Okay, we'll slide you back and show you some images."

The bed slid back and Mike looked up. This time a screen appeared above his head and a series of slides flashed across it. First there were landscapes: mountains, trees, rivers. Each slide was visible for about three seconds and then it was replaced by another. Landscapes gave way to animals. Animals to people. Images of people clothed became images of people naked, both men and women. Images of adults were replaced by images of children. Naked young girls appeared in provocative positions, and Mike understood what Dr Sibthorpe was doing.

Then the screen went blank and the bed slid out again.

"Now, Michael, I'm going to ask you some questions. Just speak normally."

The bed moved Mike back under the machine again. Sibthorpe began asking the same questions as the day before. What had Mike seen in New Orleans? How did he feel? Describe the murder and so on. At last the bed slid him out again.

"Thank you, Michael."

Mike got off the bed and went through to the room next door. He was taken to change into his clothes, then back to his room. Dr Sibthorpe said nothing, other than that he would probably see Mike tomorrow.

Back in his room, Mike sat on the chair and looked out of the window. He felt uneasy. This whole thing was strange. The telling of his story yesterday had been fine, even with the pads stuck to his chest, but this was different. People showing him pictures or asking him questions and looking to see what was going on inside his head. He didn't know what it was they were looking for. He didn't know what the patterns would show. The pictures had been predictable: neutral at first building up to the naked girls and then pornography. Suppose there was a pattern of thought that was typical of a paedophile? Suppose Mike matched that pattern? Nothing he could say then would make any difference; he would be faced with a mountain of objective scientific proof. There would be no escape. He'd always thought he was normal apart from the dreams, but perhaps the dreams made him abnormal. He knew he needed to keep calm, especially here where he was on his own, and yet not really on his own.

In the office on Tuesday, Laura looked again at Marie's file to see if there was anything she had missed. There were other reports, though there seemed to be nothing else substantial. She looked quickly at Charles's file too. He was the elder of Rose's two sons and nearly three years older than Marie. His file was even bulkier than hers. Laura skimmed it; the evidence of violence and crime, much of it alleged, stood out clearly. A colleague came to the filing cabinet so Laura had to leave it, but the picture was pretty clear.

Laura left work early and drove to the Hawthorns estate, then looked around it for the road where Marie lived. She had been on the estate before and had never realised what a warren it was. With a map open on the seat beside her, she eventually found the street and drove slowly down it, identifying the number of the house. There was no sign of anyone. Laura didn't stop. Instead she drove to the end of the road and turned the corner so she was out of sight from the house and then pulled in. She looked at her watch. It was quarter past four, and Lottie's school finished at twenty to. If Marie had been at school it was probably a thirty minute walk away. Laura looked at the map and tried to work out which way Marie would walk home, then she drove back along the route. Soon she began to pass little knots of pupils. Some were walking on their own, some in pairs or groups. Laura pulled over and parked on the opposite side of the road. She picked up the newspaper she'd brought with her and pretended to read it, watching the pupils as they went by. There was nobody that fitted her image of Marie and the flow had become a trickle. Laura was just about to drive off when another group turned the corner. First came four older boys, two black and two white. They were walking together and talking animatedly. She guessed they might be Charles, Marie's cousin, and his gang. Then two girls turned the corner about ten metres behind the boys. They were tall, but the one closer to the kerb was taller. They both had golden brown skin and long hair that fell in bunches of curls. The shorter one's hair was longer. Laura assumed that she was Yvette, making the one on the outside Marie. The black school skirt had been hitched up to reveal her long legs in the regulation tights. She had already taken off her tie and undone the buttons on the white blouse to show off a bit of cleavage.

Her face was turned away as she listened intently to her sister, so Laura was able to take a long look at her over the newspaper as she walked by.

Mike and Lottie were both right. Marie was strikingly attractive. She moved and held herself in a way that radiated sexuality. Laura wasn't surprised that Mike had been unable to resist her.

She waited until the girls were out of sight, then started the car and drove to the childminder's to pick up Alice. The image of Marie filled her mind. Laura's original intention had been to find out what she could about Marie from the records and above all to actually see her. Now she had done that, her curiosity was still not satisfied. Seeing Marie had made Laura even more determined to talk to the girl, but she realised this was very risky.

Once Alice was asleep, Laura went into her bedroom to change. She put on a V-necked grey sweater, jeans and trainers, then chose a short black coat with deep pockets. After a moment's thought she opened the bottom drawer in her cupboard. This was where she kept her self-defence kit. Whenever she was travelling on her own, or on holiday with her friend Lottie, she had learnt to take no chances, and over a period of time had acquired a number of items useful for personal protection. There was a mace spray bought in America; a metal comb with a pointed handle that had been filed down to make it extra sharp; a telescopic baton; and an alarm that sent out a high-pitched bleeping. Sometimes she'd take an item from her kit if she was having to home visit a particularly problematic family. Laura looked at the items. She didn't necessarily want to make a lot of noise, but she needed to be able to protect herself. Finally she chose the mace spray, the metal comb and the alarm, and put them in the pockets of her coat.

Downstairs she stood for a moment by the front door. She was probably being incredibly stupid, but she had to try. Earlier Laura had asked Pauline if she could babysit for an hour. She had told Pauline that Alice would be asleep and to help herself to wine from the fridge. Once Pauline had come round, Laura got into her car and set off.

At the Hawthorns Laura drove slowly round the estate on the off chance that Marie might be out on the street, but she wasn't. The streets seemed deserted. Laura drove past Marie's house a couple of times. It was nearly half past seven, and it was beginning to get dark. Laura found a place to park further down on the other side of the street, from where she could see Marie's front door. She switched off the car's lights and sat back to wait.

Laura wondered, as she sat in the dark, what she was really doing here. What was it she was trying to achieve? She didn't really have a plan, just the feeling that she needed to confront Marie and talk to her face to face. Laura didn't even know what she was going to say, nor did she really think that she had any chance of persuading Marie to leave them alone, but she had to try. As a woman fighting for her man, and a mother protecting her daughter, she had to show Marie that she wasn't going to give up. She wasn't a pushover.

So Laura sat and waited. By nine she'd seen nobody and was beginning to think she'd have to give up and go home. She couldn't leave Alice with Pauline for much longer. Then the front door of the house opened and Marie came out. As she stood in the doorway, talking to someone in the hall behind her, the light caught her for a moment. She was wearing a very short skirt, boots and a white hoodie. Marie shut the door and came out into the street. Laura was in luck; Marie was on her own, and the street was empty. Marie walked past where Laura was parked. Laura let her pass, then quietly got out of the car and followed her.

"Marie," Laura called softly. Marie turned. She was right under a street lamp, whereas Laura was in the shadows.

"Who is it?"

Laura stepped into the circle of the light. Marie looked at her and smiled. "Oh, it's you. I wondered if you'd find me. I wondered if you'd come."

Laura was surprised. She hadn't thought that Marie would know who she was.

"What do you want? I suppose you've come to fight for your man." Marie's tone was amused; she stepped closer to Laura.

Laura stood her ground, determined not to be intimidated, and they stared at each other. Laura saw fine, high cheekbones, sensuous lips and blue-green eyes that seemed to draw her in.

"You can have him back, I've finished with him now. Give me what I want and I'll withdraw my statement. I can say that I made a mistake, or that I made it all up. I might get into trouble for wasting police time, but he'd be free and back with you in twenty-four hours."

Laura said nothing, just stared into those eyes. Marie stepped closer and took Laura's hands in hers. They were standing against each other, their bodies and their faces almost touching.

"Laura, there is no need for us to be enemies. I want us to be friends." Marie's lips brushed Laura's. Laura could smell her scent. "Mike was okay. He was good in bed, but he was so stupid. He kept asking questions and he could never put the answers together." Marie's voice was soft, almost a whisper. "You're different. You're smart and pretty. You're like me."

Marie kissed Laura on the mouth. "Men are useful, don't get me wrong. They need us to organise them. They can give us pleasure, but we can give each other pleasure." Marie kissed Laura again; this time her tongue gently probed into Laura's mouth. She let go of Laura's right hand, slipped her own inside Laura's coat and touched her breast. She found the V in Laura's jumper and slipped her hand inside Laura's bra. Laura gave a sharp intake of breath at the touch; she had never been touched or kissed by a woman before. The softness of Marie's hand excited and aroused her. She closed her eyes. "See?" Marie whispered, gently caressing her breast. "I can give you more pleasure than you would think possible. Join me Laura. Let us be friends. You can have Mike back if you want him, or you can leave him where he is. Together we can have so much power, and so much pleasure. You, I and Alice."

The word reverberated around Laura's mind. To protect Alice was the real reason she was here. Laura broke free of the embrace and stepped back.

"No. You're not having Alice."

Marie stepped forward again. "Laura, listen. You think I want to hurt Alice, but I don't. Alice is as precious to me as she is to you. She has great power and she must learn how to use it. I am to be her teacher. Together we can guide her to her future."

"No, you're not having anything to do with her." The spell had been broken. Laura felt stubborn and determined.

"Think about it." Marie's voice remained soft and soothing. "Mike will go to prison. The court may decide you are not fit to be a mother.

Why put yourself through all that? I can solve the problem, take it away. You only need to agree to let me teach Alice."

"Teach her what?"

"To understand the spirit. To understand the dreams. To use her power. We must start when she is very young."

"No. I don't want her to have anything to do with it."

"You can't stop it." Marie's voice was harder now. Laura could see the gleam in her eyes. "I will have her, and I will teach her. You can't prevent it, but you can make it easy for yourself."

"You'll never have her." Laura turned away and walked towards her car.

"Think about it," Marie called. "You can make a different choice."

Suddenly a group of four youths appeared between Laura and her car. She recognised them as the group she had seen walking in front of Marie earlier.

"Is this one under your protection too?" one of the African Caribbeans called out to Marie.

"Not entirely," Marie replied. "You can take her and play with her for a bit, but don't damage her too much and don't cut her. Bring her to me when you've finished. Maybe she'll see reason then."

The four walked towards Laura. The two African Caribbeans were in front of the other two. They swaggered as they walked. The one who had called to Marie looked at Laura. "Now white bitch, it's time to suck some black cock." His voice was silky soft.

Laura stood still. In her pocket her hand closed over the mace spray. She realised that she had only one chance. Surprise was on her side, but she had to be quick and accurate. She stood motionless, as though petrified, while they walked slowly towards her. They had to be near enough. Quickly she took out the spray and gave each of the African Caribbeans a short blast in the eyes. They collapsed holding their faces, and Laura ran.

Marie was laughing. "Pathetic little boys," she shouted, her voice full of contempt.

Another voice shouted "Get the bitch" and Laura heard the sound of running footsteps. She glanced over her shoulder and saw the other two youths running after her. If she stopped to unlock her car they'd catch her, so she ran on. Seeing an alley on her right, she took it. She might have enough of a start to lose them. That was her only chance. Although she was fit she would never outrun them. Another alley crossed the one she was on, and she turned left, then right again. There was a half-open gate on her right, so she went through it and stood in the darkness behind a fence, trying to control her breathing and listening. Somebody ran down the alley on the other side of the fence. There was the sound of shouting and then more running, further away.

They must have split up. The estate was a maze of alleys; the boys knew them, and she didn't. If she wasn't careful, she might run right back into the youths. She'd have to risk it. Taking the metal comb out of her pocket and holding it in her right hand, she moved cautiously out from behind the fence and into the alley. Then she pressed on, moving quickly and quietly, stopping occasionally to listen. The alley came to a road. She stood back in the shadows and looked down both ways. It seemed empty. Laura didn't know if she was safer in the alleys or on the road. She was more obvious on the road, but it was less easy to be surprised.

Whatever happened she couldn't stay here, so she ran across the road and into another alley. She turned right and followed an alley running parallel to the road, trying to visualise the map of the estate. It was different in daylight, and in a car. She had to work her way off the estate to streets where there were people.

Laura came to another road. Again she stayed in the shadows and looked down it. Once she was sure it was empty, she ran across it to the alley opposite. Behind her, another shadow crossed the street further up. Laura stopped and listened; there was no sound. At the intersection of alleys she turned right, again moving parallel to the road. Hopefully this would take her towards the edge of the estate. As she reached the next intersection of alleys, hands reached out of the darkness and grabbed her.

The youth tried to wrap his arms round her. She smelt his breath close to her face. Getting her right hand free, she brought the metal comb up hard into where his face should be. There was a howl of pain and the hands let go of her. She ran on down the alley to the road.

A voice shouted, "She's here." There was an answering shout somewhere to her right. As she reached the road, Laura saw a bus stopped in traffic at the far end and sprinted for it. Behind her came the sound of running feet. Reaching the end of the road she turned right towards the bus stop, and reached it just as the bus started moving. She waved wildly, trying to attract the driver's attention. He saw her and pulled in. Panting heavily she got on.

"You're lucky love, I nearly didn't see you. What do you want?"

"Thanks very much. A single to Birch Lane, please." Laura paid and the bus started off again. As it left, two other figures arrived at the bus stop. The bus was only half full. Laura chose a seat with other passengers immediately in front and behind her, and tried to get her breath back. She had never felt so relieved to be on a bus among people. Her escape from the nightmare of the alleys had come so suddenly that she felt stunned. She couldn't believe that she was sitting in apparent normality. Numbly she looked out of the window as the bus followed its route into town. Her brain seemed to have stopped functioning. The sense of numbness was so great that she almost missed the stop at the end of her road. She rang the bell just in time and thanked the driver.

Warily she looked down the road to her house. It appeared empty. The estate was a good twenty to thirty minutes' walk away, but nothing seemed certain anymore. Laura felt in her pocket for the comb, which she had pushed out of sight when she got on the bus. Cautiously she walked towards her house, looking to her left and right, especially where there were shadows. She tried to keep away from the street lights. A cat ran across her path and made her jump. At last she reached her front door. She paused for a moment, almost expecting figures to appear out of the shadows and drag her away. There was nobody. She shivered, then went to the door and let herself in. The front room was a bright glow. Pauline was sitting drinking a glass of wine, watching television. She stood up as Laura entered the room.

"I'm sorry I've been so long," Laura said. It was nearly ten o'clock.

"That's alright. There's not been a sound out of her." Pauline gestured upstairs. "Laura, are you alright? You look a bit shaken."

"It's nothing. I had a problem with the car, so I had to leave it. I rushed back as quickly as I could. I'm just a bit out of breath, that's all." Laura was surprised how easily the lies came to her, but how could she explain what had really happened?

"You shouldn't have rushed. I'm fine."

"You're very kind." Laura wanted Pauline to go. She needed to be on her own.

Or did she? Did Laura really want to be on her own in the house? Pauline sat down again, and was in no hurry to go. She drank her wine and chatted away about her children, nephews and nieces. Laura listened politely, despite the turmoil inside her. She even offered Pauline more wine. Thankfully Pauline declined it. That seemed to be a trigger for her. She got up to go and then talked some more while standing up, and again on the doorstep. Laura looked beyond Pauline into the dark street, fearful that she might see shadows waiting.

"Are you sure you're alright?" Pauline asked again, picking up something of Laura's tenseness.

"I'm fine, really." Laura tried to inject a jolly tone into her words. At last Pauline went and Laura closed the door behind her. As soon as she was sure that Pauline had gone into her own house, Laura locked the door and put on the safety chain. She hadn't really bothered with it before. Then she checked the back door and went round the windows, making sure they were securely locked as well. She drew all the curtains and turned all the downstairs lights off, then she fetched Mike's bottle of whisky, poured herself a large glassful and sat in the darkened front room, listening. Even in her own home she felt vulnerable, as though any minute someone would break in and drag her out. She went upstairs to her bedroom, from where she could see the street. Through a crack in the curtains, standing back so that she couldn't be seen, Laura peered out. The street was deserted. There were no dark shadows. She sat on the end of her bed and suddenly began to shake uncontrollably. She took a gulp of the whisky. It burnt her throat, but it seemed to steady her nerves and eventually she stopped shaking. Crossing to the window she looked out again; still there was nothing. She went back to the bed and lay down, propping herself up on the pillows and sipping the whisky. Only then was she able to think back over what had happened to her.

Laura realised she had been incredibly lucky. She had surprised herself by how quickly she had reacted. But if she hadn't – she shuddered at the thought of what the gang had had in mind for her. She was so glad she had taken the mace with her. They weren't expected that;

they'd thought she was easy meat, unable to put up any resistance.

Then she thought of Marie. Now she understood. Mike wouldn't have stood a chance. Laura had never been kissed by another woman or touched in that way, but she had been mesmerised, drawn in, seduced by the soft words and the caresses. Even the memory of Marie's hand on her breast sent a thrill through her. It would have been easy to give in, to listen to the sweet persuasive voice that was so reasonable and was offering so much. But she hadn't. She hadn't for Alice. However guilty or unsure she had once felt about her child, Laura knew now that she would do anything to protect her daughter. Getting up, Laura went into Alice's room and stood for a long time, looking down at her pale face in the darkness and listening to her breathing. She would never let anything harm Alice.

"Alice, they shall not have you. I will do anything in my power to protect you." But what actually would she do? What could she do? She no longer even felt safe in her own house. She had to get away with Mike and Alice. Their plan was right. They had to get out of England, go somewhere where they could disappear, out of reach of both the police and Marie. And they had to go soon.

Laura drank another glass of whisky, then lay down and closed her eyes. Sleep didn't come easily. She kept going over and over what had happened. This merged into nightmares in which she was pursued down a dark alley by black shadows. At the end of the alley Marie stood, laughing and holding Alice by the hand.

Laura woke early the next morning, even before Alice called, and lay looking at the ceiling. She remembered what had happened. Her head ached from the whisky. She got up, made herself a coffee and tried to think. The first problem was her car. She had left it parked near Marie's house. It wasn't too much of a problem; she could use Mike's as he'd left the keys when he'd been arrested, but she ought to try to go and get it. That would mean walking to the estate. Perhaps during the day would be best when the girls should be at school. Not that they always went to school.

Alice woke. Laura got her up and gave her breakfast. It was Alice's day to be at the nursery, so Laura took her in. On the way home Laura drove through the estate to decide what to do about the car. As soon as she saw it, she realised there would be no need to walk back into the estate to collect it. The windows had been smashed, the tyres slashed and the words "We'll get you, bitch" had been spray-painted on the side. The degree of damage shocked her, and she drove home quickly. She parked in her drive and looked carefully around before going into her house. After locking the door behind her and putting the safety chain on, she went upstairs to her bedroom. It was impossible to stay in her house. She knew she would have to leave as soon as possible. On Thursday afternoon she had an appointment to see Dr Sibthorpe. Perhaps she would have the chance to talk to Mike and plan what they were going to do. After that, she would take Alice and go to her mother's.

At nine o'clock on Wednesday morning Dr Sibthorpe came to collect Mike for another interview. This time his focus was on the dreams. He got Mike to talk him through each of the dreams in turn. Sibthorpe listened, made notes and asked questions, then divided the dreams into two groups. The first group contained dreams that appeared to foretell the future, and the second those where Mike claimed he had gained knowledge of past events.

"Michael, what do you mean when you say that you dreamt you would meet Laura?"

Mike thought carefully. "I saw her image very vividly. I also saw her in a particular place. The place where we met. I dreamt that she would take me back to her house. That she would like me."

"So when you saw the person from your dream it made you more confident when you approached her?"

"Yes. I've never really been that confident with women. I tend to get tongue-tied. I don't know what to say, but with Laura it was easy. I knew she would like me. I knew that whatever I said it would be okay."

"Is it possible that it was your confidence that attracted her to you?"

"Yes. I guess so."

"So it wasn't the dream itself, but the way you acted that made the relationship work?"

"Yes." Mike paused. "But don't you see? If I hadn't dreamt of her, if I hadn't recognised her, then I wouldn't have been so confident."

"Did you ever see another woman that you thought was the woman in your dream?"

"Once or twice, when I got close to them I knew they weren't."

"How did you know?"

"It's difficult to explain. I just did."

Dr Sibthorpe wrote some notes for a while. "Let's talk about the dream that led you to Marie."

"Okay."

"You knew you were in the right place because of the roundabout?"

"Yes. The playground in my dream was very distinctive. Not just the roundabout, where the swings were. Lots of things."

"The roundabout was the key?"

"Yes, because none of the other playgrounds had roundabouts. I went to a number, but none of them were right. None of them had roundabouts."

"The woman in your dream about the playground wasn't Marie?"

"No, she was the dancer from the club in New Orleans."

"So your dream wasn't about Marie?"

"No."

"Was she wearing the same dress as the woman in your dream?"

"No. The first time I went to the playground she was just a girl on a swing. I didn't really notice her until I was just about to go."

"Then what happened?"

"Her hood fell back and she looked just like the dancer. My head was spinning. I didn't know if I was seeing a girl or a woman. A real person or a ghost."

"So you went back again?"

"Yes. I had to be sure. Even then she looked and behaved so much like the dancer, not like a girl. I was confused."

Sibthorpe wrote again for a while. Then he stopped and put his pen down.

"Have you dreamt while you've been here in the hospital?"

"Only the dream I've told you about. The one where Alice is at the playground with Marie and I can't get to her. I think that is just projecting my fear. I don't know that it is a dream telling me what is going to happen."

Dr Sibthorpe looked at him. "Michael, tomorrow Laura is going to come and tell me about her experience of your dreams. What I would really like to do is scan your brain while you're dreaming. I don't know if it will tell me anything, but I'd like to try to see if your brain acts in any unusual or different way."

"Okay, although I can't control when I dream." Mike felt and sounded doubtful.

"I know that, and you're not likely to fall asleep lying on the brain scanner. I would have to sedate you and scan you while you are sedated."

"Yes, I suppose so."

"There is no guarantee that you will dream while you're sedated. It's possible the sedation might influence you. To get you used to it I would like to sedate you tonight, then on Thursday night I want to try to keep you awake all night. How do you feel about that?"

"If it helps you to understand then I'm happy to try."

"Michael, thank you. Now I think we'll stop there." Dr Sibthorpe closed his notebook, stood up and phoned through for a nurse to take Mike back to his room.

Laura picked Alice up from the nursery at half past two. She took Alice to the playground nearby for a while, and then they went to do some shopping. Laura drew some more money out on Mike's card and bought some more euros with hers, then they drove home. As they came in Alice picked up a piece of paper from the doormat and handed it to Laura. It was folded in half and looked as though it had been torn out of an exercise book. Laura unfolded it. As she read it the uneasiness that she had been trying to push to the back of her mind since she'd seen her vandalised car became a sick feeling in her stomach. The note was written in blue pen, in neat, precise handwriting.

White bitch. We know where you live. We'll get you sooner or later.
Give us what we want or we'll take it. And we will make you suffer.

Laura dropped the note on the floor. Quickly she returned to the front door that was still open. She closed and locked it. Panic filled her. They had put a note through the letter box. Could they already be inside her house? She went frantically from one room to another to see if there was any sign of forced entry. Alice trotted after her. "What's matter,

Mummy?" Laura picked her up and hugged her.

"Oh, Alice," she said. "Go and play for a bit. Mummy needs to think." Alice went into the front room to get her toys. Laura sat down at the kitchen table, then immediately got up again. How could she have let Alice out of her sight? She rushed into the front room where Alice was choosing some toys from the toy box. People could see into the front room from the street. That had never bothered Laura before. Now it did.

"Let's play upstairs." Laura picked Alice and her toys up and took them to her room. She put Alice down and walked through to her own bedroom. From there she could look down on the street. There was nobody. She sank on to the bed. What should she do?

Should she go to the police? What could she say? She had tried to make contact with Marie. That could be seen as interfering with a potential witness. Marie would lie. Laura had no witnesses to what had happened. She had not been assaulted. The gang would deny any knowledge of the damage to her car. The note was anonymous. There was little she could prove, but there was a real danger that it would compromise her and threaten Alice. No, she couldn't go to the police.

Laura knew that she didn't want to stay in her house that night. If it had been just her, then perhaps she would have stood her ground. But Alice. She didn't dare put Alice at risk. Suppose Marie and her gang tried to break in? Realistically that was unlikely because it would have given Laura something definite to go to the police with. Her house had no garage, so Mike's car would be left on the street all night. There would be nothing to stop them coming in the middle of the night and slashing the tyres or smashing the windscreen. If she and Mike were going to escape to Spain they needed that car and they needed it intact. Laura thought of driving to her mother's, but it was a four-hour drive and she would have to come back tomorrow to see Dr Sibthorpe. She sat for a while considering her options, then took out her phone and rang Lottie.

"Lottie," she said, "I need to ask you another favour."

"Go on," the voice at the end of the phone said.

"Could Alice and I come and crash out with you tonight? We'll bring sleeping bags and towels and stuff."

"Of course. What's the problem?"

"I'll explain when I come over. There are reasons why I don't feel safe being here tonight."

"Okay. Come over whenever you like."

"Lottie, thanks so much. You really are a star. We'll be over in about half an hour."

"I shall look forward to it. You are going to tell me what this is all about?"

"I promise." Laura put the phone away. She looked out of the window at the street. It was still empty. She went into Alice's room.

"We're going to stay at Auntie Lottie's tonight. Won't that be fun?"

"Auntie Lottie?"

"You haven't seen her for a while. Choose some toys to take with you." Laura put some things into an overnight bag. She took the pounds and euros she'd been collecting, put them in a money belt with their passports and put it on, pulling her top down over it. Tomorrow she'd come back for the cases she'd been packing. If she stayed with Lottie tonight she could drive to her mother's tomorrow and stay there until she'd decided what to do. She would take Alice with her to the hospital. Mike could look after Alice while Laura was with Dr Sibthorpe. She hoped she would have a chance to talk to Mike as well. Twenty minutes later she was taking Alice to the car with her overnight bag and a sleeping bag. There was still no sign of anyone on the street.

Colin Morris was just thinking about going home when Dr Sibthorpe arrived. Morris had been on an early morning shift and had intended to get away earlier, but some things had cropped up.

"Got a few minutes?" Dr Sibthorpe asked.

"Have a seat." Dr Sibthorpe sat down opposite him. "Well?" Morris asked. "How are you getting on with our friend?"

"Very interesting."

"Any conclusions?"

"It seems pretty clear that he had a very traumatic experience in New Orleans."

"You think that's true then."

"I am fairly certain. I think he suffered significant shock as a result.

Because he never really recognised or talked about it he never had any treatment. As a result I think there is a part of his mind that is very vulnerable and open to suggestion."

"And the dreams?"

Sibthorpe sighed. "I'm focusing on those at the moment, but I doubt very much whether I am going to come up with anything conclusive. It is impossible to prove that someone can foretell the future. As a scientist I would regard it as irrational. However, if you believe certain things will happen you can behave in a way that means they do, then you can claim you predicted them. It's called a self-fulfilling prophecy."

"So it's all a trick?"

"I'm not saying in Pearce's case it's a deliberate trick. I think he made things happen and then convinced himself that his dream had predicted them. He began to believe that he had a special power."

"So he has fooled himself into believing it?"

"Something like that."

"What does that mean in terms of the charges?"

"I don't think he is your usual paedophile. I believe somehow he met this Marie, who he claims looks just like the woman he saw murdered. He was vulnerable, and she was able to take advantage of that and exploit it."

"It certainly fits with what we know about her. It's still rather tenuous though."

"I know, but I think it's the best I'm going to do."

"What about the sister? He had sex with her too."

"He claims he was pressurised into it by Marie."

"He would say that, wouldn't he?"

"Yes, if you believe this is all a story he's made up."

"What's the motive? I mean for Marie. She didn't seem to be getting that much money out of him, a tenner a time. She could get more than that from punters behind the station."

"He could be lying about how much he paid. Perhaps she's blackmailing him in some way. I don't know."

"What does Pearce say?"

"To him it's all to do with his daughter, Alice. He says the girls want to gain control of her. That's where the voodoo comes in."

"Voodoo sounds like mumbo jumbo. Do you think this is all part of his fantasy?"

"It could be. He claims that the murdered woman was some kind of voodoo queen. That is why she was killed."

"Well, it's either a fantasy he believes or a fantasy he's telling us to try and get his sentence reduced. When will you be finished?"

"I've got a couple of things I want to follow up. I haven't had a chance to talk to his partner yet. I'm seeing her tomorrow. I would think by next Wednesday at the latest."

"Okay. You can have until then, but I'm nervous about him being with you. I would much rather he was back here under lock and key."

"I'm sure you can have him back next Wednesday. Then it's up to you to decide what you do with my conclusions."

"For me there's nothing strong enough to justify any mitigation."

"Has he got a solicitor yet?"

"No, not yet. I asked him about it when he was arrested, and at the time he wasn't interested. He certainly needs one, though I can't see it making much difference in the end."

"Maybe not." Dr Sibthorpe looked thoughtful. "Well, that's all for now. Of course I'll write my notes up properly and let you have them by the time Pearce is transferred back to you." He stood up.

"Thanks, Richard. I appreciate what you've done."

"Actually it's been very interesting. I've never come across a case with this sort of postponed shock before."

"If it's real."

"Yes, of course," Dr Sibthorpe said, and went out into the corridor.

Lottie and Laura sat next to each other in Lottie's front room. Lottie's small and modern flat was on the top floor of a building on the other side of town from Laura's house. They had made up a bed for Alice on the floor of the spare room, which doubled as Lottie's study. Laura had brought a sleeping bag and said she would sleep on the settee. She had fed Alice earlier, and played with her while Lottie did marking and preparation. Then Laura went out and bought them a Chinese takeaway. They had eaten that, and now they sat back on the settee.

Laura knew she had to tell at least part of the story to Lottie. She had spent time wondering how to shorten it, and which bits to miss out because they seemed too fantastic. In the end she had given up. Lottie was her oldest friend so she had better tell it all. Lottie already knew about Mike's power to dream, although she had been very sceptical of it. Laura told the whole story from the beginning, including her confrontation with Marie the previous night and what had happened after it. By the time she'd finished they were halfway through their second bottle of wine.

"So," Laura said, "I just felt I couldn't stay at home tonight. If it was only me then I would take the bastards on again and hope they would give me some evidence, but with Alice I can't take the risk."

"I still think you should go to the police. What they did to your car is outrageous."

"I know, but I can't prove it was them. And I approached someone who is a key witness in the prosecution of my partner. If I make a fuss then I'm sure she'll accuse me of trying to persuade her to drop the charges, and she'll probably produce her sister or her cousin as a witness."

Lottie was silent for a long time. "I see what you mean. So what are you going to do?"

Laura looked hard at her. "I think we're going to leave the country if we can."

"So that was what it was all about. Leaving things with me because you were going to go away."

"Yes."

"Don't you think you should stay and fight it? I'm sure Mike could get lots of character references."

"It won't help. He is guilty of having sex with underage girls. Even if they accept some mitigating circumstances he'll go to prison. He may go on the sex offenders' register. He may never be able to live with Alice and me again because he'd be seen as a threat to her. If I protest and take him back they may declare me unfit as a mother and take her into care. I'm sure that's what Marie is scheming for. She wants to get hold of Alice. If she can do it legally it would be so much easier for her."

"I really don't think it would be quite as easy as that."

"You would be surprised. I've seen these things at first hand."

"I'm still not sure. Leaving the country will be seen as a sign of guilt. You could never come back."

Laura said nothing for a while. "I know. It means leaving my mum, my house, my job, my friends, you. It's not something I want to do, but there seems no other way. If we go away we could start again somewhere else, free of all this."

Lottie leant over and hugged Laura. "You know you can trust me. I'll do anything I can to help you. "

Laura hugged Lottie hard. She could feel the tears welling up inside her and tried to keep them under control. "I'm so lucky to have a friend like you."

Lottie smiled, breaking the embrace. "You'd do the same for me. When do you think you'll go?"

"I don't know, it'll be soon. We've got to find a way for Mike to escape. It's bound to be easier while he is in the hospital."

"Try to let me know where you end up. I don't want to lose touch."

"I will, I promise, but I don't want to get you into trouble, so be careful."

"Don't worry, I will. I must say, I fancy a job in Spain myself. It's got to be better than being here." Lottie picked up the bottle and filled their glasses. "A toast," she said, "to new opportunities and brighter futures."

"And friendship," Laura added.

"And friendship," Lottie echoed.

On Thursday afternoon Laura sat in Dr Sibthorpe's office. She had explained to Dr Sibthorpe that her neighbour was busy so she'd had to bring Alice with her. They had decided that Alice could stay with Mike in his room. It was a bit irregular, but Dr Sibthorpe didn't feel there was any risk. Alice, of course, was delighted to be able to see Mike and have him to herself.

Laura sat sipping the glass of water she'd asked for. Before coming to the hospital she had gone back to her house. She had approached it with some apprehension, but everything seemed to be in order and there was no sign of another note. After she had finished packing the cases to take to Spain, she'd phoned her mother to say that she was coming to stay for a few days. Her mother was used to such short-notice visits, and had sounded glad to have the chance to see them. Alice, meanwhile, had been in her room, choosing her favourite toys to put in her own little bag. Then they had popped in to see Pauline next door. Laura had said to Pauline that they were going to stay at her mother's for the weekend and might not be back until the middle of next week. Laura gave Pauline a spare key, and asked her to keep an eye on the house. Finally, she went back to her house to change.

Laura wanted to impress Dr Sibthorpe. After musing for a moment, she chose some of her work clothes: a white blouse, grey skirt and grey tights. Then she applied a little discreet make-up and tied her hair back. Finally she checked herself in the mirror and was satisfied; the image she saw reflected back was of a calm, competent professional.

Just before she left the room she stopped to look around it for what could be the last time. Something on the pillow caught her eye. In the centre of the bed was a doll with its head on the pillow and the duvet drawn up to its chin. Laura hadn't noticed it while she was packing; her attention had been focused on choosing a few of her nicest things to take with her. She picked the doll up and looked at it with a sick feeling rising in her stomach. It had brown hair like hers and was dressed in a red summer dress, a miniature of one that hung in her wardrobe. Someone had inserted a large pin under the skirt and pushed its point between the doll's legs and into its crotch. To Laura the meaning was clear. With a sudden feeling of revulsion Laura cried out and dropped the doll. Somebody had been in her house, in her bedroom.

Alice came in to see what was the matter, dragging her bag behind her. "Mummy alright?" she said, looking up at Laura. Then she saw the doll on the floor and bent down to look at it. "Mummy got a doll like Alice," she said gravely. She rummaged in her bag and pulled out another doll which she held up for Laura to see. This doll was made in a similar way, but it had hair that fell down to the shoulders in curls, blue-green eyes and a blue dress. There was no pin pushed up between its legs.

Laura looked at it. "Where did you get this, Alice?"

Alice looked up at her. "Auntie Marie gave it to me when I was very little." Then she added with a sigh, "When are we going see Auntie Marie?"

Laura stared at her, speechless. She had never talked to Alice about what had happened or mentioned Marie's name. To hear Alice say it in such a longing way shocked her. Someone had been in her bedroom, and her daughter now wanted to see the person Laura was doing her utmost to protect her from. Laura bit her lip.

"Come on, Alice. We need to go or we'll be late." Laura went downstairs to put the cases in the car. She didn't want to stay a moment longer in what no longer seemed like her home. Alice started to follow, then went back, picked up both the dolls and put them in her bag.

Now Laura sat opposite Dr Sibthorpe, trying to be the calm, competent professional she had seen in her mirror, and put out of her mind the thought that her whole world seemed to be disintegrating. On the small table between them was a copy of the book she had written about Mike's dreams. Dr Sibthorpe picked it up and looked at it.

"Laura, tell me about the book," he said in a friendly way. "How did you come to write it?"

So she told him of the story Mike had told her. How she had researched it and wanted to try to find some empirical proof. "My training is in the social sciences," she said. "I couldn't just accept what Mike had told me, although I believed him. I needed to try to get some kind of proof. To prove precognition is simply not possible. He would have to have a dream, and then we would have to wait to see if it came true. But of course our awareness of it might influence the way we behaved."

Dr Sibthorpe nodded. "The self-fulfilling prophecy."

"So I had to try to prove his claim to have retrocognition. He told me that the first time he had experienced it was in America, in in a room where a woman had committed suicide, so I set out to look for hotels where some dramatic event had occurred. It took ages, but eventually I found the Pheasant. It was in the country, and somewhere Mike said he'd never been. In the 1950s a murder had taken place in one of the rooms. I persuaded him to go away for the weekend to do some walking, and arranged it so we could stay in the actual room where the murder had happened."

"And he dreamt?"

"Yes." Laura went on to tell Dr Sibthorpe what had happened, then how they had managed to find Robert, who had confirmed everything that Mike had said.

"So you believe the dream was genuine?"

"Yes. I know there is no convincing scientific explanation for it, but I believe it was."

"Do you have the tape recording you made that night?"

"Yes, I brought it with me as you asked."

"May I borrow it?"

"Of course." She took it out of her handbag and passed it across the table to him.

"Why did you write the book?"

"Different reasons. First we wanted to tell the truth about what happened. Then it seemed to me that, if Mike had this power, perhaps we could use it to some benefit."

"To make money?"

Laura felt defensive. "Yes and why not? Mike had carried this burden and it had made life difficult for him. Why shouldn't he benefit from it? I thought it might make a new career for him on television. Lots of people are fascinated by the supernatural or the paranormal."

"But it didn't work."

"No. Mike doesn't really have the confidence. He felt awkward in front of the cameras. Some of the team were very sceptical and that intimidated him. He just didn't seem to have the determination to make it work. It was a shame."

"You did."

Laura felt herself flushing. "I thought it was an opportunity for him."

"And for you too."

"Not really. I had my own career."

"Ah yes, you're a social worker. Not the best paid job in the country."

"No, but it's one I believe in."

"I am sure you do. On the other hand, the chance of making some money out of people's fascination with what they don't understand must have been appealing, even if it didn't quite fit with your social science test of validity and reliability."

"What do you mean?"

Dr Sibthorpe picked up the book again and flicked through its pages. "It's a good story. It reads well, and you could have made it all up."

"I could have, but I didn't."

"Why should I believe you?"

"Listen to the tape. At first all I wanted to do was understand what this was about. I believed and I didn't believe, so I set a test to try and see if there was any truth in what Mike said he could do. I found there was. It was such a great story I thought we could use it. I thought it might help Mike to confront and take control of whatever power he has."

"And did it?"

"No. I don't think Mike is able to do that. It is as though he is a medium for a power which he doesn't understand and cannot control. I know that seems vague and unscientific, but it is what I believe."

They sat in silence for a long time, Dr Sibthorpe writing methodically in his notebook. Then he put the book down and took off his glasses. "Thank you," he said. His tone was gentler than it had been during their recent interchange. Laura said nothing. She stared at him, feeling hot, flushed and defensive. She hadn't expected him to challenge her so directly. "I'm sorry. I know this isn't easy for you."

Laura remained silent, looking down at the table between them. Then she looked up and met his eyes. "So what do you think?" Her voice was defiant.

Dr Sibthorpe picked up his glasses and polished them. "I think Michael had a highly traumatic experience in New Orleans. This caused severe shock, for which he has never been treated. It has left him very vulnerable, and prone to accept things that are merely suggestions as true. He thinks he can predict things, when in fact he behaves in a way that makes them happen. Coincidences are seen as evidence of this power to predict. This makes it easy for other people to exploit him."

"You think I exploited him?" Laura did not break the eye contact. Dr Sibthorpe looked back at her calmly.

"I don't know if you exploited him. I do think this girl, Marie or whatever her name is, probably has."

"Will that make a difference in court?"

"I can't tell you that. It might, you will need a good solicitor who is sympathetic to your case." Dr Sibthorpe paused. "Michael has committed a crime and he will go to prison. The question is, for how long?"

"Would your findings send him to a mental hospital?"

"That might be part of his sentence if my views were seen as conclusive. However, in an age of care in the community we are trying to lock fewer people up in mental hospitals."

"Thank you for being frank with me."

"My job is to try and illuminate the truth. I am not on your side, nor am I against you."

"I know." Silence fell between them for a while. "Would it be possible to see Mike for a while?"

"I'm sure I can arrange that. Let me ask one of the nurses to come." Dr Sibthorpe got up and crossed to his desk. He picked up the phone and dialled a number. He spoke to someone on the other end, turning his back slightly to Laura.

"A nurse will come in a minute and take you to Michael's room." Sibthorpe sat down opposite her again.

"Thank you." Laura thought, then she spoke with great conviction. "He did have that dream you know, the one in the book. I heard him tell it to me. You will hear him on the tape."

"How can that be?" Dr Sibthorpe smiled slightly. "How can someone possibly see in a dream what has happened in the past?"

"I don't know. I only know that he did and what he dreamt uncovered a truth that had been hidden." At that point the nurse arrived, and Laura got up. Dr Sibthorpe got up as well.

"I will listen to the tape," he said, and then she left the room.

The nurse led her down the corridor to Mike's room and unlocked the door. Mike was over by the window, looking out of it with Alice.

Laura greeted him. "Dr Sibthorpe said I could see you for a while."

Mike looked at the nurse, who was standing inside the door. "Alice really wants to go outside in the garden for a bit. Is that okay?"

The nurse looked uncertain. "I suppose so, but I'll need to stay and keep an eye on you. You're not allowed outside on your own."

"That's okay. We won't be long," Mike said.

"I've got to go soon anyway," Laura joined in. "I'm driving to my mother's tonight for the weekend."

"Okay, I'll just check with Dr Sibthorpe." The nurse led them back along the corridor. Alice walked next to Mike, holding his hand. The nurse went into Dr Sibthorpe's office and left them alone in the corridor for a moment.

"I need to talk to you Mike," Laura whispered. There was urgency in her voice.

"I know, but not in my room. Everything is videoed and recorded. It's much better outside."

The nurse remerged from the office. "He says it's alright as long as I stay with you."

"That's fine," Mike said. "Thanks a lot, we really appreciate it." The nurse led them down the stairs and out by a side door into the gardens. Alice jumped up and down with delight.

"There's a small lake with fishes in, Alice. Would you like to see them?" Alice clapped her hands, which was a defined yes. Mike led them over the lawns towards a group of trees that surrounded a small lake. He tried to get out each day into the gardens, and had gradually explored all of them. It made a break from sitting cooped up in his room and allowed him to form an idea of the layout of the grounds and the perimeter wall. He wanted to find out how easy it would be to escape. It was soon clear that leaving the site from the grounds wouldn't be a problem. The real difficulty was his room; once locked inside, getting out seemed impossible.

They reached the lake and knelt by it, looking at the fish. The nurse watched them for a while and then sat on one of the seats that surrounded the lake. Pretending to point to a fish further away, Mike gradually led Alice and Laura around the edge of the lake, so that they were far enough from the nurse not to be overheard.

"Mike, we've got to get away." Laura looked ahead at the water, continuing to point at the lake.

"What's happened?"

"I met Marie." Mike turned to her, then quickly looked back at the lake.

"I told you to be careful."

"I know, but I had to see her. I had to talk to her. It was the only way I could understand."

"What happened?"

"There isn't time to tell you now. Marie offered to drop all the charges if I let her be with Alice. Then she tried to persuade me to forget about you so that she and I could bring Alice up together in the way she wanted."

"What did you say?"

"I refused. I'm not giving up Alice, not for anything. But I'm scared. I'm afraid they may try and snatch her away somehow. I stayed with Lottie last night because I was too frightened to be at home. They've vandalised my car so it's a write-off. That's why I'm going to my mother's."

"Can't you go to the police?"

"No, they would never believe me."

"Why don't you tell Dr Sibthorpe?"

"I don't trust him."

"He seems to take it all very seriously. I think he's really interested in my dreams."

"Sibthorpe may seem to be interested, but he doesn't believe them. He doesn't believe that you can predict the future, because scientifically it's impossible. He doesn't believe that you can dream about the past. He seems to think I put you up to it to make money. His diagnosis is that you're suffering from shock because of the incident in New Orleans. The best you'll get is a reduced prison term, and that's only if we get a good lawyer."

"He seems really genuine."

"He may seem genuine. He is genuinely interested in your case because it is unusual, but it's not going to make any difference. If you go to prison then I'm sure they'll find a way to take Alice from me."

"I think we should wait until he's finished his report."

"Mike, we can't. Once you're back in the police station we'll have no chance of getting away. If we're going to escape we've got to do it while you're here."

"It won't be that easy here. Getting out of my room will be really difficult. Even now we've got someone watching us." Mike looked back at the nurse.

"Yes, but what if that person was distracted? Within a few minutes we could be in the car and away."

"I'm not sure."

"Please, Mike. If you really love Alice and you really love me, then help me. We could start a new life together, the three of us. If you won't, I'll go on my own."

Mike was quiet. He looked at the lake and the fish and the trees. Alice came and put her hand in his. "You know," he said, "you make me think of Robert and Anne."

"We're not them. We are us."

"I know, but..." Mike trailed off uncertainly into silence. When he spoke again there was a new determination in his voice. "We'll do it. I don't want anything to happen to Alice, or to you."

"I'll book the flight for Saturday. I will come and see you on Saturday morning. We'll come out here again. I'll think of a way to distract your minder." They embraced each other.

The nurse had got up from his seat and was walking towards them. "I'm sorry, we'll have to go back inside now. I've been paged and I'm needed on one of the wards."

"That's okay," Laura said. "I need to get on my way. I've got quite a long drive. Come on, you." She stood and picked up Alice. "Do you think it would be alright if I came back to see Mike on Saturday?"

"I should think so. But I need to hurry you now." Mike and Laura embraced again, then Mike kissed Alice. The nurse led him back to the building. Laura put Alice down and they walked across the grounds towards the car park. She went slowly, looking around to see how the grounds were laid out and where the car park was. Possibilities were already beginning to suggest themselves to her.

Thursday night was the night that Mike had to stay awake. On Wednesday he'd been given a mild sedative and slept through the night without being aware of dreaming at all. When he reported that to Dr Sibthorpe, Mike had again said he was afraid that the sedative would stop him dreaming, so the staying awake had become even more important.

Dr Sibthorpe had brought Mike a DVD player and a stack of DVDs to help him through the night. Mike had asked especially for some music ones; he wasn't that interested in films. Laura had persuaded him to go

255

to the cinema a few times, but he was without any real enthusiasm. Laura liked lots of films, and she and Lottie had often gone to the cinema together before she had met Mike. He was okay with thrillers and sometimes action films. To him they were better than novels, left to himself he wouldn't have bothered. Filmed concerts were different. It wasn't like being there, but in some ways, because of the way they were recorded, the sound was often even better. He inspected the selection. There were some old classics from before his time like Pink Floyd, and some more recent ones like the Red Hot Chili Peppers, the Foo Fighters, Arctic Monkeys. It was just after nine. It was probably too early to start watching one now; the night was going to be a long one.

Mike crossed to the window and looked out into the darkness. All he could see were parts of the grounds, illuminated by the lights from the hospital. He thought of their moments by the lake and wished he could have talked properly to Laura. Since arriving at the hospital he'd been drifting, waiting to see what would happen. He had hoped that Dr Sibthorpe might find some way to prove his story. Although it was Mike who had suggested the plan to get away to Laura, he hadn't expected them to act so quickly. Now faced with doing it, he wasn't so sure. Would it be better to stay and face it, and call Marie's bluff? Running away would make it look like he was guilty and the dreams were just a story. He didn't want to go to prison, but he would do it if he had to. If it was the best thing for Laura and Alice. He didn't like to think of them on their own and the pressure they might come under. Mike stood for a long time looking out. Then he sighed. He couldn't talk to Laura. Tonight there was nothing for him to do except stay awake. And tomorrow he would try to manufacture a dream to give Dr Sibthorpe some proof, something that would overcome even his scientific prejudices.

Mike turned back into the room. He selected a DVD at random and prepared to lose himself in the world of music; a world where life was much less complicated. He made himself a coffee and sat down to watch.

Just after two in the morning he was beginning to struggle. He did some press-ups and sit-ups, and had a cold shower. After another coffee he found a Foo Fighters DVD, hoping that the loud rock would help to keep him awake. It was best to focus on the group. If he listened to the music the temptation was to close his eyes and let it sweep him away.

At six he showered again. Then at seven a nurse brought him an early breakfast. The fresh, strong coffee and rolls helped. Just after eight the nurse came to collect him and took him to Dr Sibthorpe's office.

"Good morning, Michael, and how are you?" Dr Sibthorpe's greeting was cheerful. He seemed in a very positive frame of mind.

"Awake," Mike responded wearily.

"Good. I think we might try without the sedative to start with. Let's go through." He led Mike through to the scanning room. "We can pipe some music through the headset if you like?"

"Let's just see how it goes first. I feel really tired." Mike undressed and put the white coat on. Then he lay down on the bed. It wasn't fantastically comfortable, but at least he could stop trying to keep awake. He lay back, and looked up at the white ceiling and fluorescent lighting.

"Could you dim the lights, please?" he said into the microphone. Dr Sibthorpe raised his thumb to show he had understood. The lights went out. Now the room was dark apart from the glow of the scanning machine. The only sound was the slight whirring it made. Mike closed his eyes and listened to the sound. He let his thoughts wander back to the club in New Orleans, and shivered. No, he didn't want to replay that yet again. He'd seen it too many times. He thought about the first time he had met Laura, watching her and Lottie dancing in the Corn Exchange, and his first meeting with Marie, when her hood had fallen back and the girl on the swing suddenly metamorphosed into a ghost from the past.

Alice. He was walking with Alice. They were on a promenade by the sea. He was holding her hand. Laura was walking on the other side of her. They stopped to look at the beach where people were swimming. Somebody waved to them. It was Marie, wearing a bikini.

"Come in," she called, "the water's lovely."

Alice looked up at him. "Can we, Daddy?" she said.

Mike was shaking his head. He didn't want to let Alice's hand go. "We'll take Alice swimming for you," Marie said, smiling at him. Yvette was beside her, also in a bikini. "Why don't you come in too?" Alice was tugging at his hand. Mike was trying to say no, he didn't think it was a good idea. He turned to Laura, but Laura wasn't there. He looked round for her frantically. Then he saw her. Two men were dragging her away. They had put tape over her mouth. She was struggling; they held her arms. She twisted her head and saw Mike. Their eyes met, and she called out to him for help.

Just then, Alice tugged at his hand. "Can we go swimming, Daddy?"

"Come on," Marie said, and stretched out her hand to Alice. Mike turned, Laura was still looking at him. He tried to pull Alice away, but Marie was pulling her back.

Mike woke. He was standing in the room next to the scanner room, wearing a white coat and looking in through the window. The room was different. The scanner was gone. Instead there was a bed with straps for the arms and ankles. There were electric wires attached to it, and what looked like terminals. A man was standing waiting; a young man with a beard and dark hair. He took his glasses off to polish them. Mike saw his eyes and recognised him as Dr Sibthorpe. The door opened and two men came in. Between them was a figure in a white coat. The figure's head was covered with a hood. The two men held the figure tightly by the arms. Once inside the room they pulled off the hood. Mike saw that the figure was a man with black hair. His face was pale and tired. As soon as he saw Dr Sibthorpe and the bed he began to struggle desperately. He appeared to be terrified.

"Please," he screamed, "please don't do this to me."

Dr Sibthorpe ignored him and gestured to the bed. The two nurses lifted the man up off his feet and put him on the bed. The man screamed and struggled. One of the nurses held him down while the other secured him with the straps. He lay helpless. His wrists were secured above his head and his legs were apart so that he was spreadeagled. All the time he was sobbing and pleading with them. Once he was secured the nurses stood back.

Dr Sibthorpe approached the bed. "Calm yourself," he said, looking down at the man. "I know this is going to hurt you." His voice was firm though gentle, as though he were speaking to a small child. "You know it's part of your treatment, don't you?" The man sobbed and nodded. "You do want to get better, don't you?" Again the man nodded, still sobbing. "Then you must accept the pain like a good boy."

"I can't," the man shrieked. "The pain is too much, I can't stand it."

"There, there." Dr Sibthorpe patted the man gently on the shoulder. Then he undid the buttons of the white coat and pulled it open. Mike could see that underneath it the man was completely naked. "Now where shall we start today?" Dr Sibthorpe spoke as though he was thinking aloud. "The ears. Yes, I think the ears first. Attach the electrodes to the ears." One of the nurses stepped forward and attached two of the electrodes. "You take the controls." Dr Sibthorpe gestured to the other nurse, who went over to some switches on the wall. Dr Sibthorpe moved so he stood looking down at the man. "Now," he said, "low power to start with." The nurse flicked a switch and moved a lever. The man's head juddered and he let out a terrible scream. "More," Dr Sibthorpe shouted above the screaming. The nurse pushed the lever again. The convulsions and the screams increased. Mike could smell burning flesh. He felt sick.

"Enough." The nurse reversed the switch, and the convulsions ceased. "Now, where shall we try next?" Dr Sibthorpe said. There was a strange pleasure in his voice that shocked Mike. "The nipples, I think. The nipples next." One of the nurses moved the electrodes on to the man's nipples. "We'll leave the genitals till last. Something to look forward to. Let's try full power this time." The nurse by the controls pushed the lever right down. The figure on the bed writhed in agony, and his screams were more piercing than ever. After what seemed an interminable time, Dr Sibthorpe said, "That's enough. Now the genitals."

Mike heard the man pleading again, and couldn't bear to watch any longer. Turning away from the window he looked for a door out of the room. All he could see were white walls. The screaming started again behind him and he was desperate to get away. At last he saw a small door right in the corner. The handle turned in his hand, but the door seemed stuck or locked. Frantically Mike pushed at it. Suddenly it gave beneath his weight and he was through it.

He was in a long corridor. The floor, walls and ceiling were all pure white. Mike felt dazzled by it, and disorientated. At the far end he could see a grey door. He started to walk towards it, but it didn't seem to be getting any closer. The sound of footsteps came from behind him and he thought that the two nurses were following him. Then he realised that he was to be the next person on that bed. He began to run. He had to reach the door. His legs were heavy, his heart was pounding. Hands grabbed him. He tried to fight them off.

Mike woke suddenly. He was lying on the bed in the scanner room. One of the nurses was shaking him by the shoulder.

"You were so fast asleep we thought you were never going to wake up." Dr Sibthorpe was smiling down at him. Mike sat up. The memories of the final dream, of the bed and the eclectic shock treatment, were still vivid.

"Are you alright? You look shaken."

"It's just... It was a deep sleep. Could I have a glass of water?"

"Of course. Nurse, get him some water." The nurse went to the dispenser on the wall and handed Mike a glass of cold water. Mike drank it.

"Now go and get changed, then let's have a chat." Sibthorpe turned away. Mike went to the cubicle.

Ten minutes later Mike sat in Dr Sibthorpe's office, looking at him over the coffee table.

"Well Michael, would you like to tell me what was going on in your head? The scanner certainly recorded a lot of activity." Mike looked at Dr Sibthorpe, uncertain what to say. He thought back to his first dream.

"I was with Alice at the seaside," he began. He described what he'd seen, how he had been pulled in both directions. "And then..." He stopped.

"And then what?"

"It was really weird. I thought I had woken up. I thought I was looking through the glass panel into the scanner room, but it was different. There was a bed that seemed to be attached to electrodes. There was a doctor, a young man. Two nurses brought a man in. He was hooded. As soon as they took the hood off him he saw the bed and started screaming. They ignored him and strapped him to the bed. Then the doctor supervised something, I am not sure what. I suppose it was some kind of electric shock treatment. It was awful to watch." Mike stopped. He was aware that Dr Sibthorpe was looking at him intently. "Was that room ever used for electric shock treatment in the past?"

Dr Sibthorpe started at the question. "No, I don't believe so." He stared at Mike. "What happened next?"

Mike described the corridor and the feeling he was being pursued.

"How very interesting," Dr Sibthorpe said. He seemed to have recovered his composure. "What kind of a dream do you think it was?"

"I think it was a dream from the past. In those dreams I am always a spectator. I can see what is happening, but it's as though I'm invisible. I do not interact with the people I see or with what they are doing."

"But in this dream you did interact. You tried to get away at the end."

"Yes, that's true. Up until then I was just a spectator."

"So you think what you saw might be true? Might actually have happened here in the past?"

"Yes, that's why I wondered if you knew whether the room had ever been used for electric shock treatment. Wasn't it an approach that was tried at one time?"

"It's possible it might have been administered here, though it would have been well before my time. These buildings are quite recent. Certainly there has been no use of electric shock therapy since they were built."

"What was on the site before?"

"There's always been a hospital here. The old hospital was partly knocked down and partly converted when the new one was built."

"Is it possible that electric shock therapy was used in the old one?"

"As I said, it was before my time so I've really no idea."

"How would I find out?"

"I really can't tell you that either. There may be records somewhere." Dr Sibthorpe shut his book. "Don't you think it's just as likely that the dream was a fantasy induced by your surroundings?"

"No. Dreams from the past are different. I can tell that."

"Really? You're very sure." The note of scepticism in Dr Sibthorpe's voice was unmistakable.

"Yes, I am."

"Well I think we'll leave it there for today." There was finality in Sibthorpe's voice. "I'm afraid I have other patients to attend to. I'll write your report up once I've studied the scans."

"Will you want to see me again next week?"

"I doubt it. I think I'm pretty much finished. We might need a brief final chat on Monday, after which I'm afraid I will hand you back to the boys in blue."

"And your conclusions?"

"I'd rather wait until I've put my final ideas together if you don't mind. Now I really need to get on." Mike had a sudden feeling that Dr Sibthorpe was desperate to bring the interview to an end. He seemed to be preoccupied in a way that Mike had not seen before. Dr Sibthorpe got up and phoned the nurse, asking for Mike to be taken back to his room.

Once Mike had gone, Dr Sibthorpe went and sat behind his desk. For a long time he stared out of the window. Then he said aloud to himself, "That is really quite extraordinary. I would never have believed that it was possible. So interesting, but what a pity." He opened his notebook and wrote for about five minutes. Then he closed it and locked it in the drawer of his desk. He sat thoughtfully for a moment longer, then picked up the phone and dialled a number.

"Colin. Just to let you know I've finished. I will need to have a final interview on Monday, then you can have him back." Dr Sibthorpe paused to listen. "Yes, I'll have it written up by Monday." Another pause. "What do I think? Well it's difficult. There is no doubt he is suffering from shock, although he may be using that as an excuse. He is also prone to fantasy. The dreams I think are just fantasy. He's a good storyteller. You would almost believe that he can look into the past, but of course that's not possible so it has to be fantasy." Dr Sibthorpe put the phone down and smiled grimly to himself.

Mike lay on his bed, looking at the ceiling. He went through the dream yet again in his mind. The more he thought about it, the more he was convinced that it was a dream about the past. He knew by now the sense of detachment, the feeling of being the unseen observer. It was true that at the end of the dream he had felt he had to leave, to get away. What he had been watching was so terrible that even in his dream he couldn't bear to see it. That had never happened before. He also knew that running down a corridor to escape from pursuers was a common dream, but he was convinced that what he'd seen was something that had actually happened.

He was also convinced that the doctor, the man in charge, had been Sibthorpe. Yes, he had been younger, how much younger he wasn't sure? Mike thought about it. Sibthorpe had probably been late twenties or early thirties in the dream. With hair and a beard he looked different, though his mannerisms were unmistakable and so were his eyes. So the events in the dream must have happened twenty or thirty years ago. Sibthorpe had denied it, had dismissed it as fantasy. Why was that? Was it something he didn't want to remember? Had something happened to the man on the bed? Mike wished there was a way he could find out. He felt that this had changed his relationship with Sibthorpe completely. Before, there had been no sense of hurry. Sibthorpe had seemed interested, even fascinated, by Mike's case. Now his investigation was abruptly over and Mike would be back in a prison cell next week – or that was the intention.

It made Laura's desire to leave seem even more sensible. And yet, what if Mike had dreamt of something that had happened? If there was a way of proving it, it would support his whole story. He needed to find a way to prove it but if it was something that involved Sibthorpe, then he would try to suppress it or deny it. There would be little Mike could do about that. Sibthorpe was an expert, and highly regarded.

The phone rang. Mike had forgotten it was there. He had avoided the temptation to use it, because he was sure that everything he said on it would be recorded. He stared at it for a moment and then picked it up. It was the switchboard who had a call for him. Could he take it? He said he could, and next Laura's voice was on the end of the phone.

"Hello," she said, "how are you?"

"Okay."

"How did the scan go today?"

"It was interesting."

"Did you dream?"

"I think so."

"Do you want to tell me about it?"

"Yes, but not now." He knew he had to be very careful about what he said.

"Look, I'm going to take Alice away for a few days. I think we both need a break."

"You said you might." Mike knew exactly what Laura was talking about.

"I'd like to come and see you again before we go."

"That would be nice."

"Time's going to be a bit tight. I'd like to come about half past ten."

"I'm sure that'll be okay. I'll talk to the nurse about it in the morning."

"We've got quite a long drive ahead of us so it would be ideal if we could see you in the garden, like we did yesterday. It would give Alice a chance to run around for a bit. Then she might sleep on the journey."

"I'll ask if it's alright. I think it should be, as long as the weather's okay."

"The forecast is fine for the morning and rain later. If we can meet in the garden that would be lovely. It would fit in with our plans. We won't stay long because we need to make a quick getaway."

"I promise I won't do anything to delay you."

"I know you won't. I like the garden. The trees are so pretty and it has such a sense of freedom."

"I know what you mean."

"Good, I'll see you tomorrow then."

"Just one thing before you go."

"Yes?"

"In my dream I was watching someone use electric shock therapy in the hospital."

"Really?"

"I wondered whether you could try to find out if that was ever used here. It would have been about twenty or thirty years ago."

"I don't have internet here so I'm not sure I can help."

"It might be of historical interest."

"I'm still not sure I can help, but I'll try."

"Thanks."

"See you tomorrow."

"I'm looking forward to it." Mike put the phone down. He lay back on the bed. So Laura had booked the flight tickets and she had a plan. He just had to make sure he could meet her in the garden.

*

Just before ten thirty on Saturday morning Laura drove into the hospital car park. There was plenty of room and she chose her space carefully. She checked that the travel rug was pulled over the cases on the back seat, then she unstrapped Alice and lifted the little girl out of the car. They walked together to reception. Alice was skipping happily along. Laura had said nothing to Alice except that they were going to see Mike and afterwards she and Alice would be going on holiday. In reception Laura explained why she was there and the receptionist rang through. After a brief conversation the receptionist told her and Alice to go into the gardens. Mike and the nurse would meet her by the lake.

Laura said that she needed to go to the loo first and asked the way to the ladies'. The directions were clear and she soon found it. She washed her hands while Alice watched. Then they both came out again, and Laura found a door into the grounds. Before she went through it she looked down the corridor, searching for something. Once she had found it, she checked that she had her geography clear. The ladies', the door into the garden, the corridor leading to reception. Once she was confident she knew where these things were, she took Alice out into the grounds. They reached the lake just as Mike did with the nurse. Luckily it was the same one who had been there on Thursday. He went and sat on one of the seats by the lake, and left them to themselves. Just as before, they moved a little way around the lake until they were out of his hearing.

"Listen carefully," Laura said, not looking at Mike.

"I'm listening."

"I'm going to put the keys to your car on the grass in front of me, then move away a bit. You need to follow me and pick them up."

"Okay." Laura put the keys carefully on the grass, shielding what she did with her body, then she moved on a little. Mike moved to where she had been sitting, as though he was naturally moving to be close to her. "I have the keys."

"Good. In about ten minutes I'm going to need the loo. I'm going to ask the nurse where the nearest ones are and leave Alice with you. As soon as I get inside I'll set off a fire alarm, then go straight to the car. It's parked under the large beech tree near to the exit. When the fire alarm goes, pick up Alice and tell the nurse you are going to look for me. Hopefully there will be enough chaos for you to lose him. Go to the car. I should be there by then. Give Alice to me and get in the boot."

"In the boot?"

"Yes. If the nurse comes he mustn't see you in the car. I'll tell him you've gone back to reception. With a bit of luck it'll give us enough time to get away."

"Okay." Mike was surprised at how carefully Laura had thought out her plan. They played with Alice for a while, looking at the fish in the lake and getting her to run from one of them to the other. Then Laura whispered to Mike.

"I'm going now. Do exactly as I told you." Mike nodded. Laura stood up and walked over to the nurse. They spoke briefly and he pointed back to the building. Laura walked slowly over, not hurrying, taking her time. Mike watched her cross the grass and disappear. A few minutes later the fire alarms went off, and people began to come out of the building. Mike picked up Alice and walked over to the nurse.

"You'd better come with me to the fire assembly point," the nurse said.

"But I need to get Alice back to her mother. I know they've got to go soon."

The nurse looked doubtful for a moment. "I'm a fire marshal, I've got to clear an area of the building. Can't I take you to the fire assembly point first?"

"No, I think Laura will want to go right away. Look, you go and do your duty. I'll take Alice to her mother and then come to the fire assembly point. I won't be long."

"Alright, but be quick and don't go through the building."

"Thanks." Mike walked off quickly through the grounds. People were still coming out of the building. There was a lot of milling around. Staff knew what they were doing, but they had to look after patients. Members of the general public had no idea where they were supposed to go. It was easy for Mike to make his way through. Soon he was in the car park. He spotted the beech tree and his car underneath it. Laura was already there waiting. As soon as he reached the car, Laura took Alice from him.

"Quick, into the boot," she said. Mike went round to the back of the car, opened the boot and climbed in. Laura shut the lid down on him. The boot was dark and uncomfortable. He had to double himself up to fit in. He heard Laura talking to Alice while strapping her into her seat, then he heard Laura get into the driver's side. The car started and began to move. The jolting was even more uncomfortable.

Laura reversed the car out of the space and drove towards the exit. Just as she was about to leave the nurse came running towards her. She stopped the car and wound down the window.

"Where is Mr Pearce?" he said.

Laura looked at him with surprise. "Sorry, I thought he was with you. He brought Alice to the car and then said he was going back to the fire assembly point. You must have missed him in the crowd. If you don't mind, we need to get on our way."

"Okay, I'll go back. Thanks."

"No problem." Laura wound up the window and drove out of the exit. She turned left and followed the road down to a roundabout. She then drove right round the roundabout and back past the hospital. Laura knew that the entrance was covered by CCTV. It was only a question of time before the police started looking for her, so she wanted to do anything she could to confuse them. She drove for half an hour, then pulled off the road into a supermarket car park. Earlier that morning she had left a car there that she'd hired to drive them to the airport. She stopped and looked around. Although it was a Saturday morning it was relatively quiet. She got out and opened the boot, and Mike struggled out.

"I couldn't have stayed in there much longer," he said.

Laura ignored his comment; she knew there was no time for pleasantries. "Get the cases and bring them over to this car," she said. "I'll bring Alice." Mike did as he was told. Within five minutes they were in the hire car and on their way. Laura had chosen the busier airport of the two. It was a longer drive, but it had a greater choice of destinations. In theory travellers had to check in two hours before their flight, Laura didn't want to spend too long at the airport. She had worked out that an hour should be fine. Flights were normally called half an hour before leaving. It was a Saturday in October, so the airport shouldn't be too busy. Half an hour to check in and go through security ought to be enough, though the timing to get there would be tight. As long as there were no serious delays on the way they would be alright. The route Laura had chosen was by back roads to avoid the motorway and its cameras. She wanted to leave as few clues as possible about where they had gone.

The journey proved uneventful. Checking in was relatively quick. Soon they were sitting in the departure lounge waiting for the flight to be called. This was the worst time. There was nothing to do but sit and worry. Laura wondered if at any moment police would enter the departure lounge and take them away. They bought a newspaper to try and pass the time. Mike took Alice to look out of the window at the aeroplanes. It was the first time she had ever been to an airport. She loved every minute of it and was delighted to have Mike back with them. Laura hadn't told her that they wouldn't be coming back.

The departures board said the flight would be called in five minutes. Five minutes went by and there was no announcement. Ten minutes; the sign on the departures board hadn't changed. Mike looked at Laura anxiously. The last thing they needed was for the flight to be delayed. Laura could feel the tension mounting inside her. She tried to keep calm, and put her hand on his to reassure him. They had hardly spoken a word to each other on the drive or at the airport. They were far too preoccupied with their own thoughts to be able to enjoy the pleasure of being together. Mike immersed himself in Alice. For a moment Laura felt a pang of jealousy. She had looked after Alice and she had brought them here; now it seemed she was being excluded. She suppressed the feeling. There was no time for that now. Once they were in Spain there would be time to do the readjusting they needed.

At last the tannoy system came to life. "EasyJet would like to announce their fifteen forty departure to Barcelona. Travellers with speedy boarding should go first to gate number eight." Trying to hide their relief Mike and Laura sat and waited for the announcement that would invite passengers with children to come forward. It duly came. Laura approached the gate with dread. She still expected a policeman to appear at any moment, or the attendant to ask them to wait to one side when she saw their passports. But the attendants merely gave the passports a cursory glance. Soon they were on the aeroplane, Alice sitting on Laura's lap, her little seatbelt attached to Laura's. Even now

Laura wondered if they would be dragged off the plane. At last everyone was on board and the aircraft's doors were closed. It taxied onto the runway. Laura looked out of the window as it gathered speed. She heard the note of the engine rise and felt the plane lift away from the ground. She looked down at the road and houses, the green fields, the groups of trees already turning yellow and brown, and wondered if she would ever see this country again.

Then a thought dampened her sense of relief. They still had to get into Spain. Was it possible that the police could find out which plane they had caught and telephone through? Could it be that even as they thought they had escaped they would be apprehended at the point of entry? They had taken one step on the way to a new life, but they were not there yet.

At the hospital the nurse was searching for Mike. It was nearly an hour before everyone was back in the building, and it took him another half an hour of searching to convince himself that Mike really wasn't on the hospital site. He couldn't believe that Mike had actually vanished. Then he wasn't sure what to do. He knew that Mike had been transferred to the hospital by the police, but he had no idea who to contact. He rang Dr Sibthorpe, which was the obvious thing to do. There was no response from Sibthorpe's home phone, and his mobile was turned off. The nurse left a message, but it was another hour before Sibthorpe got back to him.

"You're sure he's gone?"

"I've looked everywhere. His things are still in his room, but there's no sign of him."

"Damn. You'd better contact the police. Colin Morris is the person you need to speak to. If he's not there, talk to the duty sergeant."

Getting through to the police was a nightmare. The nurse spoke to some central admin reception that connected him to Morris's extension, but Morris didn't answer. The nurse had to phone again and went back through to central reception, where he spoke to someone different. They put him through to the duty sergeant. There was no answer there either and the nurse had to leave a voice message. The nurse didn't feel happy with that, so rang the central reception again, where he spoke to a third person. This time he managed to get across how urgent his call was and eventually spoke to someone at the local police station. He explained what had happened. The officer who answered seemed to have some trouble in understanding the situation. He said he would see what he could do, but the local football team was playing at home and most of the officers were deployed on that. He would send a car up as soon as he could.

Just after half past four a police car arrived at the hospital. Unfortunately the officers had not been given the name of the nurse they needed to contact, only the name of Michael Pearce, so there was a further delay before they found the nurse and he was able to explain what had happened. Then the officers methodically began to do what they could. They wrote down a description of the car and the number plate, and radioed it out across the county, then across the United Kingdom. They looked at CCTV footage from the car park, and identified the car leaving and the direction it had gone in. It was not until Sunday afternoon that the car was found in the car park of a supermarket, only half an hour away.

6

Spain, October 2009 – May 2011

They walked out of the airport into the evening sunshine. The heat of the day still hung in the air; the brightness of the light, the colour of the people's clothes and the vibrancy of the language flowed over them. For the first time since she had made up her mind that they must go, Laura relaxed. She'd felt her heart beating in her chest at passport control. The young, uniformed man behind the glass window seemed to look at her for an extraordinarily long time. Then he had smiled, and said, "*Buena sierra, Signora*, welcome to Barcelona." She mumbled "*Gracias,*" smiled at him and moved quickly on. Mike breathed in the air and felt free again.

Eventually they found the bus mentioned in the guidebook and bought tickets to Playa Catalunya. The journey into the city reminded Laura of the family holidays she had gone on when she was eight or nine. The most exciting bit was the journey from the airport, being in a foreign country where everything was exotic and the feeling that the holiday stretched out before them. This time, the holiday might last the rest of her life.

Taking Alice on her lap, Laura held her so she could look out of the window and pointed things out to her, telling her some of the names in Spanish. Laura was surprised how much of the language had already come back to her. Half an hour later they got off the bus in the square. Unmistakeably they were in the centre of a big city. It was Saturday night and everyone seemed to be out on the streets. They crossed the square to a tourist information kiosk, and Mike waited with Alice while Laura went to find somewhere to stay.

In a few minutes she was back with a map. She'd managed to book somewhere nearby. It wasn't too expensive and it would do at least for a couple of nights until they got their bearings. She led them south of the square into a maze of medieval streets. The buildings rose above them like cliffs, the narrow side streets were fissures leading into the rock. Laura turned left and then right, checking each time with the map. Soon they were standing in the foyer of the hotel. The smiling receptionist checked them in and gave them a room key. They took the lift to the fourth floor and followed a narrow corridor. At last they reached room 428, opened the door and went in.

The room was larger than Laura had expected. It had a double bed and a small single one for Alice. They put down their cases and embraced. First she and Mike hugged each other, then they lifted up Alice so she could join in. Laura had only one thought: we are here. She almost needed to pinch herself to make sure that she wasn't dreaming. They stood together like that for a moment: then they separated. Alice went off to explore the bathroom, Mike crossed to look out of the window at the street below and Laura sank down on the bed.

"I'm starving," Mike said. "Let's go and find something to eat before it gets too late. After all, it's way past Alice's bedtime already." As soon as he spoke Laura realised that she was hungry too. They had bought Alice a sandwich at the airport, but neither of them had felt like eating.

"Okay," she said. "We can unpack later." She took the guide she'd bought out of her handbag and looked through it. "If we find our way to Las Ramblas, that's supposed to be one of the main streets. There must be places to eat near there."

Outside it was dark, but the streets were still full of people. Laura led Mike and Alice along the narrow street the hotel was in and turned right. Here the street was illuminated by the lights from the shop windows and it was even more crowded. As they walked along it they passed some arches on their left. Mike was curious and crossed the street. Beyond the arches was a large square full of restaurants. He called to Laura and Alice, so they followed him under the arches. Chairs and tables were set out beneath bright awnings on the cobbled stone. Many were already full. In the centre of the square, groups of people were sitting and talking around a statue. Laura led Mike and Alice from one restaurant to another, looking at the menus. The first ones seemed very expensive, but in the far corner they came to one that did tapas. Laura explained that tapas meant a selection of small dishes. The restaurant was typically Spanish. The prices seemed reasonable and it was popular, so they stood looking around the square while they waited for a table.

Fortunately a couple left and soon they were sitting looking at the menus. Mike left it to Laura, who ordered a selection of dishes, a bottle of Rioja and lemonade for Alice. They all felt hungry and the basket of bread the waiter put in the middle of the table was soon empty. Mike looked around with interest, absorbing the sights, sounds and smells of the new city. It was a while since he'd been abroad and he'd never been to Spain. He felt renewed and excited. There was a whole set of experiences waiting for him and he was free. He felt incredibly happy. Alice, too, was fascinated by everything around her. Laura watched them both and her own sense of pleasure grew. She had brought this about. She had lifted the shadows that had been hanging over them and, despite having left her beloved house behind, she too was ready for a new life.

The drinks came and they clinked glasses, even Alice. Laura savoured the red wine. When the food came it was exciting too. Laura had chosen a mixture of fish, meat and vegetables. They talked about what they would do tomorrow. Laura said they should explore the city. There was a beach and they deserved a real day of holiday. On Monday they would need to start looking for an apartment or a flat. It would be better to be out of the tourist heart of the city. In any case, the hotel was too expensive for them to stay in for long. They needed to find for work of some kind. Although they had plenty of money for now, it would soon go if they weren't careful.

After they'd eaten and paid the bill, Laura insisted they go as far as Las Ramblas before they went back to their hotel. It was only a few minutes from the square where they'd eaten. They stood on the pavement that ran down the middle of the street and looked at the flower stalls, bars and restaurants. Everywhere was crowded with people. Then they turned back. Alice was tired, so Mike carried her. By the time they reached the hotel she was fast asleep. In their room they didn't turn on the light; Mike laid Alice gently in her bed and drew the sheet over her. They both stood looking down at her and listening to her breathing. Then they embraced.

Laura's lips found Mike's and they kissed. He pulled away from her and looked at her face. The lights of the street filtered through the curtains.

"Thank you for freeing me. Can you forgive me for what I did with Marie? For ruining our lives?"

Laura looked at him. She remembered the touch of Marie's lips on hers and Marie's hand caressing her breast. How could he have resisted? She shivered. Then she pulled him close to her. "I will try."

"Thank you. You know I love you. I never wanted to hurt you."

Laura kissed him silently. She undid the buttons on his shirt and slid her hand inside, touching his chest. They undressed quietly and lay down on the bed. It was so long since they'd been in bed together that there was a pleasure in touching each other's bodies. They didn't make love; Laura was too aware of Alice being in the room. Instead they lay in each other's arms until they fell asleep.

They all slept well, even Alice and didn't wake until after nine. Once they had showered and Alice had had a bath, they went out and found a cafe where they had a breakfast of coffee, rolls and fruit juice. Then they went to Las Ramblas which was already busy. They followed it down to the sea where there was a big statue of Christopher Columbus. Beyond that was the harbour.

They found a wooden walkway and followed it. To their left was a marina crammed full of luxury yachts. To the right was what seemed to be the commercial harbour, where there were ferries and a big ocean liner tied up. The walkway sloped up and they realised that they were on a bridge that crossed the entrance to the marina. As they reached the middle of it they heard blasts on a whistle and shouting behind them. People began to hurry in whichever direction they were going. Mike and Laura weren't sure what was happening, but Mike picked up Alice and they hurried too. They reached the other side and turned back to see the bridge was moving.

"It's a swing bridge," Mike said. He was right and they soon saw why it had moved. Three large yachts with tall masts were leaving the marina, the bridge had moved to let them through. Everyone watched fascinated as the yachts sailed past. Their owners looked up at the crowd and waved. Once they'd gone, the bridge swung back and people began to flow across it again.

Laura, Mike and Alice followed the walkway out for a while. There were shops and cafes. They wandered around, enjoying the sunshine and feeling lazy. "Beach?" Alice said suddenly. For her, being at the seaside meant beach and sand.

"There is a beach," Laura said. She took out her guidebook and looked at it. The beach was further round. Laura thought it was about half an hour's walk. They debated going back to get the metro or a bus, but Mike said he was happy to walk. After days cooped up at the police station and then the hospital he was pleased to be outside. So he put Alice on his shoulders and they set off. It was a warm Sunday morning and they took their time, exploring the streets and restaurants. Eventually they came out behind a sandy beach with umbrellas and sun loungers, already filling up with people.

"Beach," shouted Alice from Mike's shoulders. He put her down and led her on to the warm sand. As soon as they were on the beach they realised that they weren't equipped for a day at the seaside. They had, after all, set out to explore a big city. Laura left Mike with Alice by the water's edge. She had noticed a market and some shops behind the beach and went off to see what she could buy. Mike took off Alice's shoes and socks, then his own. He rolled up the legs of his jeans to the knee. Alice was better prepared in her shorts. Taking her by the hand, he led her into the water and they paddled together. The sea was beautifully warm and the sand felt firm beneath their feet. Little fishes darted to and fro around them, making Alice squeal with excitement. In a few moments Laura returned with a large beach towel and a bucket and spade. She spread the towel out on the sand a little way from the water's edge and sat down on it.

As soon as she saw the bucket and spade, Alice wanted them. She went over to Laura, who made her sit down and put some sunblock on her face, arms and legs and found Alice's hat in her bag.

"You'd better put some sunblock on too," she said to Mike. "The sun is quite hot." He did as he was told, while Alice went off to fill the bucket with water.

"The water's lovely," he said. "Are you going to come in for a paddle?"

"Maybe in a bit." Laura lay down on the towel, propping herself up on one elbow so that she could see Mike and Alice. She took her sunglasses out and put them on. The sun was hot and she felt relaxed. She watched them playing, digging holes and building sandcastles. It really was like being on holiday and reminded her of the days at the seaside they'd had in the summer. That seemed like such a long time ago, as though it had been in a different lifetime. Everything had been so normal then; now it was different. They were here together, which was all that mattered. Tomorrow there would be things to do; today they could pretend they were on holiday. A breeze swirled around Laura. She felt drowsy. Now that she was beginning to relax, all the tension of the last few days washed over her in a wave of tiredness. Lying back on the sand she could feel the warmth of the sun and hear the lapping of the water and the sound of children playing.

Mike turned and saw that Laura was asleep. He kept Alice away from her and left her in peace. After all, he thought, she deserved it. She'd had a tough time, without her determination they would never have made it. The way she had taken charge of everything had surprised him. He had always known that Laura was very capable, but never to that extent. For a moment Alice was engrossed in the sandcastle she was building, so Mike walked back into the water. He loved the feel of it against his skin. Looking out to sea he thrust his hands into his pockets.

His right hand encountered something hard. At once he knew it was the ivory figure. He pulled it out of his pocket and looked down at the carved shape that he had carried with him for so long. At first it had kept alive the memory of what had happened all those years ago. Then he kept it because he thought it held the key to his dreams, as though if he lost it he would lose that power too. Now it made him think of Marie. He didn't want to remember her, or what had happened. The power of the dreams was a burden he'd carried for too long and it had almost ruined his life. It was time to be free of it. He grasped the figure firmly in his right hand and threw it as far as he could out to sea.

On Monday, Laura began to look for alternative accommodation. By Wednesday she had found a modest apartment in a small square north of the Diagonal, the motorway that cut the city in two. It was well away from the tourist areas. Laura hoped that here, in a nondescript suburb, they could disappear from view. The apartment was not far from the

Joanica metro station, on the second floor of an old house. There were two bedrooms, a bathroom and a large room that served as a sitting room and dining room with a tiny kitchen. It smelt musty and in places the wallpaper was peeling, but it was cheap and they could move in as soon as they wanted to. By the end of Thursday they had unpacked and were making themselves at home. Laura opened all the windows and left Mike and Alice scrubbing down the surfaces while she went to buy bedding. She found a market a few streets away and was soon back with everything they needed. Then she went out to find the nearest supermarket to stock up on food. Her Spanish was improving all the time. She had a good ear for the language and picked up vocabulary quickly.

By the evening the musty smell had gone, the surfaces were clean, the beds were made and their two cases unpacked. The three of them sat round the table in the main room, eating the paella that Laura had made. It wasn't like the house she'd had to abandon, but they were a family again and they had at least the beginning of a home.

After they had washed up, Alice went to bed. Laura and Mike were properly alone for the first time since Mike had been arrested. They opened a bottle of wine and sat at the table, talking. Mike was able to tell her the whole story of his dream and his relationship with Marie and Yvette. As she listened, Laura could picture Marie and could understand how Mike had been unable to resist. It was still hard for her to accept that it had gone on for so long and she had never even sensed that anything was wrong. After he had finished he reached across the table and took her hands.

"Can you ever forgive me for what I did? For what I have done to you and Alice? I have turned our lives upside down." He looked unflinchingly into her eyes. Laura met his gaze and looked away. She was quiet for a long time, then she met his eyes again. She spoke quietly and deliberately, trying to express honestly the mixture of emotions she felt.

"I do understand. Having met Marie I know how she could have seduced you. She nearly seduced me too. But you did betray both of us and you did break my trust. In one way I can forgive you. If I couldn't then I would have left you in the hospital and come here on my own with Alice. Saying that I forgive you, doesn't make everything alright. Trust that has been broken isn't easily mended. You must rebuild it by what you do now. You must help us build a new life here. If you ever betray me, or Alice again, I shall leave and you'll never see either of us again."

"I understand. I promise I'll never, ever keep anything from you. You have given me a second chance. I will make it work." He bent his head and kissed her hands.

She lifted his head and pulled him towards her. Then she kissed him hard on the lips. She stood up and, taking him by the hand, led him to their bedroom. Since the first night in the hotel they had not touched each other, so conscious had they been of Alice's presence. Now they had the privacy of their own room. Laura let Mike undress her and they made love. It seemed as though they hadn't done so for years. As they came together, she felt the same sense of being moved by his power as she had at the Pheasant. But this time she knew what it meant and she welcomed it.

Afterwards she lay in his arms. She told him properly about her meeting with Marie and her terrified flight through the alleyways of the estate. He propped himself up on an elbow, looking at her in amazement and concern. Again he was surprised by her determination and resourcefulness. Then they both felt that they had said everything they needed and slept in each other's arms until dawn.

The next day Laura began to look for work. It didn't take her long to find a job as a nanny to a well-off family living closer to the centre. Both parents were working and they had two children, one older and one younger than Alice. They'd had a series of young au pairs who had not settled. Laura's maturity and experience and her ability to teach the children English, impressed them. The money wasn't great, but it would cover their rent and what they needed to buy food. This meant that they still had most of the money they'd brought with them. Laura was happy. They had a home and financially they could cope.

Their new life was beginning to work.

Colin Morris looked at the pile of papers in front of him with deep frustration. It had taken a week to piece together what had happened. Within a couple of days the police had found Mike's car in the supermarket car park, which had confused them. It suggested that Mike might be hiding somewhere in the area. Finally an analysis of airline manifests of flights from local airports had revealed a family of three, travelling under the name of Pearce's partner to Barcelona on the day of Mike's escape from the hospital.

Sibthorpe had dropped in to see Morris to present his report and had apologised for the apparent ease with which Mike had slipped away from the hospital.

"Well at least you know where he is." Sibthorpe tried to sound positive.

"We do, but it's not much help. Extradition from Spain isn't easy. Finding them in Barcelona, even if they stay there, will be impossible unless we get some sort of lead."

"So what are you going to do?"

"Leave the file open and wait for him to make a mistake. There's nothing else I can do." Morris's tone was gloomy. "Did you have any indication that he was planning to do a runner?"

"Not at all. We had a good conversation on Friday after the scan of his dream. I did rather tell him that I thought his dream wasn't convincing, but I had no idea he was planning to leave. Did you get any clue from neighbours or friends?"

"Not really, although the next door neighbour seemed to think that the partner, Laura, had become very anxious and stressed about something. On the Wednesday she didn't stay at her house and then on the Thursday she came back but went off to her mother's. The neighbour also noticed a group of youths hanging around on the street, but she didn't really think anything of it."

"It sounds to me as though something scared the partner."

"Perhaps, but then why didn't she come to us? Now we can't ask her, so we don't know."

"What about the alleged victims?"

"Marie and her Aunt? They're very angry that Pearce has escaped. They want to know how it happened, where he is and what we are doing to bring him back."

"Have you told them where you think he is?"

"Of course not, that's classified police information. I have no intention of sharing it with them."

"Good. Do you think they could have threatened the partner in any way? Both she and Pearce seemed to think that they wanted the daughter for some reason."

"I really don't know and I have no way of finding out." Morris's voice was full of exasperation. "As I said, I am just going to have to leave the file open. Perhaps in the future we may have a chance to resolve it."

A few weeks later, Mike and Laura were sitting at the table drinking wine. This had become their custom, to spend time together after Alice had gone to sleep. Laura suddenly said, "You never did tell me what happened at your final session with Dr Sibthorpe."

Mike looked at her. "No, I didn't. Were you able to get an answer to the question I asked?"

"I didn't have time to do any research myself, but I asked Lottie to. I had completely forgotten about it. I'll email her tomorrow. I want to let her know that we're safe anyway. Tell me what happened."

Mike described the scan and the different dreams he'd had. "It was very strange. When I described my dream about the electric shocks, Sibthorpe seemed to change. He tried to tell me my dream was just a fantasy produced by being in the hospital. To me it felt as real as the dream I had at the Pheasant. I just wondered whether there was any truth behind it."

"If there was then it would prove that your dreams about the past are real."

"That's what I thought, but he just dismissed it and quite quickly brought our interview to an end."

"How strange. I will definitely email Lottie tomorrow and see if she's found anything."

At six o'clock the next evening Laura went to an internet cafe a few streets away. She had left it late, hoping that Lottie might be on the internet even allowing for the time difference. Laura knew Lottie often checked her emails when she came back after school. Laura went on to Hotmail and set up a new address: bestfriendabroad@hotmail. co.uk. Then she logged in and typed:

We are safe and well and somewhere. Hope you are too. Any answer to the electricity questions?

Laura went on to her old Hotmail account and looked through the emails, seeing whom they were from without opening any of them. Then she went back on to her new account. There was a message waiting for her.

Glad to hear your news. Hope I can see you sometime. Research was not easy but see attached. Might answer your question.

Laura opened the attachment. It contained copies of two articles from the local newspaper that Lottie had scanned in. Laura skimmed them and printed them. She folded the two pages carefully and put them in her handbag, then she logged off and went home.

Once Alice was in bed and Laura was sitting with Mike, she fetched the pages and spread them out on the table. One article was dated April 1976 and the other June of the same year. The first described how a patient suffering from mental illness had died while undergoing a new kind of treatment. There was a picture of the patient. His relatives had expressed concern about the nature of the treatment and an inquiry was to be carried out by the hospital.

Laura passed the article to Mike. He took one look at it and said, "That's him. That's the man I saw in my dream, the one who was strapped to the bed. He was wearing a hood to start with, but I saw his face clearly once they took it off."

"You're sure?"

"Definitely."

The second article was headed: *Local Doctor Cleared Over Patient's Death*. It carried a named photograph of a young-looking Dr Sibthorpe, and explained how an inquiry had been held into the death of the patient. The inquiry had examined all the evidence and absolved Dr Sibthorpe from any responsibility. There was a brief statement from him in which he expressed deep regret at the patient's death. He maintained that the treatment he was developing was not new and had been used effectively in the United States. The death was unfortunate and was due to a complex combination of other medical factors. It was really nothing to do with the treatment. The chief consultant psychologist at the hospital was quoted as being satisfied that Dr Sibthorpe had acted correctly, although the use of the treatment had been temporarily suspended.

There were also comments from the patient's brother. The brother was very angry, claiming that the patient had been physically healthy when he had begun the treatment and had died as a result of it. He claimed that important evidence had been suppressed and that the real truth was being covered up. The report, however, noted that the brother was beside himself with anger and grief and was clearly not looking at the matter rationally. It observed that relatives in these situations often jumped to conclusions and invented conspiracies because they needed to blame somebody. There had been a "very detailed and thorough investigation", to quote the words of the consultant psychologist and there was no evidence of any wrongdoing, just of a young doctor trying his utmost to find a way to treat a profoundly sick patient.

Mike read it carefully. "That is the doctor I saw in my dream. I was sure that it was Sibthorpe even though he looked so much younger." He thought for a moment. "Why did he deny it?"

"Isn't it obvious?" Laura said. "You saw the truth of what happened. To admit that you were right would not only prove that you can dream about the past, but it would also raise questions about the inquiry and its findings. Sibthorpe had read all about the dream at the Pheasant and how it established what had really happened."

"That would certainly explain his sudden change of attitude. He seemed very uncomfortable and very dismissive."

"It would be in his interests to dismiss what you were saying as fantasy. He had to do it to protect himself."

Mike shook his head. "You know, I really trusted him."

"It's hard to know who you can trust these days," Laura said.

Philippe sat on his haunches, his wares spread out on the blanket in front of him. There were fans, sunglasses and carved wooden figures; anything to tempt the tourists. His was a good pitch, just behind the beach and close to the little market. He had got there early and had been there for over an hour before two others turned up and set out their blankets next to his. In that time he'd sold a few things and made a few euros. Now there was competition it was harder, but it didn't seem worth moving.

Street selling did make Philippe some money, though not enough.

He had other businesses as well that made much more. He bought and sold anything that would make money – drugs, information and, at times, people. Despite that, he still liked to spend time on the street. As a street seller he was both conspicuous and invisible. People noticed him, but only because he was selling things. They never gave him a second glance and could not distinguish him from those selling next to him. It made it easy to move about, to watch and to pick up intelligence. In the evenings during the rush hour, Philippe would travel the metro looking for easy pickings on the crowded trains. Despite Barcelona's reputation for pickpockets, which had made locals more wary, he could normally find some tourist who was tired or disorientated and whose camera, wallet or handbag it was relatively easy to remove. Put it all together and Philippe made enough money for a one-roomed flat, so he didn't have to sleep on the street like some he knew.

Spain was very different from his own country, the Ivory Coast. There it had been hard and dangerous. Tribal violence and civil war made life cheap and uncertain. After escaping from one of the militias, Philippe had decided that he had to leave. The journey to Europe had been difficult too. He had been able to steal enough money to get to Mauretania and pay for the final stage to the Canaries. The leaky and overcrowded boat had only just managed to reach the islands. Then he had spent months in detention while the Spanish authorities tried to decide what they were going to do with him and the other illegals. The guards at the detention centre hadn't been particularly vigilant, so when it seemed that Philippe might be deported back to Africa he had escaped and make his way to Spain.

Eventually he'd ended up in Barcelona. It was a big city, a place where it was easy to disappear and where there was plenty of money to be made, even for someone who didn't have any papers. It had been hard at first, but now Philippe knew people and was known by the right people. These contacts made it easy to dispose of stolen goods and to be asked to do other jobs. He'd gained a reputation for being reliable and discreet; someone who would ask no questions, get a job done and not talk if the police picked him up. So things were good and the pile of cash beneath the floorboards was increasing.

Philippe sat back on his haunches and watched the people going past him to the beach. Watching people was a skill that came naturally to him, though one he'd made an effort to develop. He was able to assess the wealth, the vigilance and the relationships of the people who passed. They all represented opportunities for profit as victims or clients. A family with two little girls approached. The girls were hot, the mother was irritated. He picked two brightly coloured fans as they drew near.

"Two for a euro fifty," he said. He spoke in English because he'd heard them use that language. Learning languages was something he had also worked at. Now he was fluent in English, as well as Spanish, French and several African languages. He could get by in German and Italian if he needed to. "Special offer for two pretty girls." He smiled at them.

"Please, Mummy," one started, a whine in her voice.

"Okay," the woman said. She felt in her bag for her purse and fished out the coins. "Give them to the man." The girl came over and handed him the money in exchange for the fans. He noticed that the mother had not pushed the purse right down into her bag and made a mental note to find them later as they went home. A mother distracted by children might not be vigilant about her purse. As they walked off towards the beach he looked after them, noticing where they sat down.

Then he heard three sharp whistles and looked up quickly. A boy was standing on the pavement waving. It meant the police were coming. Quickly Philippe folded his blanket together, tied it into a bundle and set off to the beach. It was against the law to sell from the pavement. Lots of people did it and the police knew they did. Every so often they decided to enforce the law and would arrive trying to catch people. It was as much to make a point that they were the ones in charge as actually to have any effect. The street sellers knew this and had their own system to avoid arrest. There was always a lookout who earned a few cents by watching for the police and warning the sellers if they approached.

Philippe walked across the sand between the people on the sun loungers until he came to the water's edge. He walked along it, letting the sea wash over his bare feet. It would be best to walk for a while and then circle back. The police would soon have gone and he could resume his pitch, as long as nobody else had got there first. The sun was hot, but not as hot as in his own country. Moving slowly along the sand he looked to his left at the people on the beach, always alive to any opportunities – a bag left open, a camera left in view.

At the end of the beach he was just about to turn to start his loop round when his foot touched something. He stopped, put his bundle down and felt in the sand. His fingers touched something small and hard. It wasn't a stone. He pulled up a small object covered with sand and washed it in the sea. What he saw made him start. It was small figure of a woman, carved in ivory. Although he knew exactly what it was, Philippe hadn't seen one for a long time. He wondered what it was doing here on the beach. Had someone dropped it, or perhaps it had been washed up? Either way it was unusual. He dried it carefully on his tee shirt and put it in the small pouch he wore under the shirt against his skin. Casually he looked around. Nobody would have seen what he'd found. He picked up his bundle and turned up the side of the beach to make his way back to his pitch.

Philippe was thinking hard. This was very unusual. Someone must have lost this figure and would be looking for it, he was sure of that. The message would need to be put out that it had been found. There were networks within his community that linked to other communities. A message like this would spread out like ripples on a lake when a stone was dropped in. The ripples moved slowly and they could take a while to reach all the edges of the lake, but eventually they would reach them and Philippe was in no hurry.

It was exactly a year since they had come to Barcelona and Mike decided that they should go out to celebrate. A lot had happened in that year. Laura's feeling after they had made love on the first night in the apartment had proved to be correct. James had been born in July and was now nearly four months old. The birth had been much easier than Alice's and Laura had felt happy and relaxed about the pregnancy. After the birth she had started child minding. When she worked as a nanny Laura had soon discovered that there was a market for this service. It meant that she could look after James and earn money at the same time. Mike had redecorated their main room. Laura had bought some second-hand children's toys and cleaned and repainted them. There was the little garden in their square and a larger one not far away if she needed to take the children outside. The parents brought their children first thing in the morning, and collected them late in the afternoon. Alice helped too, although she would be starting school soon. Mike had found it harder to get any kind of steady job. He occasionally helped with gigs and did some construction work when he could get it.

So tonight they were celebrating the first year of their new life. They had gone to I Piccolo Spazio, a small pizzeria at one end of the Placa Joanica. The owner knew them because they'd been there a few times over the year. He welcomed them, had a brief conversation with Laura in Spanish and then showed them to a table towards the back of the restaurant. Mike's Spanish had improved after a year and he could get by, while Laura had become really fluent. James was asleep in his buggy. Laura ordered a selection of tapas, a bottle of wine for them and lemonade for Alice. Alice, too, was picking up Spanish quickly, though they made an effort to speak English at home.

Laura looked around the table happily. For the first few weeks after they'd arrived she still occasionally felt on edge. If a police car suddenly drew up it made her anxious. Weeks turned into months without any attention from the police or anyone else and so she relaxed. Although she missed her house, she loved Barcelona and she loved her new life. The whole episode had really brought Mike and her together again. Eventually she had forgiven him for what had happened with Marie, though she made him swear that he would tell her if he ever started to dream again. She had kept in touch with Lottie by email and discovered that, although the case had received some local press coverage, it had soon died away. It seemed that they had successfully buried themselves.

As the food came they clinked their glasses, not missing out Alice and celebrated their new life and their happiness.

Charles Cameron sat at a table in the bar, drank his beer and waited. He had arrived early for his meeting and had studied the bar for a few minutes from the other side of the street before crossing and going inside. The interior was unremarkable: wooden tables and chairs, a brightly lit bar. Charles had chosen a table in a corner where he could see both the entrance and the rest of the room. When the waiter came over he had ordered a beer and spoken the message he'd been told to give. Then he sat back, watching the door.

Charles had been to France a few times and once to America, but this was his first visit to Spain. The flight had been on time and he had followed his instructions, taking the bus into the centre and then the metro to the stop he'd been given. From there he had easily found the small hotel he was booked into. When he had asked for his key at the desk he had been handed a folded sheet of paper. Written on it was the name and address of a bar. He had looked at the map and discovered it was just a few streets away. The meeting time was at nine and Charles had reached the hotel at five. He went to his room for an hour and lay on the bed, flicking through the TV channels, trying to find something he could understand. He did find the BBC, but it was all boring, so in the end he'd settled for a cartoon channel and watched that until seven. He went down to reception and asked them to for the name of a good place to eat. He wasn't that hungry, but he'd felt he ought to have something. The night ahead was full of uncertainty and a full stomach always helped. Charles wasn't used to being on his own. At home he went out with a group. In fact, he spent most of his time with his crew of three and sometimes more. Alone he felt exposed and not sure how to fill the time. He would have had a few drinks, but he knew he needed to keep alert.

Now he looked around the bar at the other customers. The majority were black, the rest Spanish. This was not a place you would find tourists. The customers were mainly men, although there were a few couples. They hunched over their drinks, engaged in animated conversations in low voices. In the background speakers churned out a mixture of English, American and Spanish music. Charles wasn't sure what he expected to get out of this meeting. When the message about the figure had reached Marie, Charles had been very sceptical. He had said that going all the way to Barcelona to meet a man who might have found a figure was a waste of time and money. There were lots of other little schemes he was working on and he resented being taken away from them. His mother had insisted and he knew it was no use arguing. Marie couldn't go, so it had to be him. He had suggested that she or one of the others come with him, but that had been turned down too.

The bar door opened and a tall black man came in. He crossed to the bar and said something to the waiter. They spoke briefly, the waiter gestured in Charles's direction. The man looked across and then came over. Charles watched him warily. He was not only tall, but powerfully built, his white tee shirt stretched tight across his chest. Charles made no move to get up to greet him. The man sat down in the chair opposite. The waiter came over and put a glass of beer down next to him. The man was very black, his cheeks scarred with tribal markings. Charles guessed that he was from somewhere in West Africa – Senegal, Liberia or the Ivory Coast. When he spoke his English had a touch of French, which confirmed Charles's thought.

"You are a man who wishes to buy something?" A pair of eyes looked at Charles steadily.

"And you are a man with something to sell?"

"If the price is right."

"Let me see it."

The man put his hand under his tee shirt and brought out a small object wrapped in tissue paper. He unwrapped the object and laid it in the middle of the table between them. It was a small carved ivory figure. Charles recognised it at once. It was the one missing from the necklace that Marie always wore.

"May I?" Charles moved his hand towards the figure.

"Of course." The man's glance was unwavering.

Charles picked up the figure and held it so he could see it. He turned it round carefully, then placed it back on the table.

"Very pretty."

"You want to buy?"

"How much?"

The man looked at him in silence for a moment as if making a calculation. "Two thousand euro."

"That is a high price for a little thing."

The man's face remained expressionless. He picked up the figure and held it between his finger and thumb. When he spoke, his voice was considered and without emotion.

"I know it is a thing of great power. You have come a long way to see it, so it must be worth a lot to you."

"Where is the man who had it?"

"I don't know. I found it in the sand on the beach. It had been dropped or washed up, I don't know."

Charles felt in his pocket and took out a photograph. He pushed it across the table. "This is the man who took the figure. Do you know him?"

The African pulled the photo towards him and looked down at it. He shook his head. "I do not know this man. There are many men in Barcelona."

"Could you find him?"

"If he is in Barcelona, I can find him." He paused and then added, "If the price is right."

"He is more valuable than the figure."

"How much?"

"I will give you a thousand euros now for the figure, and five thousand when you find the man."

"My price for the figure is two thousand, I told you. Finding the man will take time. Time costs money." The African's voice was as expressionless as ever. Charles stared at him.

"Fifteen hundred now. Five thousand when you find him. A bonus of another five hundred if you find him quickly. Then there may be more work for you."

The man was silent for a while. "Okay, a deal." Charles took out his wallet, counted out the money and handed it over. The man took it and gave him the figure. They shook hands. The man did not move.

"And when I find this man? What then?"

"Then you let me know. Here is my number and my email." Charles pushed a folded piece of paper across the table. The man looked at it then put it away. "There is a woman and a child too." Charles took out two more photos and passed them across the table. The man looked at them and placed them in a row next to the first one. "I want photos of the man. I want to know where they live. I want a photo of the place. If he is in this photo too, that would be good."

"And afterwards, I can offer you other services?"

"Perhaps. I will decide then. Be careful, I don't want him to know I'm looking for him. I don't want him disturbed or frightened. I want to find him alive. Then we'll see."

"As you wish."

"I will wait for your call. How long do you think it will take to find him?"

The man shrugged his shoulders. "Who knows? Barcelona is a big place." He picked up his glass and emptied it.

"You are sure you can find him?"

"As I said, if he is in Barcelona I will find him. I'm very good at finding people. I am also good at making them disappear." The African got up, walked across the bar and out into the street. Charles sat and watched him go. He would have liked to leave the bar straight away, but he knew it wasn't a good idea. The man might be waiting outside for him. He might think that Charles had more money and taking it would be easier than having to find someone. You never could tell, so Charles ordered another beer and drank it, watching the people in the bar and listening to the music. After half an hour he asked the waiter to order him a taxi. He'd decided it was easier to take no chances. At the hotel there was a small bar containing a couple of guests and a girl who was on reception and serving drinks. Charles bought a couple of beers and took them up to his room.

He turned on the television and lay on the bed watching cartoons. He took out the figure, unwrapped it and looked at it. He took a photo of a white woman out of his pocket. For a long time he stared at it, thinking of a night when this woman had made a fool of him. He could still hear his cousin laughing at him. Looking down at the carved female figure it seemed to him to resemble that woman. He would have his revenge. The meeting tonight was the first step towards achieving that.

Philippe laid the three photographs out on the table in his flat. He looked at each one, studying the image carefully, searching for distinctive features. He had a very good memory for faces once he'd internalised them. After a few minutes he picked the photographs up and crossed to the side of the room. There on a small desk was his laptop, linked to a scanner photocopier. Once Philippe had settled in his flat, his next purchase had been the laptop and scanner. Although word of mouth passing between people on the street was still one of the best ways to send a message, he knew the value of technology. It could send the information quickly and clearly to a hundred people in a few seconds.

Carefully he scanned the three pictures into his laptop. Then he set up a new Hotmail address. It would make it easier to monitor responses and harder to trace it back to him. He wrote an email in Spanish, French and English, attached the photos, and sent it to his contacts. The next day he would go to a cheap print shop and make copies of the photos. As he moved about the city he could hand them out. Not all of his contacts had laptops or phones so the old ways were still needed, but by using both he should get the quickest results.

The job interested him as a challenge. Barcelona was a big city with a large population. He had found people before, but normally there had been more to go on. There had been a district of the city, or someone who knew them. These people might not even be here. The link to the figure was tenuous. If they were here then he was sure he would find them sooner or later. He took the pictures and stuck them up on his wall where he could see them, so he could keep looking at them until he had memorised them.

Now he stared at them again; a tall, well-built man in his early thirties with blonde hair and a beard; the woman was younger, attractive with a good figure; the little girl was pretty in the way that little girls are. Philippe didn't care who they were or what this was about. They represented a job and the money was good. He wondered if he should have tried to drive a harder bargain and push the boy a bit more. On the other hand, the price was okay. He was not the only person in Barcelona who knew how to find people and he wasn't the cheapest. The boy didn't know that, of course. Philippe was pretty sure that this was the boy's first time in the city; he'd toyed with mugging him to see how much money he had on him. However, he must have good connections. Philippe knew the power of the figures and those who owned them. There was no point in making enemies for no reason. Besides, he guessed that once he had found these people there might be more work to do.

Finding people was a challenge that Philippe enjoyed. Making people disappear could involve pleasures of a different kind. He looked again at the photograph of the woman. He was sure he could find a good market for her, if there was anything left to sell. It was a pity she wasn't blonde, but that could be changed. Little girls always fetched

291

a good price, especially pretty ones like this, but he was anticipating too much. First they had to be found.

Towards the end of April, Mike and Laura decided to take the children to see the magic fountain, a spectacular display of light and water that took place each night. Giant fountains shot water high into the air at different angles while lights played on it, turning it into different colours and projecting images. The combination of water, light and music was completely mesmerising, and entirely free. They had gone with Alice to see it shortly after they'd arrived in Barcelona. She had loved it and was desperate to go back. Mike had taken her again before James was born. After that they'd waited until James was old enough to enjoy it. By April he was sitting up and crawling and his attention span was longer. Early one evening they set off to get a place at the tables by the cafes, being free the entertainment was always busy.

The display was by the site of the international exhibition, so they took the metro from their local station Joanica to Espanya, making two changes on the way. From there it was a walk up the long avenue and across the bridge over the road. They soon found a good place at one of the tables. Mike went off to the cafe and bought a beer, a glass of wine for them and the usual lemonade for Alice. She was very excited. James sat in his buggy, fascinated by everything that was going on around him.

Once the show started, Laura took him out of the buggy and held him up so he could see properly. He couldn't believe his eyes. The fountains rose and fell; they became bright towers, then waterfalls. Everyone watched, completely entranced. After an hour, James's eyelids began to flutter. He desperately tried to keep awake, but fell asleep in Laura's arms. She looked across at Mike.

"I think we should go."

"Oh please, just five more minutes." Although Alice was tired too, she didn't want to leave.

"I need the loo," Mike said. "You can watch until I come back. Then we're going to go." He stood up, walked over to the cubicles and joined the long queue, looking over to the fountain as he waited for his turn.

"Mike." He didn't know the voice and turned without thinking at the sound of his name. His eyes met those of a tall African standing behind him in the queue. He wondered if it was someone he'd met when doing casual work. There were people of all races working; Mike met them and then didn't see them again. The African's eyes showed no recognition and no interest in him. Mike looked around to see if someone else had used his name, but he saw nobody he knew. Maybe he'd imagined it. After all, he'd had a couple of beers. Or maybe it hadn't been addressed to him at all. The queue moved on and he went into the cubicle. When he came out the tall African was nowhere to be seen. Mike walked back to Laura and the children, dismissing it from his mind.

"Come on, Alice," he said, picking her up and putting her on his shoulders. "Now it is really time to go." She didn't protest. Halfway down the road he took her from his shoulders and cradled her in his arms. By the time they reached the metro she was asleep. The metro was crowded, but they soon got on a train. The changes on the way back seemed more tedious and it was difficult with the buggy in the crowds. Although Mike felt tired too, he tried to be vigilant, not that they really had anything worth stealing.

"I'm glad we waited till James was older," Laura said as they climbed the stairs to their apartment. "Did you see his face?"

"Yes, it really is a magic fountain. Even I could sit and watch for hours."

Laura unlocked the door and they went in, locking it behind them. Mike lowered Alice gently into her bed. She opened her eyes briefly when she felt the pillow underneath her head, saw Mike, smiled, then turned over and went back to sleep. He pulled the sheet up over her and went into the living room. Laura followed him, having just put James to bed. He turned and embraced her.

"You know, this whole place is magic," he said. "I'm so glad we came." Laura kissed him, they turned and went into their bedroom.

Philippe could not believe his luck. For weeks it had seemed that his search was in vain. Even with his network of contacts there had been little success. One report turned out to be mistaken when he'd checked it out, but tonight he had come face to face with the man he was looking for.

Philippe had gone to the magic fountain as he often did. There were crowds there, lots of tourists, people often had too much to drink and

293

were distracted by the fountain. It was an easy place to steal cameras and wallets. He'd had quite a good evening and had decided to hang around the toilets for a while. That too was a good place. Suddenly he noticed a man who looked familiar in the queue. Philippe wasn't sure to start with, so he moved to stand behind the man. Then, just as a test, he had called out the name. Sure enough, the man looked up. Philippe acted as though he hadn't spoken and the man had looked around in confusion. Philippe knew then that the man was definitely the one he was looking for.

When he'd seen Mike go into a cubicle, he'd left the queue and waited to one side for him to come out. Then he watched Mike walk back to the woman. To his surprise there were two children not one: a toddler as well as the little girl. He followed them to the metro and then on to it. They moved slowly with the buggy making it easy to keep track of them, despite the crowds. And they were not expecting to be followed, so they hadn't noticed him. He was just another face in the crowd, invisible. When they got off the metro it was not so crowed and he had to be more careful. He dropped back to make sure they were unaware of him and kept them in view until they went into a building. Crossing the street he paused, looking at the windows until a light came on, on the second floor. Then he noted the address and went back to his flat.

The next day Philippe was up early. By seven he was outside the apartment again. Slowly he walked around, exploring the area. The house the apartment was in stood in one corner of a small square, the Placa Joanica. In the middle there was a park with a few trees, flowerbeds, an open sandy space and some seats. On the other side there was a pizzeria. It was just opening up, probably hoping to catch the trade of people on their way to work.

Philippe went inside. He ordered coffee and a roll, went to sit by the window and read a newspaper. The window was directly opposite the door of the apartment building. From where he sat he had a clear view of anyone entering or leaving. In that sense it was a good observation point, but not a suitable place to take photographs from. He sat slowly drinking his coffee and reading his paper. The place filled up, emptied and filled up again. People starting work at different times surged in like waves on the beach, and then withdrew again.

Philippe ordered a second coffee. By eight o'clock he was beginning to think about moving on. Most people stayed only ten or twenty minutes. If he were to stay longer than an hour he knew he would begin to stand out. Just then he saw Mike come out of the door, turn right and walk along the street in the direction of the metro. Seeing him in daylight confirmed his identity for certain. So that was the first part of Philippe's job done; now he just had to get the evidence. He paid his bill without hurrying and left the cafe.

Philippe didn't follow Mike. He knew where the apartment was so there was no need. Instead he walked to where he could not be seen from the apartment, stopped, took out his mobile and made two calls.

In the middle of the morning, during her child minding session, Laura was surprised to look out of her window and see two African street sellers in the little park in the square. She normally only found them by the beach or in the tourist areas and she didn't remember seeing any on their square before. She thought about taking the children out to look at what they were selling, but then decided not to. By the afternoon they'd gone. Probably they'd discovered that it wasn't a good place to sell. It would have been better by the metro station. She didn't notice the battered white van that had appeared, parked a few doors away from the entrance to their house. Vehicles came and went on a regular basis, so there was no reason why she should notice this one among all of the others. She and Mike didn't have a car in Barcelona, and vehicles weren't really of any interest to her. The fact that it stayed in the same place for the next few days did not in any way seem remarkable to her. Nor did it to Mike, when he came home early in the evening after a day helping at a small recording studio. He had enjoyed himself and although it had only been a day's work they had seemed impressed by his knowledge and skill. He hoped that at last he might find something permanent. It was the only thing that frustrated him about their new life. Laura had found work effortlessly and then had set up the child minding business with no difficulty. He had struggled to find anything other than the occasional back-breaking stints on building sites, where he ended up with all the hardest unskilled work. If he could get something permanent that he enjoyed in the area, then everything would be perfect.

The following night Philippe sent an email. He attached two of the best photographs he had been given. His message was simple.

> I have found what you are looking for. Look at the attached. See there are now four. What next?

He deliberately did not send or give any evidence of the address. This was the most valuable part of the information and he didn't intend to hand that over until he had his money.

He didn't have long to wait for a response.

> We are very pleased with your success. I will meet you in the same bar on Friday night at 9.00. Please make sure you continue to know where they are.

Philippe read it, then replied.

> Okay, I will be there. You will have the money? There will be an additional charge for the extra work.

The reply came right back.

> Of course, I will pay any extra costs.

Philippe was satisfied. Today was Wednesday. He just needed to keep things in place for two more days. That would be easy and wouldn't cost too much, but he could charge a high price for it. His employers would need to understand that he had to employ others for this.

This time when Charles came into the bar he saw that the African was already there waiting for him. The African was sitting where they had sat before, drinking a beer. Charles sat down opposite him. The waiter came over and Charles ordered a beer too.

"You have the address?"

Philippe put an envelope on the table. "Here are the photographs you asked for. In one of them the man, Mike, is outside their door. There is another photograph with the name of the street. I have also written the address for you. You have the money?"

Charles also took out an envelope. "Five and a half thousand euros, as we agreed." They exchanged envelopes across the table. Charles took the photographs out and looked at them, while Philippe counted the money. The photographs were of good quality. There were several of Mike on his own, one in front of a door with the number forty-seven on it. There were also several of the woman with the little girl and a buggy.

"Good," Charles said, "you've done well." He paused. "And you're sure that they don't know you've taken these?"

"They don't know a thing." Philippe took a drink of his beer. "There is also the cost of keeping them under observation for you."

Charles looked at him. "How much?"

"It is expensive," Philippe replied. He spread his large hands out on the table. "To watch them all the time I have to employ other people. It's important that they do not suspect they are being watched, so I can't use the same person all the time. I have other businesses to run too and this has taken a lot of my time."

Charles waited, expressionless. He was used to this justification of cost and knew that there was likely to be some haggling done.

"How much?"

"Normally I would charge a thousand euros a day. That would be two thousand from Wednesday night. Because I like you I will do it for eighteen hundred, but I am hardly making any money myself."

Charles thought. He was tempted to drive the African lower. The man could see he was young and might think he was an inexperienced pushover. On the other hand, Charles knew he would need more help from him. They could go to someone else, but it would take time to set up the contacts. Besides, the African had done a good job. Charles had been sceptical, even after their first meeting. Barcelona seemed so big that he had wondered if the task was at all possible.

"Okay, but I want to look at your set-up. Tomorrow you take me to see the house for myself." Charles was trying to assert himself without giving offence.

"If I take you tomorrow I must keep my people there for another day. There will be an extra cost. Another five hundred."

Charles realised that his manoeuvre hadn't worked. "Yes, if I think it's worth what I'm paying."

Philippe nodded and for the first time he smiled at Charles. Then there was silence while they both drank.

"And after tomorrow? Now you have found them, what next?"

Charles looked up. He was loath to give away too much, but he needed the Africa to work for him for longer, so he had to say something.

"There are certain things that have to be put in place. The man will be removed and then the little girl will be taken."

"I could remove the man for you and then snatch the girl. It wouldn't be a problem."

"No, it has to be done in a certain way."

Philippe sighed. "It sounds complicated."

"It is. If it was up to me I'd do it your way, but I have my orders and they must be carried out. It will take one or two weeks to arrange. I'll need you to keep an eye on them until then. It doesn't have to be as intense as now, or," he added with emphasis, "so expensive."

"I am sure we can come to some arrangement. After you see tomorrow you can tell me what you want. And the woman and baby? I could get a good price for the woman. In North Africa they like to have white women. She's older than most, but still attractive."

"I don't know about the baby, he wasn't part of our plans. Maybe we will take him with the little girl. If not, he is yours if you have a use for him. The woman I have some business to finish with. Afterwards you can have her. You can keep her or sell her, whatever you like. She can be a little bonus for you."

"Good." Philippe took a pen out of his back pocket and wrote something on one of the drink mats. "Meet me at this metro station at seven thirty tomorrow morning." Then he stood up and left the bar.

After two hours with Philippe, Charles was satisfied. He had seen Mike, Laura and the children come out of the apartment, so he was happy that the information he'd been given was correct. Philippe's organisation impressed him. It was clear that the African knew exactly what he was doing. Charles was convinced of the need to retain his services and his goodwill.

Afterwards, Philippe took him to a cafe. They had coffee and rolls with cheese and ham. Then they discussed the next part of the operation and agreed the price. Over the breakfast the relationship between them changed. The wary suspicion of their first two meetings was replaced by something more akin to business associates. They had agreed a deal and they were both happy with it. They knew that, at least for a short time, they would be working together, so they stopped testing each other out and trying to get an advantage over the other. Charles respected Philippe's ability to get the job done. Philippe accepted that the young Englishman was tougher and more experienced than he'd thought. Not that either ever relaxed their vigilance; both knew that their relationship was about mutual benefit and that this could change at any time.

Once they had finished eating, Philippe asked Charles what time his flight was and how he wanted to spend the time until then. Philippe offered to provide Charles with anything he wanted: a woman, drugs, transport to the airport. Charles was tempted, but didn't want to run any risks. He politely declined, pretending that he had some other business to transact. Philippe looked at Charles closely as if he knew this wasn't true, though he didn't insist. So they parted company. Philippe agreed to keep an eye on the family, and Charles promised that he would contact Philippe once the final part of the plan was in place. For this he would return to Barcelona.

On the Tuesday of the following week an envelope arrived at the police station with "For the Personal Attention of Colin Morris" typed on it in bold letters. The postmark was London. Morris looked at it carefully and had it scanned before he opened it. Letter bombs were not uncommon occurrences these days. When he finally opened it he found a sheaf of photographs and a piece of paper with Michael Pearce's name and an address in Barcelona. Morris immediately took them to Inspector Hayes, his superior.

"Michael Pearce. Didn't he do a runner in October 2009?"

"That's right, sir. We thought that he might have gone to Barcelona, but we didn't feel we had much chance of finding him there.

"Well it looks like someone has done the job for us. Do you think it's genuine?"

"I've no idea."

"Well get on to Barcelona and check it out with the Spanish authorities. If it's true then I want you over there as soon as possible to bring him back. I should take Ogilvy with you, I think he speaks a bit of Spanish. In fact, if you go and talk to him now it might be better if he made the official contact for you."

"Yes, sir."

"It's strange, though. We don't normally get anonymous tip-offs about petty villains on the Costa del Crime, do we?"

"No, sir."

"I suppose it could be some tourist on holiday who's come across him and recognised him."

"And has gone to the trouble of finding out exactly where he lives and taking some very professional photographs?"

"I see what you mean."

"I think there's someone who wants him back here and in court even more than we do."

"You could be right, but whoever it is they seem to have done us a favour."

Following that conversation things moved very quickly. By Thursday evening Morris and DC Ogilvy were on the plane to Barcelona with an international arrest warrant. Charles Cameron was on the same flight. His contact within the police had let him know of Morris and Ogilvy's planned departure. Also among the passengers were a well-dressed couple. The man was tall, in his mid-forties and wore a dark grey suit, blue striped shirt and matching tie. He carried a smart black overnight bag and an overcoat. The woman was younger, slim and attractive with carefully styled hair. She was dressed in a grey two-piece with a white blouse, and carried an elegant coat and a leather briefcase. They travelled business class with the air of professionals for whom this was a matter of course.

At Barcelona airport Morris and Ogilvy were met by Spanish police and driven away at high speed to the central police station. Charles was met by Philippe in an old blue Renault. Philippe drove him to the small hotel with which Charles was becoming familiar. The couple took a taxi to a smart hotel in the business district.

After a brief discussion at the police station, it was agreed that Morris and Ogilvy would present their warrant to the magistrate at ten the next morning. Once that had been done they would arrest Pearce either on Friday afternoon or Saturday morning. They wanted to do this, if at all possible, away from the family to avoid any kind of scene and preferably on the street. The woman would be informed of the arrest, although there were no plans to take any action against her at this stage. She would be left in Barcelona unless she wished to return. It was possible in the future that social services might become involved, but Morris hadn't had the time to inform them of the operation. His focus was to get Pearce back to the United Kingdom. The Spanish police were fully in support of this approach and were keeping Pearce's movements under surveillance. Once these discussions were completed, Morris and Ogilvy were taken to an inexpensive hotel nearby.

Charles and Philippe spoke in the car on the way from the airport. Charles explained how the plan would work. Once Mike Pearce had been arrested by the police, Charles would alert a third party. The third party would visit the woman and remove the child, then he and Philippe could go in and finish off. It was important they knew as soon as Pearce was arrested. They would then wait outside the apartment until the third party had completed their role. Philippe said he would have someone follow Pearce from the next morning. He knew the police would need to get the approval of a magistrate so nothing would happen that evening. Philippe dropped Charles off at the hotel and offered to show him a good place to eat. Charles didn't want to refuse a second time, so he agreed to meet Philippe in an hour. He went up to his room and dropped off his bag. Then he took out his mobile and sent a text. "Everything is in place."

He waited for the response, which came quickly as a simple "OK."

For the first time since they had come to Barcelona, Mike had a dream. He was sitting on the beach with Laura, Alice and James. Suddenly a shadow fell across Alice. It was a long, deep shadow. He turned to look. A man was standing there. The sun was so bright and fierce behind the man that Mike could not make out his face. The man was very tall and thickset, with a hat. As Mike tried to make out who he was the man began to move forward, towards Alice.

Mike got to his feet and as he did so he felt hands grab his arms. He was turned round and found himself face to face with Morris and Sibthorpe. They laughed at him and waved a piece of paper in his face. "Thought you could fool us, did you? We've got you now." Morris was in plain clothes, but Sibthorpe was wearing a white coat.

"Bring him over." Sibthorpe gestured to where there was a bed set up with wires and terminals. Mike twisted to look over his shoulder. The large man with the hat was walking towards Laura and the children. They had their backs to him and didn't see him coming. Mike tried to shout to warn them, but he was being pulled away and they couldn't hear him. Then suddenly they turned and noticed the man. Mike saw the terror in their faces. Laura looked for him and her eyes met his, then he was pulled away towards the bed. Sibthorpe was saying "Strap him down. Oh, I think we'll start with his genitals."

Then Mike woke. Laura was awake beside him.

"What's wrong? You were shouting in your sleep."

Mike turned to her. "I had a dream," he said. "I haven't dreamt all the time we've been here."

"Tell me." She sat up in bed and turned the side light on. Her face was anxious.

Mike described the dream.

"What does it mean?"

"I don't know. Perhaps it's just a jumble of images. Perhaps it means nothing."

"Can you tell if it's just an ordinary dream or if it's special?"

"It's difficult. The shadow on the beach makes me think it is special. But Morris and Sibthorpe giving me electric shock treatment? I don't know."

"This is the first dream you've had since we arrived? You haven't had any others?"

"I promise you, I would have told you if I had."

"Could it mean they know where we are, that they're coming for us? Could it be a warning?"

"It could, but I would have thought they'd have forgotten all about us by now."

"They never forget."

"If it is a predictive dream I would normally have it several times before it comes true."

"But you can't be certain."

"No. I'm not even certain it was that kind of dream."

"You haven't noticed anything unusual, have you?"

"No." He wondered if there was something, but he could think of nothing. Laura was asking herself the same question. Things like an African street seller in an unusual place or a battered white van parked in the square were not unusual enough for her to notice. "Let's go back to sleep. There's nothing we can do now. We can talk about it in the morning."

"Okay." Laura put out the light and lay down again, but she couldn't sleep. The sick feeling had returned to her stomach, the one she had felt when she had read the note pushed through her door and found the doll in her bed. The one she had felt the whole day of the escape from the hospital and the journey to Barcelona. She had forgotten all about it, now it was back.

Suppose the dream was a warning, what should they do? Move was the answer; move out of Barcelona and go somewhere else. If they had been found or were about to be found then they needed to disappear again. They could take the train north to France and then cross to Italy. In the EU nobody bothered that much if you crossed borders. It was a pity because they'd built up a good life here. With two children it wouldn't be easy to move quickly. Perhaps they should just go to the coast for a while. They could always come back in a few days and check things out. It would be best to go at once, which meant tomorrow, but that would be a problem because Laura had children coming at eight thirty. Her mind kept working, exploring possibilities and weighing up different options.

Eventually Laura must have slept, because she too dreamt. It was a dream she had not had since the difficult months after Alice's birth. She was in the front room of her house in England playing with Alice when the doorbell rang. When she went to answer it, standing on the doorstep was a smartly dressed couple. Laura knew at once they had come for Alice and she tried to close the door on them, but they forced it open and pushed her aside. Then the dream followed its usual pattern of Laura being tortured to sign papers, and the couple taking Alice away in a silver car.

This time, though, the dream didn't end there. Instead another scene formed in Laura's mind. It was as though she was looking into a room. The room was dimly lit, the walls hung with drapes and tapestries covered with erotic pictures. In the middle of the room a young girl was dancing to music. The girl must have been about thirteen with long blonde hair that reached to her waist. Laura knew at once that it was Alice. The girl was wearing a blue dress with a very short skirt and cut low to reveal her developing breasts. Around her neck she wore a necklace of ivory figures, just like the figure that Mike had shown her. She danced with her eyes half-closed, as though in a trance and Laura noticed on her arms the scars of injection marks. A man and woman entered the room.

"It is time," the man said. "Is she ready?"

"I think she is still too young." The woman's voice was pleading.

"You have said that for three years. She is thirteen, so she is ready. He is impatient. He wanted her when she was ten."

"I know, but both the body and spirit must develop or the union will not produce want we want."

"So you keep saying, he will not wait any longer. He wants her now."

"If it must be?"

"She is so full of heroin she will hardly know what is happening."

The woman looked at him and sighed. "Only a man would think that." She went into the room and put her hand on Alice's arm. "Alice, you must come with us. There is a nice man who would like to see you dance." Alice looked at her, eyes still half-closed, face expressionless and nodded. She walked with them down a long corridor and into a large hall. Then they took her up a grand staircase and along another corridor. Halfway, they stopped in front of a door and knocked.

"Enter." The voice from behind the door was rich and booming. The room they entered was spacious and luxurious. The carpet was thick, the windows covered with hangings that reached to the floor and the air was full of the smell of incense. In the middle of the room was an enormous four-poster bed and on the bed was an equally large man wearing a gold silk dressing gown. Around his neck was a necklace of ivory figures, but larger than Alice's.

The couple went into the room with Alice between them and bowed their heads slightly, showing their respect. "This is Alice," the woman said.

The man rose from the bed and came towards them. "Alice, Alice." He spoke the word slowly and deliberately as though savouring it. "My precious flower, I have waited so long to meet you." Stopping in front of her, he put his hand underneath her chin and raised her face to look at him. "She is as pretty as you said." He spoke to the woman. "The spirit is strong within her?"

"Yes, but I am not sure that she is really ready. I think it would be..."

"I will be the judge of that." He cut her off in mid-sentence, and she was silent. He turned back to Alice. "Take off your dress and let me see your beauty." Alice reached up to the straps of her dress, pulled them down over her shoulders and let it fall to the floor. Beneath she was completely naked, her skin a flawless pure white. "Leave us," he ordered and the couple bowed slightly and left the room.

"Do you want me to dance?" Alice spoke for the first time.

"Alice, I will show you a new dance that we can dance together." His voice was soft and he undid the cord of his silk dressing gown.

The woman closed the door behind the couple. The man walked away, but she stood outside in the corridor, listening. "Please." She heard Alice's voice. There was a low response that she could not catch. Then Alice again said, "Please," her voice full of fear. After that the screaming started. The woman turned and slowly walked away down the corridor. She was crying.

Laura woke and lay rigid in the bed. James was moving around in his cot. It was six o'clock. The image of Alice and the sound of the screams were still vivid, as though they had been burnt into her mind. Inside her head a voice said, "If that is the future, I will never let it happen."

Laura felt tired and tense as she got up and went into the room James shared with Alice. Alice was awake too, although she hid under her sheet when Laura came in. Then she suddenly said, "Boo," and popped her head out. Laura managed a laugh of surprise; it was important to keep things normal for the children. She lifted James out of his cot. He immediately started to explore the room, crawling then pulling himself up on things. She knew he would be walking soon. Laura went through to the main room. She opened the fridge and took out some juice, put some in a beaker and handed it to James, who was just arriving. Alice followed him, so Laura poured some of the juice into a plastic glass for her. Then she made coffee for herself and Mike and went back into the bedroom to wake him.

"Well?"

He drank some coffee, taking time to come to. He looked at her. "I don't know. It could be a prediction, it may be nothing."

"What do you think?" Laura wanted to tell him about her dream, but somehow she couldn't.

"I haven't dreamt for a long time. I think it is better to be safe."

"We should go away for a few days."

"Yes, I think that would be best."

"If we go north along the coast to one of the resorts, one of us could come back and check out the situation."

"How soon should we go?"

"Today, as soon as we can get away."

Mike thought for a moment. "I need to go and see Sebastian this afternoon. He said he had a job for me next week."

"Can't you phone him?"

"I'll try, but it would be better if I go and see him, especially if we're going to be away. It's only round the corner. You have the children coming anyway."

"I'll see if I can finish at lunchtime. Their parents are sometimes okay about that on a Friday. We'll go as soon as you come back from seeing Sebastian."

"Okay."

"I'll pack a couple of weekend bags." Laura sat on the bed, not moving. Mike reached out and took both her hands.

"It will be alright," he said. "After all, it was only a dream."

"Yes." She got up, went into the other room and busied herself getting food ready for the children. She could hear Mike in the shower. When he'd finished she went and showered herself. The sick feeling was there in her stomach again. It was a feeling of dread, of uncertainty. Suddenly everything they had was at risk. She put on a pair of light blue jeans and a red short-sleeved blouse, then she fished her money belt out of the cupboard. Bending down, she felt under the bed and lifted the loose floorboard where she hid their money. They had not used banks or credit cards since they'd arrived in Spain to avoid leaving any traces of themselves. It was easy to arrange to be paid in cash and caused no surprise in a city where there were many casual workers. Laura pulled the money out, put some of it in her purse and the rest in the money belt that she wore out of sight under her blouse.

Was she being silly and alarmist, she wondered? Laura had always believed it was best to be prepared for anything, a strategy she had no intention of abandoning now. For that reason she found the pepper spray and sharpened metal comb and put them in her handbag. Then she pulled out a small weekend bag. She packed some underwear and a change of clothes for her and Mike.

In the kitchen Laura made breakfast, though she didn't feel at all hungry. Mike got the children up to the table and settled them to eat. This left Laura free to go into their bedroom and phone the parents of the children she looked after. They were all fine apart from the parents of a little girl called Isabella, who would be busy and couldn't come and collect her at lunchtime. Laura said that she would take the little girl to her grandmother's. It wasn't far away.

"How would you like to go to the seaside for the weekend?" she asked Alice and James as she went back into the other room.

"The beach?" Alice asked, meaning Barcelona's beach which they had gone to when they first arrived.

"No," Laura said, looking at Mike, "we thought we'd go north to the coast, and stay for the weekend."

"Yes please," said Alice. She loved the seaside. Laura could remember the first time she and Mike had taken her to the beach in England. James banged his spoon on his plate in agreement, catching Alice's excitement.

"Okay. After breakfast go and put a few things together for you and James. Not a lot, just what you need for the weekend. I have rung the parents and I'm going to finish at lunchtime today."

"Oh good." Alice was full of enthusiasm.

"We've got to take Isabella to her grandmother's. We'll do a bit of shopping, and then we'll go as soon as Daddy comes back from his meeting."

"Can I go and pack now?" Alice asked, already sliding off her chair.

"No, finish your breakfast and your drink. Then you can."

Alice's enthusiasm helped to lift Laura's mood a little. It would be nice to get away to the seaside for a while. Perhaps it would be just a break and afterwards their lives would return to normal.

At ten o'clock Morris and Ogilvy presented themselves with their warrant to the magistrates. The formality took only half an hour. By eleven they were being driven across Barcelona. They parked several streets away from Pearce's apartment and transferred to an unmarked blue van. The officer who had been keeping the apartment under observation reported on the current situation. He explained that nobody had come out of the apartment yet that day. Children had gone in because the woman was a childminder. Then the officer drove Morris and Ogilvy to the square where the apartment was, parked on the opposite side and they settled down to wait.

On the other side of the square Charles and Philippe sat inside the dirty white van, also waiting. They had been there since eight o'clock, not sure exactly what time the police would arrive. At about quarter to twelve Philippe received a text. He read it and looked across at Charles.

"The police have just arrived," he said. "They are in a blue van on the other side of the square." He slid one of the panels in the van's side open a little and looked out. "I see them. Your English friends are with them it seems."

"Good," Charles said. "Now we must wait for them to make their move."

"Your plan begins to work."

At quarter to one the parents began to arrive to collect their children. By one o'clock they had all gone apart from Isabella. Laura set out, with Alice and James in the pushchair, to take the little girl to her grandmother's. Once they had gone it would be time for Mike to go and meet Sebastian. Hopefully by the time he returned Laura would be packed and ready to go. She came slowly down the stairs of their apartment building with James on her shoulder and the folded pushchair under her arm. Alice had taken Isabella's hand and was helping her down the stairs. Outside on the street, Laura unfolded the pushchair and put James in it. She adjusted it slightly and fastened the belt that would stop him from getting out. As she was bending down, she looked to see where Alice and Isabella were. Beyond them she saw the same dirty white van that seemed to be permanently parked in their square. For the first time she noticed a small panel in the side which was like a window. At the window was a face. Laura froze for a moment. There was something about that face she recognised; something that triggered the sick feeling in her stomach. She stood up quickly and turned away.

"Come on, you two," she called to Alice and Isabella. "Time to get Isabella to her Granny's." She spoke the words in Spanish and they moved off towards the corner of the street. Her mind was working frantically. Surely she couldn't be right? It was difficult to tell, because she could only see the eyes and part of the nose. It was a black man's face, she was sure of that. A black man she had seen before. She could not be absolutely certain, but she had the strong feeling that the man looking out through the side of the van was Marie's cousin, Charles.

The thought raised Laura's anxiety level. Her immediate impulse was to pick up the children and run, but she suppressed it. If she was right and Charles was there, it was important that he didn't realise she had seen him. So she acted as normally as possible and shepherded the children slowly along the street to the end of the square. She crossed over and then turned left. As soon as she was out of sight of the square and the van she stopped, took out her mobile and phoned Mike. Above all she needed to warn him. If it was Charles then he was probably watching the flat. If he didn't know that she had recognised him then they could be one step ahead of him.

Laura needed to tell Mike to pick up the bag when he left. He had to know not to go back to the apartment after he had met Sebastian. They could meet somewhere later and go straight off to the coast. Mike would need to be careful, though, in case Charles followed him.

Mike's phone was engaged. Laura cursed and started to walk off down the street. He was probably ringing Sebastian to say that he was about to leave. She would have to try again in a few minutes.

As she walked Laura looked warily around. If it was Charles, was he just watching the apartment and was he on his own? Was it possible that she was a being followed as well?

She passed two African street sellers sitting outside the metro.

Charles held his breath. He had been looking out of the van when Laura had come out on to the street. She had looked over towards the van for a moment and he wondered if she'd seen him. There had been no sign of alarm from her and the observation aperture was small. She had only seen him once as far as he knew. It was unlikely that she would remember him.

Morris watched the parents come to collect their children. This was a bonus; he had thought they might have to wait all day. Then he saw Laura come down with three children. She went off out of sight. Morris waited. He wondered whether to go in and arrest Pearce in the apartment now that everyone else seemed to have gone. There was too much waiting around for his liking; he wanted to get on with it. He turned to his Spanish colleague, about to make the suggestion when the man gestured across the square. Morris saw Pearce come out of the apartment building, cross the road to the little park and begin to walk towards them. Juan, in charge of the Spanish police, immediately switched on his walkie-talkie and spoke into it. Morris saw two plain-clothes policemen appear behind Pearce. He opened the door of the van and got out.

Mike had got halfway across the little park when his mobile rang. He took it out of his pocket and stopped to answer it. Laura's voice, full of anxiety, was in his ear.

"I think I saw Marie's cousin watching our apartment. He was in a white van. After you've met Sebastian, don't go back to the apartment. I'll meet you at the main train station. Be careful, they might be following you."

"Okay," Mike said. Then he looked up and saw Morris getting out of a blue van. "Marie's cousin isn't the only one watching our apartment.

I think I'm just about to be arrested. Laura, whatever happens don't let them get Alice, any of them." He shut off the phone and turned round, only to walk straight into the arms of the two plain-clothes policemen. Turning back he found Morris coming towards him.

"Michael Pearce, I have a warrant here for your extradition to the United Kingdom for sexual assault and statutory rape."

The two policemen were on either side of Mike now. He said nothing as they handcuffed him. Morris led the way to a waiting car. Mike was pushed into the back. The police got in on either side of him. Morris spoke to Ogilvy.

"I suppose we need to inform his partner that we've arrested him."

"I think we should, but she's gone out and there's no point waiting around. We don't know how long she's going to be. I can always come round later, before we go to the airport."

"Good idea." Morris was keen to get back to the police station. He got into the front of the car and it drove off, followed by the blue van.

From inside the white van, Charles watched the arrest take place. Once the police had driven off, he took out his mobile and sent a text.

"He has been arrested. The woman and children have gone out, but should be back soon."

Then he sat back and relaxed. The first part of the plan had been achieved. He had just put the second into operation. Now he could look forward to the third part and the opportunity to settle his unfinished business.

Laura had just reached Isabella's grandmother's when she finally managed to contact Mike. Her relief at reaching him evaporated at his words. She stood for a moment, holding her phone to her ear and listening to the silence at the other end. If Mike was arrested what should she do?

"Mummy, are you alright?"

Alice's voice cut across her thoughts. Laura looked down at her daughter, standing there holding Isabella's hand. The first thing they needed to do was to deliver Isabella.

"Yes, of course. Let's drop Isabella off."

They crossed the street and rang the doorbell. After a few minutes the door opened and Isabella went inside. Laura turned away, thinking quickly. She could not go back to their apartment. Perhaps that was all part of the plan; once Mike had been arrested, Charles was going to come and snatch Alice away. No, Laura needed to leave Barcelona at once. That was what Mike had been telling her. It was lucky she had put on the money belt this morning, so she had plenty of cash. It was a pity that their things were back at the apartment, but it couldn't be helped.

"Alice, I think we'll go straight to the station and to the seaside. Daddy will bring our things and join us later."

"Was that him on the phone?"

"Yes. Don't worry, we'll see him later." Laura hated lying to Alice, but she had no choice. There was no point in upsetting her daughter. They set off, back towards the metro station.

About thirty minutes after the police had left the square with Mike, a silver car arrived and parked close to the entrance of the apartment building. A well-dressed couple got out. The man was tall and well built. The woman was slim and attractive and carried a leather briefcase. The man produced a set of keys and opened the door to the apartment building. Another of Philippe's jobs had been to obtain copies of keys that would let them into the building and the apartment itself. The couple walked slowly up the stairs to the second floor. They went to the door and rang the bell, just in case there was someone still inside. Nobody came to the door and there was no noise.

The man put the key in the lock and opened the door, then walked around the apartment, going from room to room. He went into the main bedroom and found the half-packed overnight bag.

"It looks like they were planning to leave."

The woman put her attaché case down on the table and joined him. She picked up the bag, looked in it and turned it upside down so its contents fell on the floor.

"There will be no need for them now," she said.

They came back into the other room, then went into the children's bedroom and saw the pile of things on the bed.

"These we might need," the woman said. She went back into the main bedroom, picked up the empty overnight bag and brought it into the children's bedroom. "It will be better for them if they have some familiar things to start with." She carefully packed the pile of things – clothes, books and a few toys. Then she zipped up the bag, brought it into the living room and put it down by the door. She came back and sat on one of the chairs.

The man went into the bathroom to complete his inspection of the apartment, then stood at the window, looking down on the square.

"You should come away from the window," the woman said. "We don't want to do anything to scare her off, do we?" He turned to look at her and nodded. "I think it would also be better if you relocked the door. Then when she comes in we will have the advantage of complete surprise." The man crossed to the door and locked it and sat in a chair opposite the woman.

"You have the papers?"

"Of course."

"Just relax and wait. I'm sure she'll be back soon."

By the time Laura reached the metro she had a plan. She would leave Barcelona straight away and go to the coast. Mike's arrest had changed everything and she needed breathing space, a time to think. The police would take him back to England to face trial and prison. He was probably already on his way to the airport. Their plan had been to go to the coast together and if necessary move to another country where they could start again. Now Laura was on her own. She bought tickets and manoeuvred the buggy on to the escalator. To get to the central train station she would need to go one stop and change lines.

It wasn't the police who really worried her now, it was the others. She knew there was a danger, if Mike was convicted, that social services would take the children into care, especially as Laura had helped him to escape. It might be that she would be charged too. She wondered why the police had arrested Mike and not all of them. From the conversation they'd had on the phone she knew that he had just come out of the apartment, so the police must have been watching the apartment too.

Laura reached the platform. It was lunchtime and it was not too crowded. There was a train due in three minutes. She stood and waited.

It was the others: Charles and whomever he was with. Laura knew they wanted Alice. Now that Mike had been arrested they would try to find her. She shuddered at the thought of meeting Charles again. The last thing Mike had said to her was not to let them get Alice, not any of them. Her hands clenched on the handle of the buggy. She wouldn't let him down; she would do anything to keep Alice safe. As if somehow sensing that something was wrong, Alice touched her hand.

"Are you alright, Mummy? You look very serious."

Laura forced a smile. "Yes, of course." She gave Alice's hand a squeeze. "I'm just thinking of the best way to get to the seaside." Then the train arrived and they got on.

Laura wondered if she was being followed. She looked around the compartment. It was three-quarters full. They were all just people. Spaniards; Africans; men; women; some smart; some casual. If someone was following her she had no idea what they would look like. Perhaps if someone turned up on the next train it might be a clue. Anyone who had seen her go out must assume that she would come back. That meant they were probably waiting for her now. They wouldn't know that she was aware Mike had been arrested, or that she had seen Charles. Now she was sure that it must have been him. If she was not being followed there was a chance to escape and disappear. If she was being followed she still had the advantage of time. They didn't know where she was going. At the moment she was just taking the metro. She could be going shopping or to visit a friend. Once she went to the train station though, it would become obvious that she wasn't coming back.

The train reached her stop and she got off. The changeover to the other line was easy, but this time the wait was longer. A train had been leaving just as she reached the platform. Laura looked around her. About ten metres away there was a tall African in a pink shirt. She had a feeling that he'd been on the last train too. It was probably best to assume that she was being followed. Always assume the worst scenario, someone had once told her.

At last the train came in and she got on. The African in the pink shirt got into her carriage. He could have got into the next one, but he chose to get into hers. He was sitting at the far end. She looked towards him. His eyes met hers, his face was expressionless. This journey was longer. Laura found some sweets in her pocket and gave them to Alice.

James was looking all around him, fascinated as usual.

"We're going to go on a big train," Laura said to Alice quietly, trying to sound jolly. Laura wondered where she should go. This morning she and Mike had talked about the Costa Brava. Somewhere like Lloret de Mar or Tossa de Mar; places out of Barcelona, but close enough for them to come back after a few days. Now things were different and Laura wondered whether she should take a train straight across the border into France. She felt reluctant to leave Spain. Perhaps there was still a chance that she could hide away for a few days, then come back to collect their things. Deep down something told her that this was unrealistic, but she didn't feel ready to uproot completely. Not yet, she needed time to think things through, come up with a proper plan.

They reached Sans, the stop for the main railway station and Laura got off. Glancing back she saw that Pink Shirt had got off as well. Could that be coincidence? She took the escalator up and came out on the concourse of the central train station. It was large and confusing. She stopped for a moment to get her bearings. Pink Shirt was talking to one of the African street sellers. He had knelt down on his haunches and seemed to be deep in conversation. Laura set off, following signs to the information centre. After some discussion she decided that she would initially buy tickets to Girona. That left her options open. There was no direct train service to either Lloret de Mar or Tossa de Mar, but she could get a bus to either from Girona. It was also possible to get a train to the border from there and it had an airport as well. It would give her more time to think. There was a train in half an hour.

Laura came out of the office. Pink Shirt was nowhere to be seen, but the inevitable African street sellers were there. She looked at the departure board and located the platform. It was too early to go to the platform, especially if someone was watching them, so she paused for a moment, thinking.

"Mummy, I'm hungry," Alice said, tugging at her arm. Laura realised that it was nearly two and they'd had breakfast at seven. She walked to the far end of the station where there were shops. There she bought bread, cheese, some bottles of water and some fruit.

"We'll have a picnic on the train," Laura told Alice. That satisfied the little girl who loved picnics. Laura looked at her watch. To kill time and confuse anyone who might be watching, she went down the escalator back down to the metro. Buying a ticket, she took a train two stops down the line. Alice was confused, James loved it.

Laura looked around the carriage. There was no sign of Pink Shirt though there were a number of other Africans in the carriage. Was one of them the one that Pink Shirt had spoken to at the station? It was hard to be sure. For some reason she assumed that anybody following her would be black, probably because Charles was black. But there were Africans everywhere, and they couldn't all be following her. After two stops she got off, crossed the platform and took the next train back.

She reached the main station again ten minutes before her train was due to depart and headed straight for the platform. Stopping by a fairly empty carriage she took James out of the buggy, folded it up and carried him and it on to the train. They found four seats together on the side away from the platform. The train began to move slowly out of the station. As it did so, it passed a tall African in a pink shirt, who seemed to be looking into each of the carriages as they went by while talking on a mobile phone. Laura bent down as though to get something from the bag with their food in, hoping that hasn't seen them.

Charles sat waiting in the white van. It had been over an hour since Laura had left the apartment and Mike had been arrested. He kept telling himself to be patient. After all, a woman going out with two young children might be doing shopping or something.

Philippe's mobile went. He listened intently and said something in French, then turned to Charles. "The woman with the two children just got on a train to Girona."

"Shit," Charles said. Philippe spoke again into the mobile.

"My friend says she seemed very wary, almost as though she thought someone was watching her."

Charles swore again. "So what now? Is your friend on the train?"

"No, but it's not a problem. I have friends in Girona."

"So where do you think she is going?"

Philippe shrugged his shoulders. "Who knows? To France? To the airport? Perhaps to the Costa Brava – Lloret de Mar or Tossa de Mar?"

"So what do we do?"

"I text my friends in Girona. I send them a photo. A woman with two young children will not be hard to find. We drive to Girona. It's only seventy kilometres. If my friends see her they will try to find out where she's going. Then they will text or phone me."

"Okay. I need to make a call. Let's get on our way." Charles took out his mobile and dialled a number as the van's engine spluttered into life.

Upstairs in the apartment, the smartly dressed man and woman sat in silence opposite each other. A phone rang. The woman reached into a pocket of her coat, took out her mobile and put it to her ear.

"Hello." She listened intently. "How did this happen?" She listened again. "Do you think she suspects something?" Again she listened. "What is the plan of action?" She paused. "Okay, we'll follow you. We have a Sat Nav, but keep in touch. I don't want her to get away, do you understand?" There was sharpness in her voice that betrayed her irritation. She snapped the phone shut. The man looked at her inquiringly.

"She has taken the children out of the city by train. They think they can track her."

He stood up. "Why did she run?"

"Who knows? Maybe something's scared her. We need to follow them."

"Do you know where we're going?"

"Girona."

"I'll set the Sat Nav."

They went to the door and unlocked it. They were going out when the woman stopped. She came back and picked up the bag that she had packed with the children's things. "We may still need this," she said and went out locking the door behind her.

Laura got off the train in Girona. There had been no sign of Pink Shirt during the journey. On the train Laura had entertained Alice by playing I spy, with James trying to join in. At the same time she was weighing up her options. If Pink Shirt had seen her, Charles would know she had got the train to Girona, but not where she would go next. The trains ran every hour, so she had a couple of hours' head start.

Laura had four choices. She could go to the airport and get a flight back to the United Kingdom; her passport was in her money belt, but the police might arrest her on entry and the children would be taken into care. She could take the train on across the border to France and then perhaps Italy. With the two children and no clothes it would be a struggle. The children would soon be tired and she would have to tell Alice the truth. Alternatively she could go to one of the resorts, Lloret or Tossa. She had never been to either of them. They had always made do with the beach in Barcelona. Lloret was bigger, so perhaps that would be better. There she could blend in with the tourists and lie low for a few days. In the short term money wasn't a problem, so she could find a hotel. Then she could buy a few things and move on.

So once she left the train, Laura went to the tourist information and asked where she could get a bus to Lloret de Mar. Then she set off with the children to the bus station. She was glad her Spanish had improved, otherwise it could have been difficult. As she left the station she passed a group of Africans selling their goods. They really were everywhere. In Barcelona she'd hardly been conscious of them. That was probably because she had lived out of the tourist areas.

Laura bought the tickets. They were lucky: there was a bus in twenty minutes. They sat on a seat and waited. It was hot. Alice was good, but James was beginning to get niggly. Laura gave the children the last of the water. One of the street sellers had packed up his things and he came to sit near to them. He seemed to be waiting for the bus too. As soon as he saw the children were bored he spread out his things, obviously sensing the possibility of a sale to a distracted mother. He had the usual things: carved wooden figures, fans, sunglasses. Each was held up in turn as he tried to tempt the children. Alice wanted a fan because she was hot, and James pointed to one of the carved figures. The man picked up both.

"Both for one euro," he said in English.

Laura wondered how he knew they were English. She supposed that she still stood out. It was a good deal, so she said "Yes" and handed over the euro. The things would help to distract the children and keep them going until they got to a hotel. As he handed them over and took the money, he reached into a bag and pulled out a small doll. It was a girl with long blonde hair, wearing a blue dress with a short skirt.

"For the little girl, madam," he said, pointing at Alice. He smiled at Laura. Laura looked at it. It was just like the doll she had found in her house when she had come back from Lottie's. The only differences were that it had blonde hair, not brown like hers and it did not have a pin stuck up between its legs.

"Oh pretty," Alice said. "Please can I have it, Mummy."

"I don't think so," Laura began. "I've already bought you a fan."

"Madam, there is no charge," the man said, smiling at her and showing a row of white teeth. "It's a gift. It will bring the little girl good luck." He thrust the doll into Alice's hand, then rolled up his blanket and went back to his seat.

Alice was overjoyed. The fan was forgotten and fell on to the ground. She cradled the doll in her arms like a baby, talking to it.

"She looks just like me, so I shall call her Alice too. I am big Alice, and she will be little Alice. Don't you think she's pretty, Mummy?"

"Yes," Laura said, picking up the fan and fanning herself. "She's very pretty, but not as pretty as big Alice."

"And," continued Alice, "she's just like the one Auntie Marie gave me. I put it on my bed, so when Daddy comes I'll have two. Then they can play together, like Auntie Marie used to play with me."

"Yes," Laura said, staring at the doll.

The bus came in. They all got on it, including the African. He sat at the back of the bus. Laura felt him watching her. Then a thought struck her. It was the doll that made her think of it. The doll reminded her of the one that had appeared in her house, even though all the doors and windows had been locked. It brought the dream of the early morning dream back to her. Again she saw Alice in the room, dancing in the blue dress. The thought made the feeling of sickness rise in her stomach. She'd thought she'd been very clever. She had thought she could throw them off, find somewhere to hide. But did they have spies everywhere? Could they know where she was now? Were they already on their way? Every African street seller suddenly seemed like a threat.

Laura pressed the palm of her hand against her forehead. This was too fantastic. She was losing her grip and letting her imagination take control of her. It had to be a series of coincidences. The African on the bus could not possibly be working for Charles. It was important she kept calm and thought things through properly. But what if she wasn't imagining it all? In that case, wherever she went they would track her down. There was nowhere she could hide. Nowhere that Alice would be safe. She remembered Mike's final words on the phone: "Don't let them get Alice, any of them." Again the dream came into her mind. If that was really the future then it must not happen. But what could she do? She was on her own, with nobody to help her.

The white van was stuck in a traffic jam. It seemed on this Friday afternoon that lots of people were leaving the city to head north. Charles sat in the middle, between Philippe and another African who was driving. Occasionally the driver pressed the horn and other drivers did the same; it made little difference. They moved for a bit and then they stopped again.

Philippe's mobile rang. He listened for a moment. "She has taken the bus to Lloret de Mar. My friend is on the bus with her. He will tell us where she goes. This is good. Once we get out of the city we can drive straight there. We do not need to go to Girona."

Charles took out his phone and relayed the information.

Further back in the same traffic jam, the woman in the silver limousine answered her phone, looked at the map spread out on her lap and reset the Sat Nav.

"Excellent," she said. "Soon we will have the girl."

Laura got off the bus in Lloret de Mar and headed down towards the promenade. She no longer looked behind to see if the African was following her. Somehow it no longer mattered. It was a game that she knew she couldn't win. On the promenade she took the children into a fast-food restaurant. They were hungry, so it would be better to get them something now. Once they had eaten there was more chance that they would sleep. She ordered a burger and chips for Alice and asked the servers to do something for James. That was no problem; they were used to babies in Lloret. This was a real treat for Alice and she seemed so happy cradling her doll and eating the junk food. She pretended to feed chips to the other Alice, with whom she was having a long conversation.

Noticing that Laura wasn't eating, Alice said, "Mummy not hungry," in the ambiguous way she had of making something both a statement and a question.

"I'll eat when Daddy comes," Laura lied, looking out of the window and wishing that it was true. Alice accepted it without question and returned to her conversation with little Alice. Laura focused on feeding James and tried not to think of anything else. She knew exactly what she had to do; she only hoped that she was strong enough.

After the children had finished eating, they all went to look for a hotel. Laura chose one in the row behind those on the front. It was an instinctive choice, because she knew it would be cheaper. Not that it mattered anymore, she thought, as there was plenty of money for a one-night stay. At reception she booked a family room for the weekend. To the unasked question about her lack of luggage, she explained that her husband was coming later by car and was bringing the bags. She and the children had got away early to avoid the rush. It was another lie that slipped easily out of her mouth. She had never thought it would be so simple to manufacture the truth. People were eager to believe what they expected her to say. The polite young man on reception certainly accepted it and, smiling, wished her an enjoyable weekend. Then Laura took the children up by the lift to the ninth floor where their room was.

Once in the room she released James from the buggy and let him explore, then she locked the door and put the chain on. It was quite a large room, with an extra bed for Alice. The receptionist had promised to send up a cot for James as soon as more staff came on duty. Laura had told him there was no hurry. The room also had a balcony looking out towards the sea. She made sure that the door was properly closed so the children couldn't get out on to it. After ten minutes of exploring they began to look tired. Laura put them both on the double bed. It was quite wide and low, so once James fell asleep he wasn't likely to roll out. Then she turned on the TV and found a cartoon channel for them to watch. This was a treat too, because they didn't a television in their apartment.

Laura opened the minibar. There was no white wine, so she took the small bottles of gin and vodka. There was no tonic either. As she had no glasses, Laura took a plastic cup from the bathroom, then quietly let herself out on to the balcony.

The beach was visible between the hotels in front of her and she looked out at the sea, sipping the neat gin and thinking of what she had to do. Charles was probably already on his way, so she didn't know how much time she had. But she needed to prepare herself and she could not rush.

The pillow covered the child's face completely. She pushed it down with all her strength. He woke, struggling, fighting for air. The child put his tiny hands up to try to pull the pillow away. He tried to shout, but she held the pillow firmly, blocking his nose and mouth and covering his eyes. His struggles became more frantic. Her knuckles were white; the veins stood out on her forehead. At last he was still. His sister stirred for a moment in her sleep, but did not wake. The woman removed the pillow and looked at the little face. Then she bent again and once more kissed his lips and forehead.

Carrying the pillow, she walked round to the other side of the bed. Her daughter was nearly five. The woman knew this would take all her strength. Again, she stood beside the bed for a moment. She took two deep silent breaths, then she placed the pillow over the little girl's face. The movement woke the girl at once. Her cry was partly muffled. She got her hands up to the pillow and tried to push it away, but the woman held the pillow down hard, pinning the little girl to the bed. It took longer as the girl fought for her life, but finally her arms and legs stopped thrashing about and she was still. The woman let the pillow drop from her hands. She bent over the little girl and kissed her lips and forehead.

The woman sank down into the chair. She sat for a long time, taking deep shuddering breaths. Her whole body shook. She wanted tears to come, but they wouldn't. At last she stood. She picked the pillow up and replaced it on the bed. Then she crossed to the telephone and rang the police.

The flashing lights of the police cars and ambulance parked outside the hotel soon attracted crowds of the curious. Word quickly spread of this bizarre and tragic event.

Reporters worked the crowd, trying to find someone who might know something. Local television crews arrived as the two little bodies were carried out by grim-faced ambulance men. Tourists of different nationalities tried to say something to kindle human interest and give them their thirty seconds of fame on broadcasts set to hit the main evening news.

Finally the mother came out of the hotel, walking between two policemen. The onlookers gaped at her incredulously, not knowing what judgement to make. They needed the journalists to give the deaths some meaning that they could comprehend. Suicide? Accident? Murder? Until it had been neatly labelled and fitted into its paradigm, they didn't know what to make of the event or how to react to the mother. Was she victim or villain? Nobody knew, so they simply stared as she was ushered into the police car and driven away.

A smartly dressed couple had reached the front of the hotel just as the bodies of the children were being brought out. They watched and then walked in silence back to where they had parked their silver car.

Mike sat on the aeroplane between Morris and Ogilvy. He hadn't spoken a word since his arrest, except to confirm his name. Ogilvy had tried to break the news to Mike's partner, but the apartment had been locked and empty. As the plane taxied to the runway, Mike stared straight ahead at the back of the seat in front of him. He felt the wheels lift off from the tarmac as the ground was left behind. Everything had happened so quickly, he was finding it hard to come to terms with where he was. If only he could pinch himself so that he would wake up and find that it had all been a dream.

Lightning Source UK Ltd.
Milton Keynes UK
UKOW05f0935281014

240675UK00003B/42/P